# FIBONACCI TALES

# FIBONACCI TALES

*Dust Tales*

**eLBe**

Fibonacci Tales by eLBe

This book is written to provide information and motivation to readers. Its purpose is not to render any type of psychological, legal, or professional advice of any kind. The content is the sole opinion and expression of the author, and not necessarily that of the publisher.

Copyright © 2018 by eLBe

All rights reserved. No part of this book may be reproduced, transmitted, or distributed in any form by any means, including, but not limited to, recording, photocopying, or taking screenshots of parts of the book, without prior written permission from the author or the publisher. Brief quotations for noncommercial purposes, such as book reviews, permitted by Fair Use of the U.S. Copyright Law, are allowed without written permissions, as long as such quotations do not cause damage to the book's commercial value. For permissions, write to the publisher, whose address is stated below.

Printed in the United States of America.

New Leaf Media, LLC
175 S. 3rd Street, Suite 200
Columbus, OH 43215
www.thenewleafmedia.com

# CONTENTS

| Chapter | Title | Pages |
|---|---|---|
| 1 | A Cow in the Well | 1 |
| 2 | Becoming Unforgivable | 1 |
| 3 | Conservation and Other Curious Customs | 2 |
| 4 | Crew Boss | 3 |
| 5 | The Barren Wife | 5 |
| 6 | The Killing Field | 8 |
| 7 | The Killing Field Redux | 13 |
| 8 | The Angel Garden Redux | 21 |
| 9 | The Unblemished Calf | 34 |
| 10 | Moon Bird | 55 |
| 11 | The Mark of the Master | 89 |

| Total Pages: | 232 |
|---|---|

# A Cow in the Well

"You have to believe me. I'm not lying. I *promised* I would not lie to you. You have to help me get the cow out of the hole before it drowns. It fell in and can't get out, and it's too big, and I can't pull it out by myself. Please come..., you have to help me. The girl replies, chin raised, eyes lowered - There is no deep hole in the grove, nor anywhere else for that matter. You're lying again," judges Sister with conviction formed from tradition, pushiness, and her harrying hating habit.

"'I'm *not* lying!" the boy defends, "And I'm not asking you anyway." Turning back to the girl he pleads "*You* should *believe* me, I don't lie to you. I promised I wouldn't, and I don't.

"You're afraid that if you come help me they won't play with you again" the girl veils her eyes in shame, "and they probably won't. But if you *don't* help me, a cow will drown and Daddy will be disappointed in us because we let it die and didn't even try to save it."

"How did the cow get into the hole?' the girl seeking a middle ground where she takes no stand, nothing is omitted, and nothing dies.

"She was thirsty, and there was a cover over the hole and I pulled it off soshe could drink. Then se fell in, and I'm too little to get her out alone. You have to help me. *Please*...."

Never taking her eyes from the boy, Sister hisses a sinister soft threat: "If you go with him, we will *never* play with you again. You decide, but know that you choose between him, and us."

"You can't say that for everyone!" The irl protests pointedly.

She looks at each sibling in turn, then back at the girl "I just did," she hisses furiously fiece.

"She won't play with you anyway!" The by shouts, angry now. "She's mean. You don't even *like* her. You *have* to believe me."

The girl settles back and pronounces: "There is no hole. You're lying – again."

Betrayed, laid bare and exposed the boy spins away heading for a never land of his own making while Sister delights in the drama of her design.

# Becoming Unforgivable

"Will I be guilty of killing my brother when I'm seven? Will I be sent away like Cain?" The boy's voice twists through octaves as he cowers under a silver sword delayed by a hair.

"Don't be silly," Hester snaps. The age of reason isn't about guilt or innocence. It's about learning right from wrong; and then making wise choices so you won't *feel* guilt. Most seven year olds can make right choices; but seven is a number, and the age of reason isn't about numbers. It's about choice, and the wise use of free will."

"Well, what happens if a boy was bad before, and then he becomes seven, is he guilty on his birthday?'

'It isn't about guilt, son,' *He focuses on retribution and avoids the right use of the power of choice.*

"Will - I - go – to - hell - when - I'm - seven?" The boy demands fiercely furious with frustration.

"I believe you must die before you go to heaven, or to hell." Into the stirring silence she whispers: 'Did you know that "sin" is an ancient archery term meaning to miss the mark?' She seeks the light of understanding in the boy and finds that power center derelict and deserted. *Is one who is amoral therefore innocent?*

The boy puzzles his mother's words carefully and long and then poses: "if I become a good archer and never miss the mark, then will I stay innocent even after I'm seven?"

"You can *choose*, son; and that is a powerful thing. Life is not penance. But if you focus your thoughts on penalty and punishment, penalty and punishment *will* show up in your life, and yours will be a hard life.

"Or, you can learn instead to monitor your thoughts and keep only those that make you feel good here" she taps his chest, "and makes you smile," she touches his cheek, "then you make yourself the master of your fate..., and fortune will not desert you."

For an infinite instant the boy abides in peace and life is abundant and fair.

Then the boy's faithless fear and faithful doubt returns to savagely strip his heart of courage, leaving him small, bitter and isolated within the minimal margins of his solitary stingy singularity.

*E.G.O. Edging God Out.* Hester mourns his loss of innocence and his cell block locked up wanton will.

# Conservation and Other Curious Customs

"How come there are so many rabbits this year?"

"What do rabbits eat?"

"Anything that's green and isn't bigger than it."

"How much rabbit food was there last spring and fall?"

"A *lot*! Oh, I get it, lots of food means lots of what eats it."

"What eats rabbits?"

"People…,"

"*And* coyotes."

"Well done, my sons. How many coyotes were there last year?" He watched them return across time to see the plains a year ago and hear the nights they enjoyed coyote concerts.

"I don't remember coyotes howling last year…, I've heard a lot of them *this* year though."

Jacob grins "are they all adult dogs you hear calling?"

"Oh…, no, there are coyote puppies singing too."

"What else preys on rabbits?"

"Hawks, owls, and big hunting birds."

"I hear more owls hooting, even in the day time."

"I see more hawks now too, and" backhanding his brother, he asks excitedly, "remember that nest we found with all the eggshells in and around it?"

"So, who's the climber that sucked the eggs – they were sucked, right? – and then grounded the nest?"

"Most of the eggs were sucked, and we think it was a raccoon that grounded the nest…. *Wait*, Dad, we'll tell you why. 'Coons are climbers," he ticks off fingers, "there are more 'coons this year, a 'coon is big enough to win a food fight with an owl; and a 'coon heavy enough to down the nest getting away from an aerial attack.

"Some of the eggs broke when the nest hit the ground because there was egg yolk and albumen in it; and later, something with a big tongue came to lick egg off the shells. Coyote, maybe…, the Trickster." The boy grins.

"Good eye, sons. Trickster? What have you been reading about the coyote?"

"Myths, Dad, legends of the Southwest Indians and other native people, Jung's archetypes. The Trickster is a nature spirit whose role is to hoax people into seeing their vulnerability so they willingly come back to the safety, security, and, *I think*, into conformity with the tribe."

"Unh, such a Rebel you are." Jacob grunts. "Are we living as a tribe then?"

"No, Dad, we're living in a bloody *commune* with you and Mom as the spiritual, mental, and emotional divinities. The problem with communes is that being unique is not valued, and so the uniqueness of each person makes no difference *whatsoever*."

Seeing the unity, and the duality of life, complicates loving those who don't. Respectful moments later, Jacob asks, "you got time for a paradox?"

"How long does a paradox take?"

"How long is a piece of string?"

The boy shrugs "we're here clearing debris from a gully so spring rain will flow and not flood so yeah, I guess I got time for a paradox. Make it a good one though, Dad. Housework – even Mother Nature's – doesn't need much of the mind in getting it done. What's your paradox?" He teases a grin into Jacob's eyes "it wasn't that piece of string thing was it?"

"What you resist persists. What you receive recedes."

The boys turn from their work to face Jacob, seeking the purpose and the boundaries of the puzzle he has set for them. "Okay, we talked about rabbits and coyotes and coons and hunting birds…, and then, we talked about the Trickster, and then, communal living."

"And that's when, Dad named you Rebel in our tribe…. So, wise elder brother, maybe your lesson is that the longer you deny and resist the Trickster, the longer you stay trapped in the Rebel archetype. I'm getting tired of your Rebel by the way. What *else* ya got, bro?"

"Little brother, you keep forgetting that *I am* the eldest and I *know* more than you do."

The younger boy chuckled, chunking debris "How's that working for you?" Three-as-one throw back their heads and arch their spines in laughter, and the Trickster turns from the gully to seek more innocent game.

# Crew Boss

They didn't much like me when I was crew boss for the Missouri Pacific laying a Transcontinental Railroad tributary line across the plains. The crews didn't like me because they thought I did nothing and was paid too much. The bosses didn't like me for the same reasons.

The crew thought I was too young to lead. As long as I got the work done and kept crewmen alive, the bosses didn't care my age. I could starve or work the men to death and that would concern the railroad men only if I failed to deliver the completed miles the owners and investors needed to measure their success in brute muscle taming nature to yield even more profits ever more reliably.

Because we build rail lines over the plains where herds of buffalo were slaughtered from trains, rail workers get hazardous work pay even if we don't use nitro. The plains Indians do not forget why there are few buffalo since the iron horse came to their land, and those that live are skeletons walking.

They say a man is three days away from begging for food, five days away from stealing to eat, and eight days away from killing to stay alive. It seems clear then that the plains Indians are men because they *will* kill for the food we have and they need to stay alive.

Like the game they call, they willingly stand before my rifle trusting my sure shot to take their life without pain.

I *was* too young to boss a crew of sun hardened men the age of my Papa and too untried to anticipate the harshness of this rich flat land. I knew I was too young, and so scouted ahead, looking for firm soil below every foot of every mile of track just as carefully and well as any proud German would do.

Then I found ways each man could benefit from our work and taught and showed them how to deliver the daily mile challenges I set for them, and how and why to be proud of that. I let them see the other ways I stood up and looked out for them and never did they see me weak or unsure or uncertain. My crew delivered our mile targets on or ahead of time every time with fewer men killed, lost, or gone AWOL than any other crew on any tributary line.

Few knew the hazards of laying rail lines over the high plains or saw the dangers hidden in the grasses, gullies, and swales. Those who rolled west by wagon saw only tedious miles of grass, and did not see the wind washed beauty of land and sky. Eyes firmly fixed on the distant continental divide they prayed to a remote rigorous god for deliverance from hungry natives seeking food and a sustainable life.

Only Cookie and our half-breed guide knew I took food when we scouted ahead to find firm land for our rail bed and left caches of food where the guide told me to leave it. In a few weeks, we'd see skinny Indians waiting near the drop spots to receive the provisions for their family tribe. In exchange, they left fresh greens, gourds, grains, and roots; and that made Cookie whistle and grin as he prepared our daily pot of food.

Fresh food is another reason my men lasted longer, worked smarter, and stayed strong and willing. Leaders, you see, are in front leading; they are not behind pushing the slow or the uncommitted.

Yes, that is how my crew made its mile targets and why we lost fewer men than other crews, any rail line.

Call it trading with the enemy as you will…, but I wasn't trading, I was leading.

Yes, I did get my land grant all but free. What's never mentioned with that complaint is that I made the Missouri Pacific offer fair homestead prices to my crewmen too. And my willing, fiercely reliable men quickly became contributing citizens in the townships we established and formed into strong, vital, and engaged communities.

There's no point owning land if you can't make a living from it and enough extra to pay it free and clear before you're old. A man needs to leave his sons a safe place to sleep and to raise their families.

## Agelessness

They say I will not age if I drink living blood each full moon night.

I'm not sure I want to live forever. Nor even to live longer than a man's normal span of years.

Nature cycles even as man does, yet man denies it. Nature fights and kills to eat and live and none call it sin…, except when *man* behaves as nature does. The puzzle of that incongruity gnaws at me. The effects of man's punitive judgments against his fellows is disturbingly more intolerable than not drinking blood full moon nights.

Reason rarely trumps addictions, so this aversion is a perplexing conundrum to me.

Observe and you will see the great unnatural man turn his face against nature giving no regard to the Divine expressed as earth, air, wind, and water, nor to the cycles of life that begins at breath and ends at death. Unnatural man denies man has a right to take a life, placing that right below man's responsibility to give, to nurture, and to preserve life. *Que tonto! Que increable estupido!*

The blind judgments of man must make the Divine weep with despair at the people he created as caregivers of earth and its riches intending for us to make gardens of Eden all over this blue planet. Instead we created wastelands. Man callously kills natives, animals, and birds; and takes trophies of every kill. Then boasts over our battles and calls them good because we still live.

Walking wounded, we are.

The circle of life turns with or without my consent.

I *will* spin the whirling cogs of that wheel to shape the life I mean to live.

# The Barren Wife

"The Daughters should have a say in what's done about Father. It's our children too who are spoiled by his randy love. The Daughter mothers *should* also have a say in protecting our children."

"And the Sisters…?"

Hester flashes a lopsided grim grin, "The Sisters got their message to Hester speaks of the pregnant nun who retired to the nunnery. Our sons and daughters came at risk then."

Jacob nods amiably, "the Daughters have as much at risk as the Knights." He looks away, irritated, then snaps: "And, Father would not have owned the problem in the presence of women, nor would he have willingly been part of the solution, and we didn't leave much but agreement for Father to contribute."

Hester steps away to refresh their coffee keeping her eyes averted. Firmly replacing the pot on the burner she says "he never…," She frowns tight, "Father didn't do anything to *our* sons did he?"

Jacob chortles, and when Hester looks up he beckons her back to her chair. "Remember when I invited Father to come bless our herd, and I just *happened* to be castrating a yearling when he arrived?" Hester nods; Jacob continues, "Well, they say a picture is worth a thousand words, so I gave Father a picture so crystal clear that he didn't need one spoken word to take my message." Jacob's eyes dance with glee, "The boys were helping with the gelding, and when Father saw me with my pliers and both boys helping with the castration, he went a *very* unlovely bilious yellow and excused himself until we finished. As Father left the barn he assured us our new steer would get a very *special* blessing when we were done. Our sons' eyes blessed *me* when Father left us to our work; and we shared an openly conspiratorial clucking, crowing, bawling laugh." He nods agreement, "Unrepentant…, to the man."

Hester studies her husband and murmurs "You *planned* that. You gelded that animal for the sole purpose of showing Father what he puts at risk if he *doesn't* keep his pants zipped when performing his priestly duties."

"With intention, planning, and premeditated aforethought; yes, I did." He adds a defensive, "I feel bad about the bull though! He'd have sired *many* fine calves to the herd." He winces and moans "and *so* much money lost in stud fees...."

"Husband, you are disconcertingly like your father when you have decided on a thing. You are one eyed and uncompromising to the end." she grins despite herself, "and you do it with sinister innocence." She is silent a moment then asks? "What if Father had *not* gotten the message? "Wait, Jacob. On second thought, I do *not* want to know." Smiling faintly she adds "I am continually thankful that you are on my side. Tell me what happened in the Knights' meeting with Father."

Jacob frowns then slides a hand over hers. "Father admitted that he is a randy son who winked at the vow of celibacy and took the penitent's path of silent and frequent confession and 'purifying' self-castigation. Knowing that complicity inspires secrecy Father made it an *honor* to be chosen to 'help' him on the altar and always stressed the need to keep their secret forever, and to never tell anyone."

"Jacob, *stop*! Hester gasps; "you *must* not tell me this. I too know how to use your *special pliers* and I am *sorely* tempted to use them for an altogether other objective other than growing large meaty beef for the table. This man is our parish priest...." Fighting a grin and failing, she revels in glee "It would not *do* for a Daughter to castrate her Father; and throw his balls..., to the sea, I suppose. Our parish is far too small to house that mighty myth, Jacob.

"Tell me about the Knights' solution instead."

"Hedda Geis is a Daughter isn't she?" Hester nods with an arch-browed frown; Jacob sips coffee. "Well, as it turns out, Hedda loves Father – her words, according to Reinhold; and she will happily serve as housekeeper and cook for Father, and take care of his physical needs while she's there." Studying the steam curling off his coffee Jacob whispers surly sour stoic "so that Father can keep taking care of *the spiritual needs of his parishioners*." Despite himself, his last six words come out as a judgmental growl.

Hester inhales sharply, and whispers "Hedda's barren." Jacob nods. "What did Reinhold say about this?"

"I quote. 'She's barren. She loves sex. She'll take care of me before, and after, she takes care of Father. I'm retired. The extra income will help.'"

"He said it that *dispassionately*?" Jacob nods. "That is *painfully* cynical."

"Or purely practical." Jacob defends to the jury of his cup, then adds "Words don't change reality, Hes. Perfect solutions are of God's realm. They are as rare as hen's teeth where man lives. Human plans cannot anticipate all the ways an issue shows up in life." Sliding a hand over hers, he adds "life is imperfect, wife-mate, sometimes only an imperfect solution meets a life need."

Hester sighs "I know. Still, I want to protect Hedda from what she knows is wrong and wants *anyway*!" Lowering her eyes she admits softly "I have a passion to punish Father for the harm he's done the people he came to shepherd and to protect. Why *not* ask the Church to assign him to another parish, or to another role in the Church?"

Jacob numbers the reasons on his fingers "That moves him to other people who don't know his problem. That's avoidance, not a solution. There is nowhere *else* to move him. He's too young to retire. We are a small parish, insignificant to a global church *with* a past Popes who took the name Innocent to declare their blamelessness for being born *the son of a Pope*." He clicks his tongue and spits, "I'm not over that yet…, and it's only *been centuries* ago.

"We either resolve the problem with Father, or we keep living with the outcomes and adapting to them because ignoring the truth *does not work*. There is no perfect solution, Hes, but this one works. Hedda and Reinhold will make it work," his fierce eyes meet hers, "with or without Father's help. Reinhold agreed to the plan first to protect the children, then for Hedda," he shakes his head in perplexity and awe, "for her *good love* for Father; and then for the parish, and for the community."

The couple silently studies the order of the willing Knight's advocacy aims, and Jacob speaks. "Sheriff Ben was there. The Knight in him goes militant when talk turns to the pregnant nun, and it did. He wants to go strike the head off a serpent, or dethrone an arch-demon, or some other-worldly worthy deed."

"I think Father remembered my special pliers because he glanced my way, and *quickly* assured Ben that when he became a priest he believed he could be celibate, that he *could* manage his urges by censure, denial, and penance. Now he knows better, and willingly accepted the Knights' solution."

"Did Father tell the truth, do you think?"

"Truth is more a journey than a destination, Hes. When she prepares the favorite meal of a guest, Hedda will eat with Father and his guest. Father will *never again* call children from school to 'help him'." Jacob scratches his palm vigorously, "My hand *aches* to use my good tool on our good priest."

He sobers sipping coffee, "Maybe Father heard the truth this time and let it set him free to be the priest he always hoped to be. He's not the first to feel shame for his physical needs and act in guilty, shameful ways. Did you know Father was zealous about mortification to discipline the body into obedience? I'd hate to be his dog." He grins and shrugs, "Maybe not; for I surely *would* bite the hand that feeds me."

"Father owns some punishing beliefs, Hes, and has scars to tell the power of those beliefs."

"Scars?"

"Before Father arrived; and after the Knights were sworn to confidence, Reinhold told what Hedda said him about seeing Father's scars when she was 'cleaning his private office'."

"Private office?" Hester's eyes dancing dangerous delight, "Tell.…"

"I *thought* you would go there…, the Knights certainly did. It seems that Hedda sometimes prepared special meals for Father and quickly noticed that each special meal she prepared was the favorite food of Father's guest. One day, after talking with Reinhold, Hedda asked Father if she could prepare for him *her* favorite meal and be his guest to eat it. Before Father could catch his breath to speak, Hedda quietly and pointedly confessed to Father that she was barren and could bear no child.

"As it turns out, Hedda's favorite meal *is* Father's favorite meal, and soon the Knights are calling it a shake and no bake meal; and that rampage continued until our watch Knight came to say Father was on the way so we could settle down and be knightly before he arrived."

"You *planned* this? You set a watchman?"

Jacob nods sober as a judge, "Indeed we did. We Knights did *not intend* to need Father's forgiveness *before* our meeting with him began. The unexpected blessing of spending our anger in high camp is that no one got down the ceremonial sword and rebuked Father into a gelding before the meeting began." Hester tips back her head in opening, easing, healing laughter.

"It was an uncommonly dramatic evening, Hes," Jacob stifles his glee enough to add: "it was one of the oddest Knights gatherings I have *ever* participated in."

# The Killing Field Redux

"*Stop.*" Comes the running demand from behind the men as they work. "*Stop* it, now!" The fierce cry comes nearer, carried on fleet furious feet. The men turn to watch a girl with streaming hair, dirty face and gritty livid eyes approach. Curious or wary the men set the safety and lower or holster their guns.

The girl eyes each man as she comes to a panting stop by the pit. One is dressed nice, *like an official* she thinks. She moves along until she finds a face and eyes she knows will hear and not merely listen. She focuses her attention him and speaks with the unbridled power of her anger expecting every man to listen, and *to* hear. "If you cannot kill clean *with one shot* you have no business with a gun!"

A yearling calf with a curiously colored coat bawls bewildered protest for the hard hurting inside his body that overwhelms even the barren taste of salted tumbleweed and dust infused water. This pain is inside him, dominating, overpowering and pinning him like a mouse caught in a cat's cunning claws. Though none notice, the yearling reacts to the unfamiliar rage in the voice of the girl and is puzzled, but glad she has come and he bawls out pain to her who only loved, fed and petted and prettied him in all his days. He knows with simple surety she is come to make the hard hot hurt in him go away.

Looking at the men holding silent downward guns the girl sees who they have become and who they were, cowboys, farmers, fathers, men who came to the plains or were born to the living land for a long enough time to learn to love it and living in it.

Before the dusters came. And came again, and still again. For *these* dusted gritty men the girl adds softly, gently, "And none of *you* have any duty or cause to do this hard cruel work."

Bam White flinches at the flint in her words and the fiery hard sparking truth of what it is they do for a daily wage when none other is offered. Each man thinks of his own kids, and the other gritty men on the crew who *do this cruel work*, and Bam defends them and him, "these men are good shots, every one. No man hits the target 100% of the time."

Looking into the pit of breathing skeletons with unblinking eyes the girl snaps "whoever shot that calf" she jabs a finger at the yearling "*hit* the target. *That* is not the problem. And it's not the solution either."

"We only get one bullet per animal," says a hangdog defensive man.

"If your target is the whole calf," she snaps, "then you hit the target. And you *still* missed your mark." Her blue gold eyes glint hard as sapphire and amber ablaze in sunlight. "There is a reason the red center of a target is called the bull's *eye*," she snaps. The defender blinks perplexed, and she cocks a brow and demands "What's behind the eye of a bull?"

"Why, why" the man stutters. "The brain is."

The girl nods grim agreement. "When the brain dies," she snaps fingers a sharp pop, "it *cannot* send pain messages to the rest of the body." She shoots her arm out to Bam White "give me your gun."

Bam hesitates, checks the safety lock, then spins the trigger guard on his index finger and slaps the gun grip into the waiting hand of the girl. She receives the weapon, cocks the trigger, sights down the gun, raises a brow, sets the safety, pivots the gun and slaps the weapon back into Bam's quick hand.

"*With* a bullet in the chamber" she snaps eyes fixed on the bodies of the dead and dying animals, arm stiff and waiting.

Bam looks to the CCC man overseeing the shoot, he nods once. Bam chambers a bullet, sets the safety, rotates the weapon and slaps the grip into the palm of the girl. She widens her stance, pivots her arm at the shoulder, sights down the barrel, locks elbows and wrists, and aims at the eye of a Holstein milk cow. The name *Queenie* blooms in her mind and she steels heart and eye, and pulls back the hammer.

A calf marked from nose to tail one half white, the other black with a spot of the other shade, one on a shoulder, one on a hip, bawls its puzzled pain in the face of the girl. Quick as no thought she sights into the eye of the yearling and fires before anyone can blink or inhale to protest.

The girl stands frozen in the echo recoiling memories of each day in the life of the calf. She does not blink but a tear pools at the edge of her eye that slips garnet, onyx and amber down her cheek until the liquid is absorbed by the dust powdering her face.

She does not look away from the calf as she locks the safety, spins the weapon butt-out pivots her arm to Bam. As Bam takes the pistol in hand he lays a finger gentle and comforting on her thumb resting in the hollow a chamber giving soft pressure and thinking of his own kids and how he will convey the weight of wisdom the girl bears into them without damaging their still springing innocence. When the girl releases the weight of her words and the gun, her arm drops motionless at her side.

Relieved of the weight of the weapon the girl turns and walks seven solid paces into the setting sun where she stops unable now to bear the weight of what she and the farmers and the government have done to prophesy and preordain this day in a killing field in a raped and pillaged land she loved from its deepest roots to the farthest reaches of its bleak blistered sky as barren of rain cloud as the land is of grass and grain and green. Tears fall freely now, the sun burning them dirt dry on her cheeks, her body shudders for she cannot cry or wail or scream, her throat is bereft of sound and word, her lungs and heart forlorn shorn of capacity to tell this day or the events of it.

Her head bows of its own accord and she surrenders her full measure of pain and anger and rage at the sheer desolation that shatters life and the living of it. She bears the hopelessness pressing down her spirit and feels it as dry and cracked as the streambed where water once ran, splashed and played among deep rooted bog plants and green was forever the color of the day. When morning and midday and sunset were still causes for blazing irrepressible joy and delight.

Into the setting sun she pours it all, the heavy weight of disappointments, losses, discontents, pain, and the insidious, abiding absence of life and joy in living it that rode the angry dark dusters and stayed far too hard and long choking hope down to its deep parched roots. She let it all go, she just let go.

| Shawn Gallaway – The Truth |
| --- |

Having mourned losses and things left undone, the girl recalls times when brilliant stars shone through a midnight blue sky and sang odes to the joy of life and living it. She sees anew the fiery riot of colors of autumn on the plains, the gilded tassels of grasses, the heads of wheat, rape and rye coming ripe for harvest. She savors anew the reds, the golds, and the undulating umbers of spring, summer, fall, and the dazzling iridescent whites of winter. She delights again in the luminously alive green of wheat pushing through the sunny silvery snow. The spring of spring springs reborn replenish the girl, hope returns, and she can smile again. Some of the mud caked on her cheeks shatters and falls away.

"Young lady –"

She starts at hearing her new name, and thoughtfully focuses on the voice that speaks and what it will say to a *lady*. "I'm with the Civilian Conservation Corps," The voice falls silent a long moment then continues. "The CCC has a one bullet per animal limit when we do kills" he says apologetically. "That half black, half white steer got two bullets, which means I will have to explain to the CCC why that happened. I don't want to do that.

"So, here's what I will do – *because of you* – young lady." He says sternly. "I will account for that second bullet," he rubs his neck, "somehow. And I will teach other CCC workers about targeting on the eye of the animal, as you have done, and they will teach it to their crews, and so on." He pauses to compose himself for what comes next, and then continues, "and I promise *you*" thinking of his own child "that I will do everything I can do so that your yearling is the last to suffer because of a bad target," he casts a hard eye to the shooter who flushes and lowers his eyes, "and because of the CCC's one-bullet rule."

The girl finds a smile within her and says "thank you" soft and firm. Thank you for that." She closes her eyes against a hard truth, and sees the humanity of his mission to change her place, her people, and her distressed land for the better. *He is a good man*, she thinks, and pours a smile gratitude into the setting sun asking the sun to use it as a template for all her tomorrow days. In reply, the sun smiles and sings.

| Shawn Gallaway – As You Are |
|---|

### The Healing Field

Bam and the others hear the song of the sun, and in the silence that follows, he speaks gentle, as to his own girls, "We take all the animal hides to a tanner to have them cleaned, cured and distributed for re-use." His head bows under the liquid weight of the words he has to, will, and must speak.

"I will save aside the hide of your calf for you; and when it's cured, dried and rubbed smooth inside I'll bring it to you." He grins a crooked apology for wrongs too weighty to be endured by one alone, and adds "I'll be sure Tanner knows the value of this rare hide and who it's for, and when it's ready and done, I'll 'distribute' the hide to you," he pauses to shoulder a curious weight of pain and pleasure in equal measure, and adds "and, I will be the one that brings it to you."

The girl raises her head and nods him thanks. Bowing again she lifts her hands to shield her face from the eyes of the sun and silent poignant tears slip away at the thought of seeing and touching the hide of Paradox without Paradox in it.

> Shawn Gallaway – All Shall Be Well

All the men in the killing field hear the song and each smiles as the child within reawakens and frolics again for an infinite eternity in their hearts. Bam White touches hand to his heart receiving the return of the bright child of light who dances there unyielding before the carnage surrounding the older outer man he is and gently welcomes his innocent child back safely home again.

*I can't wait to be home again,* Bam reflects, realizing as he does that the aspiration rises like a morning bird from deep inside his newly healed heart. He smiles knowing it is already done.

> Shawn Gallaway – Healing Happens

Opening her eyes again to the setting sun, the girl lifts her weight of woe up to the great furnace and pours it in with careless grace, not saving any at all for another day. She gathers up all the anger and stubbornness that lives in her, all her imagined inadequacies, her ensuing willfulness, and all her irritated irreverence for what others hold dear. Imagining the very absolutely hottest spot in the heartless heat of the sun, she dumps it all in. She reserves nothing of who she thinks she is and how she imagines, and how finds life to be presenting itself to her. She let go. She *just* let go.

> Shawn Gallaway – The Wind Is Always

In the great wind of release the girl enters a space of the possibility of *another* ending, another path of destiny, and a wholly other outcome for Paradox. She prays for and receives Source guidance embracing, penetrating and filling her with incomprehensible hope that melts itself into another shape and form of a whole other destiny for her, for her land, for *her* animals and *her* grasses and *her* trees.

She feels herself embraced in abandoned surrender, falling passionately in love with the very idea of love. She open heartedly calls love forth into her awareness with the hope and the expectation that it is *already done*. She utterly and passionately loves *all of it* with an aching bowing ever filling renewing and flowing fullness; *and the rain came, soft and gentle, sweet and clear.*

While rain falls in another dimension of reality, Bam offers the girl an amendment and apology in a few small words, "that bullet hole in the hide, I'll have the tanner cut it out before I bring it to you."

"No." It is a report retort, a terse passionate protest freighted into a single word that resounds and reverberates like echoes of thunder in a canyon. "Leave the hole in the hide where it lays," she breathes the command arresting and sounding the immutable reality of facts of their life and the living of it. She is determined to find, own, and allow, the powder dry authority of all her perfectly parsed parched proofs, and send them up to the sun to be purified and redeemed and released. She just lets it all go.

For it was these hard dry facts that led, pushed, prodded, and steered her – and each of the shooters – to this place and time, and ordained for all of them to stare steadfast and unbowed into the soulless eyes of fickle fate and to leap into it anyway. And so she does.

And an ancient strong wind whispers truth: "*be careful for nothing; but in every thing, by prayer and supplication with thanksgiving, let your requests be made known unto God.*" Philippians 4:6

The girl searches out and collects every longing loving memory she has, and some she recently dreamed, of rain, and the cooling deep cleansing of it. In faith and hope and love, she tips back her head sticks out her tongue and dances in the rain of new life in a fluid flow of alternate fates and a wholly other reality she never dared see or say. The endless rain washes her clear, clean and whole again.

Soaked and sated the girl springs light-footed and assured through the treacherous terrain of mind fields well sowed with deep-rooted memories and littered through with love and the detritus of mind bombs violently detonated in the happenings of life.

She senses that the infinitely vigilant inner Presence knowingly left them rooted there to await the fullness of time and of healing. Memory stalks and stirs moving like a restless wind over a killing field at the end of an infinite abiding struggle in the moral mortal contest inherent in Spiritual warfare. A silent knowing blooms in her inner warrior who is aware and at choice actively untangling and mending the fabric of life on the bleak barren plains.

Golden gouts of joy gush and guide her and the silent men to the path of power showing the way to just let be what is while holding firm and fast to a higher vision of what *might be* instead.

"I need that black burned hole," the girl speaks simple and true, "and I cannot tell you the why of it. I do not know..., not the whole of it..., nor even a whole part of it. I know only that *I must* see and feel the seared edge of that great black hole when you bring the hide of Paradox back to me.

| Shawn Gallaway – Living Without Edges |

In an infinite and eternal space within the girl envisions another outcome and tracks the ways a story arch must alter to lead to a different outcome, another reality, another possibility. She sees and feels the other happier outcome, *a paradox for Paradox*, she thinks with a smile and experiences that truth *as if* it were the only real reality. And so it is. She knows that before it happens and she just lets go to a higher will and wisdom incipient with the power of chosen change.

She hears the gravelly gentle voice of Bam behind her say to the men "any man here who is not absolutely certain and sure he can kill clean with one bullet, step over here and I'll teach you how to do it – so you can go back to your wife and children with a and calm cheerful heart."

The CCC man is the first to step to Bam's side willingly submitting to being tutored by the killing master of this cowboy crew of meager mortal men working for two dollars a day in a desperate battle to relieve the abiding scrape of the dusters ravaging the resilient topsoil of a land that during the global war was called 'the bread basket of the world'.

As the shooters form a line behind the agent, Bam's thoughts stray to his eldest son Melt who newly knew of his Native American heritage and, still seeing only with his white man eyes, cannot yet receive nor savor the worthy wisdom, dignity and resilience of the new-found ancient elders of his family tribe.

| Shawn Gallaway – Cross That Bridge |

Dense with the grit of the plains and the mystic mystery of it, Bam bows to the wisdom of the tribe of his wife-mother of his children and humbly asks for grace and guidance in the walk and work of melting Melt's frozen heart from the persistent angry and forbidding weight of his new old legacy. Bam prays and praises the Mother for doing the work of freeing Melt of his hard heart so he reclaims and receives the eyes, the heart and the wisdom of his ancient ones, and comes to own, allow, and celebrate the blood heritage gifted him by his mother in her last breath that delivered him to life and the living of it.

Melting into the comfort of the song sung for Bam and his native son, the girl surrenders all the cherished hopes and dreams that no longer work and willfully dumps them into the cauldron of the sun watching as they melt and are purified, renewed and refined. The sun and the abiding wind sing and play a truthful melody to her.

| Shawn Gallaway – The Real More |
| --- |

And the girl is the Real More. She opens her arms wide to the fresh falling rain, tips back her head, pokes out her tongue, and dances in the torrent of new life vibrant and alive with promise. She conceives and sees a moving picture showing of alternate possibilities teeming alive with wholly other realities never before dared, never before seen nor spoken. She lets the endless rain wash her pure and clear and clean and whole again.

In a daisy strewn bluegrass field in a distant infinite neighboring galaxy the girl frolics in the sun with a calf marked from nose to tail one half black, the other white, each with a spot of the other shade, one on a shoulder, one on a hip. Together they cross rain washed lush green grass and into the rising sun on the first eternal day of a pleasant and fertile land that could be her own in an unimagined future.

### The Paradox Hide

True to his word, the CCC agent sends Bam White with the black and white hide of Paradox wrapped in brown paper from Smithy's Farm and Implement store. Shy and sheepish, Bam extends the wrap to the girl and places it humbly in her hesitant hands.

The girl's lids flutter three rapid blinks as she feels the hollow weight inside the wrap bereft of the spirit of Paradox.

With infinite reluctance she reverently pulls aside the paper to reveal the Paradox hide folded neat and sweet to display both the black and white of it.

Stifling a swelling scream the girl shakes open the hide searching frantically for the hard black hole in the black side of the hide, when she finds it, she pushes a finger through, and turns a weak moist smile on Bam.

"Thank you, Bam," she whispers husky, "you're a good man."

The good man starts in wonder hearing his new true name. He colors a bit, highlighting the shy smile he has for the girl, and then awkward again, he adds, "Guess I'll be going then," he speaks to the room and to Hester in it, "but I'll come back when I can, to look in on you good folks and see how you're doing."

Bam cocks a lopsided parting grin at the girl and adds: "and to see what you make of that fine hide of yours." He turns to go and turns back again,

"I almost forgot *the most important thing*. Smithy said to tell you that he'll let you use his leather punch, his other tools, and his needles, *on the condition* that you come to his store often enough that he can teach you how to use his tools *'on the leather,'* the man said, and not on your own hide."

The girl grins up at him and Bam sees an intimation of mystery and magic in her laughing eyes, and knows without asking that she will not share what's behind them. He bobs his head and turns to go.

When the clop-clop of the mule hoofs fade into the music of the ever restless wind, Hester silently studies the girl nuzzling the pelt, finger through the burnt black hole and watches as crystal drops of tears fall on the finger and slide around and into the seared black hole left by the bullet.

The girl eases her finger back watching the tears slip and slide into the void black hole, and with a heart full smile she gently massages the salt and water into the burn until the blemish of the scorch softens and the hole in the suede eases soft and supple again.

Without raising her head or asking the girl snatches the paring knife from her mother and stabs it cruelly into the finger poking through the hide hole, then slaps the knife handle into Hester's still open palm. The girl lovingly massages the blood into the scar and Hester imagines, or sees, the burnt ring soften, plump, and become whole again as the hell fire agony is eased from the hide and the hole in it.

"Why did you do that?" The question is a sharp command demand prayer for reason and hope, and Hester returns to the reliable rational root of the Earth to peel away the brown skin of a potato.

She is poleaxed for knowing certain and sure that she pares away the health carrying cover of the spud as surely the wind pared away endless eras of whole rich earth baring the inner core and heart blood of her beloved plains to the ravages of drought, and the restless wrecking wind.

Leaving the peel where it dangles, she quarters the potato and drops it into the cooking pan with a splash.

"You aren't peeling them?" the girl asks.

"No," she snaps, "all the vitamins and minerals of a potato are in the peel and few or none in the flesh. Hereafter this family shall have the empty flesh cooked *inside* the healthy cover the Creator made for it.

The girl returns to painting the black hole red. "*Why* are you doing that?" Hester rephrases her question and drops her gaze to the bloody finger caressing the hole in the hide.

The girl is silent for long and long and Hester is patient, knowing without reason that the answer will tear through her, and her child, with an icy manic fury packing the pitiless raging wrath of the Four Horsemen, returned and now riding the punishing winds and dark clouds of Black Sunday.

Ecological disaster born by the folly and faults of man.

Hester watches the girl as she works and is startled breathless to see her raise palms to her face in a harrowing image of The Scream by Edvard Munch.

**The Scream, Edvard Munch 1880 - 1916**

Profoundly moved by the stark power of the colors and the image when she saw it, Hester cut it from the magazine out and tucked it in her Bible at a random page of Armageddon never to think of it again. Now she prays, *Mother Father God be whole in me this day – for I need you wholly whole in me this day.*

Gently taking the hide from the hands of the girl, Hester raises it searching the black hide side for the hole in it. Finding it, she lets her own tears fall as she gently salves them into the torn bloody circle feeling soft suppleness reestablished in the burned edge. Turning back to the sink, she takes up her knife, poises it over a finger and aborts the plunge down and in, when her child cries out.

"*No!*" With firm tenderness the girl takes the knife from her mother, dropping it into the sink again.

"Tell me why you did this," Hester demands pushing the wet hole at the girl, fiercely firm.

Head bowed, the girl's voice is made tender by the demanding pain as she whispers a soft confession. "When we had only salted tumbleweeds to feed the calves" her eyes squeeze tight against a profound terrible truth, she whispers "I gave Paradox some of my blood... every day."

Stunned blinking blind by the words and the weight of them, Hester cannot speak nor yet breathe.

Into the cavernous maw of the silence of infinity, the girl whispers, "I think it helped him, Mom; that my blood gave Paradox something he needed to live, that kept his coat shiny and his muscles strong." Almost apologetic she adds "he stayed healthy on empty food the other calves became..., as they were when they were shot." A fierce protective anger freights and weights the last word to its knees.

*I'll ask Bam when he comes again what happened on that killing field and why the bawling calf fell silent.* Still, the hole in the hide uploads its tale into her mind whether true or not. Hester decides then and there to *not* to ask Bam to give voice to the deeds of that unhappy day in the killing field.

Hester takes the right hand of the girl turning the finger tips gently to her face and sees the web of scars from a knife point, crystal white and luminous like cross-hatching of ice on a window, telling the reality without words. Freeing the right hand, she raises the girl's left hand and finds a cross hatch of scars weaving a pattern of amazing grace and truth. *The weave of the Heart*

*Cloth* Hester perceives, then gives herself over as her heart sings a burdened mournful sweet triumphant tune.

> Shawn Gallaway – Breathe A Little Magic

A week of days later the girl comes to her mother wearing a sleeved vest of black and white leather stitched together with ribbons of rawhide, calling out "Mom, look!"

Hester turns and sighs a soft breath "why that is *stunning*, child. What an excellent job you have done cutting and sewing it, it fits you perfectly." Looking closer she frowns and snaps "the bullet hole is over your heart – as if it struck *you* there."

The girl tucks her head and speaks a soulful certainty: "It did," she says simply.

Hester puffs and pipes: "well it is just ghastly *ghoulish*. You cannot wear it. I won't allow it. Take it off." She watches the girl's lips fall into a sharp line, her face harden like flint flashing inner fire. She knows she has lost her case before pleading it. Her heart wails and weeps although her eyes do not.

"I'll put a red rose over it like the ones our rose bush had before...." She falls silent facing unfathomable fickle fate and explaining it is beyond her. Instead she pulls from a pocket a piece of red felt formed in a golden curve of perfect coiling petals swelling into the sweet curl of outer edges releasing a faint fragrance of the earthy life scent of a rose. She places the rose in her mother's palm and says "put your fingers like this," she demonstrates, "and turn it about a quarter turn."

Hester does and is dazzled to see the petals curl and arch up, the embracing curl of the center petal lifting and inspiring the other petals to follow in their turn.

"That's brilliant! What a clever design, so simple, and yet so deeply inspired."

"Freedom said I should give this to you, and I think you should embroidery over the felt with red embroidery floss to make the petals shine. She put a pin on the back so you can pin it to anything."

"Freedom made this then?" the girl nods with a satisfied grin. "And..., what will you put over the hole in the heart of your Paradox coat?"

"This one," she says pulling out another rose crafted from leather, laying it in a palm and spinning it into its full bloom, smiling all the while.

"Smithy used Paradox's white ear died red to cut the rose, see how the small petals curl like a calf's ear? I need to use some of your red embroidery floss to attach the suede rose over the hole in the Paradox coat," she explains pulling out Hester's last skein of rose red embroidery thread, "can I use some of your embroidery floss to do it?"

Hester cannot stifle the gleeful giggle that bubbles up from her gut to blast warm and soft through her sacral chakra, then tarrying awhile in her heart before meandering to her mind and mouth collecting sound and finding a puzzled but happy voice. "Yes, you can!" Frowning now she asks "*How* will you attach the rose to the leather coat?"

The girl grins "Smithy showed me how. I'll need ten or twelve inches of floss to attach the rose along these dots around the bullet hole to the center of the rose." Hester nods. "That's how I'll sew the rose to the Paradox coat."

Hester giggles as gleefully as a child splashing in the spouting spray of a fountain. "And this you will do with your bare fingers?"

Grinning the girl pulls a pair of black leather gloves from a pocket of the coat and presents them to her mother who snaps "So…, you will push a needle through a leather hide using *glove leather* and *that's* your plan for protection?" The girl turns a glove finger inside out and presents the inner tip to her mother. "Oh, *two* layers of glove leather instead of one – *that* is your solution?"

Pushing the inner tip out, the girl points to the leather patch and says "tap here with your fingernail."

Hester hears a metallic ring and smiles, "sounds like tin," the girl nods.

"That's brilliant! I'll take Smithy a dressed goose for teaching you his art and the craft of it, and for letting you use his tools. Smithy *loves* bird better than any other meat, and goose better than any other bird. 'Blessed with the Divine spark' Smithy swears."

"Divine spark?" the girl queries doubtful.

"Everything eternally carries the spark of the Divine. Man alone may know, own, allow and *choose* Truth as a *functional* reality…, or keep on doubting and denying Truth experiences simply because they can't be proven.

"Truth is eternal and cannot be weighed, measured, or shaped into a physical form. Yet it is still functional to the one who knows how to use Truth wisely and when."

The girl cocks both brows and amends *"wisely* and *well?"*

"No. Wisdom is not wise if it's applied at a time when it won't work well at all.

*When* you apply your art is always more vital to pleasant outcomes than applying it *well*."

"*Example*," the girl demands.

Hester grins, merry eyes dancing "Had you tried to sew your blooming rose to the Paradox hide while Paradox was wearing it he would have objected *mightily* to make you stop poking him with a needle."

"Mo-o-o-m" the girl wails, "that's just *rude*."

"But *effective* – don't you think?"

The girl grins, gathers tools and thread and turns away to finish adorning her Paradox coat.

---

**eLBe recommends**: *The Worst Hard Time: The Untold Story of Those Who Survived the Great American Dust Bowl* by Timothy Egan, New York Times national enterprise reporter and author.

# The Angel Garden Redux

"Tell me what you can see of The Angel Garden." The girl asks absently, arms crossed and linked around her knees.

*That is not a casual question!* Hester thinks casting a sidelong glance at the girl. She's feeling set up for a fall, and she does not know why.

She defaults to her habitual value, her small self-consciousness. She feels safely familiar there.

Safe....

Safe in a habitually benign self-sabotager's crooked way. Negating safety through dedicated devotion to her small self-awareness of who she is, and why she is here. Not against her will, oh no, not that!

The serpent that lured Hester to her free-fall from grace was her own indwelling powerless, knowing-less, *witless*, devotion of who it is she *thinks* she is. Who she thinks she is, is 'The Whole Truth' of the small self who it is she *believes* she came to be. *I see through the glass darkly.* She concedes the small truth that rides her, a wicked wyvern, with claws hooked hard deep and disabling into her self-esteem.

Hers is a stunning fall from grace without the net of faithful faith in a truth of reality that does *not* arise from faith, but needs the strong uplifting wings of trust in grace asked for and received. And then the ball-buster for Hester: Why is it that she is *here?*

Why am I *here*? Why *here* on this Earth-bound and wingless in a barren land filled empty with wilting withering rootless life set sundered and airborne in the relentless ruthless reckoning wind of Terrible Thundering Truth?

*Why* are *you here?* The D.O. waits awhile and then answers, knowing Hester is currently incapable of getting, nor saying aloud and proud, her truth in her own soul. *You are here to mother the girl.* Hester's self-installed low-slung glass ceiling does not shake, shatter, nor break.

The D.O. sighs a more irritated and impatiently insistent, and leaps full force like a blast furnace into the breach in Hester's self-awareness that gapes stark, bare, wind worn torn and twisted into her tight, tiny, and torqued empty core of withered faithless faith in grace. The D.O.'s shouts the fury of His frustration intending to shatter the deeply rooted faithlessness faith that shelters safe and sound in the heart, mind and brain of the woman who would be Mother and not just *mother*. *The big 'M', what a shift it creates.*

The D.O. hears the empty echo that resounds through her body, mind, brain, and fully and faithfully revealed in her vacant face, and faith. *Her inner eye great eye is as peacefully, and innocently closed as a babe before the breath of life is blown into its eyes, nose and mouth, animating the Earth suit even as it inspires the quickening breath of life.*

The D.O., who imbued the Third Eye to all of mankind as a gift of grace free-given and fully formed, and not yet received, is *not* amused. He shouts: *Why are you here?*

*Nothing..., not even a blink of an eye. Mesmerized....*

*I gave you free will!* The D.O. thunders, and in that moment the voice of Zeus the Thunderer inspires the Spirit of Thunder to sing an ode to joy amplifying the power of praise in full vibrato thundering True voice, and Truth has its way, and its sway. *What's a good God to do but give what is needed, even it's not what she thinks she wants? What a determined bull-head bitch she's become, hide-bound and determined to have it her way, and make others responsible for the consequences of her willfully negligent choices. Hester is a slow learner. I judge that it is high time for her to take a wild wildcat coaster ride on the back of a dragon that makes The Polar Express look tame.*

Dragon, snaps finger and thumb, and to Hester it sounds and feels like thunder too far away to change anything in the here and now.

Here and now is where a desultory dragon impatiently paces whipping its tail and stirring up dust clouds that coil like dark twisters bearing a wicked weight of dust and turmoil.

Hester is at a choice point, standing in the V of a fork in the great red road of life. Each choice may be wrong. Each choice may be right. Does she declare the inner sub audible truth of her and ride the Dragon? Or not? She dwells awhile in silence heeding only inner inaudible voice of a peaceful piece resounding alive with echoes of thunder.

*You are here to guide her safe and true along the straight and narrow way that is* eternally *littered with mesmeric tempting and fruitful looking forks in the road.*

*Your way is to walk the way of the Mother, by accepting what is, and then finding the ways and the will to change it for the better.*

*'I may not change the world, but I will* not *leave it the same'. You were inspired by the Kayette motto Does it inspire you still?*

*You know this, Hester! You've taken those fruitless forks more than once in this lifetime, and in those in an Infinite* Eternity *of lifetimes past. You probably don't remember in your present body, mind, brain Earth suit because the conscious mind – where the co-Creator lives – lacks the processing capacity to comprehend the mega-data that the D.O. can parse true and clear, in a nanosecond.* He snaps his thumb, meets her eyes and says: *That fast.*

*I recycle. In case you weren't aware of that.* The D.O. proclaims with a patently pleased pride. *The subatomic particles currently inhabiting and dynamically enlivening* your *body, mind, and brain Earth suit,* have *inhabited countless Earth suits over the eternal infinite instant. Each and every 'differently bodied' incarnation of the Spirit of you was inspired to life by the breath of thunder stirring in all creatures universally. Ancients knew thunder as the voice of Zeus, the Thunderer.*

*And now, some mysterious energy is eternally stirring the internal stew in the pot of you, and is recombining your singular DNA. That is happening for two reasons:*

*First so that you live long and prosper.*

*And primary before the first..., because I recycle.*

*Sub-atomic particles of Life Light and Love infinitely bubble and stir the zesty stew of life. The recombined DNA of me is currently and eternally manifesting into human form. Remember Macbeth's three witches?* Hester nods hesitant, like a dog head hung low meekly yielding to the higher power of 'The Master'.

*Trust me on this one, you have everything you need to do everything you came to do in* this *lifetime.*

*Deal with it! But don't get attached to it. The body has a 'best-by' date. Always has done.*

*Is that worthy enough for you?* Hester nods, thinking she's done this before and logic won't work.

*Now, wounded wary one, are you ready for a dragon ride?*
*Dragon ride?*
*Me?*
*Ready?*
*When?*
*How long will I be gone?*
*STOP dithering!* The D.O. demands in command form actually, but who's keeping score? The D.O. is. He mislikes obedience, and he does not admire humans who submissively obey.

Hester's riding the fence like it's a wild bronc. Obedient. But not compliant. The D.O. is not amused.

The only obedience he admires is to traffic laws; and he doesn't much like admire *that* either. He admits, owns, and allows though that negligent and willful disregard of traffic laws makes His people *dead*. I*t is He, the D.O., who* gets to choose the best by date of each an every one of humans he makes!

*I have an undeniably love/hate relationship with man.*
*Woman too – if truth be known.*
*So, willful woman, answer me and tell me true: Why are you here?*
*No answer for that? Then* tell *me* how much *can* you see of The Angel Garden.

*Not much.* Hester murmurs abashed admission to her feet.
*I – I – can't even see the gate.*
*Nor the chain link fence.*
*Nor the weeds and vines that always grow beside it.*
*I can't see anything inside.*
*I hear there's a dome....*

The D.O. giggles, joyful, belly wiggling glee and asks: *Would you like go inside and see for yourself?*

*Yes. But if I can't see something, I can't go inside it; and I can't see the gate, nor the fence nor any other part of it, inside or out! How can I go inside something I can't even see?*

*Believing is seeing,* the D.O. replies evenly. *Have you ever considered that conundrum? Ever pondered it? What if both answers are true? What if seeing is believing,* and *believing is seeing? What then?*

*Now, tell me new and true: Why are you here?*
*To be a mother, that is what I came to do.*
*True that.*
*Drill down.*
*I came to be a good mother.*
*What do you mother?*
*What? Or who?*
*Start with 'who' first, get that out of the way, it's easier to scope, and easier for you to cope....*
*My children.*
*All of them?*
*Equally, yes.*
*Are all your children equal to all the rest?*
*In my mind, yes.*
*Get out of your mind now. Answer from your heart.*
*Are all my children equal...? Are you asking how I think of them?*
*No. This time, answer from your heart, and not from your head. The heart knows an earlier and more inclusive love and wisdom. The heart is dividing cells, creating bones, marrow, muscles, brain, nerves and nerve endings for six weeks before the heart sends that little blue line from the heart to the head and activates the synapses in the mind/brain. That's a whole other shift in consciousness, Hester. Music tames the savage beast....*

Shawn Gallaway – The Shift Is On

*Did you know, Hester, that the energy of the heart is five thousand times more powerful than that of the mind/brain? This time answer from heart wisdom. Set your mind/brain to the busy work of taking notes. For your own enlightenment and future reference, of course.*

*Why are you here?*

In her mind's eye, Hester sees a descending golden spiral approaching at an amazing pace with glittering grace of a shooting star.

She is breathtakingly bewildered in shock as the form approaches at dizzying spiral speed and she begins to see the outline of a massive lizard body borne aloft on a pair of glistening strutted fibrous wings.

Like Dorothy watching the tornado come, Hester is gob-smack stunned stupid blown away. She loses track of everything she ever knew, everything she ever thought she knew, she even easily forgets her most devout faith in the paltriness of who she thinks she is. She just lets go.

She feels no fear as the glittering gilded dragon king (it *had* to be a king among dragon kind) spirals to a smooth graceful landing, eyes cold fire forged gold, like a boulder on a road. *You ready to ride, Hester?*

*I – I – I don't know how to ride a dragon,* she protests shakily.

*Well this is your lucky day, little lady, because* I am known *among dragon kind as the absolutely best able to keep my rider astride! Even at warp speed.*

*Warp speed?* Hester gasps.

*Take a chill pill, chick. I haven't lost a rider yet.* The dragon leans close and whispers, a spark of pride in his eyes, *I am the current No Lost Human Cargo champion among dragon kind. I ain't losing my title for you and your trivial understanding of speed! Get over it. Then get on board.*

*Am I dressed to ride a dragon – at warp speed?*

*No.* The dragon wiggles its brows like Groucho Marks on a wickedly witty night, and says: *You will be dressed in dragon rider clothes when I beam you aboard.*

*I will?*

*Of course you will! I have my pride to protect.* The dragon sniffs snootily.

*That said, the real truth of the dragon rider clothes requirement is that it's to protect my precious pretty dragon scales – among Dragon kind – known as 'damage-by-dunce dragon riders'.*

*I'll have you know that I'm known among dragon kind as the Wardrobe Master of the Gods.*

*You are probably clueless to this, but 'Wardrobe Master to the Gods' is a title among wise wyvern. It is a* great *honor among dragon kind to be titled master! Of anything! Because* all *dragons do everything furiously, frightfully, rightfully, and enduringly well.*

*You have no respect!*

Hester giggles, she can't help herself.

The dragon lowers its head to eye-height with Hester's, cocks a beetling brow and steam hisses: *Did I say something* funny?

*Um – no – and yes.* Hester replies balancing on a point of faith and an urgent call for Angels, S.T.A.T.

*You see:* It's a hard point that holds her up, so Hester quickly explains: *the answer turns wholly and solely on what* you *mean by 'respect'.*

*For* I do *respect your Dragon Master title.* Hester assures quickly and sincerely and stays on target. *What I do* not *respect is your bossy bullying demanding obedience! Que tonto! Que totalmente estupido!*

*You saying I'm stupid?* The dragon goes dire in one blink of his eyes. Hester is chilled. But not stilled.

*Will you* stop *putting words in my mouth, and then, demonically demanding I defend* your *words for you! That whole passive/aggressive trauma-drama shtick of yours is precisely what I do* not *find worthy of respect in you. You..., you...,* you *dim-bulb dire dragon, have been playing the dumb dragon trauma mama drama far too long.'*

Hester pops him a knowing smile. *It's separation from source anxiety that you're feeling.* She touches her heart and adds: *it's the feeling you get when you have utterly and completely forgotten the truth of who you* are.

She hears the sound of distant thunder and yields to Spirit of Thunder to sunder and shatter her into Perfect Mind. Complete Mind, where the D.O. speaks, and is finally heard in the thundering silence.

*Why you are here? Why are you here with the dragon? Dragon is a guardian spirit! Yet the guardian energy I find in you, is your own timidly terrorizing 24/7 driven drive to guard your self-deceived E.G.O.*

*E.G.O.?*

*Edging God Out.*

*The spirit of Dragon opens new realms of possibility before you and around you. Will you just* play *in the silence with that awhile?* Hester shorts a smile as though recently remembering a really important thing. She shares. *Dragon energy protects creations, and controls emotions.*

| Shawn Gallaway – Choice Point |
|---|

*That being the case, you will just stop blowing smoke and fire simply because there is* so much *hot piss and tart vinegar in your tummy it aches with acid; and dear one, that is a* definition *of self-destruction. Dragon energy acts* only *from inner balance and self-control. The change begins in you, dragon a mine.*

*When does it end?* The worried wyvern wonders.

*Never! You witless worm! Who is an eternal being that has willfully, and functionally, and firmly forgotten that! You should be ashamed of yourself.* Hester stifles a grin and giggle, for that shaming *is a case of the pot calling the kettle black. Never mind.*

*Pot..., kettle..., black.... I don't get it. The wyvern wonders*

*I said never mind! There's something else I want to ask you about anyway.*

*What's that?*

*Um..., can you see The Angel Garden?*

*Yes.*

*Can you see inside The Angel Garden?*

*Yes.*

*What do you see?*

*Death, destruction, devastation, damnation. It's a curious conundrum for me, as an eternal being. I want to know how long will that fast fall will last!*

*Until it's healed.* Hester offers off-handedly casual. *That's why you're here isn't it?*

*Beg pardon?*

*You are here to take me into The Angel Garden*

*Why do you say that?*

*Because I have eyes to see, yet I do not see. Because I cannot be, what I cannot see. Because I have not asked for the grace of Spirit to inspire the breath of life in me. To make me clean, to make me whole, to make me new again; and, because the Master said: 'you have not because you ask not'.*

*Have you asked?* The wise wyvern wonders.

*I'm asking now! Will you fly me into The Angel Garden?*

The dragon smiles, a wise-wyvern-who-was-right-and-he-knows-it, full toothy grin. It's true after all. *Yes. Glad you came to your senses without stuffing common senses down to distant echoes of thunder.*

*Well let's go then.* Hester suggests, suddenly impatient.

*Not yet.*

*Excuse me!*

*You got a ticket to ride, lady? A ticket that's time stamped showing ETA and ETD of an unscheduled flight on The Dragon Express?*

Hester crosses her arms tight, and staccato stamps a foot in angry impatience. The dragon ignores it. She inhales fully, holds it for a count of ten, then letting the lungs rest deflated into emptiness. *Ready.* Hester stays awhile, yet is fully present when the body's oxygen needs compel her lungs to fill and begin anew the rhythm of life within her body/mind/brain Earth suit. Awareness inspires. *Mine is a most excellent Earth suit, Divine Mother. Thank you. Exquisite tailoring too, fits me to a T.*

Welcome.

*So, dragon, when are we leaving this Popsicle stand?*

When everyone we need is here.

*Who are we lacking?*

The girl.

*The girl?*

Yes, the girl. For two reasons: First, she is the only one of the three of us who been in The Angel Garden, second: because without her, neither of us can go in at this stage of the siege, and come out alive.

*I thought you were a mystical magical dragon of power. Don't dragons live forever?*

You are as annoying as a mad, nagging magpie, Hester! The dragon spits fire, the words lash like whipping tongues of fury, flame, and fire. She hears hair sizzle, she smells an acrid stench and hisses: *Damn it! I just got a perm, and my hair was looking* good*! She self-corrects. Okay, let me try asking a different way, what's the risk of going in* without *the girl?*

None!

*O-o-o-k.... If there's no risk of going in without the girl, why don't we just go in without her?*

Because we can't!

*Why?*

Because the Archangels won't let us in.

*Excuse..., no, wait. Just tell me what the Archangels have to do with me going in The Angel Garden.*

Because the Archangels fell from grace. Since then they have behaved like the two cats from Kilkinney.

*How do you know this?*

The dragon does not meet Hester's eyes when he replies. *Bam White told me. Bam's a picker and a grinner and a tall tale spinner; and Bam always tells all tales tall and true. Bam is the reason I am here to get you inside The Angel Garden S.T.A.T. so you can see what is happening in there.*

Dragon touches her chin with the knuckle of a claw. *And mother The Angel Garden healed, healthy, and hale again.*

*What are we waiting for then?*

*The girl.*

*The girl. Why?*

The dragon grins. *It's a disturbing thing,* He says*: But true. The girl breathes a little magic, you see? Things change in a blink of an eye when you breathe a little magic,* the wily wise wyvern whispers.

---

Shawn Gallaway – Breathe A Little Magic

---

*And where is Bam?*

*He'll be here. He's driving Becky in with his buck wagon. The girl's with him.*

*The girl's with Bam? How does that work?*

*You weren't worth* shit *at dot-to-dot puzzles because they aren't orderly or predictable, and reason doesn't rule! 'Reason' is your Cardinal Rule. And there's not a whit of reason in puzzles. That's why they're called puzzles. So, puzzle it through, Lady Lazy Lame-Brain human cargo. I got time to wait.*

Hester's not fond of quiet time. She's nothing to do but twiddle her thumbs until Bam arrives. So twiddle she do. The dragon's soft sleeping snore winds a rhythm of waves lapping repetitive and gentle up a distant inner island fruit full of contentment and luscious lavish peace. Hester lays down her weary head in the crook where the dragon's shoulder muscles flesh mesh into those running along the beast's ribs and side over lungs like a forge, and heart like fire.

The day-dreaming dragon watches the fire hot forge in Hester's heart and smiles. Softly, Dragon raises a wing knuckle and fans fins to cover her in shade. The wise wyvern mother raises her head, eyes bright love on fire watching a child sleep in heavenly peace. *Bring her home, Master. She's lost alone in a weighty worldly wind that shreds her deep roots and drives her slow silent fall from faith and grace.*

*When you say 'bring her home' do you mean make her dead?*

*No.*

*Good. That would be counter-productive. There's a great need of Hester's present, prescient awareness, and there is need for her to demonstrate her new-found faith in rushing redeeming grace. I think she finally gets that she* can only give as willingly and openhandedly as she is willing to open heartily receive. She has thin skin too, but that may be a human defect.

The D.O. chortles in glee and says: *So you think I fucked up? Is that the bottom line of it dragon a mine?*

*Well, now that you put it that way, no, I don't think that. I have faith that you gave the hairless apes bigger brains for a reason. I need to know that reason because the heavy psychic weight of Hester's false faith grounds me deep-rooted where I stand when she comes anywhere near me.*

*The ground zero of Hester's psychic waste is deeper, broader, longer and more thoroughly twisted than the uprights of World Trade Center after it was bombed to rubble and to fire. She is one taut, twisted, tormented woman, D.O.*

The dragon lowers his eyes and admits: *I have very strong doubts that I will be able to lift off with the weight of her separation from source anxiety. She's so insanely ingrained and entrained in her small self-awareness that she lacks the capacity to make another choice.*

A wise one once wrote 'Once you get over the fear, then it's a cinch. And then she leaped into a mountainous and unexplored region of her heart'. *Name your fear dragon a mine.*

The dragon whips its head hiding her eyes but not her will. She leaps like a hunting hound released and free to jump into mountainous and unexplored regions of her heart. That works for her. She's a dragon. She's a mythical magical beast. She *likes* playing on the edge. She delights in running on empty and still running strong with a full heart, full throated bellow echoing like distant thunder while shattering ramparts of perception. And, perhaps it was only the sound barrier shattering. Again.

Not that anything changed for the D.O. for it is time for the arrival of Bam White. Bam would be a game changer. The Angel Garden would never be the same again. But it would be better than before, and it was a step in the direction the D.O. wanted to go. The D.O. is a good God. He is a generously loving one. He willing and freely sends angels to anyone who asks.

*Grace is freely given for the asking. It is theirs to ask. I gave them free will. Let them* use *that gift. Let them lift up the voice of their hearts! It's a reason I like Bam so much. When he can't see or find a way, he calls out to me and he asks for a smelt small share of my amazing grace. What's a* good God to do but generously give his Earth bound expressions of self a free overflow of grace given in full measure as I promised I would do? Bam walks the walk. And look, here Bam comes now.

*I hope the mother-bitch-on-wheels is healed enough to Mother again. I hope she's stopped navel-gazing enough that she can now look up and ask for amazing grace.*

That was the dragon talking, gentle reader, not I, the D.O. That said: Frankly, I agreed with the wise wyvern with a bad barbed whip for a tongue on that point. It's why I called the dragon in the first place. Only a drama queen dragon with an acid tongue and astounding acting chops could make Hester straighten up and fly right…, into the face of her deepest fear…, into The Angel Garden.

To Hester, the garden is a deep dark, teeming and mysterious place so vastly void and quietly pacific that she only faintly hears butterfly wings as they pass nearby. She does see the light and shadow play of leaves and shade the domed structure of it. But nothing else. Everything else was lost to her when the girl knelt and demanded God to send Angels to protect their garden, and God sent Angels.

*When I called, God didn't even hear.* Hester mourns a penitent's stingy acceptance of God's good grace.

*You're jealous of your kid? Really?*

*No! I'm jealous of you! I am simply keen green envious of you because the girl talks to you, and she* doesn't *talk to me.*

*Then how do you know she talks to me?*

*She tells me so.* Hester snaps surly sour.

*Then she must talk to you, no? What are* you *missing here? Because I'm missing it too; and I want you to get strait with me. Get straight with me now, Hester, in* this *infinite instant of time,* not *the next one. Your body/mind/brain Earth suit won't last that long. Do it now, Mother a mine, do it from your heart, not from your head, for else, you'll not fly but fall when you ride the dragon.*

*Ride a* dragon? *Oh my! Surely, surely, surely, dear, dear God, I do* not *have to ride a dragon.* Tears pool in her eyes but do not fall. *Please say it isn't so, say I do NOT have to ride a dragon.*

*Ever known me to lie? Ever known me to just jest? Reluctant warrior?*

*Warrior? See now, D.O., that is simply and clearly a case of mistaken identity on your part.*

*What're the odds of that?* The D.O.s left brow arches eloquent elegance, his eyes steady on hers. *No place to hide!* Hester knows the truth, the question in the D.O.'s mind is: *Will she let truth set her free? All my chips on this craps table of life are on Hester. And this is not a game that I am willing to loose.*

*Dragon dude, to me, S.T.A.T.* The D.O. calls in his favorite and most reliable reinforcement.

The wired weird wyvern spirals Earth-ward bound light as a feather and giggling glorious golden trills of glee set free. The D.O. giggles his usual homing call to the dragon he made for delivery of amazing grace to the human race. And today's race card is specifically vital, for it is a race for life of a woman. It is a race for the life of a girl. It is a race for the life of a man named Bam. It is a race for faith in saving grace for The Angel Garden. It is a race to revive and renew the deep faith of the caring people of this barren land for they will starve if The Angel Garden remains under attack from within the roam of its dome.

*Hester is the saving grace. And her saving grace arrives on the wings of the dragon.* The D.O. smiles seeing the dragon's two heads on one sleek wyvern body, and one lashing rudder of a tail. The dragon's gleeful grin lights his face and the air around him in a corona of light. *It is so good to see the light of me reflected in thee, my dear dire dragon. You are my crowning glory. I am content with that, for you will live co-eternal and forever one with me, always reflecting the light for all the world to see, and to be.*

*U-u-u-h, that's a step process for humans, the dragon cautions. Most of my human cargo are entirely incapable of taking that quantum leap of faith that's needed to propel them away from the 'safety' of the known, let alone to leap into and explore the uncharted regions of their heart.*

The D.O. pats the dragons near knee with a smile and says: *That's why I called on you, my dear transformer extraordinary.*

*So, what's my mission? And why does this mission make you whole-self-smile with eager anticipation?*

*We're going to save The Angel Garden, that's the initial target. When that's done, our mission shifts to healing this barren land that* once was *so lush and fertile!* The D.O. moans fingers tracking failure lines down his face.

The dragon doesn't laugh, nor even grin. He does blow a little smoke though when he says: *That means our mission shifts to teaching, showing, and ingrain training the good peeps living on this barren land how every-day actions can be forever directed from the heart so composing and recycling to enrich and stabilize the soil, and using ground-water wisely is an essential fact and duty of Keepers of Mother Earth. How far they fall in greed spawned in separation from source anxiety,* is all dragon does not say, knowing the D.O. hears his thoughts anyway; and knows and cherishes the secrets of his heart.

*That is precisely why I called on you, my wise wyvern*

*Excuse me? Why me?* The dragon dares, gold bold eyes flashing warning lights into the D.O.'s eyes.

*Have you forgotten who made you, dragon a mine? Have you forgotten why I made you? Have you forgotten why I gave you free will?*

The dragon ponders the puzzles presented by the Divine One, and, the curious-er puzzle still, of the *real* reasons why he fell. He's stumped, stuck, stone still mired in some gummy goo that seems to coat him toe to head. *Yuck!* The dragon declares, dry pawing the sticky stuff off him. And mostly succeeding in transferring it to his hands, so now he leaves paw prints the size of dinner plates. *I don't get it.*

And then he does. *Now his mission shifts to show and tell. In real life that means teaching by showing, and telling. It means ingrain training these deep rooted folks barely scraping a living off this barren land, how day-to-day actions can be directed from the heart, so that recycling and composting to enrich and stabilize the land becomes second nature again. As it was before.*

*So that henceforth, what is planted in the dirt of this land roots vibrant and deep, hangs tight, and keeps on growing, and withstands the wind. That means teaching man the ways and whys of wise use of ground-water, a core and essential function and reality and responsibility, of Keepers of Mother Earth. Most true Earth Keepers are Mothers, but there are wise men humans too who are Keepers.*

*Most Daughters are mothers,* Hester muses. *The Daughters own the fellowship hall and kitchen in the basement of the school.*

*It speaks!* The dragon meowls like a pissed off cat with a stepped-on tail. His eyes glare anger darts into Hester's saucer round eyes.

*You're an ass!* Hester hisses back. *And that is an insult to Becky, who is a mule, but she is not an ass! Judging by your current behavior, Foul Fiend, you have been the world champion title holder among asses of all ilk since before the beginning of time. Now, either be part of the solution, or go away.*

The dragon blinks once, cocks a brow and says: *Then I'm staying. You ready to ride, bitch on wheels?*

*Ride?* An unsettling memory Hester had tucked away deep inside her subconscious mind in the dark behind cupboards and closets of ancient memories comes stirring whirling alert and awake, not at all unlike the dead hearing the clarion call to rise up on Judgment Day. She shudders. She looks the dragon in the eye and asks boldly: *Where are we going?*

*Into The Angel Garden.*

*What will we do there?*

*Heal it! That's what mothers are for, fool. Mothers are not* merely *baby-makers, they are world shapers. How do you intend to shape your world, Hester?*

Hester quirks an off-sides grin and asks: *Does my shaping have anything to do with The Angel Garden?*

*It does indeed.*

*I am a healer. But I can't even see* inside *The Angel Garden let alone go inside it as I am supposed to do.* Hester's eyes pool with tears, and in the trembling sparkling puddles collected there, dragon sees the color of truth, the power of passion, and a radiant rainbow of liberal uses of Mother's healing love that courses through the Self of her. He lowers his head in the universal dragon sign of submission and purrs:

*Ready to ride?*

*Yes.*

*Time to wait?*

*Um – sure – you're my ticket to ride. I go when you do. What're we waiting for?*

*Not 'what', 'who'. Who? Bam White and the girl.*

*Why?*

*Do you ever get tired of asking questions?*

*No! I'm a mother, that's part of my job. Why are we waiting for Bam White and the girl?*

*We are waiting for Bam because he can ride a dragon at warp speed and stay on board and alive. We are waiting for the girl because she's the only living being who has ever been inside The Angel Garden, and The Angel Garden needs a whole lot of open hearted loving S.T.A.T. Do you know the girl cries when she cuts an earthworm in half when she's hoeing? She cries even though she knows the two half-earthworms will grow in a pair of whole ones, and all is well. The D.O. made earthworms to heal and replicate that way. The term for that in the language of my human cargo is 'compassion'.*

*The girl's got it. In spades. Besides, Hester, if you* cannot *reconcile yourself to being the amazing mother of a remarkable child then The Angel Garden will die. People will starve and be turned out of their homes to join the hordes of hungry hobo's riding the rails looking for a chance and food once in a while.*

*I could change that?* Hester gasps grasping tight at the straw of hope in the dragon's words, that fuel to awaken the faint fire of faith flickering in her heart. The flicker flames into a raging fire. She inhales full, deep, and slow, feeding her passion fresh and hot in her heart.

*She glows!* The dragon thinks with a smile. *Perfect time for Bam and the girl to arrive.* And so they do. What *else* does a good God to do?

"Mom!" The girl cries, scrambling down from Bam's wagon as Becky comes to an easy stop before the invisible Angel Garden that the girl can see, and Bam too. Always could. "We're going on a dragon ride!" the girl jumps up and down in glad glee, "and we'll land inside The Angel Garden, and make it healed and whole and fruitful again like it was always meant to be!" That mission totally scrambles and cavitates Hester into whirring racket and sunders her. Well, only her E.G.O., her lifetime habit of Edging God Out is at risk of rupture. The dragon handles it masterly and wickedly well. He lowers his eyes to Hester's, smiling true gold bright and laser sharp into her eyes and poses: *What scares you stuttering, shit-dribbling stupid, about The Angel Garden?*

*I can't see it!*" Hester cries, stunned under the weight of her admission of truth.

*Did you never hear a wise worm say 'You cannot see because you do not believe'?*

The Alice in Hester is back in Wonderland again and it's even more mysterious and magical and musical than it was when she was about

Alice's age. *So, weird wise wyvern, answer me true: if I believe in The Angel Garden, then I can see it?*

*What would Alice's caterpillar say?*

*He'd blow smoke in my face..., to clear a space for amazing grace.*

*Let me do the honors then since the caterpillar isn't here, and I am.* The dragon pulls deep and full from a hookah sitting tall and glittering proud in the space between his paws. His inhale is a sorrowing sigh, his exhale a sweet release of joy-filled grace. Hester is captivated, blown away by the curious coiling of smoke as the dragon exhales soft and slow. The aroma embraces her as calm and smooth as grace come soft fleet on dragon's amazing grace. *The Dragon guardian has come. New realms of possibility open for me. I* protect *creation. I control emotion. I act only from balanced self-control. I am Earth Mother to The Angel Garden. That is why I'm skunk drunk on the intoxicating faith in amazing grace. I can ride a dragon, and live to tell the tale tall and true, for its origin lies in a saga of a furious fall from grace, even as mine does.*

"So, dragon a mine," she asks patting his glittering gold plated knee, "When do we ride?"

"Soon as Bam and the girl arrive."

Hester frowns. "Haven't we been through this before?"

"Yeah." The dragon allows. "You're a slow study. Take a chill pill. Go with the flow."

Hester lets go everything falls into place like clockwork without effort or command and control function from her. *It's a Small World After All spins through her mind a reminder of times of amazing grace when everything dear was within her reach. She became a wife and mother and all that changed.*

*Except in truth. There nothing changed other than the outer boundaries of the ways and whys I think myself small, helpless, powerless, victimized, and likely left alone and lonely. Abandoned to fickle fate! Scared shitless I am. But Who I am is enough. My work is to keep it true, unvarnished, earthy, and whole.*

The dragon hears, and smiles. *Well done, Mother a mine, Are we ready to rock and roll?*

*If you're waiting for me you're wasting time, dragon a mine.*

*Good. I got a trifecta of human cargo to deliver to The Angel Garden. To do that, I must hit warp speed, shatter the sound barrier and wing us into saving grace space of The Angel Garden. Let's kick butt and take names.* The dragon's full-body grin purrs like a kitten lapping cream.

## Maiden Flight of The Dragon Express

*All aboard that's comin' aboard!* The dragon calls in a voice like a gong. *We've got a narrow window of time, and no time for delay because Bam and the girl are here!*

*I – I don't have a ticket...,* Hester protests feebly.

*Of course you do, silly woman. Think about the missing ticket in The Polar Express. Same-same for Dragon Express.*

Hester giggles poking three finger through the new, and not yet torn, hole in her apron pocket. *I seem to have lost my ticket to ride, or, it was not given to me yet. So, dragon fine a mine, where is the conductor of The Dragon Express who has my ticket to ride in his pocket?* The dragon grins. It is a disconcerting, disturbing, and disorienting thing to see. *Stunned stuttering stupid! Again.* Hester worries her teeth against the oft gnawed knuckle of her habitual harsh humility and self-effacement.

It gets her nowhere. Like it always did. Like it always does. *Exactly where is the conductor of The Dragon Express?* She asks pleasantly through gritted teeth. *The one who has my ticket tucked safe in his pocket?*

"That would be me!" A familiar favorite voice announces behind Hester. "And I got your ticket to ride The Dragon Express." Bam slaps the ticket into her hand, grins, and says: "I kept it in *my* capable hands because *you* weren't ready to believe in dragons, having lost all faith in amazing grace. For the same reason, you would have lost your ticket to ride The Dragon Express, as certainly as the boy lost his. Just like you, Hester, that overtly *obedient* boy was nose-to-the-grindstone busy, busy, busy, being 'responsible' trying to 'save' someone *else's* ticket, and, in the process, he *rendered himself incapable of being compliant* with the will of the One! Obedience does not work!

"Let me put it another way", the wyvern whispers wisely. "The D.O. gave man free will. That *means* the D.O. does *not* expect obedience! You are such a dim-bulb sometimes Hester a mine. The Polar Express had one simple rule, 'stay in your seat while the train is moving'.

"The Dragon Express has the same rule, but re-phrased more profound and true: 'You *cannot* save anyone else *unless* you save yourself first'. What salvation do *you* need, Hester? "Are you *will*ing to accept what is for what it is, the good, the bad, *and* the ugly? Are you *will*ing to *ask* for amazing grace? Is your E.G.O., your Edging God Out, *will*ing to ask? Are you *will*ing to sing praise and gratitude *before* you see proof of the effect of grace? It's is a test of faith, w*ill* you receive the grace of faith without proof? In case you don't know, 'faith' is the perceiving power of the mind linked with the power to shape substance. Got faith? Willing to forgive? Willing to shape a sacred space inside for you and the D.O.?"

"Yes. Yes, I am that. I am one with the Indwelling One. There is no place where I AM is not."

"Ready to ride?"

"If you're waiting for me, you're wasting time. What are we waiting for?"

"Bam White and the girl, I already told you that, dim bulb!"

"Why?"

"Told you that too. Bam's the Dragon Rider. The only one. The girl's the only one who's been inside The Angel Garden. She's the guide.

"You are the only one who's NOT been inside The Angel Garden. It scares the drizzling shits out of you because you *can't see* it! The art of believing is having firm faith in the *unseen*. Your faith is strong. You're ready to be tested."

---

Shawn Gallaway – Soul Friends

---

"Mom! Mom!" Hester turns to see the girl tumble jump from Bam's wagon and run to her singing: "We're going on a Dragon ride and we'll break the sound barrier and then we'll fly into The Angel Garden together and get it fixed and healthy again." The girl sobers suddenly. "Two of the angels are being bad. They're fighting like furious fiends instead of best-bud mates; and they're naked as jay-bird babies, scab scarred and scratched! They sound like a basket *full* of angry cats from Kilkinney."

"Well, Bam to the rescue then, little miss! We got a dragon ready to ride, a lot-a fixing to do, and lot-a miles to go before we sleep. See this shallow where the dragon's wings and neck connect?" The girl nods. "That's where you'll sit for the dragon ride, sit, and get comfortable. I'll help your mother up. Hester, you sit here just behind the girl.

Keep her safe as a good Mothers always do. I am the dragon jockey extraordinaire. I'll sit behind you and keep you safe. Dragon a mine, are you ready to fly?"

"That I am. We'll be at warp speed in ten, nine, eight, seven, six, five, four, three, two, and one! And blast off!" No one on that dragon ride had an ear to hear nor even feel the psychic blast when it happened, jiving lost as they are in the infinite instant and eternal now. Shift happened anyway.

They enter The Angel Garden at warp speed in a steep controlled downward spiral. *What happened here?* They think as one, except the girl. She knows. She remembers. She can't un-ring that bell and she dammed well wants to. Hester susses the scene. It ain't pretty. She opens inner awareness to feel into the void in The Angel Garden. She rests there awhile. "Angels," she says in quiet grace, "to me. Now!"

"I am getting *damned well* tired of this!" Michael snarls landing like cat in attack mode. Gab-re-EL falls slit-eyed and growling ripping soft. "Me too!" Gab-re-EL's growls eyes locked on Hester the intruder.

Hester gives a small smile and notes: "I have heard it said that the definition of insanity is doing what you've always done and expecting a different outcome. *Estas locos, tus Angeles? O, Estas totalmente estupido?* What the *fuck* are you doing here?"

There's nothing like a tart tongued woman talking dirty to focus attention that's not otherwise available. "What is your mission?" It's a demand. Politely phrased to sound like a simple request. It ain't.

"It's not a mission! It's a demotion, it's an insult! And *I* don't deserve it!"

"Me too. On all counts!" Snarls Gab-re-EL looking for all the world like an arch-back growling cat with snapping, sparking furiously angry eyes, and pugnaciously poised to pounce. Instead she hisses: "And what's it to you, *you pissy peasant proletarian puta!*"

To her utter dismay, Hester looks level into Gab-re-EL's eyes, a tickled amused sparkle dancing in her eyes. Her chest heaves silent mirth, her cheeks raise up as smooth and unwrinkled as the girl's. "Do you know that it's practically predictable that ones who *cannot* answer a reasonable question descends, like you two squalling angels, to spewing passive-aggressive pugnacious, perverse, pejorative, and *preposterous* language? *Dammit* The D.O. made both of you of finer stuff than the bare-butt-skinned-cat persona you project now. Hester words hit the Archangels like a powerful stomach punch. Both fallen ones fall again, this time cloaking their soft sensitive parts with shoulders and bowed heads. *Cowed cats! How true human body language reveals the animal spirit that's active and alive in the body.*

"This time speak *truth* when you answer: What your mission is here in The Angel Garden?" Silence resounds. "Michael, you are the D.O.'s first knight, you start. *Why did* the D.O. send *you* to here?"

Michael cannot raise his head full heavy with riotous remorse and self-incrimination. He answers still: "I am here to be the strong center pole of The Angel Garden. I was furious for getting such proletarian job. I am the D.O.'s First Knight! I can't *wear* knight's armor when doing nothing but supporting a dome! My anger arose from a willful a furious fall from grace. I was insulted, personally, and professionally."

"*Professionally*? I didn't know Archangel *was* a profession, nor that knight's garb could *lucidly* be the *only* clothes an angel can wear! *Que tonto! Que totalmente estupido!* Yours is a *stunning* fall from grace!

"I see the disappointment in your eyes. I see it in your bodies. I hear it in your voices. It echoes in the words you say, you who sang 'Amazing Grace' a' Capella and didn't leave an eye dry, nor a heart broken, nor even one stray sheep of a human mind unchanged! How can you *possibly* condone your willful disobedience to the D.O.? Mutiny' would be an answer. If so, what would a pair of admittedly fallen Archangel *do* to make amends, and come back to God's grace?"

"Fix it. Then fix it in habit," The Archangels speak in one voice. "Then make it a habitual practice." They look each other in the eye, and as one say: "Oh, what fun it will be to make The Angel Garden a thriving space of amazing grace. And, we'll compete and cooperate and collaborate while we perform our missions because we work as one team." They laugh until they cry and say: "Just like always!"

Like helium filled balloons the two fallen angels rise up in a narrowing spiral until they join hands, heads, and hearts on their one mission in two angelic forms. They laugh gleeful joy so their rise is as fast and smooth as the Dragon's rise was.

And the rain came, sprinkling down like golden joy drops that wash the air in The Angel Garden, to fall copious, rich, vibrantly alive and nourishing on the withered plants they'd started in early spring. Hester smiles healing grace on the whole space, as a mother healer would do.

She looks up into the dome and sees the angels clear, and bare as the day they were born, and calls: "Angels, to me, now." This time they don't grouse, or snarl, nor hesitate, or argue, they just comply.

"So", Hester says, scratching her head, with a worried mother frown. She meets their eyes and holds. "Tell me, why are you two still as naked as the day you were born? Don't you believe that you have redeemed your self-imposed fall from grace? Don't you think that you have earned your angel wings back *again*? The Master did say 'you have not because you ask not.' Did you ask? With gratitude? As though it's already given, but yet unseen? Look into my eyes and see what *I see* when I see you."

They do. They like what they see and become that. "Wahoo! Wings again and bright white gowns too."

# The Unblemished Calf

They came early one morning in the spring when ice still crusted tire tracks and the road was treacherous with soft mud and frozen hazards for those tempted to forge a new trail.

Morning visitors at a working farm signals separation from the cycles of life. That alone brings the whole family out to see and to hear as the black sedan slides to a sliding muddy stop.

Four men wearing plaited beards and hair emerged.

"Welcome to our land and our home," Jacob says. What brings you all the way out here on eleven miles of muddy road, and you arrive with the sunrise?"

"We come to tell you of our search for an unblemished yearling calf to be offered in atonement for the sins of our people, and to tell you the requirements, and the payment we will make for the chosen calf."

The driver with the body of a running back or a pugilist, and a flat nose broken at least twice by a well-placed blows, hands Jacob a sheaf of papers, which he takes and rolls into a tube without looking at them.

"Let me introduce you to my wife Hester." Hester smiles and says hello to each of the men. "My kids will tell you their names – if they decide to talk to you at all – farm kids tend to be silent observers around strangers.

"We were about to sit down for breakfast before beginning our day, would you care to join us?" He sees their hesitation and adds: "We have enough food to share, and Hester made pancakes, *and* the syrup we'll pour on them. We have coffee too." The visitors are looking at their shoes. *Interesting....* Jacob thinks.

Hester nudges him and whispers *Hassidic*.

Jacob gives her a 'probably so' nod. *So what do we do?*

*Bring the table, three extra chairs, plates, cups, coffee pot, and silverware out here.* She nods to the flat area beside the kitchen garden. Jacob grins, nods and turns back to the silent men.

"My wife thinks you might be Hassidic." Their eyelids flash up and then back down again.

"Hester suggests that we bring our breakfast out here" he motions to the flat space Hester pointed out with her eyes. "I'll need help bringing the table and bench out, but me and the kids can handle the chairs, and we will all help Hester bring the food out.

"I would hear the prayer *you* offer to bless the food you are about to eat." He feels a hesitation and offers, "And then I will lead us in *our* prayer to bless the food we are about to eat." His grin is infectious. They all catch it and pass it on.

The most senior of the plaited ones signals the driver who leans in, listens and smiles as the driver looks at the man and his wise wife. "I will help you move the table and chairs out here, Jacob, and help move anything else that's heavy too.

"And when we're done eating, I'll help you put it all back too.

"How did your wife know that we are Hassidic?"

Jacob smiles though his eyes are sad. "Hester's mother was a Jew who married a Catholic when she was still young enough to believe that love could bridge cultural and religious biases, even those based on fundamentally different social and faith practices.

"So tell me, gentlemen, why did you ask *me* that question instead of asking my wife..., who prepared this food we blessed and share together today?"

Jacob turns to Hester and says: "Perhaps he thinks you are mute?

"Or, maybe he thinks we have a tape recorder under the table, and that we'll use the tape *to get them in trouble*?" Jacob gives his most sinister silly grin making Hester giggle.

She looks at each of her guests and says: "Jacob is right about the tape recorder." She grins mischievously and snips: "You should know that you are *simply not* that important to us.

"Anyone need more coffee?" She asks with the pleasant smile of a gracious hostess.

Laughter is an ice breaker. Stiff formality is gone as though it never was. Now all speak one language. All hearts blend in one harmony.

The first Rabbi looks to Hester with warm eyes and a soft smile and asks: "Will you tell us about your mother?"

"The children know little...."

"Perhaps it is time for them to hear."

Silence extends profoundly, moderated only by the sounds of cows lowing to be milked, and calves bawling to be fed. Hester does not move, and she scarcely breathes.

"Perhaps the time has come for you to tell your children about their grandmother, so they know how life was for her as a Jewess married a Catholic. It cannot have been easy for her.

"And with your profound compassion, Hester, it cannot have been easy for you.

"I confess that I *personally* and deeply want to know how that tension effected your mother. I want to understand how that altered her relationship with your father.

"I want to know how that affected *you*. I want to hear how the dissonance between them echoed into you and your siblings."

### The Confession

Hester pulls a hanky from her pocket and blots her eyes. She keeps it in her hand knowing she'll need it again.

Jacob lays his left hand on hers so their rings touch with a tiny ting that centers her in the strength she needs for a true tall tale telling that is, by its nature, an admission. One that is not solely hers to make. Hester turns her hand to lace Jacob's fingers through hers. She receives his steady strength and releases what is, and what was. She prayerfully and knowingly creates a space for what can be healed and made whole again from what was broken and bereft.

*Mother, help me tell tall and true how that was for you. Speak through me so that I feel your presence, so that I feel your forgiveness of the torment you suffered when Daddy took us to Catholic services every Sunday and holiday, but forbad you to take us with you to went to your own faith services and celebrations.*

*There is but one God!* Hester wails silently.

*There are countless faith practices that honor the same One God of a thousand names. And still, people want and even demand obedience. Que tonto! Que increable estupido!*

*You gave man free will and that can mean nothing* except *that you do* not *expect obedience from us. But you* do *expect compliance. Make me compliant with your will. Use me.*

*Make me your instrument. Speak clear and true through my voice. Make the power of truth ring through my words and dissolve error thought, for it is my will to heal the past, the present, and the future.*

> Shawn Gallaway – I Choose Love

Hester feels the Divine One smile and is warmed through and through. She melts when she hears the D. O.'s silent words. *That is what I brought you to life to do, daughter of mine.*

*A gift only becomes a gift given when it is received. Until then it's just a box wrapped in pretty paper with a sparkly bow on top. Open yourself up! Give the whole gift of you.*

*Shred the small powerless obedient self you always believed was your only truth. Receive and use the true power of compliance that I placed inside you and in all of my creations.*

*Use your true voice rightly and well, and be my instrument of healing and change. Do it for your mother. Do it for your children.*

*Do it for all of my children, Hester.*

*Do it for these three wise men from afar whose belief is that I require the blood sacrifice of an unblemished calf in order to forgive them and love them unconditionally.*

*Que tonto! Que increable estupido!*

The D.O. mourns, head in hands, and Hester smiles small willfully bridling the laughter that bubbles up like seltzer water from inside her. The D.O. brings her gently down and centers her in the heart of peace, healing and wholeness.

*Be my voice, Hester. Be my voice of love that welcomes them home on mother Earth.*

Hester smiles at her guests and at her family all bundled in coats and hats to conserve body heat. She does not laugh aloud, but she *really, really,* wants to.

Her laughing eyes do the merry magic anyway, and everyone is warmed from the inside out. As the sun rises bright and clear to gild the air with golden light, Hester begins her Mother tale.

> Shawn Gallaway – Keep Gettin' Up

"My mother was a Jewess. She married a Catholic, and as required by the Church, she agreed that her children would be raised in the Catholic faith.

"She was okay with that. Catholic services are on Sunday morning. Jewish faith practices are held on Saturday evenings. Her children *could* be raised in the Catholic faith as she agreed, and, they could come with her to learn the faith of their mother too.

"That worked very well for them for a quite while actually." Hester bows her head letting the D.O. show her where next to go in the telling. She nods and takes up her Mother's tale again.

"Every community has busybodies with a keener interest in what's happening in *other* people's homes and lives than what's going on in their own.

"Perhaps that is the way people blind themselves from clear seeing the truth of what's really going on in their own homes and in their own families.

"Maybe gossiping and maligning others is to divert attention from the dysfunctionality in their *own homes* and in *their own families*. In their noisy nattering over nits and tittles they persuade themselves their slander did no more than *pull the masks off others*. They package it in their minds as a service to the community. They then assume it is their divine right, and duty, to prove their gossip is true through the shunning and the shaming of their victims.

"That's what happened to Mother. That's what happened to Daddy too when he took us to church with him on Sunday mornings.

"That is what happened to *us* when we weren't allowed to attend Sunday school after Mass with other kids our ages. We were not welcomed. It was guilt by association.

"In the end, Daddy wasn't even welcomed unless he came to church alone. Without even us.

"History, and fiction, repeat this story over and again. This is not a new story.

"This is what the green-eyed monsters of 'the true faith' did to Mom. That's what they did to Daddy. It's what they did to *all* of us, to all of their children. That's what happened to their innocent children who were shunned and shamed and left with no space or place to honor *any* faith practice or to learn and know any intimate and personal relationship with Source.

"The religious zealots left Father with no choice and no way to exercise his own free will. He could *not* honor his marital promise to Mother that we *would* have diverse spiritual training so that when grown, we *could* freely make our own free will choice of the faith practice to follow.

"The Church of obedience left *us* with no middle ground where we could exercise free will, and learn to honor the Divine One from the heart of us, and not solely from the minds of us.

"The Church gave *us* no quarter. They left us no space or place where we could learn and experience the Divine by our own lights and forge and know a personal relationship with God in his infinite loving generosity. *Sinat chinam* – senseless hatred. That's what it was and *is*!

"The church *was* unkind. But it is our neighbors who make up our churches. Obediently, our neighbors libeled and slandered us, never once considering that all of us are given free will, and therefore, the D.

O. does *not* expect obedience. But *she does* expect our willingly chosen compliance with the Law of Love that teaches: 'first, do no harm'. *We* abandoned *ourselves* to an indifferent and navel-gazing God who sprang full formed from the meager mind of man.

"A god created by man is *necessarily* jealous, weak, powerless, self-absorbed, and navel gazing! *Que tonto, que increable estupido.* How small a god man made to delude ourselves that the One God of all and everything *can* hate, *can* slander, *can* shun, and therefore must accept and excuse that behavior in man, his highest and most innovative creation. A punitive god is what we deserve for we are that!

"When did a free people *ever* accept 'good enough'?" Hester puzzles with a frown. "Never! We the people of us *deserve* better – for we are co-creators with the Divine! We *can* do and be better than we were before.

"But that can only happen when we freely and consciously choose to *stop* slandering and shaming others over *which* of the thousand names of the One God is the one and only true name of the Divine One, and which faith practice is the one and only *true* religion. This is *man's* judgment run amuck out of holier than thou one up-man-ship! This is *not* Love! God must *weep!*" Hester is silent awhile composing herself and surrendering to what is so she can choose what is to come and what will be.

"We were hurt and confused by the division between our parents that let Daddy deny *us* the right to learn other ways to love and honor the One God of a thousand names.

"We cried with our mother every Sunday morning when Daddy took us to Catholic services and Mother was forbidden to come with us. He punished *us* for breaking his marriage vow to love, honor and respect Mother.

"We cried with Mother every Friday evening because we were forbidden to go with her to her faith services. And, like most women then Mother didn't drive. And Daddy *would not* drive her to the Jewish center.

"In fear of his own shaming by the church Daddy obediently denied Mother the comfort of *any* faith practice whatsoever. He lived in fierce fear of his own shaming by the church and the people in it if he failed to be entirely obedient to the church's demand that he annul his marriage as though he'd never made marital vows to Mother. Because his spirit was broken by the Church's shaming, Daddy beat and cursed us if we cried because of his meanness in denying Mother *any* faith practice whatsoever.

"Mother wept every Friday when Daddy told us that we could not go with her to church even though we begged to go so we could learn another way to honor and love God.

"The church *was* unkind!

"And churches are buildings. It is the clergy and the church members who did the shunning. It's the *Christian* members who gossiped, slandered, judged, and shamed my family. It was our neighbors who looked down their noses and slandered us in the greater community. Our *neighbors* called us half-breeds and rewarded their kids for being hateful to us and for doing cruel things to us. They gave them sweet treats for the ugly names they called us.

"Eventually even Daddy was shamed by what he allowed to happen to us while he was fiercely trying to obey the Church in what it required him do to *atone* for his *sin* of allowing his children to exercise their God given free will and to learn life lessons from the mistakes we made.

"He began to listen to Mother again and to respect her thoughts and opinions. Daddy didn't apologize in words. But he did in his deeds. My parents went together to interview public school principals. They got the standards of student conduct and mutual respect set by the school, and copies of student curricula by grade.

"Mother asked each Principal how teachers handled differences of opinion among students, and how they addressed anger and aggression exhibited by them. Daddy *always* asked if students were encouraged to ask probing questions about what they were learning.

"It was a grand celebration for all of us when Daddy and Mother renewed their marriage vows and became two in one again. One Friday afternoon in front of all of us, Daddy asked Mother if he could go with her to her church, and if he could bring all of their children along with them.

"We all cried and hugged necks and laughed and we healed. Then we bundled into the car and went to find and honor the One God in a temple in an unfamiliar tongue. Healing happens.

---

Shawn Gallaway – Healing Happens

---

"My brothers graduated high school and left home to find work and earn a living distant from where our family lived. They married and raised families that we saw at Christmas time – when they still came to visit us.

"Daddy was uneasy and anxious if we gave Mother a Christmas gift, even a utilitarian one. He believes so profoundly in a punitive punishing god that Daddy cannot forgive himself for *loving* Mother unconditionally. He is scared stiff because he loves *her* children in the same way.

"*Her* children..., as though we were inspired and born whole cloth from Mother *without* the inspiration of Daddy's seed into her! *Que tonto! Que totalmente estupido!*

"*This* is the predictable consequence of *Sinat Shalom*, senseless hatred.... God must weep!

"All of Daddy's children learned that you *can* love your father unconditionally, and still want passionately to kill him for his craven and unrepentant cruelty to your Mother.

"The church *was* unkind, dammit!

---

Shawn Gallaway – Wake Up America

---

When she composes herself again, Hester takes up her Mother tale: "My sisters and I went to dances in nearby towns, and each of us met our husbands there. When we married, we moved to where our husbands lived – as young women are wont to do – and together birthed and raised our children." Hester's hand is still in Jacobs, their wedding rings still touching.

"The distance between us sisters is physical. Mentally and emotionally we were connected. There isn't always safety in distance, but distance *does* afford a vital shift in understanding that owns and allows what is, and then *chooses* better and more heart centered outcomes.

"We sisters, and our sisters-in-law, always send birthday and holiday cards with letters inside that tell what's new and what's changed in our lives and the lives of our families. Mostly we write about our children and our grandchildren as mothers always do. My sisters and sisters-in-law became God mothers to our children, and we sponsored children of theirs.

Hester smiles a sweet memory. "We sisters devotedly and eagerly spent weeks with a pregnant sister who asked us to sponsor their child's baptism. The baptismal sponsor sister stays at her sister's home for at least two weeks before the baby's birth. She stays until after the baby is baptized and the mother is strong enough to care for the baby, and her home, without the 24x7 support of a sponsoring sister.

"During this time the Sponsor sister develops a heart connection with the baby's energy long before the baby is born. That bond between the sponsor sister and the baby deepens and expands as the sister oils and massages the mother's belly and feels the shape, the energy, and the position of the fetus in the womb. Hester smiles a warm sister memory, "The Godmother connection with the baby is fully formed and lovingly powerful weeks before the baby is delivered and draws its first breath.

"At its birth the baby knows the joyful and unreserved love of both mother and Godmother. The babe learns that its smile muscles are already formed and fully functional when it is born because it is born into unconditional love and the blessed babe can but smile and laugh.

"At Christmas we sisters always remember our God children by writing their names in the holiday letters we send our siblings.

"It's a small thing for sisters to do, but it matters to the children to hear their names spoken with a smile and in a voice that is overflowing with infinite love and gratitude.

| Shawn Gallaway – Infinite Love And Gratitude |

The coffee has gone cold in the pot and in the cups and no one really minds because Hester's tale and her telling of it inspired forgiveness and self-acceptance in each of them. The visitors are no longer sure there *is* a need for a new Solomon's Temple in the Western hemisphere, or for an unblemished calf to sacrifice in it.

"That said, the rabbi are on assignment and are expected to make a full report of their search, and to give recommendations for a suitable location of a recreated Solomon's Temple. They are also expected to locate, identify, and pre-purchase an unblemished calf to sacrifice in the Temple when it is built. The head Rabbi sips his cold coffee and smiles enjoying the flavor better than when it was hot. He returns to his mission statement.

"Jacob, you asked us what brought us out here so early this morning. The answer is that we are seeking an unblemished calf to sacrifice in a new Solomon's Temple we will build in America.

"Everyone we talked to yesterday said you are a master at turning calves into strong, healthy, meaty beef that would be perfect for sharing with many worshipers when the Temple is built.

Jacob is silent a long moment, then with a small frown offers: "Yours is a timing issue then, I think. It seems premature to me for you to seek an unblemished calf if you must first buy the land for, and then build a temple like Solomon's was."

"Why is that?" The Rabbi asks, with a frown of concern.

Jacob chuckles and replies: "By fall the unblemished calf will have matured into a bull. If the farmer already has a bull that sires healthy calves he *cannot* introduce an uncastrated bull into the pasture because the two bulls *will* fight each other to *death* to be the only living and the one unchallenged sire of the herd.

"It's a testosterone thing, and it's not only bulls that demand to be the dominant male, humans do it too. Hester's daddy tale should teach you that. The unblemished calf you seek now will necessarily have been castrated so the feed and grain it eats turns into muscled meat that's tender and lean when it's butchered and eaten."

"How often do you butcher a calf?"

"Annually," Jacob laughs. "We also butcher a pig we've grown so we can have pork roast, ribs, and bacon."

Hester slaps his arm and chides him with a grin: "You said that on purpose! You know they can't eat pork."

Jacob grins amiably, nods, and agrees: "I do know that, Hester. That I do.

"I also know that if a Temple is built in America and it is even slightly bigger, more splendid, or more gilded than the tiniest Catholic Church – the Church *will be* unkind! Again.

"Just as the Church was disproportionately abusive of your mother. Even more irrationally, they aggressively punished your father who *was being obedient,* and did everything they demanded – *except* to divorce your mother and to deny his own children.

"For that *disobedience*, the Church stripped your Dad of his standing as a Knight of the Church!

"Obedience was never enough for the Church. It won't be enough now if Solomon's Temple is recreated here. That's your whole problem in a nutshell.

Jacob looks back to the Rabbi sitting across from him and adds: "If you must build a temple, build a small synagogue somewhere in the U.S., and keep a low profile *except* when you are paying taxes, feeding the needy, and helping school administrators maintain open, welcoming, safe, and stimulating learning environments for children of all ages and all genders."

"*All* genders?" A Rabbi asks with patent perplexity.

"Yes. All genders includes trans genders and homosexuals." Jacob raises an eyebrow at their dismay and notes: "The Divine One created them too…, and the D.O. *never* miscreates. The D.O loves each and every one of his creations unconditionally…, meaning that God loves with*out* condition. The question for man always is: are *we*, individually, and as a community, *will*ing to love *all* of God's creations without condition or reservation even as God loves us?

"It's a tough choice for man to make because it inherently means he *must* willingly give up judging others. That means forgiving those who believe and behave differently than he does, and even those who, by our lights, have 'wronged' us in the past, and likely will do again. Yet the Master did say: 'you have not because you ask not'.

"What have you asked for – if you speak the truth – retribution? Retaliation? Vengeance? Revenge? Intimidation? One-up-man ship? 'Boasting by brick', as my father used to say it?

"Be honest with yourselves. You are here among friends you didn't even know before this morning and the birth of this new day of light. Tell us tall and true the very highest outcome you can foresee for this new day and for all the new days to come. Not ready yet? Still wanting to hedge your bets? Still wanting to stay tight wound in your separation from source anxiety?

"That same Master said: *Forgive and you will be forgiven.*

"Those words have always been a lamp in the darkness for me at any time I was hurting because of the harsh and sometimes punitive judgments of others.

"*Forgive* and you will be forgiven. What lies buried deep and unforgiven in you and in your people? Is it the destruction of a physical temple in a temporal world? *Que tonto! Que totalmente estupido!*"

"What did you just say after asking your questions? What does it mean?"

"'How crazy! How totally stupid!'" Hester translates with a smile.

The head Rabbi trims a wry grin, nods, and offers: "Those words do sound much friendlier and more sympathetic in Spanish.

"Spanish is known as the language of love." Hester explains warmly, "It is practically impossible to string together enough unloving words in Spanish to form a complete sentence, let alone to encompass and to convey a whole insufferably insupportable unloving consciousness. Hester giggles infectiously, "Even hateful words and robust rebukes are somehow charming in the language of love. Don't you find that to be true?

"What lies deeply suppressed and unforgiven within you, Rabboni?" Hester waits in the silence sipping cold coffee. She decides she prefers the taste of coffee when it's gone cold.

"If you are *still* mourning the destruction of Solomon's Temple and refusing to consider *any* solution other than the total destruction and disempowerment of the places of worship of other people, then you have chosen to make yourselves a totally worthless waste of time, and utterly incompetent to change the world in positive and healing ways.

"I have no time for you, nor for your childish king-of-the-mountain waste of daylight games of power and authority. You *totally* could be another prurient pious Pope who took the name of 'Innocent' because he too was born the son of a Pope. Only *your clothes and hair* would have to be changed for you to fit the role of a pious pope to a tee. The Church has become more clever and self-aware because it did stop numbering the 'Innocent' Popes after Innocent the twelfth, and that was mostly because of their unshakable faith that thirteen is an unlucky number.

"If you're not part of the solution, then you are part of the problem. Come, children, it's time to clear the table and get our morning chores done."

Jacob sits facing the three black robed visitors who bow their heads stunned stuttering silent at the tongue lashing Hester delivered on them like they were toddlers being disciplined for not knowing right from wrong, or worse, *doing* what they knew was wrong from the get-go. He's been there. He knows what they're feeling. He smiles recalling each of the better outcomes that followed from Hester's candor and offers a suggestion in question form.

"Why *couldn't* you explore reconciliation, and compromise?" Jacob asks. "Why not explore the option of community engagement and thoughtful collaboration as an *opportunity* to explore before imposing yet *another* religious rigidity on some community in our country?

"*Forgiveness....* I find it interesting that the word 'forgiveness' as the Master practiced it most truly and deeply means 'giving for the self'.

Jesus wasn't hard-headed, he wasn't cold hearted, and he did not insist on having all and everything his way. Jesus didn't find any 'others' because he *knew no others*. The man never met a stranger, he only saw brothers and sisters who were members of his family.

"I'm not surprised that Hester walked away from your energy, and not at all surprised that she called the children away." He turns to the chauffer with a frown and asks:

"Didn't you agree to help bring the plates and silverware and food back inside the house? And didn't you say that you'd help me take the table and chairs back inside too?"

"I did, and I will. But the Rabbi want to see the unblemished calf first."

"No." He waits until they look him in the eye. "I have no duty to be a good host to uninvited guests who are argumentative, deceitful, and misleading, and who prevaricate, backtrack, and *demand* to negotiate what is not theirs to determine.

"It comes as no surprise to me that good neighbors will not like you, and they won't want you in their communities. You are like the evil man who sowed tares in the wheat fields of a good farmer that he wanted to dispossess lawlessly, and refused to buy him out at a fair price.

"In your case, you want to cheat, disgrace, dishonor, and dispossess people who've been here for generations simply because they honor other faiths and faith practices. You *demand* the right to build a temple that is ostentatiously more ornate and gilded than any other house of worship so that you can shame them, and you will *not* let that go!

"Hester is right, you *are* a waste of time." Jacob stands and begins to scrape food scraps into a bowl for the dogs while sorting silverware and collecting plates, cups, and glasses together.

He takes the glasses inside first and steps beside Hester to give her a kiss while carefully submerging the glasses into the sink of hot soapy water. "Cups and silverware next?" She nods.

Jacob grabs a tray from the counter and takes it outside where the men with twisted hair sit stiff like they've become frozen there. He collects the cups and lines them up on both sides and ends of the tray forming a ceramic wall to keep the silverware from sliding off the tray, then sorts the silverware and puts knives, forks and spoons together on the tray and carries them inside where Hester is ready to wash and rinse them.

"You're fast," he says admiringly. "I'll be back with the plates next, and I'll take a washcloth to wash the table. And then, maybe our demented demanding guests will actually help bring the table and chairs back inside like they said they'd do."

Hester grimaces and says: "I'm not at all sure that I want the sticky energy of those two hide-bound hell-bent mean men in my kitchen even for the purpose of keeping their word to you. They want to see the calf *before* they honor their word to us don't they?"

"*Demand* it," Jacob nods agreement. "And they demand I take them *now*!

"What will you do?"

Jacob grins and his eyes dance, "Oh, Hes, do come out and watch. I *promise you* that it will be more entertaining than a barrel of monkeys with their tails tied together.

"Besides, the girl has to be there *with* the calf, and they have to see that."

"*Why?*"

"How would your mother answer that question?"

Hester gives a knowing smile, then laughs, and says: "Ah, yes! If the virgin calf has *ever* been exposed to a female, even a girl child, the calf is *not* unblemished. Well done, husband a mine!" She hands him a moist washcloth and directs him with a smile, "be *very* careful to wash the crumbs off the table and generously into their laps, okay?" Jacob laughs in head back glee.

"While you are cleaning the table and getting it, the bench, and the chairs back in the kitchen, the kids and I will milk the cows, and then the girl and I will comb, bless, and feed our calf like we always do for the calf that will feed us through the winter.

"When you know that we are inside tending our willing calf, invite our closed minded and hypercritical guests into the calf pen to see our flawless calf.

"Do you think they will change though?" Jacob worries aloud, "The twisted Rabbi are so hide-bound judgmental and narrow minded that I have strong doubts they have *any* capacity to forget and forgive ancient injustices."

"You can't un-ring a bell, dammit!" Hester explodes,

"Why don't these twisted men just *get* that and stop trying to change history? Trying to change the past *inevitably* fuck's up the present."

Jacob giggles a grins and says: "I'm glad you don't talk like that when the kids are around, my beloved potty-mouthed wife mate of mine."

Hester laughs with Jacob and says: "I'll call the kids to help with the milking. When we're done, the girl and I will go to the calf barn to pet, love on, and feed our calf like we always do for the animal that will feed us through the winter.

"*Do* require that our tight twisted guests help you put the kitchen table, bench, and chairs back in place *before* you bring them to see our *unblemished* calf." She pats his shoulder, "Otherwise our show and tell time will *not* be a lesson learned for our guests, and they will keep on proving to everyone with eyes to see that they are *idiots* who insist on doing the same things they've always done and expecting a different outcome. *Que tonto! Que increable estupido!*

Jacob laughs as he hugs Hester and says: "I am glad you are on my side, wife of mine, because you will never give less than the best you have to give; and you will not tolerate injustice or hide-bound closed-mindedness. You are a *fierce* warrior of truth. The outstanding question is whether our uninvited guests are *willing* to change and be better than they were before.

"I really do like it when you truth talk in Spanish because it is practically *impossible* to say anything that's really hateful in the language of love. *Que tonto! Que increable estupido!*"

He grins patting Hester's bottom, and calls out: "Kids, it time to milk the cows and run the milk through the separator so we have milk and cream like we always do."

"Can we make ice cream this time?" The girl asks, "Pretty please?"

"Ask your mom, she's our dairy queen. And you know that."

The girl grins up at her mother and makes an offer: "I will pick the strawberries. I will wash and slice the ones we'll need to make strawberry cream ice cream, and I'll wash and dry the rest, and cover them and put them in the refrigerator."

She can tell her mother's not sold yet. She ups the ante. "I will even crank the ice cream maker until my *arms* fall off if I have to so we can have strawberry ice cream for desert tonight."

"Hum-m-m..., maybe. But you do know the blueberries are almost ripe enough to make ice cream don't you? And you *do* know how much I like blueberry ice cream don't you?"

The girl giggles, bobs a nod, and negotiates: "Well then, let's make strawberry ice cream today because the strawberries are ripe now.

"The only *bad* thing is that we really do have to eat *all* the strawberry ice cream *before* the blueberries are ripe and sweet enough to make blueberry ice cream, and pie, and muffins. *That* is when we will make the blueberry ice cream. Will that work for you?"

Hester laughs and counters the girl's offer: "That *will* work for me *if* you agree to crank the ice cream maker for *both* batches of ice cream," the girl nods.

"And you also agree to *regularly* add ice and rock salt to the well so the ice cream thickens and sets firm enough to scoop from the maker and into a tub, and then into bowls for eating.

"Deal?" Hester asks extending her hand to the girl.

The girl grins up at her mom, takes her hand and nods agreement as she shakes her hand. "Deal," she agrees.

"Let's go milk the cows so they stop bawling because their udders hurt for being too full of milk, then we'll separate it so we get the cream and milk we'll need. Then we'll go feed Paradox and pet him and love on him so he's feeling happy and safe when the bad men come to see him."

"*Bad men?* I've never heard you say that before about anyone.

"Well, that's because it was never true of anyone I ever met before those three mean miserable men came while it was still dark this morning with their twisted hair and minds to match.

She looks up at her mother and asks: "We won't let them take Paradox will we? No matter how much they say they'll pay for him, we won't let them take Paradox will we? Please say we won't let them have Paradox." A single tear slips from one eye and she does not blink or look away.

Hester cups the girl's cheeks and smiles into her eyes as she assures: "Of course we won't give Paradox into the clutches of those greed-guts with plaited hair, noses like knife blades, hollow cheeks, and eyes as hard and black as coals in a Christmas stocking!

"There is no *way* are we will let that happen to our Paradox. Come, button your coat up and put your boots on, we're going to milk the cows and feed Paradox like we do every morning."

"Kids," Hester calls: "Let's go do the milking, feed the animals, and get our other morning chores done.

"Boys, I saw some game in the draw where you and Daddy sowed wheat and milo seeds in the spring. There are pheasants, quail, and jack rabbits. Get the birds first...," she throws up her hands and amends with a silly grin: "*Just* like your dad taught you to do.

"And," she grins again, "when the birds are dropped and bagged, call the hooved and footed things the way an Indian would, by inviting and gratefully receiving their free-given gift of life that we will dress and bless and eat through winter and spring."

"We know this, Mom, why are you telling us again?"

"Because..., because our uninvited guests do *not know any* of what I just said, and that makes me fiercely annoyed with them, and that's mostly because I can't lecture them."

"Why not?" The boys ask in one voice.

Hester blinks three times, clicks her heels (in her head) and changes her mind. "You're right, my wise sons. I *can* totally play the Wicked Witch of the West and blow the twisted ones to another state of awareness and just maybe they'll meet the Cheshire cat who'll make them forget what *asses* they are, and remember again with who they really are."

"You're a dreamer, Mom!" Her eldest son snaps stepping away. He stops, turns and amends with a lopsided grin, "But maybe we can help make this particular dream of yours come true. I'd like that. Let's go, Bro, we've got time for talking and planning while we bring the cows in and get them into stanchions in the milk barn.

The eldest son turns to Jacob and says: "Dad, you go back outside and sit at the table with our black-head guests and keep them occupied while Bro and I do what needs to be done to help Mom have her way with them. *We* will keep our unblemished calf ourselves as we planned to do on the day it was born.

"Well, *that* assignment will be as boring as watching dirt dry." Jacob grumbles as he pats their backs appreciatively and follows the boys outside, then turns to sit silently facing the black suited tight twisted ones. He pours the rest of the cold coffee into his cup, sips, and holds the cup in silence. He lets it go and opens an inner space for something good to come of what is.

*I do enjoy the peaceful silence of the morning. It has been a long while since I took the time to just sit still, to be wide open, and to wait peacefully in the silence. That's one good thing.*

*Lord, you've got to help me here if there other good things that to come from this visit.*

*They came to this place in this time, on this day, and to your home, in order to be challenged to change the scope of what they accept as true. They came to know the whole truth of life, and the whole truth of who they are, and who they came to life to be and to become.*

*They don't know this. They have not yet remembered their true purpose for being in this place in this lifetime. They are lost souls, my son.*

*Why did they have to get lost all way out here at* our *place, God? What's the deal with that?* Jacob hears the D.O. laugh and lowers his eyes to hide the glee he knows is dancing there.

They will find the truth of their souls again here. And that finding only begins here on your farm with your family and with your precious unblemished calf.

They don't know you do the same thing with a chosen calf every year. They want Paradox because they assume and believe that he is a one of a kind unblemished calf. And he is.

Yet he isn't. Everyone who sees Paradox wants him. You know this. Most of the men who want him are farmers who want Paradox to strengthen their herd. Farmers aren't nearly as brazenly closed-minded and as determinedly bull-headed as these cagey men are.

Stay on your plan and let me lead you along the way you and Hester have devised. Your plan was divinely inspired, in case I need to tell you that.

Jacob was never good at sitting still and doing nothing. He can't stand the irritating twitchiness that shudders through his muscles when he sits still for too long a time. This morning is no exception. Tensing and relaxing muscle groups from head to toe isn't doing it for him. He wants to hit something. Hard. And what he wants to hit sits across the table from him even meeting his eyes. Worse still, they will not speak to him. Even though Hester's gone to the barn to milk cows, separate cream from milk, feed the pigs, and the cats who keep mice from the house, and Teddy, their Malamute wise watch dog, gets meat scraps, veggies and milk.

And Jacob's muscles are twitching and jumping. This is not a good sign.

"Why did you come here this morning? I've asked you that before and get only squishy responses that *aren't* answers." He bangs the table with both fists and holds them there white knuckle tight. His eyes flash dangerously as he snarls: "You won't even give me the courtesy of looking me in the eye and that is *not acceptable* behavior on the part of *uninvited* visitors.

"What the *fuck* did you come here for?" Out of the corner of his eye he sees the driver look away from his twisted passengers, to hide his smile and laughing eyes.

"Uh-uh-uh," stutters the most knife nosed visitor stunned by the four letter word Jacob used. "We..." He clears his throat. It's still squeaky. "We came out this morning because we heard at the Feed and Grain that you are the best stockman in three counties. The men there were all from only three counties – and that's still 100%.

"We seek an unblemished calf to sacrifice on the altar when our new Solomon's Temple is built in the U.S. All the men we talked to said you were the man who would have such a calf.

"We came here to see your calf and decide if it's the one we want."

Jacob hasn't seen Hester and the girl come out with the pail of milk for the calf. He waits as quietly and patiently as he did when it was *they* who were sullen and silent and impolitely indifferent to common courtesy.

He watches the chauffer stand and walk away hiding his silent laughter from his passengers. He sees the man spot Hester and the girl carrying a pail of milk to the calf barn. Jacob watches as he connects the dots, smiles, nods in appreciation, then turns to look in another direction.

When Hester and the girl are in the calf barn, Jacob slaps both palms on the table calling their eyes to him. "So, you came all the way out here just to see my unblemished calf?" They nod. "Well then, time's a-wasting, let's go get this done so you can get back to finding a place where you can build your grand new Solomon's Temple and *boast by brick*, as my Papa used to say it."

Jacob gets up and walks briskly toward the calf barn. The men have to step lively to keep up with him, and they never really do, Jacob's already inside the calf barn when they arrive.

The chauffer opens the barn door for the men to enter, then steps in after them, all senses on full alert. He feels the angry dismay of the men at seeing Hester and the girl combing, currying, and feeding the calf. He waits for the explosion he knows will come. How dumb.

"*This* is not an unblemished calf!" The first Rabbi snarls pointing a trembling finger at Paradox.

"There is no blemish on this calf!" Jacob disputes indignantly. "If you *truly* believe there is any flaw, or blemish, on this calf, point it out to me. Do it *now*." He snarls, "You have wasted more than enough of my time this morning...."

The two men see and feel Jacob's extreme ire at their claim that Paradox is *not* unblemished calf. They step toward the calf with respectful caution. Hester does not move nor look away.

The girl smiles up at the men, her arms around the neck of Paradox. "Isn't Paradox beautiful? "She strokes the calf," There's not a blemish on his coat anywhere.

"That is because we keep him in the calf barn from the time he's weaned until he's old enough to butcher...," She pets Paradox's ears and head looking into his happy eyes as he gazes into her sorrowing ones. "And eat our Paradox." She says eyes spilling over with receiving in gratitude.

"Even then," the girl glares into the round eyes of the bearded men, "his Paradox coat will be unblemished.

She doesn't back down in the face of their stiff lipped silence. "*Why* do you say that Paradox is blemished when you can plainly *see* that he is not?"

"No answer for the girl." Hester notes stiffly. "Perhaps then I will ask. "*Why* do you say that Paradox is blemished when you can plainly *see* that he is not?" Silence extends awkwardly.

"No answer *for my wife?*" Jacob explodes: "Then you will answer *to me*! *Why* do you claim that Paradox is blemished when you can *plainly* see that he is not?"

The visitor's heads are unbowed but their eyes are lowered when they reply. "A pure, and *truly* unblemished calf must have no contact with any women. Or any girl."

Hester giggles and asks: "Do you have any idea how a calf is born?"

They shake their heads mutely. "How about you, do you know how you were born?"

"From my mother's womb, of course, that is *obvious*!"

"Then *you* yourself are not unblemished. Unfortunately, you make your blemishes patently obvious. *Too* obvious actually. You could at least *try* to be subtle and less in-your-face about your abhorrent exclusionary holier than thou arrogant ego. You *should* bear in mind that 'ego' stands for Edging God Out."

"A calf is born from its mother's womb just like humans are, you closed-minded buffoons! If you *haughtily* continue to believe that being born from a female, or that being in contact with a female makes a calf blemished, you will *never* find an unblemished calf.

"*You* are not unblemished by your own definition of the word. *You* were born from a female"

The girl who has been holding the calf's ears closed and looking deep into his eyes speaking silent love thoughts to the animal scratches its crown and turns to the plaited men. Her eyes spark fire flares and she yells at them although she does not raise her voice.

"You do not *deserve* Paradox!" She hisses.

"He is just a *thing* to you!

"Well Paradox is *not* a *thing*. He's *way* more than that. Paradox is a living, breathing, thinking, and loving, animal creation of God.

The girl is suddenly impatient with the visitors and the small, twisted energy of them. "Doesn't your holy book include *Genesis*?" The men are round-eyed silent.

Her eyes spark flare fire fury as she marches toward them stopping an arm's length away. The men take one step back. "Does – your – holy – book – include –Genesis?" She shouts.

Jacob taps the girl's shoulder and pulls her into his protection placing a hand on each shoulder. His eyes never leave the faces of the two men as he says: "They won't talk to you, I think..., because you are a female. If your mother were to ask them the same question they wouldn't answer her either."

"*Really*?" The girl looks up at her dad in dismay.

Jacob laughs as he looks down at her and suggests: "Let's try it another way. I think you'll see what I mean.

"Does your holy book include Genesis?" Jacob asks looking at the mendacious men.

"Yes."

"Well then, on the sixty day of creation, *your* holy book must say that God created living creatures, *cattle*, the creeping crawling things, and beasts of the earth?

"No answer *even for me*? You raise rudeness to a high art, and there is *no* consciousness that can excuse that rationally.

Didn't the Divine One make man in his image and after likeness?" The men nod cautious agreement.

"Then doesn't your holy book *also* say that on the sixth day God created male *and* female of *everything* He made on the sixth day of creation?

"*Including* man, and *necessarily* woman?

"How can you *rationally* believe that the creator of all and everything made *any* of his creations unclean? *Es tonto! Es totalmente estupido!*

"*No answer!* Not even for *me*?" Jacob poses his fierce fury.

"Well, *that* is just plain rude, and there is *no excuse* for that discourtesy from *any* uninvited guest to our home and property!" Laying hands on both men in black, he shoves them out the calf barn door, shouting: "Out! Now! Get off my land, and do not *ever* come back!"

The chauffer collects the men and ushers them to the car, opens the back doors and hands the men into the back seats of the car. "Wait here, I'll be back in a few minutes."

"And where will *you* be while we wait here?" The surly sour one snaps surly. "You are *our* chauffer, it is your *job* to take us where we want to go *when* we want to go there!"

The driver stops, turns to the surly men and says: "You do *not buy* my integrity when you hire me as an as needed chauffer.

"My integrity is *not* for sale now, nor will it ever be. You purchase *only* my navigational skills and my sure sense of direction. Never *once* have I gotten you lost, or made you late for any appointment you ever had.

"I do not work *for you*. I am *not* your employee. You *rent* my driving services and navigational skills on an as needed basis. Nothing more.

"You *can't* bargain for my integrity. That is *not* yours to command, to demand, nor to control.

"I told Jacob, *your host*, that I would help take the bench, the table and the chairs back into the kitchen *before* we leave. That is what *I will do*.

---

Shawn Gallaway – If I Could Find A Way

---

"Sit lip zipped, and *wait* until I have done what I promised to do!" It is not a request.

"While you wait for me here, pray *profoundly* for forgiveness of the evils you committed when your EGO took over and you Edged God Out of your mind and heart.

"That EGO sin of yours goes back for a *very* long time, and for an equally long time, you have *never* asked the Divine One to forgive you for the evil you do in your arrogance and separation from source anxiety.

"Begin today. Ask the D.O. for forgiveness of the iniquities you perpetrated on these good and Godly people who live here. When you have done that, begin asking for forgiveness of all the times your hidebound arrogant judgmentalism caused you to *do harm unto others.*"

He turns to walk away, then turns back: "The Master said 'you have not because you ask not'.

"Ask for *self*-forgiveness! Begin there, for until you own, allow, and forgive yourselves for the evil you have done you *cannot* forgive others.

"Forgiveness *begins* in 'giving for yourself.' Only when you truly forgive yourself of *your* flaws and *your* EGO consciousness, can you even begin to give for others.

"I will be back when Hester's kitchen is as it was before you came cloaked in your dense black cloud of evil, anger, and separation from source anxiety.

"While you wait the few minutes it will take for me to keep my word to *our* hosts, pray that the forgiving God of a thousand names has mercy on your souls for what you did here today." The good and godly chauffer walks away to keep his word and his faith.

*Even our hired chauffer cannot be paid enough to willingly compromise his integrity.... How far we have fallen in pursuit of an amazing space while never asking for amazing grace.*

The girl walks to the car and knocks on the window. When the window isn't lowered, she slaps her palms insistently against it. The men don't even look at her. She goes postal in her fury. She takes a step back from the car and begins kicking the door as hard as she can *intending* to dent it in an all-out effort to dent their hidebound judgmental pride.

"Stop doing that!" The senior man in black orders as he lowers his window half way. "*We* have to pay for any damages done to this car while we're renting it, you *stupid* girl!"

The girl grins and says, laughter dancing in her eyes: "Well *that* is a case of the pot calling the kettle black!

"As for you having to pay for any damage done to the car while you're using it..., I knew that too." Her lop-sided grin is back and her eyes are laughing a chiding challenge. "*That was* the only way that you would *ever* accept, own, allow, and admit that *you* brought this whole series of unfortunate events upon yourselves. There *is* no one else that you *can* blame for that.

"That is *mostly* because *there can be no 'other' that is* outside *the scope of the Creator of all and everything!*" The men don't get it. She can see that. She is not a happy camper.

"Your noses are pinched sharp as a knife, is that so that you won't have to smell your own *shit*?

Before they can recover, the girl adds: "Worse than that, you keep poking your knife noses in places where *your* noses don't belong!

"Plus, you're both as dumb as dirt!

"And *that's* not being fair to dirt. Dirt is inert.

"God is a circle whose center is *everywhere*, and whose circumference is *nowhere*. You *cannot get* outside of God *except* in your own minds and in your mean small-minded self-awareness.

"Animals are sensitive to energy, and they do not *like* being around people whose energy is angry and punitive. Animals *will* move away from that energy as far and as fast they can get.

"That is why mom came around Paradox and stood between him and you. She shielded him.

"You wouldn't have seen that because your hard angry eyes made you blind to the light, but mom formed an energy bubble around Paradox so that he would not take or absorb any of your judgmental never-good-enough controlling faith, and be tainted by it.

"Paradox's meat *will* be tender and sweet when we butcher him this fall because mom blocked your energy from him, and because we always pet and praise Paradox and *ask* him if he is willing to feed us through the winter."

The girl shrugs, "Our unblemished calf is *always* willing when we've made him feel special by feeding him by hand always holding the pail for him while he drinks the milk.

"We *always* give our chosen calf abundant love, appreciation, and gratitude for its willingness to be our chosen calf and to be food for us through the winter.

"Paradox *does not* like you! He doesn't like the energy of you. He wants your evil judgmental energy *out* of his calf barn.

"We *will* do that for Paradox, but we will *not* do that until you men in black are gone for good and have taken your ugly, vile energy with you.

"God made everything that *is* and everything that is not.

"I do *not* believe that the Divine One ever forgets or abandons any of his creations. Birds and animals don't forget that they were created in the mind of the Divine, that they were perfect *idea* before they ever took a physical form.

"Only humans forget that. Only humans think that the physical form is the be all and end all, and that when the body dies the Spirit dies too. *Que tonto! Que totalmente estupido!*"

| Shawn Gallaway – Shining Star |
|---|

The girl hears the chauffer approaching the car from behind her. She hears him stop where he stands studying the car, the girl and the men in black in the back seat where the door has been crumpled in by child sized feet.

"My, my," he says with dismay, "What have you done here?" He asks the men in black in back.

"What have *we* done here?" the elder one growls. "We are the victims here!"

"Well, playing the victim *is* your favorite role by far. So I am not *totally* surprised to hear you claim that a little girl actually victimized you. But *why* would you say that?

"Who do you imagine would actually believe that a polite young neighbor kid like this one *actually* kicked in the side of your rental car and did that with no provocation at all?"

"We have done *nothing*! We were simply sitting here minding our own business while waiting for you to come back and drive us back to town."

"You won't look me in the eyes when you say that – why is that?"

"Did she knock at the window first?" The men nod.

"Did she motion for you to roll the window down?" The two heads bobble again.

"Did you roll down the window?"

"You're taking her side against us." The knife nosed elder growls menace.

"I am not taking sides." He says no more, yet the men in black hear more. They know he's making mental notes of the words they've spoken and the words they've left unsaid. They know he's measuring the flavor of the energy flowing from them as force, and not as power.

They admit, perhaps for the first time, that *force* is the energy they most often use. Force is their default value. *Dark energy*. The dark ones judge with far-seeing eyes.

The chauffer clears his throat, catches their eyes in the mirror, and says: "I asked a reasonable question under the circumstance. I'll ask one more time.

"*Did you* roll the window down when the girl knocked on it and motioned you to roll it down?"

"No."

"Why not?"

"We knew what the girl would say if we rolled the window down." the younger knife nose admits with shielded eyes.

"Tell me then. I'm safe. I'm as close to a neutral party as you will ever find."

"We knew what the girl would say." The senior man in black agrees dolefully.

"We didn't want to hear that. If we heard what we knew she'd say then we'd have to admit that we *have* been closed minded judgmental jerks. We'd have no choice but to acknowledge that were self-deluded ones and that we *do not* deserve to own the girl's unblemished calf.

"We had no right to be in the same barn with Paradox." A long silence follows the admission.

"That is what we *knew* the girl would say to us if we rolled the window down.

"We knew she'd speak the truth, and truth would dissolve the hard hide-bound outside of us and reveal our true selves." He studies his hands twining together like binding spells. Or, unbinding ones if the truth be known.

"We did not want to hear that truth! We didn't want to have to look at who we have been. We didn't want to admit how insular and aggressive we have been, that we *did* want to sow divisiveness and – we *did* want to boast by brick – as her granddaddy would say it."

| Shawn Gallaway – All Shall Be Well |
| --- |

"What would you have us do?" The men ask.

"Be good neighbors. Wherever you go. Whether you're traveling to find the hometown of your new church, or to find and buy the land. Be a good neighbor. Don't boast by brick. You know how hateful and un-neighborly that is, so don't do that." He lets the silence extend into peace.

"When you have found your land and are developing the architectural plans for your new house of worship be a *good* neighbor to *everyone* in your community, not just its leaders.

"Invite all churches, all community leaders, and all your neighbors to an event that you plan, stage, and pay for, at which you share your vision for your church, and the kind of community relationship you want to have in the place where you build your house of worship.

"Tell the church and community leaders *and* your neighbors, all the ways you plan to work *with* your neighbors of all faiths to enrich the community that will be your church home.

"When you've got that rolling on its own steam, elicit ideas from, and share your objectives with community and church leaders of *all* faiths to forge mutually supportive and collaborative efforts to guide *all* faith practices to be more ecumenical and less biased and judgmental.

"The master said 'judge not lest ye be judged'. Don't judge."

"Start with yourselves. Yours is a worthy faith practice. What do you like about it? What do you *not* like at all about it? What you do *not* like about how *you* currently practice your faith?

"Until you own and allow *what is*, you remain powerless to change it." He waits a count of three, and coaches: "Awareness precedes choice, and *choice* precedes change.

"You must forgive yourselves first.

"It will make it easier if you know that forgiveness *means* giving for yourself. Only when you have given for yourself can you forgive others.

When you do that, you become good neighbors to *everyone* in your community, including all faith practices.

"If you want to make a *real* and much appreciated difference in your chosen community, openly support public schools by providing school supplies to public school teachers.

"Talk to the teachers and find out how many children by grade don't have textbooks for their grade because their folks can't afford to buy them. Buy backpacks for those kids! Buy the textbooks those kids will need for each grade. Put a ruled tablet and a packet of pencils in each backpack. Deliver the loaded backpacks by grade to each teacher before the first day of school.

The driver looks into the rear-view mirror to see his passengers. "Look at you, you're both grinning from ear to ear. It *feels* right, doesn't it?" the men nod.

"In public schools there *can be* no wrong questions. There *are* no wrong points of view. There *are always* right resolutions when all interests and concerns of your neighbors are welcomed, considered, and addressed openly and honestly.

"Children who are afraid to ask questions in school grow up to be narrow and closed minded teens, and then belligerent bullying adults who flock to churches that judge and punish independent thought and originality. This is *Sinat Chinam* against the soul and spirit of man.

"Tell me, were *you* afraid to ask questions when you were in school?" The men nod regretfully. "That didn't feel good did it? This time the senior Rabbi meets his eyes in the rear view mirror.

"You were excited to be in school. You were eager to learn what you didn't already know.

"Instead you were required to *memorize* every nit and tittle of an *already* complex and confounding faith practice. You were taught to be *obedient*.

"Yet, Divine One gave us free will, and that tells me logically that we are not *intended* to be obedient. But we *are* expected to be compliant." He gives the truth time do its healing work.

A mile later, the driver gives his summary argument. "Compliance means that you *do not* build a gigantic Solomon's Temple here. That would be politically incorrect, and counter-productive.

"That would arouse envy and antagonism in your neighbors and your neighboring churches. They would *reasonably* conclude that you and your religion are dogmatic, judgmental, and self-righteous, and that you would *not* be good neighbors.

"*Not* a good perception of you. That perception would evoke in your neighbors the same reaction that nearly wrecked Hester, her parents, and her siblings.

The driver goes impishly somber and he says: "My favorite definition of insanity is doing the same thing you've always done and expecting a different outcome." Silence follows.

"So *what if* you decide today that you do something you've never tried before? What if you *choose* to develop a collaborative approach to do what is new for you, untested, and as yet unproven?

"Wouldn't you necessarily *have* to become problem solvers then?

"Wouldn't you *have* to anticipate social opposition against your untested idea?

"Wouldn't it be *necessary* for you to consider ways that your plan to build a synagogue *would benefit* all of the people living in the neighborhood of your house of worship?

| Shawn Gallaway – Breathe A Little Magic |
|---|

"Wouldn't you *have to* support the public schools in your neighborhood then?

"Wouldn't you *have to* enroll your kids in public schools for the educational, *and* the social interaction that is inherent in public schools?

"Are you willing to let children explore boundaries? Are you willing to *help* them accept and understand, own and allow their fears so they can convert fear into tools for positive change?

"Are you *willing* to be there for people when they fall for believing they failed in some way?

"Are you willing to *be present* with your neighbors in the painful silence of their self-judgement and inadequacy? Are you *willing* give them only unconditional love and compassion?

"Every person in your chosen community *will be* your neighbor. Are you *willing* to be a *good* and caring neighbor to each and every one of them?"

The Rabbi smiles, and says: "Yes. We are willing to be a good neighbors to all of our neighbors.

### Solomon's Temple

"While Solomon's Temple was," the Rabbi narrates, "the God of Jews dwelt in Solomon's Temple. There alone did Jehovah God receive the blood of an unblemished calf in reparation for our sins. Every year in Solomon's Temple, Jehovah God forgave the sins of the people.

"Until the temple was destroyed."

An ancient sorrow haunts him. "We lost our pole star. We lost our sanctuary, our place to be alone with Jehovah God, to confess our sins, and to be forgiven."

"Forgiven for what?" The driver asks with disarming attentiveness.

"*Sinat chinam* – senseless hatred." The senior man in black replies candidly and without rancor.

"We wanted to build a place of atonement so we would have a temple where can sacrifice the blood of an unblemished calf in absolution of our sins," the rabbi replies.

"The first Temple was destroyed because of *sinat chinam* – senseless hatred." He bows his head in regret. "Since that day the people of our faith are nomads, vilified, and unwelcome wherever we go. We have no place to honor Jehovah, the God of our fathers.

The driver hears them out and notes with an amiable smile, "It is a pity Judaism did not make room in its faith to accept Jesus and his message of a loving compassionate father-God who forgives and loves *without* sacrifice of blood as evidence of repentance."

"Well-spoken..., you who take bread and wine in an act of faith that bread and wine is the transmuted body and blood of your savior who walked among men until his body temple was destroyed by the people of his land." The rabbi's eyes twinkle as he speaks.

The driver's delight reflects in the rear-view mirror. "If all men met, loved, and honored their God as true and well as you, yet held open a space in their hearts to honor and respect *all other* faith practices, ours would be a kinder, friendlier, and more tolerant world, Rabboni.

"It would be a world without *sinat chinam,* a world we would *all* delight to live in."

---

Shawn Gallaway – The Truth

# Moon Bird

The rhythmic clip-clop of the mule's hooves follow a familiar path home and lulls Bam White into an exuberant euphoria where his physical senses are profoundly alert to all expressions of life settling into the retirement of the day as fiery light casts swords and slant shadows into shade of deepening night.

Bam shares passion with all the forms that life inhabits and manifests on the physical plane. He gives praise for the life and love he shares with his wife, and for all his earnest and amiable children.

He eyes the western sky where the sun burns down like hot coals, flaring liquid gold rays across the bowl of the sky, tinting vapor clouds with the hues of fire and flame. He sees shadows extending on Earth tinted heavenly hues just for man's pleasure and joy at this one singular sunset on this one holy night.

He thanks Great Spirit for the forever growing giving gift of life, he calls for wisdom to guide him sure and safe along the twisting twining ways of his red road of life.

He surrenders to, and mourns, that sometimes his personal wisdom is purely inadequate to the tasks laid before him. In that acknowledgment, Bam recalls, forgives and releases all his shortfalls, and all those like his that appear in others.

In the release Bam is overwhelmed by a flow of certainty he never allowed his conscious mind to entertain before. It shifts his perspective to his personal sense of self, who he thinks he is, and who he thinks he came to life to be. He finds with shivering shock that he is pathetically too small for the constant confounding callings and challenges of life. He admits that he is woefully inadequate to cope with life's surprising twists and turns. He owns that.

He exhales that deficit in one powerful puff. *Release and let go*, he advises himself. Empty now, Bam gasps great gulps of air, and is filled to overflowing by the sometimes privately personal and always astonishing ways the Abiding Wisdom of Love subtly, slyly, and smoothly unspools itself into his life in fully functional ways.

*That's important*! Bam affirms with praise for the wise persistent present presence of amazing grace.

A humble man before the throne of Grace, Bam hoists his praise pack and steps from the cart. He doffs his cap and drops to his knees in exaltation before the setting sun. Reverently placing the praise pack before him, he touches forehead to earth feeling the fiery glow of the sun press inside the crown of his head to enter livid light streams embracing his mind and brain. He melts molten into his obeisance.

As amber light shot with rainbow flame filters through his skull and to his mind and brain he pulls deep slow breaths inhaling this singular grace. Holding his breath in the breadth of Spirit to a count of ten, he exhales, knowingly allowing a slow release of the small sticky stuff of life to be transformed into only love seeping slow like warm honey through him.

Bam observes his brain/mind rigorously recording mental release notes from the universe and methodically plants them to thrive and reside inside as his on-demand guide to a life practice of compassionate listening for all he meets on his red road walk.

He smiles knowing that his vision of a healed earth is already manifest although his mortal eyes cannot see it, nor his mind know how it comes or flows. He cannot even guess how Life will reveal itself in the flowing grace of time. He chooses to be a mind and heart freely and willingly made whole, to be and to become the lover, and the beloved, of the myriad manifestations of the Divine into life in this benighted land now a wandering dust desert. Wandering dirt in a land once called the Great American Plains, the breadbasket of the world..., when the war still raged and ravaged Europe.

Surrendering the pains of the day and of a lifetime, Bam gives praise and gratitude to the Source of all that is, all that is not, and everything in between. He is especially grateful for the unknown yet unseen blessings that will come for the people and the places of his beset benighted prairie.

He is awed by and gives gratitude for the indigenous people of the land, and a great respect for those who crossed an ocean with little more than the firm will and the intention to make and call this land their home. Even when their living space is but a windswept dugout.

Bam is humbled by the grace and the strength of the persistent prairie people in their diligent determination to restore fertility – albeit necessarily of a new kind – to their benighted chosen land.

Bam is grateful for the generosity of his neighbors in receiving his help and for their liberal sharing of what is presently at hand when cash is not. He praises the openhanded fair exchanges he regularly receives for the help he gives neighbors and town folks.

He holds a special smile of gratitude for the inexplicable and ever timely generosity of Lady RO. It seems she always clears her pantry and can cellar when food is more limited, or more costly, than can be had for the money he earns doing odd jobs around houses and yards. *I am grateful that you receive my special praise for Lady RO. You done a right fine job making that woman. I'm plum delighted that you guided her and her great helpful heart to live and love in our town. And so it is, amen.*

Bam rises, his surrender and praise complete and his heart healed and whole again. He picks up his praise pack and turns to his mildly munching mule, steps into the cart, pats the weighty bag beside him, takes up the reins, clicks his tongue, and his faithful mule resumes their habitual homeward way in the fading light of a day chock full with surprising burdens and blessings.

---

Shawn Gallaway – We Dance

---

### Home Again, Home Again

At ease in the abiding peace of his sunset surrender of burdens and blunders, Bam whistles and tweets bird calls, smiling anew at each reply to their nesting places along ridge rows and ditches, and to the brave branches of trees toeing roots deep enough to draw the water of life to branch and leaf. *Our land will live again. Welcome home my dear singers and tweeters,* he grins big and wide, *welcome home again!* He pats his praise pouch thinking of the 'extra chicken feed' Hester gave him and smiles warmly at the winging singing birds. His eyes fill with happy tears. He tips back his head so the tears cannot fall and warbles joy to the soil, to the sun burning down in the West, to stars blinking Morse code odes to night, and to the ever cyclic order of life amidst of, and despite, the random witless predations of man.

Though he will never tell of it, Bam sees and hears angels winging and singing odes of joy for the redemption and healing of earth that man will perform one day. When man remembers again with the making of man in the mind of the Divine. Made them to be enlightened and wise stewards of Earth, its atmosphere, its soil, and its water.

Captured in the mystical magic of Oneness with Source Bam's voice box chest and lungs expand like a gently filling balloon setting free his throat and tongue to warble and wail and trill and titter and croak and caw, and to sing in the tongues of all winged warbling, footed and hooved things living on Earth. It is, in Bam's peculiar voice, an Ode to Joy on this starry starry night.

So embraced in bliss is he that Bam sees nothing amiss until his mule stalls and stutters on the path home bobbing her head until harness traces jingle jangle in the deepening dark. Tensing the reins and talking gently to calm the mule, Bam blinks to refocus his mortal eyes to see what bothers his basically blasé beast. In the way a man does not see what is not there, so Bam does not see, then blinks to clear his eyes. He leans forward resting chest on his thighs and knees and lowering his head to mule head high. Still Bam does not see what is not there to see. Until he does.

He sits upright blinking his eyes, opening the aperture of his pupils, and sending his curiosity ahead of eyesight to lead it on; and then he sees what is not there.

*Light. There should be light where my family is.* He clicks his tongue and speaks with soft urgency and strong faith. "Let's go, Becky, let's us go see what's going on at home and put some light on the problem. If there is one. And it is sure looking like there is one. Let's go find what's not working, make it right, and get you some good healthy food."

Bam pet pats his praise pack, and breathes deep and slow. He sends faith and love ahead of his plodding mule winging swift and true to the house where now a feeble flame flickers fretful flaring light against the raised glass cover of the hurricane lamp. Their only light at night, save when the moon comes in. *It's not Lizzie, her hand is sure and quick. These hands are new, small and slow. She doesn't know how to light the lamp. She's never done it before. Where is Melt? Where is Lizzie?*

*That alone would have me worried if worry ever did any good, and it don't. Ever. Where is Lizzie?* He wail worries anyway.

"Step it up, mule, get us home fast as you can, we got some fixing to do, let's go." Contrary to her reputation as a mule, Becky quickens her pace to a steady clip-clop, tosses her head to ring the harness traces and trumpets a charge. It is unproven, but amiably claimed, that a mule is physically incapable of anything reasonably called *a charge*.

As they come to a stop, Bam grabs up his praise pouch, scrambles from the wagon and into the house where he sees Lizzie curled into a ball on the floor, Melt crouched near in fear, and his tiny eldest daughter on her toes trying to light the kerosene lamp with a stick match burning black too fast to light the wick and not singe her fingers. He drops his pouch beside his fallen wife and steps quickly to the lamp lighter touching her shoulder softly and taking the match from her fingers to fan out the fire.

"I didn't know how, Daddy, I tried, but I couldn't make it light." She is near tears but holds them back bravely, stubbornly, until Bam wraps her close to absorb her fears and free her tears.

"That's okay, Aggie" he soothe strokes her thin back and shoulders, "You tried. That's what counts. You tried even though you were afraid."

He pulls her back to look big-eyed into hers, "You *were* afraid weren't you?" She nods admission. "Because you didn't know how to light the lamp, did you?" Sucking singed fingertips she nods her head. "That is *brave*. That is *bold*. That's my *daring*, darling daughter."

Aggie giggles up at him safe and sure and home again, though she never left the house to come again. *Home isn't a house,* she thinks with conviction, *until the house has lots of love in it and people who care whether you're happy or sad, and love you anyway, no matter what.*

"So, let's learn how to open and light a hurricane lamp. Come over here you kids, Melt, Abbie, you two may as well learn how to make light safe and sure along with your sister. No shoving now," he fusses, "there's enough learning to share, and some to spare." Melt, clap a hand on each girl's shoulder, and help them *not* squirm and push. He wins Melt's grin and one from each darling daughter.

Lizzie peeps from between her fists to watch the warm, still fireless scene. *The wick can't reach the kerosene,* she thinks numbly. *There's no kerosene for the lamp. There is no light,* her inner lost child wails woe; *and no way to make or find it.* As though privy to her thoughts, Bam smiles with calm confidence and steps across her to pull from his praise pouch a thin can with the word 'Kerosene' across the label. He holds it for her to see, smiles, then return to his lamp lighting safety training program.

*Wonder what else he's got in that praise pouch of his,* Lizzie thinks but does not stir to peek, nor seek nor find any words to ask.

When the lamp is filled, the wick trimmed, children trained; and the lamp casts a warm dancing red gold glow about the room, Bam tells Melt he needs help unloading the wagon. He sees Melt stand tall and straight hinting at the man he will be.

Smiling, Bam adds, "There are some things a man simply *cannot* do without the help of another man. You're my man, son. Let's get 'er done." Man and son leave and soon return with armloads of wood cut to lay in the fireplace over a nest of kindling to flash the flame that fires the wood and prepares it for cooking, and later for warmth when banked for their sleep. When the fire is rosy warm, Bam and Melt leave and come again with wood to fill the wood box for later fires. Using hand signals Bam tells Melt the number of pieces, and sizes of hardwood they'll want to fill the fire box by the stove to lay for later meals and warmth.

Melt's stomach growls hungrily imagining what might be cooked and eaten, ignoring the fact that he'd checked every cabinet, cupboard and closet, and found no food. *I'd be glad for a hard candy Christmas,* he thinks but does not say.

*Hungry is easier when you're warm,* Lizzie weeps weak woe as her stomach rumbles restless refute that *hunger is never warm.* She waits silent spiraled in a natal coil, incapable of volition, voice, choice, nor even hope. *It's so cold, so craving craven cruel cutting cold. Bitter, bold, sharp biting chill like a foot long icicle fallen free to pierce through the soft spot and into the brain pressing it down-down-deep into suspended animation while the body breathes still breaths chill air that holds no warmth and exhales wheezing whimper blasts of cold, like black snow air, just like black snow air.*

Rushing, dark, dirty, despairing thoughts beset and burden her bright and brilliant faith in good and new and possible. *Where did all the possibilities go? Blown away maybe, with the wind and the crops and the grass land even the locusts, leaving me alone half buried in a pit full foul with sifting sliding dusty grit and dirt with nothing to hold on to, to hold on, to hold, just to hold. Dear* Lord, *give me just one hope, just one possibility, one sign, one small sign, just for this moment.*

Though Lizzie's eyes are bloodshot red no tears form to flow to wash away the darkness from her eyes, lids or dust laden lashes. *Maybe I'm dead and don't know it, like a lamp left burning warm in a dark dead house. Wonder when Bam will see and say.* She tries to raise her eyes to find him, but her eyes, suddenly disobedient, will not respond, will not even blink. *Maybe I'm dead and don't know yet.*

Lizzie sobs silent into elbows and knees and weeps. She has no hope. Nothing like faith or its substance stirs in her heart nor in her sullen, angry, withdrawn and beaten down mind with no safe space left for hope or grace. Feeling forsaken, she rejects and turns away from her bright inner core to trudge like a convict through a life without hope or power nor even enough food. Still she bows her head into her hands and whispers her last hidden prayer. *Give me grace, grace enough to hold for* just this one minute, *this one moment of this one howling hungry empty day on this hard barren land without mercy.* Her body shudders silent sundered dry sobs, *Give me* this *grace, this one gift, this one time, this one day.*

Lizzie hit her overload limit, and knowing it, she let go. She just let go. What's a girl to do? She didn't plan or practice it, she told no one, she just let go. She is adrift weightless and giddy lost from the unyielding command of gravity on her body. Yet part of her bobs along the low ceiling like a balloon untethered and beyond reach of sticky hands and minds of the physical world. With no thought she is through and long beyond the roof and into the quiet place of the infinite silent Present Presence.

Peace rushes through Lizzie with her gentle slow exhale release of things no longer working for her, clearing room within her to welcome, embrace, choose and cleave to a wise, gentle and devoted diligence. The love she longs to encompass and consume her and to enlighten and brighten her life and her living of it. *My children…, how frightened they must be when I fell, and wouldn't get up. When I couldn't get up for want of will. For want of hope.* Sundered by the total absence of love in her and standing separate and apart from the firm rock of faith that might stabilize the shifting dust that shreds her life, her home, her body, her mouth, her nose, her ears, her eyes. She is bereft of even the salty wetness of tears falling to trace her face clear and muddy along their gravity track to the dusted floor under her head. *Everything looks so big from here…, and I so small.*

| Shawn Gallaway – When I Let Go |
|---|

When the lamp is lit and burning merrily, Bam claps Melt on the shoulder saying: "I need more help from you, son, get on your coat, hat and gloves, we got man work to do."

He grins invitingly affable for he thinks he hears Lizzie's soft slow laugh and her warm inhale at the end of it. "We'll make it son, never you fear, when God's on our side, who can be again' us? None. Not one. Not ever. No matter how dark and alone we feel, we only got to remember that God's on our side.

"All *we* need do is stay on God's side and walk our red road of life in *his* stead, in *his* step, in *his* place, doing *his* work. Its fine grand work we do, and we gotta keep the faith that the Good Lord made us whole and hale enough to do the work he places before us to do each day." He scratches his head below his hat and grimaces. "We humans made it kind 'a hard for the Good Lord, tearing up his prairie like mad gophers and then walking away leaving it open raw to blow in God's bitter rebuking wind."

"Pa," Melt looks at his father, his face adult serious and sober, "I don't think God is punishing us. In any way. For any reason. He gave us free will, and mostly we just pretend we are free." The boy pauses pondering; "but when we fail to *will* a thing done, it doesn't *get* done; and nothing changes. Nothing *can* change because man *didn't* will to do a thing God wanted done, and *it didn't get done*! The outcome can be *clearly* seen, even by a blind adder. That probably *has* no faith, and *certainly* has no power of choice."

Melt tosses a lop-sided grin to his father and says: "The question is whether – or not – *we* have the sight of a blind adder, and the *will* to do what is before us to do." Bam scratches the whiskers below his nose, snort sneezes a snicker, hiding his grin behind a hand. "Your eyes are laughing." Melt says, wise to him, "Let's get our chores done, and put Becky away with some hay. I *did* see hay on the wagon didn't I?"

"You did. Let's get done all that's there for us to do this day, son." He glances back at Lizzie with a gentle smile, "Then we'll rustle up some food for us to eat."

"We got no food." Lizzie whisper whines from the icy cold floor.

"Pluck up your faith, woman! In God, if you have none in me." He grins to soften his words. "We didn't have oil for the light, nor wood for the fire before I got home neither. Don't you worry your pretty head about food, Lizzie, we men will take care of that when we get back. Hustle up, Melt, your ma's hungry and so is Becky, still standing patient in her traces *longing* for hay and grain laid in her stall in the barn."

"The barn's not *warm*," Melt hisses Soto voice.

"Becky wears a fur coat and is chock full with the fire of her orneriness." Bam replies peaceably.

"She's a good mule, Pa, you got no call saying' she's ornery!" He grins pulling the door behind as he adds "She *is a hot* little beastie though, that's for sure and true."

Lizzie grins behind the mask of her hands, slowly allowing herself to be comfortable being taken care of sometimes. Especially when the world is too big and too hard, and she too small and far too unworldly to be called wise by any ordinary measure. She puffs a soft sigh, nestles her face into her cupped hands, and closes her eyes in peace and rest.

*It is good to just let be what is. Especially when you can't fix or change it. Now I'm not alone. Bam's home. He has food. He'll cook for me, for us.* Drifting dozy Lizzie comes only faintly aware when cozy soft cotton warmth drops over her. She feels two warm bodies with *very* cold arms plop into the curve of her to rest against her and share their warm love with her and to receive warmth from her body, her arms, and her heart. Too soon, it seems to warm dozy Lizzie, Bam and Melt return, practically insisting, to no strong resistance, that the ladies stay warm and cozy while the *gentlemen* manage the kitchen duties.

When the scent of savory stew and baking cornbread make the ladies salivate in a most unladylike way, Lizzie can no longer contain her curiosity. She asks Bam to name each and every thing in the praise pouch. "Wha…, it's almost empty, there's practically nothing to say!" he protests petulant pretense. Lizzie grins. So do the girls. And Melt. He saw what came from the praise pouch to be cleaned, browned, and cut into a stew that simmer savor flavors to burst like star fire in the mouth. Melt knows that what remains hidden in the praise pouch will be tinned or crocked or canned and stowed in cupboards, but not yet. First a great healing that must come. Melt wants the healing more than anything but school that is closed, the teacher unpaid and gone home to start again somewhere else.

Sometime, later, when hope returns, Melt wants to travel with his father, to watch, to listen, to learn his trade skills, and receive his gifts for trade itself, which are very different talents indeed. Mostly, Melt wants to master the practical magic his father knows so well he doesn't know he knows it, nor even how to practice it.

*Pops can't make water though.* He thinks as he grins a hidden soft smile. *He's a natural water witch. Gets good paying work witching land to help farmers find the best place to drill* a *well into the Ogallala to make their homestead green and lush like it was once. Or never was except in land shark fliers. Liars.*

Melt never speaks these dry dirt discouraging words though. Still, a restless ruthless anger torments and tosses him when dusters come. Still come. To his beloved raped and ruined plowed planted prairie where oceans of buffalo once roamed and Cheyenne were the sage steward warrior Lords of the Plains.

*The past is done.* He reprimands himself sharply. *Only the future can be decided, chosen and lived. Only that.* Melt melts into a smile imagining watching the moon rise later tonight. He gives silent praise that it is already done. "So, Pops, the stew's stewing, the biscuits browning, Becky's fed and warm, now's time to show us what's in your praise pack. Put it by Mom and the girls, and we all get cozy nosy together."

Caught by surprise Bam yodels a chortle and joins his cozy clan on the bare board floor. He pokes about in his praise pack and murmurs: "Oh! Of *course* you want to come first…, and so you shall!" he exclaims, pulling out a fluffy sweater knit in eye bright brilliant hues, shades and tones, and drapes it close over Lizzie's shoulders and arms. He pulls the end of one sleeve to gently stroke her cheek.

She sighs a smile and stirs from the floor displacing her giggling grinning girls eyeing the bright warm prize.

"Put it on, Mama," the girls cry in harmony helping her pull the sweater over her head, across her shoulders and down her body embracing her in a warmth deeper and more complete than yarn alone can do no matter how masterfully knit and sewn.

For the first time she can remember, Lizzie feels embraced by a love as warm and light as the kiss of a butterfly wing on the morning sun. She hugs herself feeling Bam's wiry strong arms embrace her from behind. She curves back against him, snaking her knit warm arms around his neck holding him close and tender the way a mother does an anxious child. "Welcome home, Bam," she whispers near his ear. "I have missed the strong faith of you, I have missed you for that." She sighs sorrowing second thoughts and daunting doubts and yes, she thinks of barren bare cabinets, cupboards, bins and bowls.

Most soul shattering of all to Lizzy is the hope empty eyes and bare bone bodies of her children warded warm by lean muscle and thin clothes. *Bam is home, come with fire and light and love and him. He brought himself home, his homely hopeful helpful beloved self is home. I can go on. I can breathe again. I can hope. I can plan. Without hope no plan can stand against the fury of nature raped and scorned and savage mad. Lord, forgive us for what we have done to this land you love so well and true.*

"Amen that," Bam whispers fervent near her ear as though he overheard her thoughts.

"Da-a-a-a-d, what else you got in that praise bag a yours?" Abby inquires common curiosity.

"Well, let's see then," Bam agrees reaching in his praise pouch and pulling out a square tin can painted pretty and capped with a matching lid which he holds with one finger as he tips and turns the can evoking a hissing cascade from inside his impromptu percussion instrument. Melt steps close curious as his sisters who rise from the warmth of their mother to eye the handsome hissing humming box. Even Lizzie turns from her funk to see what Bam holds and spills in such enchanting melody. When all eye are on him and the singing box Bam prompts a guessing game.

"Who can guess what's in the box?" A long silence follows as conscious minds of them try to find a reply that makes perfect sense in all ways. Bam smiles like a magician about to pull a rabbit from a hat, and Lizzie sees a black silk top hat on his head. Until she blinks and it dissipates like momentary magic. "Well," Bam poses, "how else might one get data points about what's in the box?"

"What's data points?" asks Abbie, still too young to fear asking what she does not know.

Bam grins and straightens to see her eye to eye and let her see into him, "data points are information you get from the physical world." Bam pauses a time for thought outside the scope of the brain where the conscious mind lives and rules. "And when figuring out a puzzle – of any kind – you need all the data points you can get. But then you need something else."

"What?" Abbie asks innocent and open to possibilities, even the ones she can't yet know nor guess. And then she sees. "I know how." Abbie breaths attentively. "You have to let your mind go *inside* the box, so it can see and smell what we can only *hear* from outside."

"Can you do that?" Bam asks in heartfelt surprise.

"Yes." Her confidence is as clear and cool as an unruffled pond and Bam wonders what it is that she sees with inner eyes and hears with inner ears what is beyond the range of his own hearing.

It is always disconcerting and humbling to Bam when one of his children becomes his Sensi Master teacher. He waits. She grins at him holding the quiet tin. "I need to touch the box," she says doing it. Bam does not touch where her fingers and palm touch the box. He silently waits. Only that.

"It's popcorn!" Abbie whispers awe and she jumps tiny hops, "I can smell it, I can see it; I can *taste* it." She frowns out of her sock hop and adds curiously: "It's got *butter* on it." She puzzles; "And there's no butter in the can!" she clarifies her poised puzzlement.

Bam grins, "Sometimes facts just won't add up to anything worth a tinker's dam. Gotta collect 'em anyway. Ya' never know when or how they will matter, or when it'll matter that you know about 'em."

Abbie eyes him a solemn silent moment, sets an arm akimbo, and demands: "Where's the butter? I *know* there's butter, I smell it." Bam smiles as he paws in the pouch until he finds and formally presents the butter to his queerly queenly baby girl child.

*Awed again, Lord.* Bam reflects. *Nobody warned me that'd happen to a man when he's with his wee wise ones. Still, it is good to know they are wise in the ways of Spirit and can see problems coming before they start showing up on the physical plane.* "Okay!" Bam concedes cagy crafty careful as he hands her a hinge lidded clay pot with butter inside.

Abbie's smile glows with new confidence. "I *knew* there was butter," she whispers. "I knew it. And, now it's true." She turns her hands palm up and gives a 'what's a girl to do?' shrug of giddy gladness.

Aggie, the lamp lighter girl, is profoundly thoughtfully silent, then asks wistfully *"How* did you know?"

Abbie looks at her with a kind small smile and says: "Sometimes, sister, you just know a thing *so well* you don't even know that you know it. Pretend!" She commands queenly small. "*Pretend* you already *know* something that's in Papa's praise pouch. Pretend *so hard* that you can see it, you can smell it, and you can feel the weight of it like it was already in your hand. Then you will. *That's* the magic."

Aggie nods, closes her eyes, focuses her mind, and opens her heart. She is silent a long while gazing into the infinite and eternal space between what is and what is not. In that awareness she records no image or input from the outer world, and does not see the pouch nor anything inside the small lamp lit, fire warm room. She sees only from the mysterious inner eye with no lid and finds herself *inside* the praise pouch on the floor. She gasps, eyes large and wide, "we got eggs! We got eggs!" she sings dancing about like a stiff legged fawn caught in dawn delight. "We Got Eggs!" she laughs, then suddenly stops still, blinks three times, grins tentatively, as though taste testing the word for what she thinks she knows is inside the pouch. She giggles a whooping trill and shrills "We got *bacon!"* Suddenly unsure and insistent she demand begs, "Show me, Daddy…, I need to see it." Tears dance on her lower lids but do not fall.

"Proof is a good thing when you can get it." Bam smiles, "As you wish, my darling daughter." He pulls out a packet of butcher paper smelling of pork and smoke and seasoning and time. He hands it to Aggie with a papa proud grin. "Reckon you're big enough to make breakfast in the morning?"

Aggie blinks three times and says, "Not *alone!*" She drops beside her mother, and asks "will you help, Mom? Please. If you help me I *know* it can do it. But I *think* I can't do it alone. Not yet."

Lizzie chuckles and nuzzles Aggie's belly making her laugh in tickled delight. "Yes, I will help you. And we will need Abbie's help too, don't you think?"

Aggie nods full serious, "Yes, we do. I need Abbie's help, because I'm the big sister and I have to teach her things I already know.

"What do you want me to do tomorrow?" Abbie asks eagerly willing.

Abbie frowns patently puzzled, takes a full breath, and says: "I gotta know, Aggie, do you smell biscuits or bread in the praise pouch?" Aggie disappears inward awhile to see with inner eyes and heart as she breaths slow and easy, still frowning softly. "Yes," Aggie answers surely certain at last.

"*Which?*" Aggie probes with pointed brows and hungry eyes.

Abbie retires within, cocks her head as though balancing weights on a scale. "Both I think. Definitely biscuit makings though. It's biscuits for breakfast for sure!

"There's bacon and cornbread for dinner with the beans and ham in Papa's pouch. We'll need chopped onion too, so Papa, pull them out she orders." Arms akimbo Abbie faces him waiting confidently – if not patiently – for him to pull from the pouch the things she named.

And so he does. What's a good father to do? He hands them to her in the order she named them. Her smile grows and glows each time a thing she named is pulled from darkness and appears into light.

Aggie curls against Lizzie again, "When I grow up," she whispers solemnly, "I want to be like Abbie."

"Me too, Aggie," Lizzie agrees with a serene smile, "*me* too." In that eager empty peace, Lizzie holds the possibility as the truth of her and all her tomorrow days. In that confident flagrant flouting of reality, she sings "I want to be like you too, when I grow up!" She puffs truth words into Aggie's hair that now smells sweet of green grass and clover. *How I have missed that smell and I can't think* why.

"Tell me about my name, Mama."

Lizzie stirs alert to the eager focus of her child. She is eager to tell Abbie her naming story in a mythic way for only myth can sound the spirit, the weight, the nature, and the subtle substance of a naming name. *"Agatha,"* she whispers the name that came when she called the babe's spirit to tell its nature and truth. *"Agatha,"* the word breathes portents of the power of Agatha Christi's crime investigators, Hercule Poirot, and Miss Marple.

"The book I enjoyed most is titled: 'Murder on the Orient Express'," she speaks the words with sibilant dramatic flair, eyes and sparking, smile alive with enthusiasm and zest. Best of all, I *rode* with Inspector Poirot from London, through the Channel train tunnel to Calais, and then to Paris where we rested a day. Except Poirot never rests, he keeps on looking and seeing even what isn't there to be seen. It is a gift to write like this, to let the reader *experience* the excitement of boarding the Orient Express bound for Lausanne, Milan, Venice, Belgrade, Sofia, and then at last, to Istanbul. Oh, the sights I saw in those faraway places she took me to and let me smell and taste and touch and hear and see in my mind's eye plants and vistas and people and places and every wonder word I read while traveling with Poirot.

"I even smelled stale tobacco, his gin, the sooty oily smell of smoke puffing from the stack with each cylinder stroke of the diesel engine pulling that snaky train of linked cars.

"I saw the night sky cold and dark and sharp pointed with dazzling stars, and smelled the gin and the waxy odor of tacky lipstick residue at the rim.

"I went with Poirot to the kitchen to find what wasn't there, where it should be, perhaps a missing knife of the size and shape to have dealt the deepest cut. Perhaps a purloined pistol that fired the fatal shot. I followed him to the engine of the train to talk with the Engineer about "the 'hog', is what he called it.

"The minds and thought processes of Poirot and of Miss Marple; Agatha's uncommon female crime investigator whose lively mind and springing spirit that every reader came to know intimately well. I was *with Poirot*, beside inside him, behind his eyes.

"Writing like Agatha's is spellbinding, captivating, complex, and singingly beautiful and full throated. You, my quiet, observant Aggie, have that same full five sense aware attentive way with words. For this I named you Agatha. I call you *Aggie* to keep the sound of you near and dear to my heart." Aggie gentle inhales her new knowing of her old name, and gives thanks that the Agatha Christie book she feels in her hand reaches out and inclines itself to her.

Abbie, leaning and listening close and smiling, uprights herself, circles her mother to drops and curl beside Aggie facing Lizzie. "Hello, you," Lizzie coos cuddling Abbie's cheeks, "I'm glad you're back."

"Me too, Mom," she says simply as she snuggle butts into Aggie's warm embrace and leans into the curl of her mother's body. "Tell about *my* name now. Who's Abbie?" What's her big girl name?"

"Her 'big girl name'," Lizzie giggles, "how well and carefully chosen are your words, my Abbie. So very like Abigale, the wise mother of the Bible known as a woman of great understanding."

She gentles a soft strand of stray hair from Abbie's eyes, "A woman like you. A woman who can see into and through the void and beyond, all the way into the abiding abundance of life. You realize abundance, you know its appearance is a product of faith. And, you have a psychic sense of smell in the bargain!

"Remarkable gifts came alive in our life with your life, Abbie." Lizzie dotes with focused eyes and pointed purpose. "How confidently you use and apply your gifts to heal, even the invisible hurts that break and bend us. Like Abigale of the Bible, you think with your head, and you lead with your heart. You show the way to meet, learn, know, forgive, and to love ourselves as we are when we are beaten down, broken and bereft. You shine your light and reveal us, freer, stronger, more able and creative than we thought before."

"Will you read us about Abigale, from your Bible? I think Aggie would like it too, until our magic daddy finds and brings Aggie an Agatha Christie book to read."

"Yes. I will do that." Lizzie sees it already true in the eye of her heart and so she creates. "We'll nestle close so everyone can see the words as I read them and learn to read while listening." Bam smiles and snuggles close to Lizzie, setting an example as a father should, His clan cuddles all close and snuggly.

"Melt," Lizzie finds and strokes his cheek with a smile, "come close and comfy, and I will tell you how you got your name, and the true meaning of it. You too, Bam, you're a part of this story," she pats the floor and he sits warm at her side, free arm across Melt's shoulders.

"Your name was given you by your father when he saw and held you newborn gentle in his arms, his eyes full of wonder and love, filling your eyes with it too. A golden rain of love passed between you.

"'*Melt*,' your Pa whispered, looking at you with love lit eyes, you looking in his eyes, and both of you falling into love in the eyes of the other." She silently cherishes the memory, then adds strong and firm, Bam says: '*His name is Melt!*' He is silent just holding and looking at you in wonder and awe. Then tells the reason: *Because my boy…, my son…, melts my heart and makes my eyes all leaky with love.*

"*He shall be named and known as Melt. I am a father now. I am melted clean and purified of the man I was before. I am new reborn with my son, on the day of his birth.*" Lizzie's eyes smile love light gazing at Melt, waiting for him to melt and own the truth of his name and his naming. He does.

Melt toes the praise bag and finds it still heavy laden. Crossing his ankles Melt drops Indian style to the floor beside the pouch. "What else ya' got in the bag, Pops?" he asks looking at his father from the floor.

"Well," Bam replies, "there's a story behind that."

Melt hoots a giggle, and says: "There's *always* a story, Pops, behind everything you do. And, you are an *amazing* tall tale teller. Tell us your tale, Pops. And tell it tall and true, as we like it."

Bam lowers himself slowly to the floor keeping his head down to hide pain winces pinches under the bill of his cap. Melt sees and feels the reborn aches and breaks taken from XIT horses unwilling to be bear a saddle or rider. Not even by the man with standing as a first rate bronc buster and canny cattle driver.

Bam never admitted it to anyone, but Melt knows. He's been told, cautious and careful, by Mexicans and Indians and cowboys who love telling tall true tales. From men close to the earth Melt learned that Bam had a mysterious way with horses, and then, something changed. Sea change level. Bam got *better*. No one could say how, no one knew why, yet everyone knew, and all could see and clearly feel the change in the little man easy to not see. Bam was gracefully masterful now, and calm and confident in it.

First to feel, and then to think, Melt recognizes the change first, long before others sensed or saw, Melt knew. He felt the energy of his father in shift, at first subtle, seeping, slow, then expanding exponentially into a pure potent power and presence. Bam's new presence is oddly unsettling *and* comforting to the boy who long judged his father too weak, too pliable. *He gives too darn much attention to others and reserves not even the harshest stingiest shreds of compassion for himself.* Melt recalls.

This is a new man Bam. A man wholly comfortable in his skin and in his mind now governed and guided by his heart more than by mind. The new man Bam courted, cooed and cossetted trainee horses. He contracted to train the horse under the condition that he as Trainer, had six weeks alone with the horse before the owner was invited to come for owner training.

Melt grinned remembering the owner's blustery bullying that it was *his* horse and he'd *damned* well ride it when he wanted, contract be damned! The 'damned' contract said the owner is in breach, and would immediately pay the training fee in full should the owner come before the invitation at six weeks.

Bam also contracted for two months of exclusive use of the stables, training track and running field of a horseman rancher neighbor. The new man Bam was confident. He moved with fluid grace belying the effects of bone breaks badly healed and ligaments and muscles torn beyond reasonable repair.

Looking back, Melt admits he never knew clear and sure if the exclusive lease was for this horse, or if was Bam's habit and practice to contract for exclusive use of a stable when gentling and training a promising pony. The new slow and easy Bam eases his trainee horse to the weight of his hands first admiring and stroking the proud head and neck while softly whispering love sounds and praise words into the ear of the animal. He sweetly curries his honeyed generous words deep into the horse hair coat until love light shines from and through each strand even when no outer light touches it.

*Horse magic,* Melt thinks, and wonders if it's true.

> Shawn Gallaway – If I Could Find A Way

## Odd Jobs

Melt eagerly accompanies Bam on a job to break a horse to bit, saddle and rider weight for an owner who couldn't spend the time to do it himself, but could afford the fee of a top trainer who'd give him back a fast, agile show horse readily responsive to the horseman's weight and firm rein.

Being a feeler and watcher by nature, Melt felt it first, then watched to see all the ways Bam gentled the horse with praise prose and patted poetry. He feels the curried comfort of Bam's copious praise reports and his easy heartening way he raises the bridle and bit to the horse to let it sniff and snort the rig even as he slowly rubs raises the harness twined between splayed scratching fingers, to the crown of its head. Moving fluid and slow, Bam draws the bit up along the soft nose and curious lips and pauses, letting the horse explore the unknown and find peace with it. Only a heart in peace can receive the gift full.

Creeping near his father Melt watches the horse explore the bit, harness and fittings with its soft sensitive nose and lips, even as Bam eases the halter up and around the long ears of the beast. It snorts. Bam snorts. The horse eyes him, as a silent picture show passes between the two sets of eyes in which horse, and willing rider, race the wind for the clean corporeal fun of the run.

Bam lowers the halter, takes the bit ends between thumb and finger, and lifts the length to the horse's lips. It huffs. Bam's free hand finds the white star on its crown and settles there softly stroking, soothing, comforting, speaking slow low chanting charming words conveying tranquil wellbeing in the fleeting flickering mind picture images that race and run in the mind behind the star. The eyes of a man, and of a beast. Neither equal to the other. Neither as good alone. Both know it. Stalemate.

Still, to each, both, or neither, that matters not a whit. They both know it, yet both are afraid to *not* be separate, for neither knows how to *begin* to be so much bigger than their skin, nor to run wild free on the wind. True to his name Melt slips slow, easy in a silent crabwalk the ground to be near to see and hear but not be seen. Bam's not the only one who can hide in plain sight.

"Horse," Bam is saying, "You are good alone. I gotta admit that. You are *good*!

"I am good. And just like you, I'm good alone.

"Together – by choice, yours and mine – we can become something altogether amazing." He pauses dramatically, "You interested in talking?

*I'm better than good without your help*, the horse sniffs in a noble nose up snit.

Bam does not laugh. Aloud, at least. "Why with your great noble strength and spirit, combined with my estimable skill letting a horse find its own nobility, strength and power, we *can* win."

The horse bobs its head enthusiastically. "But we gotta run. Together. You and me. Me astride your back, like this blanket," Bam croons his cozy chant while stroking the pad smooth over the curve of its spine and down its sides, calming the beast's natural nervous jitters under the weight of the unknown.

"Now I'll just lay my arms across your back…," the horse shivers, still tense, "like I've done before, and I'll stroke you all the while." Showing as he tells, Bam croons soft and low: "Then, I'll put a bit of more weight on the pad so you get used to that…." the horse jerks aside, Bam follows, "And all the while I'll be stroking you and telling you what a fine horse you are. I'll whisper that you are one of the *handsomest* horses I ever laid eyes on." Horses, like all heart full beasts, respond to lavish praise and gentle coaxing stroking reassurance and affirmation. *Just like the human animal.* Bam thinks.

"And you run like the wind," Bam whisper whistle adds as an afterthought. The horse raises its head, arches its neck nobly, and then bob whinny snorts its active accord with the accurate acclaim into Bam's near ear provoking a lilting laugh. Then come Bam's soothing words: "The question is whether or not you willingly take the bite of the bit, and the weight of a saddle. For if not, you will never learn and know why God made horses love man, and made man love horses.

"And, you will never be the magnificent and singular horse you can be *because a horse needs a rider.* Just like a rider needs a horse." Without a word or thought Bam flows with inspiration heady in him. He gathers the loose reins firmly at the neck of the horse and without word or effort, grabs a hunk of mane, and jumps smoothly astride the wide-eyed dancing animal, twining legs and feet around its girth as far as they will go, and tucking them with firm resolve, into the crevasse between the forelegs and chest.

The horse jumps straight up in a stiff leg leap, eyes round wide wild, nostrils flaring in its furious indignant snit at being jumped and mounted without so much as an 'if you please.'

"But running like the wind don't mean one thing – to a horse – without a rider astride." Patting the arched neck appreciatively, Bam adds, "I'm astride you now, whether you like it or don't. So, *show me* how you run on the wind." He clicks his tongue, tugs the fistful of hair and bumps heels into the horse. Uncertain what to do in the novel situation, the horse does what is natural. It runs. Away.

Until it's running away. Not now. Not from the weight nor the smell of the man, nor from his guiding grip on its mane, nor does it flee from the firm fluid leg, knee, heel and toe muscles that wrap and relax muscles in its chest so they readily rhythmically transform shallow breaths into full long powerful pulls of pounding power that carries him and the him above on their jubilant run of pulsing pounding joy. The horse trumpets a whinny and yields to the joy held tight locked inside until it welcomed and invited rider weight, strength and wisdom on his back.

The proud beauteous beast willingly aligns itself with the command of the firm easy guiding grip on its mane and about its girth. When he does, his whole center of gravity shifts subtle soft sure and singular; and the man becomes the beast, and the beast becomes the man. *Perhaps a bridle would be better...*, the subtly stirred mute mount muses. *Perhaps it would help both of us if I learn to enjoy the warm weight and sinew strength of a two legged one on my back. Perhaps I could come to understand, and to even like, all the odd jingling ringing things he brings, to amuse me I believe. To teach perhaps. Maybe only to distract.... Ah-h-h, but there is the wind, and the sun, and the run....*

The horse finds length and strength, breath and heart, and forgets there is an*other* aboard. Forgets there is an*other* at all and knows only one on this together run.

Melt watches the run in the golden sun. He sees his father tuck his feet on the horses back and under his butt; then eases his knees atop the pumping shoulders, balancing there like an acrobat. He raises hips above his feet, balances, riding now like a jockey standing in high stirrups. *Good Lord!* Melt thinks, *I want to have thigh muscles strong enough to move like that..., when I grow up.* He grins, though no one sees.

A shrill piercing parade whistle stills every motion and thought to a startled stop, every sound to a sudden shattered sibilant silence. Bam spins to the source. He freezes, then flares blast furnace hot.

Melt is stunned hyper alert by the swift rage of his father's energy shift. He is jolted by the insight that every other father anger he has ever witnessed was less than a whisper, merely an intimation, of the scope, force, and the perilous power of the fury that possesses his father now. *Heart stopping anger...,* Melt thinks, awestruck, *and Pa ain't said a* word *yet.* He turns eyes to the shadowy intruder, parade whistle still bit in teeth. The man is perilously oblivious to the energy shift that overtook the man he hired to train his most promising horse. Across the horse pen and front yard Melt hears the man's thoughts as if carried by the wind and whispered in his ear.

A man has a god given right to see his horse when he wants, and no seedy cowpoke trainer-come-lately will change that. Not even with a signed contract will he take that God given right from me. His lips curl. "I got a gun. He pats his holster pointedly, "To back me up and protect my rights."

"You are in breach of our contract by coming here, Chester." A new voice calls.

"Under our contract Mr. White has a minimum of six weeks alone with this horse. Him and the horse. Without you. It's in the contract. You agreed to it, you signed it. You agreed that you will come here only when you receive Mr. White's invitation to come. Under the contract you agreed that on violation of that right, you're obligated to immediately pay Mr. White in full.

"Bam touches the brim of his hat, gives a bob, hard-eyes never leaving Chester's face. "I'll be over this evening to collect my fee."

"Like hell you will!" the ornery owner snaps staring down his nose at the small man who now isn't small.

"Yes...," the calm voice intrudes, "yes he will." The quiet courtly older man stares down the intruder. "I will ride with Bam and the boy to town this evening and we'll alert Sheriff Ben to your trespass on my property in violation of my restraining order against you."

He eyes the intruder calmly, "I will tell Ben and Counselor what I heard of your bullying intimidation of Mr. White while breaching the terms of your contract with him. What an ill-mannered man you are! Did no one ever tell you a man will catch more flies with honey than with vinegar? I knew from your guns and bluster that you'd not take that homily at face value nor consider intrinsic functional truth of it."

The mind of the intruder is busy parsing how his confident assertion of rights soured the sweet milk of an all-around good business deal for everyone, including the cowboy he now hates for his calm claim of right to collect his fee now. He cannot meet the eyes of his neighbor with a restraining order and a calm will to *not* allow either his contract with Bam, or the penalty for breach to be avoided under duress of threats and an impressive array of worldly weapons.

"Let's talk vinegar, *Chester*," The owner reasons, "Your puffed up bullying of this man," he points to Bam who's not small at all, "it is vinegar. Nobody wants it around. Including mosquitos. Little good can come of it. You know that. From *experience* you know that.

"Yet you are so bull block-headed dim-bulb dull that you fancy that *this* time, something good will come from your belligerent baiting bullying violation of contract signed, and that magically, you won't have to pay, or to obey.

"Delusional is the word for that. So deluded you violate your contract with Mr. White who has a minimum of six weeks alone with the horse, when Mr. White sends you an invitation. Did Mr. White invite you? If so, show me the invitation and we're done here..., except for you leaving peaceably.

"I'll take your silence for a 'no'. And there's the training you're paying for, Chester. From what I saw, you implanted a *fierce* distrust of man into that fine animal of yours. No trainer worth his salt would abide what I witnessed today." Comfy on the shaded porch, the man puffs his pipe awake and continues.

"Vinegar, Chester. You hoped I'd not get back to vinegar didn't you? You are in breach of your contract with Mr. White to train your horse for you. Under that contract, Mr. White has the right to collect his training fee, *in full* upon your contract breach by coming here before his six weeks of horse training is complete, and you get a written invitation. Contrary to your bluster, Chester, it is Mr. White's *right* to declare you in breach for being here today, and it is your contract *duty* to pay his the training fees in full, on demand. Is there any part of that you did not understand?" Chester does not reply nor raise his head.

"Vinegar, *Chester*! You are on *my* property without invitation. You are in violation of *my* restraining order against you." His eyes are dispassionately firm and fiery. "By your trespass on *my* property today with shouted threats and drawn guns. That is *unacceptable* to me."

He stares unflinching hard at the sullen horseman. "Nothing to say then? You should know I'll be riding to town this evening with Mr. White and Melt to talk with Sheriff Ben and with Counselor about these legal issues and how best and most quickly to resolve them.

"In the next day or so, Sheriff Ben will ride out to your place to tell you where and when you'll pay Mr. White his training fee." With mindful molten motion, the land owner pumps a chamber into his rifle, raises the butt to his shoulder, and sights along the barrel until he sees into Chester's eye. "You gotta know, Chester, that after I talk with those gentlemen, I can no longer kill you *'in self-defense.'* He grins amiable and annoyed at the humbled horse owner. "It is best for you to be off my spread and beyond range of my Winchester as fast as your horse can get you *gone.*" The chastened man turns his mount to spur and whip the horse until he disappears into distancing clouds of dust.

| Shawn Gallaway – Let It Loose |
|---|

### Forgiving Trespass

The land owner calmly un-chambers the shell from his rifle, pockets the shell, and notches the weapon into an elbow. He pulls a pipe and puffs it awake, inhales, and meditates awhile on the uncommon occurrences of this unusual day. He watches the lowering sun with a surrendering smile. *Guide me firm and strong to what is mine to do this day. Lead me each step of the way, my Good God, for without you I will surely go astray of your will, and of your grace.*

He adds with a grin, *"Honestly God, I do wish you could let me kill that man!"* Exhaling now, long and slow, he adds: *Forgive me for that.*

Forgiving trespass, the land owner knows, is closer to a Godly act than a manly one. He puffs an exhale as though hawking sour acid thought and tang. He snorts, clears his nose, then growling long and low, hacks phlegm into the garden by the porch, spitting the foul flavor of un-forgiveness from his mouth. He inhales now slow and long and becomes present in the Now again, full aware of the scents and flavors of the season and of the afternoon still full with hours to complete and fulfill. *And I, with hours to go before I sleep.* Smiling from his wee walk in the woods with Robert Frost, the land owner turns his thoughts to what remains for the hours of this waning day. He smiles, knowing and claiming, that it is all good.

He turns back now to his stable and yards. Bam looks frightfully like a fourth of July firecracker that didn't get to pop. He smiles warm eyed healing and moves on to Melt who willingly awaits his eye and smile. The land owner gives it to Melt's heart melting smile and a quick step to the stable door, where he clicks and coos the suddenly shy horse out from the dark and into the light.

"Bam!" The land owner cries, then waits in silence for the raised head and met eyes. Smiling inward at how keen we be to give tit for tat and slight for slap; and how great the gap between us and that, and me and them, and we and one. *Words..., the Good Lord was right. He shouldn't have given us words.*

*Perhaps to amend for that too precious gift given too soon, God gave us twin gifts of reason and feeling. There's a price to be paid for that outwardly bigger boon though. We spend the days of our lives in and through words. Most of us aren't even aware of it. Most are blind afraid we will misuse the great power invested in us by God as co-creators with him. It takes a bold and courageous heart to inhale that much unstinting love, and it needs a mind fully entrained with the soul to make the enlightened and open-hearted choices of a wise co-creator working one with the One.*

More coldly stern now, the land owner barks: "Bam! Snap out of it. Now! The man has left! How *long* will you stand there shooting eye bullets at the sand of a man whose dust is gone? That is *far* too much separation from Source anxiety anger for a man like you to contain, Bam White.

"Puff it out of you now!" Bam is statue still. "Or, I will come over there and gut punch it from you." He eyes stiff scarecrow Bam, and shouts an order "Inhale, Bam White!"

As he steps focused from the porch toward Bam, he sees the blur of Melt flying at his father from the stable where the perplexed pony stands still a bit wild wide eyed. Melt rounds on his statue still father and punches him, quick and sharp, in the diaphragm. Bam's body behaves as a body normally does when its gut punched. He exhales explosively. The body need for air demands a swift inhale. Bam obeys.

His brain gets a swift shot of blood oxygen with that gulping gasp of air. Bam winces out of his mental stupid stupor to blink shock and awe into the fierce fire eyes of his son. "I didn't know you could hit that hard, son," he wheezes, straightens, and silky strokes his stunned abs.

"I didn't hurt you did I?" Melt melts, touching his father's shoulder and arm with cautious concern. "Did I hurt you?" he whispers face to face, eye to eye. Bam shakes his head a fast no.

"I'm okay." He breaths deeply rubbing his gut, and eyeing his son somberly, "Don't ever hit me again."

"Don't ever go stupid crazy *pissed* like that again!" Melt snaps and does not soften nor melt at the edge.

"Who taught you to say foul words like that?" Bam demands.

"You!" Melt retorts, eyes sharp and cold. "You keep on behaving like that baby brat of a horse owner, then we ain't even *begun* talking ugly words, Pa!"

Bam frowns "You don't say 'ain't'! I never heard you say the word 'ain't' before in your life."

Melt's eyes hold hard and harry, "Never before today did I see you behaving like a spoiled manipulative brat, no better than that brash beast horse owner." Bam is mute. "Even *more* stupid! *Silent* stupid!"

"Stop!" Bam wheezes raising a hand. "I – I got it – son. I lost myself in anger and I became the man I most dislike." He bows his head sorrowful "I'm sorry…, that you had to see your pa behaving…," he can't stop the grin and the glee giggle that erupts as he snaps: "like a brat."

Melt giggles gleeful glad and assures: "It is *good*, for an observant son, to see his Pa behaving like a man he does not respect." He eyes his father canny, "So tell me, Pa, how are you planning to work with the bigheaded beast during *his* two week training period?"

Bam grins and cap slaps Melt's belt. "By then, son, *you'll* be ready to train the owner. Trust me on this."

---

Shawn Gallaway – White Eagle Soars

---

### Waiting for the Moon

Melt returns from his recent reverie to the warm huddle of this family nested around the mother and Bam's praise pack. He smiles fresh appreciation of his father, and of his family. *Home is anywhere you feel fully loved.* He thinks, *Home is where the heart is,* the correction pleases him. *I have a whole Divine portfolio of homes! I aim to have more. Though I need only one physical place to keep my stuff till I live in a universe of heavenly homes. Ah God is good! God is great! Praise God forever!"*

Lizzie turns to look at Bam, curling an arm cozy around his neck and shoulders, and smile invites. "Tell us about that praise pack of yours and how you came to have all the things that are inside." She narrows her eyes at him, "when nobody has *anything* green or fresh or fleshy, and when the last time was the last we had meat? Not ground meat, meat you could *chew*, meat with bones to gnaw marrow from when the flesh is gone? *Who* has greens and growing things in this dust blasted land? Who has *water* to make greens grow and carrots and potatoes fresh and firm enough to snap when they're cut into?" She grins away caution, casts a twinkle at Abbie, and adds airily: "I can smell them, Bam White. I can feel them, and I can taste them, and my mouth waters!" She says touching fingers to wonder round lips.

"Well," Bam squirms into his tale "I was about to tell you that." Raising a cautioning hand he adds, "And you won't believe it. Any more than I did." He smiles, grabs into his pack to pull out an assortment of fresh plump vegetables. "Smell," he directs his small clan. "Each and every one." Come on," he waives a hand to all, "there's enough for everyone to have a smell of each. To taste and to remember the smell of each veggie when it's fresh, and then cooked to its whole healthy goodness."

"Um-m-m this smells good," Aggie coos over soft leaf stems with dainty flowers at the top. "I want some of this under my pillow tonight."

"It's Basil," Lizzie answers, sift stroking a stem then smelling her fingers. Her family follows suit.

"What is this?" Abbie asks holding a deep soft green spiked bristled stem to her nose and inhaling fully.

"Rosemary," Lizzie replies, curling a palm around the brush of the herb and scrubbing it gently into her palms smiling as the fragrance scents the room. Abbie, and then Aggie follow suit. The guys soon follow.

"I want some Rosemary under my pillow too!" Aggie adds. She smells her fingers and reconsiders, "Or, maybe I'll just rub Rosemary all over my hands and sleep with them by my face."

"Always the pragmatist," Lizzie grins nuzzling noses with Aggie.

"I like that idea," the clan in one voice agrees. Lizzie shrugs only a tad contrite, "We *should* use the herbs while they're fresh anyway." She hears her own words, and smiles wise willful, and Bam falls in love all over again. "So, back to the source of this mysterious manna from the desert of our land," Lizzie prompts lazy easy. Bam smiles shrewdly recollecting all the whys she is his chosen one.

"The mysterious manna," Bam begins thoughtfully. "Mysterious is an apt word for it, yet there is no mystery at all. All except one, and that one I can't believe my own self. Even though I know it is true."

"You know, but you don't *believe*? How does that work?" Melt puzzles aloud and all nod agreement.

"You are my doubting Thomas, son." Rubbing the back of his neck he admits, "And I don't know if I can get used to that. A son isn't *supposed* to be smarter than his Pa."

Melt pops an arched brow, peers at is father long and deep, arches the other and observes, "Seems to me you should be giving a thousand thanks to God for breaking *your rule* that never *was* God's rule, who forever makes all things new, even musty old rules that don't actually work!" He round eyes his father and says, "Maybe it's time old Bam White made room for some *new* possibilities and fewer *old* man-made rules." He flat-lines his brows and mouth and round eyes his dad. "Else you teeter dangerous near *being* the ass of a horse owner who tied your scarecrow tongue this afternoon."

"Melt!" Lizzie snaps upright slapping his hand. "You have no right to speak to your father disrespectfully. I raised you better than that! And such a smart mouth you got on you, son! Where'd *that* come from?" Her frown is fierce fiery, and Melt melts into a bow of contrition. Lizzie chuckles, her eyes laugh into Melt's rising ones and he knows with a melting slump that the only viable choice left him is to laugh with her. So he does, with a small smile, dull eyes, and a tight-lipped 'ha, ha, ha' wheezing out.

Abbie giggles tickling a finger under his chin. He jerks his head away, beyond her short reach. She giggles gleefully hopping up to straddle his curled legs and tickling his ribs with one hand, under his chin with the other. "Stop it!" He growl shouts sourly.

"*Where never is heard, a discouraging word, and the skies are not cloudy all day*," sings Aggie, knee walking to torment tease Melt tickling his armpits and ribs to melt him into a better mood in his head. Or, he could go to his room and be alone until he's fit to be with others. She'd be okay with that too.

Lizzie sits upright and spins to full face her son. She takes his chin in her hand, raising his eyes to hers. They stay lid down, closed. She smiles and blows air kisses into his lashes, knowingly tangling them, and making him blink open his eyes at least half the time. She can work with that. *Melt is still young, still without enough life clues to know, or even guess, how to deal with impotent rage. Wonder where* that *came from*? She taps his chest where his heart shelters and asks, "What happened today?"

Melt melts away far apart from what he will not say. She clamps his jaw between fingers and thumb until his eyes and jaw pop open in astonishment and agony. "A-O-w! Stop!"

Lizzie smiles, "that's better. Nothing can change until you talk about it. What happened? Tell me."

"In front of everyone?" he asks casting wide eyed dart glances to his father and back to his mother.

She smiles. *Damn her!* Her laughing eyes join her lips in easy acceptance. She pats his knee, "you will never be a mother, Melt. You will never truly know nor fully understand the depths, and the heights, to which a mother will go to save her child. Even when it's to save him from his own folly."

"*Folly?*" Melt hoar ices, "*Nobody* uses that word anymore!"

Lizzie's brows arch dance over soft light laughing eyes, "I do." The arch warmly bids amused opposition. "Ergo, your rule of *nobody* is proven false on its face. I love homonyms, don't you?" She coos casually.

"On its *face*?" One eye challenges, ignoring her word *homonyms* and the veiled mystery of its meaning.

"Yes! The words 'everybody' and 'nobody', means there are no outliers. There can*not* be even one person who is outside the scope of those two words, 'everybody' and 'nobody'. Make sense?"

Melt chews on it a bit, nods, and says, "Yeah, in a snake eating its tail sort of way it does make sense. And, it means I can't be mad at the horse owner for being such an ass. I can't be miffed at dad for letting that bag of hot air turn him into a beached bass panting for air from water and not from the sky."

"So-o-o," Lizzie poses, "in what ways was the horse owner a commendable man?"

"Whoa! You start with the hard nut first, lady, that's hardly fair."

"What's fair got to do with it? Any of it?" She watches while he takes this in and adds, "For any of *us*?"

Melt grins and eyes his dad, "Pa, you gotta help me here you have more of Abbie's empathy than I do."

Bam giggles, "well that won't help us much either. But, together we can do it, don't you think?"

Melt shrugs, "like we got a choice?"

"Good point. Okay, here's mine: the man has a good keen eye for fine horse flesh. Your turn."

"I don't know him as well as you do." Melt gripes guarded.

"Danged near! And 99.9 percent of what I do know I don't like. Maybe we need Amos to help us."

"Think like Amos then. He's an amazing man, Pa, I'd like to be like him some day."

Bam breathes a chuckle, "We share that aspiration, son. So, what might Amos admire about the man? Maybe his passion? Do you think?"

"Passion?" Melt waivers wondering.

"Yeah, he's a wide swatch of fierce hot energy pouring through him. What's good about that?"

"He makes things happen. Fast and even furious sometimes, or so I hear. It's remarkable what a quiet lad can hear when pretending not to listen or even to care," he confesses with an unrepentant grin.

"Eavesdropper, eh?" Bam grins.

Melt matches him, "you can name it that, or you can just call it listening, mostly because adults don't want to hear what a kid has to say."

"Mom does," Abbie contends. "She hears everything we say, even when we think she's not listening."

"True that," Melt allows with a wry grin, and turns back to his dad. "So, do we admire him because he makes things happen? Even if he doesn't think it through first?"

"Even then," Bam agrees. "Well, that's two. What else you got?"

"He's passionate."

"Yeah, and dumb as a post."

"And as stuff shirted as a scarecrow." Lizzie snorts solemnly.

"That's a *good* thing?"

"Well, you can see him coming from a block away."

"And smell him a mile before that."

"That's not helpful," Bam snorts.

Melt giggles, Lizzie and the girls join. "It's an early warning system if you keep your nose to the wind so you don't meet him. *Especially* across the barrel of a gun. The man hasn't the sense God gave a snake."

"Then we could be grateful that he shows us how to admire snakes too."

"I like their skins, they are pretty and very soft and silky," Aggie says.

Lizzie turns on Aggie, "you petted a snake?" she whispers and doesn't want to hear what she already knows. "Never mind. Don't answer. And I agree, they do have soft silky skin."

"You touched a snake?" Bam asks owl eyed.

"Yes. I'd just killed it in the woodshed. I picked it up, took it outside and slung it as far as I could thinking a coyote might find a meal morsel in it."

"You feed coyotes?" It's not a question, but it begs a reply. Bam doesn't expect the stern eyed look.

"What would you have had me do with a headless snake instead?" Lizzie's asks eyes steady on his.

Bam breathes full and slow gaining time for a thought, perhaps a wise one. "That, Lizzie. Exactly that. I got another reason I'm grateful to Caleb, because except him I might not know what a self-sufficient, fearless, and disturbingly creative woman my wife is."

Lizzie begins a laugh that rings the room luring and lulling each of them into radiant rosy delight. When the energy of her people and place is joy, peace and calm, Lizzie says: "Tell me a tale of fresh vegetables that you'll pull from your praise pouch like a magician taking a rabbit from a hat. Say where you found them, who grew them, who gave them to you, and, tell me everything you know about the rain that watered them, Bam, for all the wells are dust dry; and I do so want to believe in miracles again, at least for a little while." Their eyes lock wide angle open and both forget time and its passing and simply are. There. Present. In the moment. Not expecting a thing and open to whatever comes. It's a peaceful easy feeling. The kids nestle close to be in their rose glow.

Sounding sleepy, Abbie simplifies, "Tell us especially the magic parts, Daddy. There *must* be magic parts to make a dry dusty day fetch fresh food for five of us for a week of days."

Bam smiles, "You are wise, my Abigale. I didn't see the magic before your eyes let me. Until then, I thought it was a surprise blessing come out of the goodness of God and his good people who live here.

Well, that in itself is a miracle, but it is every day magic. The story I will tell you is *real* magic. The only magic there is the magic of miracles – when what *can*not *possibly* happen – happens anyway."

Abbie's eyes brighten and sleepiness disappears. Melt, the only one to see and hear the improbable tale his Pa will tell, settles close to hear and watch and guide the weave of any story strands his father drops or omits. He grins seated at the right hand of his father, knowing the master tell teller won't miss a trick, will not negligently drop a warp strand or woof, but only pin them aside when its color, heft and weight aren't right for the pattern the tale takes weaving from his teller mouth and master muse of mind.

"Well," Bam begins as he tucks a calf and thigh under Lizzie for her head to rest comfortable on and see him well, for Bam knows Lizzie's love of tales well told. For her, he will tell his best told tale, and enchant his children in the boot. "Well, where to begin?"

"The veggies," Abbie prompts with a wide grin that Bam returns full round and deep into her eyes.

"Yes, my darling daughter, as you wish." Bam chortles, chest open, spine arched back, then settles quiet upright. "That's the major minor miracle tale I still can't believe in my logic mind. But I do see with my eyes, smell with my nose, taste with teeth and tongue, hear crunch and snap, and feel fat water full in my hand." He pulls a handful of vegetables from the praise pouch and hands them around. "For this tale is so hard to believe, I want each of you to hold, see, and smell, as I tell my doubtful tall tale."

He hears a soft nibbling like a squirrel worrying the shell off a nut. His eyes follow the sound to Aggie who is taking wee small chips from a carrot. Aggie looks up into the silence and sees all eyes on her. She ducks her head lips kissing the carrot tip but not nibbling. "He didn't say we *couldn't* taste or hear. More like he just left *out* those two senses, and I *like them*!"

The circle is silent a moment, and then Melt snicker snorts silly, snaps a sweet pea with his teeth and crunches with a satisfied smile. Bam backhands his knee, "I like peas," Melt defends with an unabashed shrug. "Hand me a tater, I plum *like* gnawing on raw potato."

Bam hands him one grudging, "Okay, but don't go spitting tater tads at us when you get over excited hearing me tell my improbable tale."

Melt's chin bobs quick up and down, eyes round. "I am most likely to spit chips then." He admits.

"You was there, son. You heard and saw, you gotta help keep me grounded under the angle wings."

Melt melts and presses a palm to Bam's spine between the shoulder blades behind the heart. "I got your back, Dad. I'll keep you under angel wings so the tale won't be too big for your telling."

To the weight of his dad's hesitance, Melt adds, "If you come to a place where you *cannot* tell even *one more* impossible thing, I'll tell the telling, so you can listen and say 'no way!' with Mom and the girls."

Now Bam laughs heartily, considers being a listener and not a teller, and remembers that every listening he ever did made him a better teller. His heart softens full and sure as he imagines hearing a first told tale narrated by his first and only son. He glows. He feels it. He sees it if he's not really trying but only allowing. He nods, "I'd like that, son. I'd like that a lot. Why don't you start then? Are you ready?" Melt's heart melting smile is his reply. Father and son butt walk, Bam back, Melt forward. He feels Bam's hand on his spine and hears the unspoken words '*I got your back*'.

"This will *sound* like a tall tale, just like it did to Pa and me." He pauses for a smile and meets eyes around the circle. His brows bob, "'It cannot have happened, you will think. "It is impossible', you will say, and I agree, that sure is sound and reasonable. We did too, Pa and me, even as these fresh sweet vegetables filled our palms and fingers to overfull. Was it magic? A miracle?"

"Was it magic?" Aggie asks eager.

"A *miracle*! It was a miracle, wasn't it, Melt?" Abbie demands impatient to know.

"What if it was *both*?" Melt consciously and conspicuously complicates the debate and in the process, magnifies the tacit tension between trust and proof. *What is a miracle anyway? Each breath, every heartbeat, every morning sun, every star strung night, even waiting for the moon to rise is wonder for the open heart to see, feel and experience. Every* heartbeat *is worthy of praise. How do I tell that tale?*

"Water," Lizzie speeds past Melt's question. "I want to know about the water that fed and held the roots into soil dark and rich enough to pop the smell of them right through the pores and put a healthy shine on the skin. Even on the skin of Melt's plump brown spud." All eyes are on Lizzie now. "Tell us that first, Melt, tell about the water." She prompts with deep thirsty eyes.

"Water is the hard part to believe." Melt grins. He bites a sugar snap pea for grounding and inspiration. "There is no proof for what I'm about to say except what's in your hands." Bam bobs a silent *amen*.

Aggie nibbles crunchy carrot chips drinking the sweet water of them pressed between her teeth. For a reason she does not know, but is sure she will if she needs to, she savors the flavor of raisins and doesn't wonder why. Easy entranced by mystery and its curious clues, she is full peaceful for Melt's water tale to unwind in its time, slow or quick, by its own rhythm, at its own pace. *I'll listen for clues,* she thinks, *just like Agatha would do. Soon enough, I'll collect enough clues I'll begin to know what to do with them. I'll watch how they relate, and how they weave themselves together clear as a puzzle full laid.*

"Where'd the water come from, Melt?" Lizzie demands suddenly impatient with the pace of the tale.

He looks her clear and steady in the eyes for three eye blinks, then replies, "angel tears."

"*Angel tears.*" Now Lizzie sits up squaw legged facing her son, eyes and mouth round.

"Don't you taste them in the food?" Melt clasps Lizzie's hand and bites her sugar snap. "They're sweeter than they'd be with even daily water from a well." His eyes pin her, "You *know* there is no other water because all the wells are low or dry and not recharging like before we plowed under the fruited plains and *really royally* pissed off Mother Nature."

Bam backhands Melt's shoulder, "*Don't* say those words around your mother, let alone your sisters! I taught you better than that."

"Yeah. And you taught me how to tell tales. Sometimes spicy words add the right tang to a tale."

"Melt," Aggie takes his hand, patting it softly and looking into his eyes, "just go back to telling your tale about the angel tears. That's all that's important right now. Ignore everything else."

Melt's brows arch over round eyes, "You're talking about *my* mother here, little sister. You should know that I am *not* planning on ignoring her, so put it out of your mind." Aggie's face falls. Melt leans close with a grin and peeps up into her eyes, and all is forgotten forgiven.

Abbie pats Aggie's hand with a pudgy palm and says "Don't worry sister, Melt's going to tell about the angel tears next. We just have to zip it until he does." She pulls thumb and forefinger over her lips, and adds, "For now, our only job is listening. We do that all the time, and we're already really good at it."

"Our first source is Hester." Melt begins, "There's something about that woman that makes me *believe* what she says even when I know that it can*not* be true in 'real' life. Plus, I saw it with my own eyes. What she says *is* true. Here's what Hester told Pa and me about these juicy fruits of her garden, which continues, by the way, to be as green and lush as Eden's glen."

Lizzie smiles soft into the swift silence that follows Melt's unexpected revelation and says, "Attribution accepted, Melt. Back to the angel tears, dear." The sisters snuggle into Lizzie's sides and in the circle of her arms where she holds them close and free in the warm embrace of mother love. The kerosene lantern flickers fleeting light visions of impossible things that may nonetheless be totally true.

Melt grins appreciating Lizzie's tale telling guidance and the ease it introduced into the task of telling the tale faithful and entertainingly well. "And then, I will tell of the angel's tears as the girl said, saw and knew it to have happened."

"The girl?" the sisters harmonize in one keenly engaged voice.

Melt bows with an inward melting smile of conscious gratitude for acting on his intention to integrate tale telling guidance from hearers. Their engaged exchanges enhances the tale telling making the whole of it more integral, full faceted and true than a teller alone can do. Raising his head dead slow Melt sets his eyes on hers and asks: "'the girl you ask, b*efore* 'angel tears'? What don't I understand about this?"

"She's a *girl*!" Abbie replies, "*That's* what you don't get!"

Melt's brows elevate cautious slow, his head bobs mechanical maniacal fast. "I get it now." He assures mock scared, "I get it," He grins fast and off-sides, peering into her eyes with barefaced bewitched enchanted love. Abbie melts. He sees that. Feels it too. He leans down to rub noses with her and grins, "perhaps I will tell her a prairie princess whose tribe is hungry and weak without food to eat and...."

"*Yes*!" Abbie interrupts, echoed almost instantly by Aggie now on her knees keen to hear the girl's story told as a prairie princess tale.

Lizzie raises her head, rests her chin on her palm, smiles, and says, "I vote with your sisters, Melt. You cannot reveal Elder Wisdom through your own telling of the *girl's* tale." The emphasis is soft supple strong. "*You* must tell her tale from a little girl's heart, as she told it to you.

"As for the girl, she is too young to be saddled with the weight of the way and the rhyme less reason of Elder Wisdom. She has neither the experience nor the right to speak it." She masks a smile with a hand, but eyes give her away. "Let her *be* a girl, Melt. She cannot tell the tale. She was only a crucial catalyst."

"Catalyst?" Melt repeats curious.

"A catalyst is a reagent, a thing that activates, facilitates and spurs reaction. Does that make sense?"

"Yes, it does, and it's exactly the right and perfect word to use when telling the girl's tale, for she was indeed the necessary catalyst and only that. She is a bit of a chemical compound too though!"

"What do you mean by that?"

"Ever hear her explode?"

"Can't say that I have." Lizzie replies uneasy as she watches dots connect to dots she'd not seen before. Lizzie peeps into Bam's mind to see a gap toothed drawing there. *Interesting,* she thinks.

"The girl doesn't do it much. Even her mom says so. But when she does, there's nothing false, and not one doubt still standing when the rattling shattering sundering explosion quiets her fears."

"Oh my! And she doesn't..., *do* anything?"

"Define 'do'." Melt arches his spine and relaxes against Bam's chest soft dropping his head on his shoulder. He can feel his father's mental distraction absorbing his weight and warmth while puzzling how *no* action can possibly produce *right* action. It's a do-loop for sure. *Doing* has nothing to do with it.

Being at peace in joy is the very energy that changes things. That, and being grateful for all of it, even the prickly parts. That's the power of the girl come to think of it. She has no power at all, and that's the greatest power of all. Melt waits comfortably until all eyes are on him again.

He speaks the words heard in the silence of his mind and heart. He watches transformations flow through them like a flight of shooting stars lancing through the places where smallness and separation hide and abide. and propelling them into healing, clearing and lighting their suppressed small lies made for supposed security's sake. Edging God Out.

Knowing what comes next and feeling the focus fixed now, Bam strums his guitar picking notes, tones, and sounds fit to engage the hearts and ears of humans and angels when Melt tells of angels come near Earth to see, to hear, and to weep. Melt melts into the sentient presence of ethereal entities of angelic faith and the presence of angel power in the company of his small clan.

| Shawn Gallaway – A Call To Joy |
|---|

When the time has come, Melt says: "First, the *highly improbable* things that Hester told me and Pa, and *then* the girl's telling of the tale. She told only me," he grins, "and, she said I could repeat her telling only *if* I told it *very* well." Everyone laughs imagining the feisty fair child putting *that* condition on her consent to the telling. As one they focus eager eyes and excited ears on Melt.

*Can it get any better for a tale teller?* He wonders idly and begins. "When Pa and I finished helping Lady RO clean out her cupboards and her canning cellar, *again*, she said we should stop in to see Hester, for there was a thing Hester needed help with. So now you know where the canned goods came from, including the pickled beets Pa just pulled from his bag of tricks known as a praise pouch." Bam gets a round of applause for his magic of turning time and effort into food and into sweaters and shoes.

"Well, Pa and I stopped to see Hester, and to my surprise, the work she wanted was help *thinning* her garden! Well, we didn't leave the kitchen for a *long* time after that. Hester's is a hard tale to tell because everyone knows before she even speaks that it *cannot* be true." He lets the puzzle rest with them as they bite and flavor the fruit of that Eden green garden that currently blooms and fruits in their minds.

"Angel tears." Abbie assures shrewdly, getting ahead of the tale – or back to it again. And, for a story teller like Melt, elevating the tension of the tale and engaging listeners to participate in the final twist of the 'tail' of the tale into a resolution that is however *impossible*. He smiles. He's *lovin'* it.

"Hester told Pa and me that she was in the kitchen doing 'kitchen stuff' as she put it, when she heard something sub audible shrill and piercing that bit into the marrow of her bones. It was agony, her word, so intensely overpowering she feared she might die, yet knew she wouldn't. It was not her time. But something else equally compelling as death when it walks in, inhabits her body mind brain, and owns it more wholly than she herself ever did. Her body trembles and she knows not why. She can't stop quaking, she can't control it. It possesses her. She is terrified she's having a seizure and no one but the girl at home to help."

"Was it evil?" Aggie asks warily suspicious.

Melt squares his shoulders, lowers his brows, looks into her eyes, and asks, "Can you *imagine* an evil…, even The *Great Evil*, *ever* winning possession of Hester's mind, and *if* it did, finding *any* comfort staying there?" The girls giggle at a tormenting demon in a personal hell hiding from Light in a circular cell.

"It was not evil. It was a sound she heard piercing pure and true in her inner ear, but not at all in her outer ears. Hester covered *both* ears," Melt demonstrates, "and nothing changed in the volume nor in the anguish of the shrill singing sound.

"The girl felt a grating rending sundering thunder like 'heaven ripping a tear through the fabric of time and space to open a new door'. A door *very* near to this place where she and her family live.

"She knew without doubt that something new and powerful would pass through the time space portal that was being rent open. She felt the portal open inside her mind and body, and she knew without doubt that the portal opened *outside* of her too. And both were true.

"What she felt, she said, was the composite force of repeated subtle soft shreds of infinite agony fiercely invoked and imposed on Earth Mother as a direct consequence of man's separation from Source anxiety. *She* talks this way…, I'm just telling.

"Yet that buckling pain riding Hester down carried welcome Hope safe and gentle in its uplifting arms, in *her* arms. That surprised Hester. It meant, she said, that the portal she now faced across space and time, was about *her*, in a very intimate way. And she wanted to know how, and why.

"Hester follows the soft sound of falling tears. *Many falling tears*, she thinks as she closes on sound she cannot hear with outer ears. Now comes the tinging tingling tune of tears dripping from high and higher onto something hard and cracked and earthy dry like clay left too long in the sun. The smell is earthy, close, careful, and intimate in an infinitely personal yet cosmically indifferent way. Her words, not mine," declaims Melt palms out and high. He grins loving his art and performance of it.

"Hester comes quiet and soft into her room where the strange weeping wailing energy is outside her window where the girl sits on the cedar chest in wide eyed weeping wonder watching something she cannot see. She moves soft and close, bending to look over her shoulder.

"She sees angels alighting in a ring around the garden. She watches as they morph into etheric gentle giants falling together in linked arms to dome the garden high. They weep fresh water tears into the parched garden. As she watches the plants transform from scarcely surviving to blatantly thriving.

Hester has blinked perhaps thrice, she says, since entering the room and watching pitiful plants miracle grow into thriving due to something rich whole and vital within the tears of the angels.

"That's where Hester's story ends and the girl's begins.

"But what *happened?*" demand the sisters in one voice at a tale ended too soon and sudden to satisfy.

"Well, next, I went to Hester's bedroom where the girl was still apparently in shock and awe; and there I sat and listened and heard what she said and what she saw happen. I wanted to learn why it *did* happen. And that's where the girl's tale of angel's tears begins.

"So, there they were, all spring and summer long, she and her mom and sibs all working hard and smart in planting and caring for their garden. Daily drawing water in pails from a weak well and tote the water to the plants they were growing. Their work was paying off, the week well still gave water."

Unexpectedly, Melt melts at hearing his retelling and the weight of what tells next. He is silent a moment slowly inhaling and exhaling. Just that. Then he opens and clears his throat, and continues.

"That afternoon another duster came pelting the plants with sand and rock hard soil." His eyes brim, his throat tightens, he drops his head, and is silent awhile, composing himself. Then thumb drying his eyes, he takes a deep breath and begins where he left off. "The duster shredded the leaves, pelleted them, tearing the well-tended plants up by the roots, and their roots from the soil.

"The girl got mad! She got *so* mad at that dirty duster that she yelled a blue Norther' straight at the ear of God for allowing yet *another* danged deranged duster rage cruel as a mad arch demon over the *very* land the Lord Himself made, and allowing it to shred to sunder the fruits of their labor! And *they*, the people who love and serve Him, would starve staring at empty cupboards, bins, pots and bowls!

"You are a *good* God of abundance and love!" She shouts soundless above the storm. "The demon duster that attacks us IS NOT YOURS! COMMAND IT TO STOP, NOW!

"WE are yours! Save *us*! Save our garden!" She does not ask the High God for this boon. She demands it. None of this did girl say out loud to the Lord. She raged silent, she yelled sub audible, she hissed words shaped and formed only in her mind where only He can hear.

"In her mind she imagines the simple smiling joy of sharing the fruits of the garden with others, and receiving from them from their own abundance, who own 'too much' that give and receive such simple pleasure from recognizing and paying *their* 'too much' forward. Or back. The girl said she could never really get *how* an Infinite God whose center is everywhere and whose circumference is nowhere, would grasp concepts like forward and back and up and down and black and white.

"Time and direction must be just so *squishy* for God." The girl tells me, "I have no idea if, or even how, we could *possibly* pay forward or back. Or why we'd even want to know," she shrugs, "I mean what *good* is there in that? With God what we call 'reality' is really just a big infinite, multi-dimensional circle whose center is everywhere and whose circumference is nowhere, forever forming and flowing."

"She talks like that?" Asks Aggie in open awe at the way and play of words that is the gift of the girl. "I want to *think* like that," she smiles, "so I can talk like her and speak music and poetry like she does."

Lizzie rubs Aggie's back and says with a soft smile, "You just did! I heard you. We all did. *Wish granted*!" She turns back to Melt, "Back to the duster, the tear in heaven, the angel's tears, and these veggies. By the way, I agree with the girl on that pay back/pay forward thing is a terrible waste of time and mind."

"Well, I reckon the good *Lord* God got an ear full because that's when the wailing angels descended to peel the sky apart, muscle through the breach, and make that *dreadful* inner ear shredding shattering sound Hester mentioned that made Earth rumble tumble and left her stumble clumsy on her feet."

Melt meets appreciative giggles, grins, and huzzas from his rapt fans, bobs a wee bow, and continues. "What happened is no mystery," Melt assures certainly. "Nor is it magic. It *may* be a miracle, but surely it is divine intervention. Whatever name we use, it was called by a girl too young to know the meaning of 'impertinence' who stood boldly before the throne of grace to *demand* God send angels NOW!

"I would laugh, but I can't inhale that deep. Awe takes less breath, and has no truck with laughter." Melt melts, allowing the power of awe thundering through him to pervade his tale and the incense sweet serene silence of wonder in the room. The soft bite kiss of crisp water laden veggies makes him smile.

He feels a yearning for more of the girl's do-it-now requisition of angels of God from God, and why her impertinence did *not* render her a crispy critter among the brown blown vegetables left by the duster.

He feels his own sweet passion for the angel tale grow and bloom in mind and heart and mouth, and knows it is time again to tell tale. He breathes deep recalling on the inhale all the words and feelings he heard and learned as the girl spun herself out, and on the exhale expelling the intimidating flow of impossibilities that spew like fiery flare flames of lava oozing and spewing from a livid lurid volcano.

Melt should speak, but he cannot. He is gut punched breathless mute and still stunned stammering stupid by the weight and measure of the girl's tale that is his alone to tell. He imagines his heart stops but he breathes again so apparently not.

"Melt," Bam bumps his elbow, "you might want to breathe now, son. Getting light headed for want of oxygen to the brain makes as much sense for a tale teller as getting dumb drunk does. Breathe!

"Do it again! Deep and slow now. Hold it, give the brain time to absorb the oxygen and for the heart to still and calm to a steady easy rhythm. That's it. Do it again, three times." Bam waits with his son in silence as he faces his dark demons of doubt without proof. Short on faith to believe what he cannot prove, Melt may not tell what he does not believe. Storyteller stalemate. No tiebreaker.

When Melt is calm and alert again, Bam smiles encouragement, sobers and says: "You are the only one, son, who heard the girl tell her telling. You're the only one can tell it true and whole." In the face of silence he adds: "I can't cover for you here, I didn't hear. *Can you* tell the girl's tale, Melt?"

His eyes are open, deep, calm, the fear in them melted to molten liquid passion. "I don't *believe* it, Pa!"

Bam grins, "A crisis of faith. I thought that'd be it. Did you ever tell a tall tale?" Melt nods. "Ever lie?" Melt eyes him flat and looks away mute. "I'll take that as a 'yes'. Did you tell a *good* lie then?"

Bam grabs Melt by the shoulders shaking him sternly shouting, "You-will-not-fade-into-fear! If you do, the devil *won* without a fight! Whites are not quitters; and you, my boy, *ain't* going to be a family first."

Melt's angry beset eyes meet Bam's stern ones without remorse or apology, but with a profound sense of doubtful distress. Bam grins toothily, wraps Melt in a bear hug and consciously and forcefully expels air from his lungs leaving him open mouthed gasping and fish eyed, a child again in his father's arms. *Pa's face ain't smiling though,* Melt frowns foggily, head bobbing.

"When you need oxygen again, nod your head" Bam coaches comfortingly.

*I gotta ask for air?* Melt thinks foggy fractious, surly sour, separate, securely denying even the possibility of miracles. *Not in this god-forsaken dust dashed desert we made by plowing too much, planting too much too soon too long, and forgetting everything we knew about making dry land farming rich and productive and ecologically sane. We became thick hick leeching life from the land we were born to live with and on. We no longer cherish the land where we work intent on making every day a good day.*

Melt's head tips softly slowly to Bam's cheek, eyes surrender closed. Bam smiles and gentles the circle of his arms as the rhythm of Melt's breath deepens and slows while his brain, still in a do-loop, repudiates and reprimands what was.

*No, God left this land we raped and despoiled and would not succor, support nor respect.* Melt breathes a deep rhythm, his oxygen fed muscles relax and ease. His neck opens and arches till his head rests soft against Bam's shoulder. *A rock. Like Peter. That's Pa, a warm strong rock. God though is more like President Roosevelt and the rain makers. They come, they see, they get money, and they go, never to be seen again.*

Bam hears this with growing unease, not all of it arising from knowing his son's deep asleep views. His face creases deep, brows bunched worried above eyes fixed firm on Lizzie's, "He thinks God left this land when we raped and despoiled it and would not give it succor, support, or respect."

Lizzie is taken a bit aback by the force of the words Melt chose. "You heard this in your mind?"

Bam shrugs tipping his cheek to Melt's crown, "He's so near to me," he explains rationally.

Lizzie cocks a brow, gives a grudging grin, then a see-through sweet smile, and notes, "It's not the first time I've known this about you, Bam. It is the first time you mentioned hearing thoughts though." She gives a playful grin, "I think being close had nothing to do with hearing his mind speak. You have the gift of knowing a man's heart, and being there with him. In minutes of meeting a man they go away feeling like they know you as an old friend, a bosom buddy, even a *womb mate!*

"That can be keenly disturbing to a mere mortal, my dear husband. Even a son. Perhaps it is good that you didn't hear his thoughts before the head touch." Lizzie stops mid thought. "You did." She touches her head. "You hear mine." She smiles, then laughs soundlessly, open eyed amazed.

"You hear my thoughts even when we're far apart. That's how you *always* and without fail bring home with you the very thing I need and am without. Today you brought staples and fresh vegetables, and you feed us from a tale that we, all of us, have powerful and abiding need to hear.

"Most of us, like Melt, are terrified *silly* at even the thought of believing in God, let alone having faith in Divine intervention and things that look *exactly* like a miracle but *cannot* be! And you, dear heart, are very likely the one who told him most about how we plowed up the Great American Plains in under a decade, turning it into a wind-blown desert of dirt." Bam bobs admission.

"Give him some slack, Bam. He' a boy, a boy avid and eager to become a man *just* like you." She chuckles, "even your passion for the land and living with it, not just on it." Bam smiles, eyes clear and bright now. "Maybe when Melt wakes up, you will ask him to let you tell the tale of the angel tears."

Bam hoots a hollow holler and says "Oh, like a true tale teller like Melt would let another teller tell *his* tale? Not likely! Besides, Melt is at the part about what the girl told that I didn't hear." His brows form firm flat over his eyes, "I can't tell it! The boy's got to be the teller. I get to be a listener."

"U-h-h-h-o," Melt moans as he raises his head, "like I'd *let you* tell my telling? Not happening, Pa," he says pushing off Bam's chest and straitens up, "I just needed a few wee winks to get restored." He pats his pa's chest, "Thanks for the shoulder to lean on. I'm restored. I'm good to tell the girl's tale, the way she told it to me." His family circle straightens and relaxes at full attention on Melt.

"After she told us her telling, Hester took my glass, nodded to her bedroom where the girl waited for me saying the girl would to talk only to me; and when I was done, I'd find her in the kitchen or maybe the garden. I hoped the garden, and if you want the truth, I got my wish.

He pauses shifting scenes and senses. "The girl sat on her knees on the cedar chest facing the window, her palms up and open as though blessing something beyond, outside. I came near to look over her shoulder into the garden that was more deeply green and in need of thinning than it was the day before.

"'*Impossible*', I thought. I leaned near the open window and inhaled the heavenly rich smell of fresh green, red, amber and gold and saw the glow of life shine through them. I was stunned stupid silent. I was. The girl felt it and turned to me with hope filled eyes and a silent prayer for humility.

"'*Humility*', I thought, curious at the choice of word. I sat beside her on her mother's hope chest and put a palm on her back behind her heart. I felt her sag almost, at some release and comfort she found in the touch. She slow pulls her lungs full, holds easy and long, then exhales through her throat and mouth.

"She does this three times, and each time she becomes stronger and more confident. I feel her heart beat slow and strengthen, her energy expand and glow through and beyond her skin like a whole body aura. I felt my hand inside her halo glow grow warm and begin to vibrate at the jubilant rate of joy.

"I must have laughed for she looked me in the eyes and was amazed to see and hear her Ode to Joy sung silent through me too. We bonded." Melt assures surely. This is what she *confessed* to me with a hand on my arm, praying forgiveness and expiation.

"I was angry. I was hellfire spitting furious with God for not making the duster stop killing everything we worked steady and smart to have, and to eat, and to share. We had nothing. Nothing but hope, and that garden, and without it, a long lean winter ahead.

"The girl said it like a reporter might: 'I was so mad I *cried*, and that's not worth the salt spilt doing it. So then I felt sappy silly, and that *always* makes me mad! At *me*. That's a snake eating its tail!'

"And so, I *yelled at* God. In my mind and heart only, where he alone can hear." She smiles below lowered lashes and makes her first confession. "My self in my mind wailed raging wild in a fierce voice fit to shake the walls of Jericho and sunder them down." She adds in a slow small voice, "And God heard and the sky tore a shrieking shred open to let the weeping angels fall through."

With wonder in her voice she adds: "The angels fell to earth like hawks dive down in a wide narrowing spiral, each landing to form a circle around the garden, hands linked, wings scooping to slow them as they soft touch down to the powder dirt of earth in a garden *decidedly* outside of Eden's bounds."

"She talks like that?" Aggie interrupts.

Melt smiles a nod, "she does."

"Good, 'cause I'm going to write like that when I grow up."

"Start now," Melt advises soberly sure.

"I can't write yet, nor even read!" she defends.

"But you *can* talk and speak." Melt counters, "and that mean you can *tell* tales." He leans confidentially close to add, "It's called the 'oral tradition' in tale telling circles. And then, when you learn to read and to write, you can *write* your best told tales quick and easy because you know them so well. When it's time to write them down, I'd start there," he advises, "writing the ones you best love telling first."

Aggie gives Melt a heart full smile. He melts. Practically predictable. "Where was I when you interrupted me?" he demands with a stern sour face and dancing eyes.

"The angels tore a hole in heaven and fell to earth to circle the not-Eden garden. That's where."

"Ah, yes, that's it. Well then, the girl tells me that the angels stretched and grew to the size of giants and then, as one, they fell together into the arms of the others forming a dome of angel and wing over the enclosed space. Then the angels wept, all the while their wings and hair were whipping into dreads in the bitter hot winds. They wove and wound the dreads into air baffles as they expanded and stretched to tower over the leafless trees in the grove nearby.

"The girl heard a sub audible tone song of longing and loss that mourned, moaned wept and wailed threaded through with sweet surging sweeping lyrical harmonies that so *ardently* loved and moved the wind that it settled into a quiet and peaceful attentive breath 'of fresh breeze that cools as it hisses through the screen to kiss away the sweat of my brow'. The girl's words," Melt explains with an outturned upraised palm.

"Methinks he protests too much," Lizzie quips to Bam provoking a smirk and a smile shared among the clan. Especially by Melt, who *likes* being seen through by an engaged group of attentive listeners. For what is measure of a teller if not the ears that hear and the hearts and minds that hold the tale?

"I'm a *teller*!" Melt hisses through smiling lips. "I must tell my tale tall and true." Then he adds with an eye wide dramatic flair. "It is yours *alone,* to deny or to believe as you will, and why.

"So then, the girl says, those mile high angels fell together catching shoulders as they went, collapsing their bodies heads arms and wings into a baffled dome over the garden. And then the angels wept." Melt has puddle melted and can't tell on just now, overcome *again* by the tale telling girl and the decidedly dubious deeds she described and the wayward timely timelessness of them.

Taking a full breath, Melt holds aloft a floridly red bell pepper like an Impromptu torch of Truth and gives a salute to proof. Melt is poised again in the center of him where the best stories always begin.

In the core of him where there still stalks the fierce and Faithless one with greedy livid eyes trapped in a rage of denial doubt. *This beast will not be bested!* Melt knows. He meets his stalker and asks: *Grandfather Teller, is this fierce conflict within me* truly necessary *to me telling this tale?*

A cat tail whips, gold emerald eyes spark flare flame, strong lithe body torques whiptails through a taut Mobius strip, eyes flaring fierce heart searing mind jolting fury. Melt is impaled and held by those eyes. He slow breathes three exhales and inhales, eyes never leaving the angry ones of the enchanting beast.

Suddenly Melt *knows,* in a silly senseless sort of way and with a certainty that both embraces and exceeds the reach of faith and doubt thereby transcending both. While opposition by opposites is a necessary and natural part of the flow of life, that does *not* mean man must be stymied and stopped when the dark side shows up in life. Melt could give a list of ways and whys he let the dark side stop and stay him on his pilgrims' path of life. He is not proud of that. Nor can he delete it from his memory.

He almost hears Grandfather Teller's amused breathy laugh and the wind whisper of his thought words carrying easy breezy release rhythm to entice, tease and ease the duals within into being and becoming a compatible fluid floating One energy, two equal, opposing and embracing flows.

"So," Melt's one word captures their eyes. He smiles. "Here's the hardest part of the telling for me. I could not find faith to *believe* what the girl told me next."

"What'd she say?" Aggie asks to be her own judge, even of Melt's doubt and blame his shame in it.

He meets and holds her eyes, silent solemn still while she takes her own measure and weight of him. Melt pulls a full breath and replies from behind shame lowered lids. "The girl said they planted, from seed, last month." He holds a dramatic pause, "Then she said the plants were only two or four inches high when the duster hit…, yesterday."

He holds the bell pepper torch aloft waiting, feeling ripples of shock break on the shores of their minds hissing sibilant across sand sucking soft away leaving sea and shore wholly changed, yet in subtle and unremarkable way, leaving sea and shore comfortably the same. Melt lowers head and inhales in the truth and scope of what he has not yet said. What he must yet say.

His family feels his retreat and without understanding it. They honor it anyway with gentle caring energy sharing. He smiles and raises his head, "Thanks, Abbie," he whispers. "I needed that."

"We know you did, Melt," she melts him with her wise smile and warm sparkly eyes. "Now, what the heck was *that about?*" she demands, fiery eyes flaring wide.

"What can you *possibly* have done that shames you so deep that you can't tell your family? We have to love you *any*way!" Into Melt's shocked face she grins a singing melting, "*That's* what unconditional love *means*!

"So, *what is it* that's so hard that you can't tell, say it to us, who must love you *anyway*? Get *over it*! *Tell the girl's tale*, not yours!" Her eyes brook no nonsense as she spins on a heel to plop where she was, draws up regally tall, and with tender firmness mandates:

"So, brother, first tell us *what beastly* thing you have done, when you did it, and how that dastardly deed fits into the *girl's* tale.... If it does.

"Then tell us how *your* despicable deed keeps *you* from telling *the girl's tale* full, true, and fair. That will be a switch-back tall tale telling unless I miss my guess – and I bet I don't."

Abbie grins, "And when you spin out the *whole* tail of your telling *of the girl's tale*," she grins lopsided sloppy indifferent, "*we – not you,* will decide if we forgive you for planning to skip important parts of the tale for the *simply silly* reason that *you* don't believe!

Now she is not at all unconditional. "That sounds like a self-rung death knell for a tale teller."

"Whew," Melt sits sharp erect, head back, eyes round. He has never before been dressed down so properly, so thoroughly, and in so few words. He lowers his eyes as her words echo in the privacy of his mind. "I think I have not been dressed down so well before today. Thank you Abbie. I needed that."

"I know you did," she agrees amiably while licking her stinging palm.

"You, Abbie," Melt presses on carefully, "from your great understanding, have thoroughly and completely destroyed my ego and its decrees about the kinds of telling I will and won't do. Without your potent protest," he touches his cheek tenderly, "I probably would have edited the girl's tale *solely* because *I would not* believe the things she told me, out of my own lack of faith in amazing grace.

"You're right, I do tell tales I know aren't true; and I do know better than to edit her story or to withhold her truth in my telling of it.

"Thank you, sister, for *demanding* I shape up so I can grow into being a true and truthful tale teller.

| Shawn Gallaway – The Artist |
|---|

"Okay then, the next part of the girl's tale is what scared me shitless. It makes no sense to me so I can't believe it happened. And yet, her telling is the only way that all the data point dots do connect and actually make any sense." He takes a deep breath and continues:

"What the girl showed me today is that the garden is growing bigger. There are new plants volunteering in the space *outside* the border of their garden.

"She took me outside and showed me where plants fill the circle where the angels wept angel tears.

He groans as though pressed down flat by a great weight, "She showed me plants that were *new*. Plants *they* didn't plant! Not from seed, nor from starter pots. She said they were volunteers from no apparent source. It is utterly illogical! And it is *real*!"

"Miracles *are* illogical to humans, Melt." Lizzie says, that is why they are *called* miracles. They defy man's powers of reason and logic." chews a pea absently and asks "When did you go athei…, no, *agnostic*?"

She growls belligerent as a mother bear defending her cubs, eyes slit to fiery stiletto prods as she roars: "An atheist has the integrity, *at least*, to take a position and make a stand for it even if it's unpopular. Sometimes even when just plain bald face *wrong* from the get go!

"Not so, an agnostic.

"An agnostic is one who willfully puts on blinders, twists in ear plugs and sourly sings 'La la la la la la, I can't *hear* you'. The antic agnostic ties on night black blinders and yells screech owl hollow loud: 'Ne ne ne ne ne ne, I can't *see* you'.

"And then, dares declares from a hoisted high place that what *he* hears and sees is the sole and only truth.

"The no-eyed man who cannot see, and the man without ears to hear, yell tell you that *they* are the one and only *right* source of truth.

"Bogus, Melt!" Lizzie snaps. "We taught you to *do* critical thinking. We taught you ways and methods to *not* let doubt and fear to turn you into the wooden headed puppet plaything of the brute pusher bully thug that lives inside you! A man like Caleb, Melt.

"Can *you* turn *yourself* into a mindless reprehensible drone? I am *very* disappointed to see and say that I believe you can. I'm looking at proof of it." She raps her word gavel on his baffled un-bowed head.

"Mama," Aggie shakes Lizzies arm firmly. When she turns, she asks, "When did we plant our garden?"

"Last month. Like every farm family did. Because the Farmer's Almanac said it was the best time to plant. So," Lizzie grins from behind a hand, her eyes spilling spewing sparkling laughter, as she says: "I personally believe we have a verifiable miracle here. And, *not one reason* we should name or claim it." She mime zips her lips, and everyone follows suit. Everyone except Melt, that is.

"So," Lizzie dares the ice hard un-melting Melt, "What's your holdout, Melt, what's going on with you?"

His eyes and one side of his mouth grin as he says: "I *promised* the girl I'd tell her tale." He lowers his head, "so she'd never have to. Not *ever* have tell that terrible telling to anyone after me."

He frowns, "I think she used 'never' and 'ever' more times than I did."

Bam giggles and claps Melt's shoulder, "It is the art and craft of the teller to tell tales tall and true. Hearers never know where the line between the two winds, loops and forks through the tale. Every time you walk with a tale it takes you down a different path, one you never followed before.

"Listeners know this. They'll only mention it though when you surprise 'em or tell 'em something they hadn't heard before. And, son, nobody but you even *knows* what the girl said. If she called it a miracle and you are telling her tale, then you *must* use her word." A small sentient silence follows.

Melt smiles and says, "You're right, Pa. If I am to tell the girl's tale, I have to use the words she used. I'm good now, Mom. I will keep my promises to the girl." He grins, "She *also* made me promise to come tomorrow and tell her how the telling went while Pa and her ma go 'pick a peck of peppers and stuff'. Her words. "Tonight is my trial telling of the girl's tale. I will tell it true, and tainted with titillating temptations to believe and to deny. Just the way she told me."

Lizzie soft strokes Melt's cheek, "there's my good boy," she says tumbling Melt back in time to each and every occasion she found to say proud words into his eyes and heart. He catches her hand in his and lets her see through to the true truth teller he intends to be and become.

First as good then better than his dad. Bam sees this. He smiles humble honored. "You make me proud son, and so very glad to see the man you will be and become when you get your whole grown up body. Enough dramatic tension, now. Back to your story."

"The girl was in the kitchen helping her ma when we got to Hester's this morning. She poured coffee for her and Pa, and the girl took my hand and led me outside. The hot red eye of the sun beat down with the power of an ungoverned blast furnace forcefully transferring its heat into us through shirts, shoes, and through the core of us. First my lungs and then my heart caught fire in me. I engaged with the thought that I would melt to a puddle where I stood just like the tar baby did.

He grins, "But unlike the tar baby I had an option. It was presented just then by the girl's easy loop around my already rosy wrist. She led me slow."

He huffs a sigh, "okay she *dragged me* slug footed to the garden gate. That wasn't there yesterday. Every step of the way, my inept beset EGO *jibbered* insanely petulant, pushy, that I DENY!

"Just *deny* anything happened and make it *not* real." Melt is silent through three slow breaths. "Even while my EGO was edgy at outright denial of data points my eyes collected and fed to my brain.

"My EGO mind and I are stunned stupid by the myriad *majorly impossible* things I see with my eyes.

"That very same EGO even now hounds me to accept and admit that what I can and do see, cannot be. In EGO's tale, well, there is nothing to tell." He releases The Great Denial and picks up the tale.

"Without reprieve or release, EGO likewise cautiously counsels and comforts that although it's nice to believe, it is *not* true that what I imagine and claim confidently will be attracted to me. EGO is like a fellow I know who's a self-lauded and self-appointed expert on everything I am and can and ever possibly become, and truth seer is not one of them. I may not be a truth teller either because all those jobs are already taken, thank you very much. *That* too is impossible, to me, personally.

"I may *not* think big, the EGO snarls slap attack and throws down like it's all that is true of 'Truth'." Teller waits for the image and experience to clear before he softly tells the EGO lie.

"I must *not* show or use my power.

"I must hold myself tight curled lest what I am be lost to me.

"I must stay small.

"I must not make ripples on the placidly submissive lake of life.

"I may only expect things small and common in life.

"I may expect that *none* of it will come generously.

"I may not say that a thing that *cannot be* there is, in fact, really there!

"I may not speak of what cannot be, and yet I see... with my own eyes.

"I must *deny!*"

Melt waits while he and they, both and one feel and find the ways they, and all, play dull and small and will not see, say, or be, anything that must not be. His inner teller knows that until the hearers own and allow what 'they' will not accept; they are powerless to end or change it, or their innate responses to it.

"That part of me that edges God out, my EGO, simply let go! That shift in awareness let my conscious mind, where the co-creator lives, capture and process *all* that it saw, while allowing time to adjust my inner eyes to see clear and well.

"It was a fierce forgotten familiar fear that made me deny out of hand – and mind – what I *knew* with all my senses was totally true.

"My inner battle was not about faith in God, nor in all the *not secret* things that God can and does do. Those things I know with firm faith, even the new and twisty ones.

"No, that battle was all over my paltry puny pugnacious petulance over *parsley!*" He slump sighs another countless remorse, this one not coarse or callow, but open broken hearted remorse. "So, I just let go.

"And on that instant I could see as though blinders were lifted, and in the lifting revealing me as a blinking lash-batting peckish pre-teen selfish naval-gazing ninny!

Bam bats his leg and in a harsh whisper says: "I taught you to talk better than that about yourself!"

Melt grins semi cocky proud and stage whispers: "I caught you up in the teller tale, didn't I? I blinded you to the arch and art of tale telling that tells both dark and light. Go on, Pa, you can admit it."

Bam quick changes into a listener scarcely aware of the teller. He hears only the next soft sweet sigh of a page turning in a teller tale now teeming alive in his ears and flitting firefly free in his mind. *Unfettered.*

The word slithers in Bam's mind hissing sibilant echoes through its twisting corridors and caverns. Blood hound like, he sniffs out scents on the word mingled and mixed in the slow eddies of Melt's quicksilver mind and melodic mouth. Bam smiles contentment. *It is good to be just a hearer with unfettered ears to hear and eyes to see..., oh my...! 'Unfettered'. I do like that word.*

---

Shawn Gallaway – Let's Play

Unfettered now, Melt returns in to walk with the girl into the garden, and into his veggie tale. "I paused as we neared the garden. I could go no closer to the shimmering *illusion* where the garden was.

"The girl stopped too, watching me with infinite attentive present compassion. I looked her in the eye knowing she'd unload on me for a faithless fickle fool I was. She did. But not once was she mean to me.

"Instead she channeled into me all the free flowing radical love and forgiveness that God gave her to flow through me. My head bows of its own weight against the weighty weightless weight of love. The Good Lord diverted all of His abundant surplus of profound love through the girl straight into me.

"I fell to my knees for I could *not* bear the ferocious force free form fall flow of His *unjustly* lavish grace. It felt like that. It felt like love gushing in liquid flow form.

"Justice has nothing to do with grace," the girl says soft gentle as though she heard my private thoughts. That brought me to my knees and pinned me to the dirt dry dust.

"Justice is powerless to initiate or to alter the flow of God as a river of abiding love." She adds, and I know that, and knew it before then. I simply did not *believe*. That is a very other proposition altogether.

"We can…" the girl frowns, "*refuse* to get in the river. We *can* choose to stay on the banks watching the river of life pass by. We can do that because we have the power to deny a thing and make it gone." She looks away far distant as if peering through the membrane of a cosmic web and into another dimension.

"Because we *have* the power to affirm a thing, to name and claim it, to give praise and gratitude that it is already done, and then, sure and certain to make it so."

A long troubled silence follows, then the girl adds frowning. "We also have the power to un-make a thing. And to destroying what is already made is easier, and sometimes more blameless, than weaving something new and other into whole cloth from threads spinning in the *mending* mind of God.

"The un-making power of your determined denial of what is," she turns her eyes away so I can't see in, and says, "the reason you will not enter the garden with me."

I am bereft. I am rejected, rebuffed, repudiated, and barred forever from entering Eden's glen. She waits there with me until I melt in the strafing stinging sun of truth.

"We do have to jump in that river though." The girl speaks soft as a whisper.

"We must do that to learn to trust and follow the flow of the river of life, and do it over and again until we feel faith in our *bones*. We inspire that faith flow as breath until faith is all we know, all we see, and all we are. In the same way that all a fish knows is a simply frank faith in fluid flowing water.

She eyes me now, testing, poking, probing, and silent all the while. "Faith acts on the conscious mind the way baking powder acts on biscuit ingredients. Faith activates the perceiving power of mind initiating a chain reaction that is *needed* to turn biscuit ingredients into something *else*, something *substantively* unlike it was before.

She nods to the garden, eyes not leaving mine, "Faith alone had the alchemy to turn Saul into Paul. I think that, like Paul, you are on your road to Damascus in a fanatic fury to throw down, destroy, punish and plague disciples…, the ones who chose to see a bigger truth than mere reality.

"So great is your anger in your own self-doubt that you feel utterly commanded to destroy the faith of others and all evidence of it, to *throw down* the altars and holy places of all the gods *you* name are false!

"Well, my young and ardent denier, in the Holy Book – all of them – there *is* no god before God. No god *but* God. From where *come* all these gods you name false if there be but one?"

"I cannot face her wide crystal clear diamond hard eyes; and I can't avoid them, it's like she's looking at me through the full spectrum all-seeing eye of Infinity. She paces me slow and appraising"

Her eyes narrow and focus on mine; "And I *know your* God!" She says staring down sharp and hard on me from the same short height.

"I know that dark disturbing detached dirge of a trying taxing taskmaster *reason*, whose warped words you hold keen in your mouth and webbed through your denying mind. He plaits you tight and tauter into the fiction that *his* words are pure gold and living water, and that the Word of God you cannot trust!

"Nor, dare you even *entertain* the *possibility* of miracle happening because your default factoid god of proofs will not allow a thing as visible as a living breathing growing thriving self-regenerating miracle!

"*Faith… boy!*" Her eyes are white sun hot as pierce searing as her words. I lower my eyes but the force of her penetrating passion sees and seeps through my lids deep into my brain, where it lays waste to my dallying dreams of brilliance and potent power over a 'false god,' a Golem god.

"Formed and fed in the womb of my brain and mind, patched together from all the hurt, anger and doubt I fiercely repressed and that haunts and hunts me still."

He sighs bowed low. "I could now faintly see foggily into God's newest Garden of Eden sparsely sheltered in a shallow bowl in a parched prairie ocean in motion. The girl felt it, she knew that I denied what my own eyes saw. She felt the weight and warp and wallop of my lack of faith.

"She said I could not enter into the garden for my doubt would shatter and sunder the miracle space the angels created, and spoil it sour and stingy and destroy the dynamic creative harmony the angels made. Then all of us would lose the gift of grace the angels had formed, and the fruits of it. The girl was fiercely cold in her rebuke. And it cut like a blade set deep and viciously twisted."

"You want us to feel *sorry* for you?" Abbie asks innocent but aghast.

I grin, I have to, she is so owl eyed wise and solemn and serious and stern. "No, no more than I'd give kindness to a golem gone on a rampage provoked by a merciless mortal.

"In its defense, the golem, lacks the power reason, knows not right from wrong, and acts reflexively obedient to the mind that gives it breath and a mission. The empathy of a golem won't heal what was broken in me. *I needed* to admit out loud, in my own voice, that *I am* the one, the only one, to induce my inner golem to rage and destroy the miracle Light

"*I saw! Yet, channeling Joan of Arc, I would* not *accept a miracle*! *My* callous faithlessness barred me from our Eden's glen! The girl Joan of Arc defended the faith, and the plant people, and the people in and near our lives who will thrive and survive on the plants grown on angel's tears."

Melt releases the pain of his self-inflicted wounds and melts into the fertile rich softness of the soil in Divine Mind. He sends tap and support roots sinking deep and spreading far to brace his faith, not in man, nor man's fearful designs, but in the incomprehensible inescapable omnipresent Presence, the shoreless washing healing stirring ocean of God's wondrous love. *A tree in an ocean, an ocean in a tree.*

Aggie, who's been a silent watcher awhile sits suddenly sharply upright, head tipped to a side listening to hear something beyond sound. She nods, frowns softly, pulls a nostril wide slow easy inhale, and then turns to Melt to demand, "Do you smell apples?"

"Apples?" Surprise puzzle pieces dissolve dismembered in Melt's face and eyes.

"Yes! You *said* the girl said there were new plants in the garden, didn't you? Ones they didn't plant?"

"Yes...," Melt agrees cautiously wondering where his solver sister will next go. Aggie demonstrates by long leg crawling to the praise pouch, poking in a hand and feeling around its bottom and sides. She frowns and wide nostril sniffs above the bag. She sits back, pale brows meshed in a puzzled arch.

Melt almost feels her brain carefully analyzing collected data points, sniffing like a blood hound on a trail for scents and clues she hasn't yet found. She comes up empty. They feel it.

Together they watch as she re-processes data points, hear her sniff small wide again, see the second frown, and, see her get second wind of will. Aggie smiles a small smile, raises a hand, frowns, then drops it, and raises the left, intuitive side hand.

As though drawn by an invisible strand Aggie's hand moves slow low and near, then plunges into the pouch and pauses. She breathes a full slow smile and in one trance dance like motion, surely lifts her hand from the pouch, turns it palm up to present an apple sparkling a red bright enticing invitation to bite, chew, savor, and enjoy.

Aggie rotates her wrist letting the fetching fragrant fruit catch the light and show itself plump proud and lusciously tempting in her palm.

There is silence. Awed silence. Silence so deep and pervasively present that when Bam moves, the soft whisper of his shirt shifting startles them to attend to him and watch as he takes the apple from Aggie, pulls out his pocket knife, and unfolds the blade. "I'll cut it for us," he explains wiping the knife blade on his pants until the juicy fruit is steady in his hand.

"Dang that smells good," Melt says, "give me a wedge."

Lillie brushes his hand away protectively dominant. "Wait!" It is an order delivered motherly polite and pointed. "It *was Agatha* who found the clues you dropped while telling the girl's tale. *Agatha* who put those clues together, and Agatha who made sense of them.

More significantly, it *was Agatha* who stayed strong, firm, and unquestioning in her faith in Source and the love He revealed when He sent his angels who came and who wept angel tears for our mindless methodical rape of our once fertile land.

"*Angels* do not chasten us. That is God's work. Their work is rebuking chasing challenging until *you*, of your own choice, turn 360 around and come *willing* and choice-fully into the healing arms of God. *Then* you could enter the garden as the girl does, and you cannot.

"*Aggie knew, without doubt...,*" Bam picks up without pause, "that if Source already creates new things to thrive in the angel tears in his mini Eden west of the Mississippi, then that same God could *certainly* make trees grow, leaf, bloom, flower, *and* fruit, in the hours between dark and dawn!

And," Bam's palm stops protest before sound, "*Agatha* will have the first cut of the apple." He leans close holding a wedge of apple against the knife for Aggie to take.

He says lover soft and sweet, "I made this cut bigger than the rest to honor your gift of sweet heart full connection with life and all that lives.

"But mostly, I made it bigger because you were *so beautifully brave*, certain and sure that there *was* an apple in that praise pouch that even though it was empty before, you were able to take yourself *beyond* doubt, *through* faith and *into* understanding power.

"It took my breath away watching you apply that powerful strong focused mind to keep faith *and know*, even in the presence of doubt. There *was* no apple there before. I looked. No apple." Abbie ducks her head and peeps between her lashes as her tongue savors the luscious liquid meat exposed by the knife.

"That *alone*," Bam continues, "would have crushed the firm faith of most, dashed the high hope of strong men. But not you.

"Somehow, my woman of great understanding, you *knew* that the God who made a rainbow of skin colors for man the day Adam and Eve were exiled from Eden's glen, could *indeed* make fruit trees root, sprout, set and flourish in what looks to man to be one single dust dirty day.

"You knew all along that God does not *get* time the way humans do. You accepted and abided with that, Abbie. That is faith firm as a rock undaunted by delay nor diminished by doubt. Powerful!"

In Bam's approving words Lizzie hears his near dear hopes for, and firm faith in, each of their children. She marvels at how easily he has melted Melt's doubt and anger by loving him through and beyond it, refusing adamantly to leave him alone in his dark night of doubt and fear.

Feeling Lizzie's attention Bam purrs a soft sensual satisfied sigh and coos "Did I ever tell you Lizzie dear, that you are my moon bird?"

"Moon bird?" Lizzie's brows dance a high arch. "No, you never told me that, Bam White." Her eyes tease tempting incitement; "I know this for certain because never before have I heard *anyone* say the words 'moon' and 'bird' together. Nor have I seen 'moon' and 'bird' side by side looking like they belong together.

"So, my dear husband, it is time for you to spell our boy teller awhile" she pulls Melt across the circle to sit beside her facing Bam, "and tell us your moon bird tale. Spin for us your best bewitching snare of moon bird tale telling tall and true and nets us deep and wide, Bam, for I need both tonight."

Lids low, Bam straightens and lengthens his spine hips and his Indian style crossed legs. He inhales slow, deep and rhythmic, setting and centering himself liquid relaxed and alert in his favorite tale telling pose.

He invites and welcomes Spirit of a bird who stays secret silent in the dark waiting to trill and tweet jubilant joy to the moon as it rises to light the star decked night sky. He smiles lost in the strong force of moon bird bliss flow through him and he cannot *fail* to tell the tale true tall and deep seeded with love.

"Moon bird…," he muses distractedly as though trying to recall a memory held deep rooted not long ago, yet gone missing without a trace at this particular pointless point in time.

*What is the point of a pointless point? No matter the time! It is good* Bam muses, *to sometimes forget the whole lot of it, every tit and tittle of a tale you ever knew. Yet this tale is new and there's little I know of it to have forgotten.* That momentary mindful mindlessness mental meandering clears a cluttered space in Bam. He enters the space to find it empty. Vacant. Void, and available for something *else*. Something *new*.

He has no clue.

But he has a trust. "Moon bird…," he begins, savoring the plump round humming of the words in his mouth, mellow between his teeth, sweet under his tongue.

*Sweet,* he thinks. *Of course, that's it! The tale is told sweet…, open…, and sincere.* He savors the moon bird telling before it even begins.

"A moon bird, my dearest Lillie," Bam begins to spin the moon bird tale, "is a bird that is as silent as a *breath* waiting for the moon to rise. When the moon rises and its light hits its eye, the moon bird sings.

"Wise ancient elders, and new ones too, say that the moon represents personal human intelligence, individual consciousness, the intellect and reasoning power of man. The moon receives light from the sun and reflects sun's light to Earth when Earth, and man, are in our daily dark time called night.

"Well, those same wise elders taught that the sun represents the realm of human conscious that has been *illuminated* by Spirit, the sun, the greater light that rules the day.

"Thus our good God gives us daily reminders of the bright light and the deep dark of His impartial, impenetrable, imperturbable abiding love for us. Each and every one of us.

"Lizzie," Bam takes her hand in his and strokes it smooth softly and meets her eyes with smile that warms and melts her to the core. "You are my moon bird, dear wife. When days are hard and horrible mean with empty apology and hungry eye, my spirit just buckles under the weight of icy doubt, serial separation, and abiding oppressive *other*-ness.

"I feel so alone, like an abandoned child on a cold dark night passing under windows of light seeping sweet smells from platters and plates piled high with food, and I feel so *damned* sorry for myself that even Becky doesn't want my company and brays and spits in my eyes." He pulls and puffs a fish eyed sigh at the trivial indignities navel gazing gathers into its deepening dark downward spiral.

He vows not to do it again. As he has done before. Bam slumps sounding so painful pitiful that everyone turns away to hide laughing eyes and hold the giggle that wants *so much* to come bubbling joyfully gleefully free.

And then it does.

First from Abbie who understands that laughter heals when it is shared, and that it *must* be shared simply because humans are hysterical, but not funny, and they can't see that when feeling sorry for themselves. *They are simply not funny then, or fun to be around either!* Abbie thinks snappishly.

Quietly, quickly, Aggie gigs Abbie to giggling gay again. "Stop! Stop." They yell at their father: "Enough already!" The girls share eye contact and unspoken words, grin as one, nod together, then index fingers at the ready, pounce on their Pa, tickling his ribs and armpits until he laughs himself breathless and can no longer bear his private powerless pity party.

Their theatrical work complete, they return to Lizzie, sit, and focus on Bam, attentive and expectant in anticipation of their father's tall true telling.

*Under the gun*, Bam smiles appreciatively. *Nothing like it to focus one's attention and sharpen one's wits.*

"I take it that I have said *enough* about my navel gazing pity parties. And, *apparently*" he suppresses a snorting snigger, "you don't *want* to hear nary one discouraging word about the mule, so all I got left to talk about is Lizzie." He takes her hand in his, and says: "my chosen mate, my beloved, my moon bird."

Her chicks click and peep as they tuck themselves into the feather warm nest of Lizzie's love to hear her moon bird mate true tell his towering tale of love in the moonlight.

"A moon bird, dear Lizzie, is a bird that sits silent as a breath," he breaths, a palm cupping an ear, "one eye on the sky," he touches an eye and up, "waiting for the moon to rise."

"The moon you see, represents personal human intelligence, the intellect, that has gathered, collected, and now reflects the light of Spirit, that realm of consciousness illumined by Spirit. The abiding present awareness of the Divine in man is represented by the sun, the greater light that rules the day.

Bam bows to the weights and woes of the world and whispers: "When I come home some days the burden of this world is too wicked and heavy for me to bear. I give all that to the sun and let the soul fire reveal my truth to me. Still, sometimes the dark weight of it tarries inside me and comes home with me.

"You are my moon bird, Lizzie, you help me sing all that away, and to praise raise the light of spirit again when the dark is deep and echo empty."

Bam's words are both admission and confession. He lifts his head high, neck turkey long, plucky playful supple, and as swift as his smile.

"I want you to know that I stopped at Smithy's to have a look at the Farmer's Almanac and I'm here to tell all of you that the moon rises at 10:15, which gives us time to pop some popcorn," he shakes the can like a castanet, "in butter, and take it outside and wait like expectant moon birds for the moon to rise."

Bam's idea, from beginning to end, is delighting and enchanting welcomed. It's an on-demand flavor savor of lifelong memories, even of the sometimes slicing slightly salty forms of love that keep man true on the straight and narrow way of the One.

---

Shawn Gallaway – The Center Of The Sun

# The Mark of the Master

Jacob pauses at the door to the common room hearing familiar voices. He inhales, holds for ten counts, and on the exhale, lets his inner and outer eyes adjust to the dark interior. He expands mindfulness into the store. Finding the familiar energies, he explores the energy of the man the woman called 'master'. He feels the power of the voice, its command of oratory forms a base line for the lyricism of his words. He hears an insecurity rare among orators. *Interesting*. Shedding his cap he inhales, and steps inside to hellos. He extends hand to the stranger: "I'm Jacob. You the driver of the Rolls outside?"

"I am the *owner* of that fine auto," the man affirms firmly. "*Before*, I was the driver," he pats a pocket, "now, I own that fine vehicle."

"And the woman?" Jacob tips his head toward the window where the cocoa woman silently sulks.

"I own the slave too." The man misses the edgy energy his assertion arouses. *Interesting,* Jacob nods to all, then to the visitor, and asks: "How *does* one man own another?"

Counselor rumbles amiable interference, "Jacob, you came at the right time. The man was about to tell those things, pull up a chair and sit." Turning to the visitor he invites: "Step to the center of the circle so you can see, be seen, and we all can hear you." He does, rises to his toes and spins, meeting the eye of each man. He tips a nod to Sheriff Ben – *the uniform*, Ben thinks – pauses before Jacob – *the skepticism*, Jacob fancies. He turns to Counselor with a bow mostly reserved for gentility.

"It's a pleasure to tell you folks how these things happened. The tales twine, so I'll tell 'em as one adding humor where I can." He supple snakes his tongue up his throat carrying his words to all who hear. I own the Rolls Royce because the master never learned to drive. He admired being delivered to appointments and festivities. When our time together ended, he gave me the auto for he could not drive nor maintain it. The carpetbaggers stole him blind. He had to send me on my way to the great American west."

Counselor murmurs, "Never before have I heard such an *extraordinarily* generous act. Surely the master knew the Rolls Royce Company would assign and send a new chauffer at his request?"

The raconteur sighs dramatically, "Yes, he did know that, and he and gave me the car anyway. The master is a saint, or will be when he dies, may that day be many years from today."

"How does your master get to his appointments and parties now?" Sheriff Ben asks, lids slit narrow.

"The folks back home love that man and will do anything for him. They'll get him where he needs to go."

Ben frowns at the double edge sharpness in the last five words and "*Why* would even a good and godly a plantation owner rely on the kindness of neighbors to get his business done when he could use his *own* car and his *own* chauffeur? Why would he allow a departing chauffeur to even use his car for a long trip to…, where'd you say you're headed?"

"I didn't. I don't rightly have a destination, for I never had I a chance to see this great land. I'm starting a new life, I will drive into the sunset 'til I find a place with good folks, settle awhile, and head off to see what's around the next bend in the road."

"Sounds like a drifter to me, Ben growls to the circle, "except for the car."

"What's a drifter?" The visitor asks anxious.

"Someone passing through with no contribution to make along the way." Ben smiles friendly, agreeable, insincere "Here on the plains, drifters are about as popular as carpetbaggers down South."

The visitor eyes Ben evenly and he says "The old master assured me he could take proper care of his business *without* the auto before he gave the title to me."

"A remarkably generous act," Counselor reiterates redundantly imposing calm courtesy.

"Tell us how you come to own the woman outside," Jacob prompts.

"The master gave her to me so I'd have someone to take care of my needs." The orator is oddly unaware of the edgy energy aroused by his last words.

"Does taking care of your needs explain the mark the woman bears?" Jacob growls tap-tapping his neck with two fingertips, "The one she calls *my master's mark?*"

"Dang, Jacob," Ben growls, "here I was thinking the woman was his *sex slave.*" Turning back to the guest he asks pleasantly. "Tell us how you come to own the woman, and about your master's mark on her."

"I got her ownership paper" the man defends, slapping his breast pocket, "the master gave her to me legal and true. She's mine, and that Rolls is mine. I can do what I please. It's *no never mind* to anyone."

Jacob growls, "*Why* would a plantation owner give a healthy young slave to a driver leaving his service and taking his only vehicle?"

"The master is a good man, I told you already that."

"You did, and we heard what you said," Counselor cautions casually. "Jacob is asking *why* even a good man would give a healthy slave to a chauffeur leaving his service." Silence extends into prickly points prodded by the steady tick tock of a wall clock. Turning to Jacob Counselor says "while our guest is auditing his *accounting*, bring the woman in so we can hear her story and have a look at that mark." Jacob comes with a woman the color of sweet cocoa and eyes round with doubt, dread and dismay.

Counselor is the comforter "Thank you for joining us, young lady. I know this is not easy for you." Her eyes dart to the orator and back to Counselor robed in black with a curled white wig. She blinks. Jacob lays a hand on her shoulder giving courage for the challenge ahead. "Come, sit by me, child." Counselor invites moving his chair to one side as Doc moves his to the other. "Somebody, bring a chair for the lady." The orator snorts, but holds his tongue for Jacob edges close on a deviant path to his chair.

"The man on your left is a medical doctor," Counselor informs the woman as she sits between them.

"Jacob tells us you wear the mark of your master." Doc invites. The girl nods but doesn't meet his eyes. "Will you let us look at that mark?" Unaccustomed to respect in matters of her body, the woman dashes a glance to Jacob who nods assurance. Holding his eyes, she releases the shawl letting it fall to show the mark. An inhale silences the room yet none but Counselor hear the words between Doc and the woman. She nods, eyes wide with dread as if she'd just agreed to jump without a rope from a towering bluff and into the infinite heart of creation. And so she has.

"This man," Counselor motions to the dandy, "is he your master?" The woman nods but speaks no word of ownership by another.

"Did he put this mark on you?" Doc asks with professional detachment, her head bobs. "When did he put the mark on you?"

"Five, six weeks ago." She sighs, "I forget things like the time, the date, when I ate last, and when I last had a good night's sleep."

Doc nods and murmurs "Does he – *urr* – penetrate you in – *urr* –other places?" The woman locks eyes on his, cocks a brow as one might to a village idiot, then turns away. "I'll take that for a yes," Doc says behind a hand hiding a grin at his silent comeuppance. He assures the woman, "we can heal that mark." She studies him, eyes slit thin with wariness born of neglect, misuse, abuse, and of primal terrors come savagely alive. *Too pale,* she thinks. *His hope of redemption is like tea when the ice is melted in the glass.* Yet thirst blooms in her and she dares not ask, know, or trust, so she simply lets go and receives hope like a cool breeze over a blistering field.

"We'll need the Daughters for the healing work, Jacob would you…?"

A chair clatters into a fall calling eyes to Sheriff Ben snatching a chair from a fast fall. Casting Jacob a grin he says "I'll go, Jacob." Stepping to his side he claps a hand to a shoulder, locks eyes, and bares a toothy grin "You know, Jacob, *he, he, he,* the ladies always come when I call." Jacob tips his head back in a chortle his eyes never leaving Ben's. "Stay *by the door* while I'm gone."

Jacob nods. "Good speed, Ben, the healing art of the Mother/Daughters is soon needed."

"What is your name young lady?" Counselor asks the woman by his side.

The woman is silent, "I – I never had a name given me." The orator's head snaps up but he doesn't look.

"Indeed?" Counselor eyes her solicitously. "Tell me how it is that you were never given a name."

"My mama was a slave. She was taken by a guest she wouldn't name. She was shamed and blamed by her people for not saying his name. She wouldn't tell about the night I was conceived. She didn't accept me. Maybe for her, or me, but *always* because of the shaming. Other slaves say mama was bright, happy and loving before me, but not *to* me. She saw to it I was clean, fed, and clothed, but she had no joy left." Words fail where memory holds no key nor cause nor reason but only nameless loss.

Counselor silently studies the evidence and turns to the orator. "What is your name then, young man?"

Caught off guard, the orator stammers "I – I. The master called me James," he says tucking his head. "James, I have an appointment, bring the auto, James, get the door, James, my guests have arrived; serve the drinks on the veranda, James.'" The orator stammers to a stop.

"And your given name?"

"I… was never given a name that I know of."

"Two strangers in our town in one day and neither with a given name. What do you make of that, Doc?"

Doc brackets his chin with thumb and fingers, broods awhile and says, "Beats anything I ever heard."

"Well, young man," Counselor cautions, "the transfer of property, chattel or slave, needs the name of the transferee to be binding, and since you have no name, I don't see how it is legally possible that you own the auto, or the woman. Let me have a look at those papers for you." He extends a palm until the papers are there, studies them, then raising eyes to the orator, he rubs his chins. "The line for the transferee on both of these documents is blank."

"Can I see?" The man gazes intently at the papers, colors, and shoves them back to Counselor meeting his eyes, "would you show me what you're telling me, please, Sir?"

"This is the auto title," he says extending the title. "See this word? That word is 'Owner', the name of the master is entered here. This word," he says, is "Transferee," it means the name of the person the item is transferred to. The line beside it is blank. That means the title to the Rolls is not in your name, the master still own the auto."

He shuffles the papers, points to the second: "The Transferee line on the slave document is blank. The Owner is her master of this woman who bears your mark."

"He *don't own* me?" Shrieks the woman punching air at all the invisible indignities that rise like ghosts to dance with her in intimations of the intimate injustices imposed on her. She paces, a cat in a cage in a rage, gulping gouts of air in a battle to find herself amidst the revelations of the day carpetbaggers came to take away the life she lived. In the safe hole again, she hears the cool reception of the intruders, their snapped sharp words, the shoving, the scuffling, the grunts, cries and protests, feels the impotent futile fury of the master's effort to protect his home, family, *and his people. How do these men not know the wrong they do to this family? How can they not stop, not go away after admitting it was all just a jolly jest, purely a punkish prank played for foul fickle fleeting fun.* The man in the safe hole with her claps a hand over her mouth, pressing a blade to her throat as the mistress cries out. She hears the stumble, her fall to the floor, she sees the woman as helpless as she trapped in silent safety. An agony of hours later the house falls silent. She is safe. As safe as one is subject to the whims of an eager sinner in the hands of an angry god. Memory ghosts dissolve to dust and she allows the dots of today connect with the old ones of the raid. She balls her fists, inhales sharply and howls "can I *kill* him?"

### Michael's Mark

The orator shrinks from the fury of the woman and turns to the faces in the circle, seeking sympathy, shelter, support, security. Finding none, he shifts. Jacob sees energy at the edge of the man's body flicker signaling a shift. He surrenders his will to the indwelling infinite Source of life. In no-thought Jacob feels a familiar dissolution of self and inhabitation by a greater power that instinctively meets and matches the transformation. As watcher, Jacob sees the visitor's clothes drift to the floor, a dark shadow take to the air wing for the door where he now stands immersed in the energy of Michael the archangel clad in shining armor. *"Welcome,"* Jacob thinks before his mind falls as empty as the orator's clothes.

*It is good to be in form when the foul sin of separation, the original fall from grace, takes a favored form of Satan himself.* Jacob feels his teeth bare into a grin worthy of the grim reaper on a mad bad night. *The master of lies, deceits and deceptions returns to stalk earth where man walks. Thanks for keeping your body in shape by the way, Jacob, I like working in you, I like working with you.* Jacob feels an angel smile rise on his face as a son of man willingly blends his service with Michael's fierce fiery grace. As one, Archangel and man step choice-fully surrendered into the endless ever-evolving multi-dimensional sinuous supple wondrous springing will of the Infinite Eternal One. *The game's afoot!*

The speed of light that is the Truth of Being, Michael's eyes track the flight of the bat across infinity through the slit in his visor. A spiraling gold wheel set with diamonds and pearls and centered with a heart shaped hiddenite stone adorns his helmet over the third eye catching light and spinning an ever evolving reel of rationality onto the flat physical plane reality. In the blink of an eye, the wheel reverses to rewind reality across time until no trace of it remains at all. *Interesting.* Dislocation overwhelms as awareness, thought, and ego, weaves into a fully present lucid mindfulness of the startlingly fluid frontiers between what is and what is not in the eye of an Archangel. All will, judgment, strength and order ever applied by man using the twelve powers to change the physical plane hold no sway where Jacob resides inside an angel peering into an infinity where a bat flies and a slave bleeds.

Michael inhales deep and touches the jewel at the bottom of the seven set in his gold breastplate from.

**Ruby**, the stone of nobility, the star fire of purity, imparts vigor and passion for life, it protectively leads to vibrant visualization, clears negative energy, and promotes dynamic leadership, strength and passion for life. Ruby is an abundance stone stimulating wealth and positive passion for life and a bold state of mind. It heightens focus and awareness, amplifies enthusiasm, stimulates power, and shields against conflict by focusing mind and heart on desired outcomes. Ruby is the resurrection stone that overcomes martyrdom, suffering, anguish, and turmoil, for ruby holds the power of beginnings and endings of all that is, was, or will be. Ruby promotes expansiveness on the spiral stairway to enlightenment, lifting creativity from the base chakra to the throat letting man direct life from higher awareness guiding to wisdom and compassion. As Michael touches the Ruby he is filled with courage, power and life force energy to neutralize negative energy in mind and body. Luke's words of bloom in his mind: *Take heed therefore that the light which is in thee be not darkness. Luke 12:35.* He knows the darkness within *him* sees and recognizes it in the bat/man. Releasing darkness into light, duality melds polarity and opens to infinite possibility. *Thy will be done*, Michael surrenders and is one with the Divine.

The ruby is the stone on the breastplate of the high priest associated with the apostle **Judas** who was scrupulously devoted to *life* as it appears on the physical plane, and especially zealous about its principal form of money. He held the purse of contributions by Jesus' followers, and he was purse proud! More than any other apostle, Judas believed *without doubt* that Jesus would escape any attempt to capture him as he had done before, that Jesus *would* face no risk of death. He believed so firmly he was blind to the willing will of the Master. He bet on the run, and the thirty pieces of silver the plotters added to the pouch of contributions Judas carried to feed the followers listened to Jesus tell Truth in parable form. Judas also knew without doubt the truth Jesus spoke, that death was not an ending, but a beginning, that Jesus would resurrect, and he *had* to die in the flesh to *demonstrate* the truth of what he taught. Through the power of in the ruby, Judas awakens to the call of the risen Jesus and is regenerated into Jude, with the surname of Thaddeus. Michael strokes the ruby absorbing the power of the stone enough to awaken a healing regeneration to animate the resurrected Judas manifesting in Michael.

Michael strokes the **Jasper** and is grounded by the truth of the self of Source bridging mind and body dualities and imparting tranquility and wholeness. The protector stone grounds and inspires shamanic journeying. He dances balancing dualities in mind, body and brain with the etheric realm and knows the assurance of support if conflict arises. Absorbing the energy of jasper Michael opts to inspire, nurture, renew and realize tranquil balance in the form of the man in bat drag winging from consequences of past choices. The decision neutralizes duality, reunites unity and opens a way to bring idea into form.

The apostle **Simon** the Zealot is associated with the jasper inspiring right use of the power of **zeal** and **enthusiasm**, honesty, imagination, quick thinking, organization, and enthusiasm to boldly come to grips with problems and transform ideas into action. Michael strokes the jasper and is filled with the power of zeal and enthusiasm to scope, resolve and heal issues, blending polarized energies as complimentary opposites and quickly transform ideas into action. Michael studies possibilities for the man bat winging across infinity on a date with destiny. He yields to the Source destiny in for the man and the woman

Michael strokes the **Topaz** and as the stone flares a pure yellow gold light he enters the abiding place of substance setting him on the path and inspiring wisdom and judgment, the twin powers of the shaman wise elder. He feels an empathetic flow of energy soothe, heal, stimulate, promote mercy, light the path to goals, tap inner resources to center him in *be*ing not in habitually *do*ing. Clarity stirs generosity, abundance joy, love and good fortune, releasing hidden pools of tension and a continuous flow of spirit energy. He can't not smile, nor resist a silly-boy grin at his passion to teach and enlighten that is the problem solver healer path of the warrior. This path is an awakening for Michael. He taps assets to find his inner problem solver to focus passion and support in manifesting Good God on Earth. Exhaling like a Zen master he opens to love and good fortune and knows the Truth that all is one, and the One is good.

The apostle **James**, the son of Zebedee and brother of John, who expresses the twin powers of **wisdom** and **judgment** bringing him into the abiding place of substance as he remembers again with truth that Judgment day is every day the effects of the body/brain choices of man and angels is revealed in life. He smiles knowing Spirit choices reveal ideas and inspiration and wonders if the duality of life prompts evil or only paradox. James applies the twin powers on the physical plane so he can *be* rather to *do* desired results. As the topaz on his breastplate flares he senses ever renewing awakening of wisdom and judgment and knows his contact with the stone inspired a spark of fire in the one on his sword scabbard.

Michael strokes the **Emerald**, the stone of enlightenment, inspiration, infinite peace, and life affirming relationships, love, bliss and loyalty and is filled with grace. He finds he has misplaced his separate sense of self and is flooded with unity enhancing love and balancing relationships. He knows negative and positive energy, and balances polarities across his meridians and up and down his body. Consciousness soars, and only positive results, decisions and actions are possible. Michael knows he *has* the strength of character to overcome the trial before him and regenerates bringing wholeness to the wounded ones. Michael intuitively accepts all who wittingly or otherwise, play roles in the unfolding bat man drama.

The apostle **James II**, James "the less," the son of Alpheus, is associated with the emerald and with the power of man known as **order** and **processes**. Those powers demonstrate that man cannot exercise true dominion until he knows who he is. Emerald imparts strength of character to overcome misfortune by applying the process aspect of order to heal and regenerate negative emotions. James demonstrates the process by expressing order into external life by the three step process of mind, idea, manifestation. Michael surrenders himself to divine order and process trusting in divine right outcomes. He touches the emerald on his breastplate and it flares, exciting a flash of greening of the emerald on his scabbard. Words bloom in his mind: *To whom little is forgiven, the same loveth little. Luke 8:47.* Perception reveals that the orator gives little, loves small, and lacks ability to see need, or believe in the grace of God's love. *He has lost himself and been cast away by his own judgment born in his own unforgiving mind and heart.*

Touching the **Blue Topaz** on his breastplate, Michael feels a rolling energy sweeping him into vitality and heightened consciousness of life in which all receive inspiration and an infilling of seed ideas. He calmly accepts a higher order of self that is forceful, energetic, objective-driven, and enlightened, and taps into inner resources before taking action. Transparency activates trust in the universe, promotes clarity, self-control and development of wisdom letting man see the macro without losing the micro in the matrix of life. The stone evokes love, good fortune, inner wisdom, and attainment of goals. Michael sees visions of a higher order of man who is self-aware, aware of others, and intent on applying Spirit resources before physical solutions. Michael is embraced by angels of truth and wisdom who welcome and join him on his mission to change the world in positive, dynamic ways. He knows his mind is a subset of Divine Mind.

The blue topaz is associated with the apostle **Bartholomew** who represents the power of **imagination**. The man *Nathaniel* fell asleep beneath a fig tree and imagined/dreamed through his third eye to see a new vision of who he is newly awakened as a man named *Bartholomew*, which signifies a field plowed and ready for seed. The awakened man is keen to see, hear, experience, and follow the Spirit call to attend a master he has not met, and rises to find and follow Truth in the form of Jesus. Eternally fired by imagination and the enchanting light of the blue topaz, Michael touches the stone knowing its twin on the scabbard sparks and flares its blue flame dance. The dance in the battle with fallen angels is gone leaving focus, peace, and the grace of a shaolin master facing a skilled rival with zest for the test.

Michael touches the **Sapphire** and feels upload of joy and peace of mind that opens intuition, dreams and passion to wisely evolve ideas into the physical world. The stone arouses collaboration at a cellular level and rejoins him with truth that when you change your mind, you change your life. Willingly yielding his militant mind-set, Michael focuses intention and joyously manifests idea/thought into form. The metaphysical realms yield esoteric principles of manifestation that expands intuitive knowing. Sapphire infuses him with the serenity of faith that when in service, spiritual attainment is accelerated. Claiming faith power, he peers into space where a bat wings fierce to exit from a physical place briefly appearing in time and space. *Interesting.* The mystic music of Sapphire pulsing through Michael he the Sapphire and is electrified to hear: *the spiritual path is not a destination, it is a journey.* He is a peaceful warrior.

Sapphire is the symbol stone for the power of **faith** physically expressed positively by the apostle **Peter** when walking on water in utter conviction that if Jesus said he could do the same impossible thing, then he *could do* the same impossible thing, and more. And Peter did! First known as Simon, he was given a new name to better show his spiritual progress to truth. Simon means 'hearing', or receptively listening to Truth with an open mind unsealing the way to the next degree in the divine order, faith. Peter means rock, or faith that is strong, unwavering, enduring, and the foundation for building spiritual awareness and receptivity Truth and expression of faith. Without the foundation of rock there is changeableness, the capacity to deny Truth. When storms of fear, doubt and faint faith plague Peter he denies Jesus. His perception plunges into a foreboding faith in the power of hostile physical forces. Peter thrice denies knowing his master. Thus, Peter shows a stronger faith in physical world things. Taking responsibility for thoughts, Michael yields to faith and hears: *"Faith never knows where it is being led, but it loves and knows the one who is leading."* - Oswald Chambers. Touching the sapphire flares it into a dance of stars on water. His dance is the grace of gazelle running in pure joy of body in fluid motion.

**Alexandrite** is a stone of regeneration that enhances rebirth of inner and outer self, expediting change in the world by producing expansiveness, creativity, awareness in manifestation as art setting the standard for bringing Divine ideas into life on earth. The stone expands joy in connecting with nature, aligning mental, emotional and etheric bodies. It attracts good fortune, stimulates neurological tissue at a cellular level and amplifies healing of body, mind and spirit. The Apostle **Philip**, whose power is **power** and **dominion**, is associated with the alexandrite. The power center of Power is the throat that produces sound to emit vibratory energies of the body. The stone is an open door between formless and formed worlds of vibrations expressing as sound. Michael assertively brings Divine ideas into reality.

*The Ancient Adversary,* Archangel Michael leers from the silver helmet sheathing Jacob's head, *still imagining he can be separate from the Creator. Still enthralled by the mad delusion of isolation from Cause, and more besotted still, willfully embracing Beelzebub's lie that a bat, man, or angel, will one day, gain more power than Source and be thus be enabled to overthrow the One. Fool! Still besotted by the delusion of separation, and the arrogant conceit of thinking it is even possible wrest from Source more power than Source has, and thus overthrow the One. Delusional!* Battle fury engulfs Michael. He tiptoes on a needle point of control, past drunk on the thrill and fill of battle fury and an impatient passion to extinguish the original sin of separation from Source. Gulping great gasps of air, he is overwhelmed by an oxygen high that melts his mind and rushes through him until he *is* the heat of battle, he *is* a lust for death and devastation, Michael *is* the Four Horsemen of the Apocalypse.

*Cool it, Michael,* comes Jacob's command. *What this situation does* not *need is two uncontrollable men, while I am stepped back making room for you in my body and mind. Or, if you wish, I can tell everyone that a man in bat form terrified an Archangel into senseless stupidity.*

*I'm not afraid!* Michael snarls.

*That was* not *a request, Michael. I allow you in; I can let you stay, or I can boot you out, your choice. Make it now. Even the Eternal can't make physical time stop forever.* Jacob grins toothily and adds, *Fear isn't the only thing that makes fools of angels and men. One wee bat can make a fool of an archangel too caught up in the past to clearly see what flies before him today, and what can now be done today to create a better world. Kill one bat, you've killed one bat.*

*I don't like you sometimes, Jacob.*

*Mutual. Check the course of bat man.*

Sighting through the enlightened stones on breastplate and scabbard, Michael checks the progress of the man bat winging through space and time. *Judas unredeemed,* he snarls; *capable of comprehending personal, worldly power in its enchantments and illusions. The Ancient Adversary, still thinking it is possible to be separate from the Creator, the first Cause of all that is and all that is not. More besotted still, willfully embracing Beelzebub's lie that he can gain more power than Source.* Ancient enmity boils through Michael. Jacob feels his passion rushing slow like molten lava to curb and cool the archangel's ecstasy that blinds him to the wisdom of the stones. Riding his polarized passion like a surfboarder over sweeps and swells of the battle fury that owned Michael during the fall from grace when he fought the angels who sought more power than Source. *Fools, skunk drunk on delusion of separation from Source and of a passion to seize all Source power and more. An arrogant affinity for separation,* Michael snarls.

*You got a wide streak of separation from source anxiety yourself, Michael. Curb your temper. Zeal, not rage, is one of the twelve powers; and rightly used, zeal can heal you and the bat man. Light the other stones, we'll need them soon. Do your sensei master fight dance this time, I like it. Good rhythm, beat, fluidity, dazzling footwork, who knows, maybe the bat will stop to watch.*

*Next time I come I'll bring you a sense of humor.* Michael snaps.

*Bring two you'll need one yourself,* Jacob replies evenly. *The physical world needs comic relief more than a militantly dogmatic archangel still fighting fallen angels from eons ago. Time to adopt cooperation and collaboration, Michael. The sapphire is the last stone you touched. Short memory for a semi-divine being.* Michael stiffens, eyes wide with exasperation. Pushing against the resistance, Jacob forces his lungs full intentionally pressing the archangel against ribcage and spine. He holds the breath on a slow count of ten forcing angry rigidity from the archangel. The champion does not go down easily so Jacob begins his slow ten count again.

*All right already! I take your point. Inhale so I have room to breathe again.*

*Still overtly crabby for a semi-divine being. Still punitive and irritable. No wonder the Good Lord doesn't give you important, world changing assignments anymore; and on that note, what* are *you doing here?*

Michael is silent, breathing slowly and rhythmically until his heat cools from volcanic intensity to mere driven purpose. Memory of his mission returns to his awakened mind. *Thank you for your strength, and for your wisdom and good judgment in calling me to task for backsliding to a time when my sword could be unsheathed in anger and vengeance.* He sighs a long release, and admits: *and for pushing me beyond the past and back into focus on the present, and my mission here and now.*

What is our, your mission this time?

*I am to save two lost souls who are gone in their own human minds, but never lost in the mind of God. I would have failed without you, Jacob. I know that. I remember how you persistently pressed the angry vengeance out of me and held me fast,* Michael chuckles, *until I blessed you. In truth, it was you that blessed me, and I'm glad it didn't take an all-night fight this time.*

*Couldn't.* Jacob replies, *we don't have that much time to complete this mission.*

*We have all the time we need, Jacob, all the time we need.* Turning attention to the five unenlightened stones among the twelve jewels on his scabbard, Michael levers the sword grip down, tilting it to cross his body like a guitar. His dancing feet lead as he strokes a thumb over the un-lit jewel above the ruby.

The **Garnet** flares, filling Michael with cleansing, revitalizing, purifying, balancing, energy and inspiring love, devotion, courage, fortitude, hope, expanded awareness and mutual assistance. Garnet dissolves habit patterns and bypasses self-sabotage by obsolete dysfunctional beliefs. Michael reforms error thoughts so they produce happier outcomes and eliminate the dark ones that beguile him to believe that what shows up in the physical world is *not* true in Spirit. Michael denounces and denies delusion that anything made by and from Source could ever be separate from Source. *Illogical*. Michael hears the words "*To whom little is forgiven, the same loveth little* (Luke 8:47). He wonders if the man in bat has forgiveness issues for always receiving small. *Except horses, they gave with no holding back, interesting. He never found that with people.*

A russet red flame quickens as Michael rubs the garnet lighting chakras and opening mindfulness so he feels and experiences the harmonies of the springing, inspiring passion that animates life. He can't *not* dance. *Pointless.* Michael yields lead-footed ingrained patterns that no longer serve, to tap around resistance, inertia, and self-sabotage. He stomps out dysfunctional ideas, antique inhibitions, a closet full of shoulda, woulda, coulda, faith in primordial enemies, and ancient taboos he picked up cheap at a rummage sale. His dancing feet step lively with joy.

The Apostle **Thaddeus**, with the given name of Jude, modeled the power of **Elimination** and **Regeneration** by open-heartedly releasing error thoughts and ideas that no longer serve, and inspiring hope for a better self and a more loving life. Thaddeus is known for compassion and the restoring power of *be*ing rather than *do*ing, and for liberal use of soul healing that instantly transforms discord into unity.

Michael strums the apple green **Peridot** gem that flares at his touch filling him with the **strength** and **courage** of the apostle **Andrew** that flows mighty streams of life, love, substance and intelligence. Andrew masters the art of asking and giving thanksgiving in the same breath knowing what is praised is increased and quickens the law of attraction magnet. Andrew has his being in reverence where he holds dialog with Divine Mind to attract God thoughts from universal mind, the positive pole of life.

The power of Peridot flows through Michael releasing old baggage, vibrations, and negative patterns. He accesses new frequencies, views new destinies, spiritual purposes, and the gifts in past experiences. Springing on the energy of Peridot, Michael admits mistakes and breaths confidence and composure in spiritual purpose and destiny forever forming. The Archangel is filled with clarity, confidence, assertion, and a fiery passion for spiritual truth. He knows people can have lived on the sense plane until they are animal in nature. In a flash of insight he knows the man took on the small self-serving nature of bat. *Interesting.* Releasing thoughts that no longer serve makes space for ideas from Universal Mind and gives thanksgiving for the healing to come. His eyes are prismatic projections of the nine powers already invoked. He takes another look at the spiritual truth of the man bat and the woman who bleeds and sees a shared destiny that lead both to this place and time. *Interesting. Whatever happens to the bat happens to both of them. It'll be grand learning the path the Divine prepared for these foes and for us!* Jacob knows confident passion without aggression. *Maybe I won't kill him then,* Michael muses.

*There's an idea whose time has come!* Jacob encourages moving to strum the next stone. Before he can, Michael touches the **Carnelian** and is filled with life force, vitality, motivation, and creativity to stimulate acceptance of what is while inciting passion for resolutions that enrich all. *That is* creativity in action. His touch activates acceptance leading to release, resolution and re-visioning of what is yet to be. Michael smiles his true smile as love and compassion fill his angelic mind, body and brain.

Carnelian is associated with the apostle **John the Baptist** is the apostle of **love** and **compassion** applied to all of life and every situation in it. John signifies a wise perception of Truth, yet one not quickened by Spirit and a mind that is zealous for the rule of Spirit. This outlook is not spiritual, but a perception of spiritual possibility and a passion for creating conditions in which Spirit rules. Passion strives with evil as a reality rather than a transitory condition. John knows culture does not make people honest nor evoke their virtues. The power of love washes away sins of separation from Source and gives birth to the inner Christ reborn in one aspect of the One. Love is the essence of life that weaves the human family, the universe, and all in it into Divine harmony. Divine love is impersonal. It loves for the sake of loving. It is not anxious with what or who it loves nor with any return of love. Love, like the sun, finds joy in shining forth its true nature. Compassion is love driven by an understanding heart. Compassionate people see error, but don't condemn.

*"Neither do I condemn thee: go thy way; from henceforth sin no more. John 8:11.* Michael finds empathy for the fear-filled man in bat and for the woman who thinks she's a slave. He opts to find creative ways to harmonize dualities and create resolutions that enrich all involved.

The **Diamond**, imparts the clarity to focus life into a cohesive whole and brings love, commitment and attracts abundance. It amplifies and harmonizes the dual poles of form to clear and purify emotional pain minimizing fear and creating space for opportunities. Diamond stirs imagination, fearlessness, invincibility, fortitude and inventiveness, binding intellect to higher mind and leading the soul to spiritual evolution. The stone links the intellect with Divine mind.

Diamond is associated with the apostle **Matthew** who represents the **will** faculty in man. Matthew (originally named Levi) was a tax collector who became a disciple of Jesus and was regenerated by the process of controlling, directing, teaching and disciplining the faculties of mind. Levi had to withdraw from his mercenary occupation and material ambitions that absorbed time and attention and dedicate himself to the master Jesus, who said: *Verily I say unto you, there is no man that left house, or brethren, or sisters or mother or father or children or his lands for my sake and for the gospel's sake, but he shall receive a hundredfold what he has left behind.* In choice, Levi made a new choice rejoicing in a deeper, purer relationship where love expands and possessions multiply. He demonstrates that the power of will *always* makes the right choice to expedite openness to truth. Before touching the stone, Michael feels a clarifying, aligning power infuse him, imparting dedication and clarity. In choosing a deeper relationship with Source Michael strokes the stone and is filled with multi-faceted visions of possibilities. He sees only light and a path to new beginnings for the man bat and for the woman who thinks she's enslaved. He is powerful, fearless, invincible and valiant. He has nothing to prove and nothing to lose. Wise and willfully dedicated to divine right outcomes, Michael names and claims his true desire: *I AM the strength to hold a space for people to return to integrity without shame or blame.* In the diamond Michael sees paths that don't serve anyone. U*seless baggage*! Michael moves with the light patterns that spangle a mosaic of life opening a way where everyone heals, grows, and blooms. He dances a joy jig.

**Amber** is not a stone but fossilized tree resin strongly bound to earth and serving as a grounding stone transmuting negative energies into higher outcomes linking everyday self to spiritual reality. The stone stimulates a drive to achieve, promotes a sunny disposition respecting tradition and easing opposition, encouraging peace, developing trust and wisdom. Amber is associated with the apostle **Thomas** whose power is **understanding**, the ability to know, perceive, comprehend, apprehend and ask. Understanding and will function as one and will is tempered by understanding. The Master showed the relationship between will and understanding when he honored Thomas' demand for proof of His identity knowing that enlightened empathy supports the right use of will by his choice to believe a dead man resurrected as he said he would. The power of understanding has a physical component (*prove it*), and Jesus asked Thomas to put his hand into the wound to *experience* Truth and initiate a right use of understanding to open the door to the kingdom by awakened mind. Will makes it happen. Understanding finds the path to well-reasoned and joyous outcomes.

The one unenlightened stone is **Peridot.** Before touching it, Michael sends his mind into the stone and receives spring green and its cleansing, energizing power. He releases toxins from body, mind and brain, plus old baggage and outside influences, and opens himself to higher power. He releases dysfunctional vibrational patterns, and moves in easy grace to release jealousy, resentment, spite, anger, fear and stress. He receives poise, confidence, and motivation to evolve on mental, emotional and spirit planes. Reviewing life lessons Michael knows that forgiveness of past mistakes empowers rebirth of hope, faith, and unity with all of mankind and with all of life.

The apostle **Andrew**, brother of Peter, represents the power of **strength** and **courage**. Andrew is the strong man with the power of mind to rejoice in the inexhaustible Source of strength and exclaims "*We have found the Messiah.*" Reuniting with his brother Peter, Andrew weaves the power of strength into the power of faith and is propelled easily through adverse experiences.

Michael strokes the Peridot and is filled with faith and the courage to rise to the challenge winging his way. Rejoicing that the man in bat and the enslaved woman are already reborn to Oneness as Truth. All stones of power now lit Michael walks the path of power into a continuum where the horned one in bat drag speeds across the void hell-bent on fleeing the outcomes of unenlightened choices through one small door in space and time.

"Touch the **hiddenite** stone on your helmet over your third eye," comes Jacob's calm command. The angel commander complies. At the touch Michael feels a sweet softening like the tender unfurling of new leaves that lengthen as they grow. The iridescent green of the stone seeps into him linking him to knowledge from higher realms to heal error thoughts and focus awareness.

He knows people who grew up fast are hard, crusty, and mean, for the early loss of innocence. Having another peek at bat he knows the innocence of the boy in the man was too soon lost, gone, and never redeemed. As he brushes the white striations of the crystal he knows the cocoa woman put on a brave face too soon and too often for want of knowing the confounding connections among the humans in her small world consisting of a kitchen and a hen pen. *The hen pen had a kinder, more lucid energy about it. The wounded child became slave to the whims of folks bigger and more powerful, and that she was not clever enough to please, nor be invisible. Interesting.* Michael absorbs the healing of the green and the clarity, wisdom and insight of the white patterns of the stone. *Thank you for that, Jacob. I trust you experienced it too?*

*I did.* Jacob nods their one head and adds: *I'm ready, are you? Prepared and ready. Have you felt the changes to my war dance? I have indeed. Good, aren't I? We are,* Jacob grins a minor course correction. Sensing the shift before it shows Michael flows effortlessly to meet the ancient adversary and joy floods him until it bubbles out in lilting laughter that if heard by a human ear might sound deranged. "When thine eye is evil, thy body also is full of darkness." Luke 12:34. Combat ecstasy erupts in Michael. The power surge disorients the bat pausing it mid-flight. *I didn't know bats could do that. Something new every day in your service, Lord, what a great and awesome God you are. I will not destroy what you have made Lord,"* his reaper grin is back *"but in Your Name I will incapacitate the serpent of deceit so the man may live free again if he chooses.* Without effort, Michael *is* where the bat flies at bat-Mach speed into the sword in Jacob's hand in the gauntlet of Michael's armor. For an instant the bat sizzles on the blade, then molasses slow slides to plop to the floor. Michael's sabaton pins the bat before Jacob's mind gets the signal his body has moved.

Ben enters the room at a run, skids to a stop beside Jacob, and grins eyeing what lies pinned beneath his foot, "Good man, Jacob, you captured a man in a bat suit," he cheers, clapping a hand on Jacob's shoulder. Wincing he pulls his hand back, lamenting, "I *never* remember to *not* clap you on the shoulder when you wear armor. You, my friend, are downright prickly when you go Archangel Michael on us."

Jacob's laughter reverberates in the silver helmet and carillons through nose and eye vents, he cocks an unseen brow. "I need three pieces of silver," he orders in angelic voice, "what have you got?"

"A pair of buffalo nickels," Ben grins holding them out, "and I already know where these buffalo roam." Dropping to a knee by the bat Ben slides a buffalo coin face up between the elbow of a wing and the spine of the bat, then places other buffalo between the elbow and back of the other, and turns to rise.

"I'm in for a silver eagle quarter," Counselor raises the ante by flipping the coin to Ben who catches it on the rise and drops again to place it prudently on the breast of the beast.

"A life was once sold for *thirty* pieces of silver;" growls a voice at the door "surely a man in bat drag needs at least *four* pieces of silver to be saved, if saved he can be." He swaggers to the bat, "I have a Walking Liberty silver dollar, and just like Ben," he elbows him aside "I know *exactly* where it goes." He stoops, rests a finger and thumb on the chest of the bat, then touches the head, sensing a moment. He looks up and announces, "The bat has a heartbeat and *very* slow brainwave activity. I think it is safe for you to remove your silver *shabaton* from this insensate creature while I place my guard on it." He edges Jacob's foot away; "and change into your regular clothes please."

"It's always a pleasure when you arrive, Luke." Jacob replies stepping back into bib overalls, chambray shirt and work boots, then bends to watch Luke.

"Counselor, I'm moving your silver eagle to put the Walking Liberty on the bat's breast. Lady Liberty *ought* to infuse the heart of the beast with the truth that liberty's light is an innate right of every being." That done, he carefully places the silver eagle in its new place and Jacob exclaims: "Oh, son, that is *just* so wrong!" Luke giggles light bright delight as he coils up and away from his mission.

"Jacob, what's Luke done with my silver eagle?" Counselor queries cautiously.

"He put it *face down* on the bat's groin."

"Oh. *Ouch*! It's enough to inspire a man to compassion for the man when he is conscious again." Casting the sentiment indifferently aside he asks "Will he shift shape before he comes to again?"

"Probably. Usually, and, as his body returns to the size of a man, the coins grow with him." Jacob shrugs, "it's something in the magic of Michael that I do not fathom."

"Oh." Counselor nods knowingly, "the magic of Michael. I should have known. Remind me to never give you reason to be fractious with me, Jacob." Turning a sharp eye to Luke, Counselor adds "as for you, *Light Bearer*, you have a *shockingly* dark side to you for one so young." Luke bobs a bow with an affable grin and takes a chair in the circle while Counselor bites a cheek to check a chortle.

## Pain Eater

"Here come the Daughters now" Doc crows the rising light.

"Led by my lovely wife in her fine regalia," beams Counselor in obvious admiration.

"May I always cherish my Hester as you obviously do your mate, Counselor," Jacob declares.

"May you always be sane enough to give praise *for*, and *to*, your mate, Jacob," Counselor counsels.

"May I always be in awe of your wisdom," Jacob replies with a puckish grin as the ringing and singing of dulcet voices fills and cheers the room and stills the sidebars.

Hester neither leads nor follows. She enters the common room sweeping her eyes to see the silver studded bat, the crumpled clothes, and the woman rising in round eyed recognition from a chair between Doc and Counselor. She bears a distinctive two-hole mark in the curve of her neck over the carotid artery. Hester swallows a cry as her world implodes into the time her untainted sense of self was assaulted, desecrated, and left abandoned without hope. Surrendering herself she consciously expands awareness to embrace only the two of them. She knows two are needed to forgive and two to heal the separation from Source that enables one to feed on the life energy of another. *Two to do the sin, two to heal it.* It is her final thought before yielding to a higher power that flows and heals through her. Fixing eyes on the woman, she lifts a hand to touch two fingers by the paired scars over her carotid artery in the place where enflamed punctures leach color and life from the woman.

The woman shakes her head, yet hope rises like the first dawn on the first day. She breathes "how?" She yields her passion to know endings, and gives an unconditional yes. She let go of that. She *just* let go.

Hester reads the silent question and responds by opening her heart to receive the pain shackling the spirit of the bowed one and time is suspended for she has slipped mortal bonds and fallen headlong into the infinite and eternal space between the formless and the formed. *Thy will be done* her heart sings. *Thy will be done through me.* Joy uplifts her as time twists and warps and does not behave well at all. No one minds for all know that when one is healed all are whole for all are one when all is done.

Pain punches Hester with the force of a blow as the cocoa woman falls boneless to the floor. She chuffs out air, then in greedy gasps inhales, force feeding oxygen to her body, mind, and brain. She exhales a soft slow sigh, eyes lancing into those of the fallen woman willing her strength and courage and hope and hope and hope. Tears flow but neither knows who first cries, who first dies, who first lives again, who finds Lazarus fresh awake, stiff still and awkward from being too long dead and separate from Source. *Lazarus is not the only one who can be resurrected and live anew. The promise is given through him even as it was given to him.* The bowed woman hears Truth Words for the first time and inhaling with Hester fills her lungs gently full with oxygen. She holds the air while blood delivers the breath of life through her body brain and mind. A smile plays on her lips knowing her resurrected self is *outrageously*, unexpectedly, and brilliantly gifted *to be* the amazing self she sees in the eyes of the woman lifting her up on love across an infinite realm of time.

Hester pulls the breath of life to fill her lungs and bronchia to capacity. She relishes the self-induced euphoria of an oxygen high and holds for a count of ten. Pumping breath like thunder through her heart Hester fires the power of love turning it to molten liquid life light joy. Exhaling to a slow count of ten she allows pain to flow and resolve to its level in the purifying passion of love. *Thy will be done,* she gasps a greedy gulp of air directing it to her heart to fuel passion knowing, loving, surrendering to what comes. On inspiration she touches her chest above her heart and is startled to feel the shape and texture of a felt rose its petals arrayed like an open tea rose. The woman's eyes round. She smiles at what cannot be yet is. Fingering petals she turns them knowing they reshape into the upright American Beauty rose.

"Breathe," Doc softly coaches the woman, "inhale deep, hold, exhale slow, relax, do it again three times, breathe deep, hold, exhale slow, relax. Pant now like a dog fresh from a run, pant, pant, pant," Doc chants a new rhythm of life song from before time began and the woman loses herself to the pant chant and surrenders to at-One-ment with the Source. Hope springs eternal, but faith is a power to be earned, learned, and won. No word is spoken, yet the woman hears Hester's gentle asking when and why she accepted herself as slave. Shocked, the woman defends that she was born a slave. *As was your mother? Yes,* the silent woman replies. *Did your mother think of herself, or behave, as a slave?* The woman blinks at the astute depth and fractal facets of the question. She knows she cannot deny or hide her truth. *No, she never behaved slavishly. She always had the dignity of one born free. If your mother did not behave slavishly but always conducted herself as one born free though owned by another, how did you come to deny the truth your mother knew? How did you come to think and behave like a woman enslaved by another?* The woman moans under the unyielding weight of a truth she could not accept, and cannot now deny. *My mother never loved me.* Hester laughs delight, and the woman knows the silliness of what she said. Hester probes *Did you have healthy food* to eat, clean clothes to wear, a warm dry place to sleep, a chance to learn things you didn't already know, a safe place to play and friends to play with? Yes, the woman admits sensing that the freedom she denied was never denied to her. *When did you begin to feel and believe you were disempowered and powerless? Hard questions, woman, why do you plague me? Why will you not face me when you accuse me of tormenting you? Who cannot own power over you when you denied it is yours alone to own and wield? Is your power available to anyone you can project blame on who will not defend themselves? Ouch! You are hard, woman!* Facing one equally hard in her self-enforced separation behind which she hides to casts darts of blame for consequences of her choices. *I did not choose this!* The woman protests in impotent rage. Hester shrugs calmly: *Passive choice counts. Which brings us back to the question of when you denied your own power and began behaving like someone outside you owns you and determines your fate? You won't let up will you?* Hester's smile is genuine; *do you choose to be healed and whole? Or do you choose to keep on slavishly allowing others to use the power you freely give daily?* The woman juts her lip petulantly and Hester interjects *Jesus always asked two questions before healing anyone, what were they?* A sullen moment of silence passes, and she replies: *Do you believe you can be healed, and are you willing to be healed.* Hester nods, *Faith, the power of Peter. Will, the power of Matthew. Both men used fear-based power before using it rightly. Like you, Peter revealed faith in* human *power and denied the man he called master. He used his power rightly by stepping from the boat into a stormy sea to walk on the water toward Jesus.*

The woman across from her frowns and says: *But he fell in!* Hester nods. *The storms of life often drop faith filled people into the hard liquid reality of life in physical form. Is that what happened to you?* The woman pauses then sighs: *If I ever had that much faith, then yes, that is what happened to me.* Hester cocks a grin, *perhaps your faith was not invested in a higher power, but really was an outwardly safe dependency on the humans you thought owned you.* The cocoa woman will not meet her eyes. Hester continues her silent lesson: *Matthew was a tax collector. It worked well for him by physical measures, yet he willingly chose to give that up to follow the master. Right use of will led him to riches on spiritual and material planes. Can you surrender your false security in dependence on physical world sources, yield yourself to a higher power, and have faith in the promised rewards of that? What security have I? Someone else to be responsible, someone else to blame, the false sense of security of dependency. What do you know, you white faced judge, thinking you can put me down because you are whiter than me.* Hester studies the woman, then opts to answer her security question, but not her white bias charge: *You have the word of the Most High God. The same* security Peter and Matthew had when faced with the choice of reality bites or taking a leap of faith.

Extending a hand Hester invites: *Come, step out of the boat you built to keep yourself safe. Leave the false security of the pretenses you submitted to and receive the promise of a better future, even if you don't know what it feels like to be free or be full to overflowing with peace and joy.*

The woman discharges the pains, slights and assaults of a life no longer a part of who she is and wills herself to stand firm and tall. "You have been very kind and I thank you, but you must stop now."

"Stop?" Hester blinks, refocusing her eyes to see the woman in her physical form again.

"Yes, stop. I tried to block the pain you took. I sent mean thoughts to you about you." She huffs crossly "that did as much good as dropping a rock in a river; the pain flowed right around it. You are a *Pain Eater*," her face crumples for being freely given more than she can receive.

Hester smiles serenely "I am that, I Am." Then she frowns puzzled, "Why do you weep?"

"What you eat you *become*!" The woman cries, "You *must not* do this, you must stop *now*!"

Hester nooses a giggle into a small smile, lays her hands over her heart, and says "watch this." Gently opening her hands like wings around her heart she invites "follow the flow of your pain, and see what becomes of it here," she taps her chest alive with heart center energy. Many in the room know what the woman sees, and watch charting her path through the implausible sight of an enflamed joyous heart encompassed in a nimbus of light, willing to freely give any essential assist. The woman's instincts are true and guided, she gasps, then pants like a dog fresh from a run. She does not look away nor take reprieve from the terrible tender anguish but inhales a breath of longing as purified liquid pain pours into her heart and shapes and forms into dazzling crystals of astonishing color, cut, clarity and size. Seeing the jewels formed from pain in Hester's heart, the woman sanctions her own cauterizing agony and intuitively eases the pain in the man bat craving freedom to enslave. *How small, powerless, cowardly, helpless, angry and hopeless he must be to sink so low. Thank you God that his has not been* my *fate for all my failings, fears, faults and frailty. Use me. Use me as you will. Use me.*

After an eternity of healing the woman sighs *"I want to do that."* Her words are longing, surrender, a dropping of defenses, a willing yielding to a higher purer power seldom known on the physical plane in body, mind, and brain of man. "Will you teach me?" she prays pleas into Hester's eyes.

Hester laughs surprised delight. "You already know how to be a Pain Eater. You are one. You have not accepted that yet, but owning that truth is all you lack."

"*I* am a Pain Eater?"

"You are that," Hester nods an assuring grin. "Touch the mark on your neck."

The woman obeys, blinks doubt, and jerks her fingers away to see the tips not red wet but only clean dry skin. She touches again softly exploring the healed dry scars like those on Hester's neck. Tears sting her eyes, "Does that mean *I* can eat pain and it turns into jewels in my heart, like happened in yours?"

Hester nods, "I'm sure of it. Would you like to try?" The woman kicks a fear habit and nods. "Ben," she smiles the name "will you come to me please?" Ben obliges warily wary. She adds as Ben approaches, "As you see from his uniform, Ben is our peace keeper." She tucks a hand in his elbow. "Keeping the peace is surprisingly more challenging than enforcing the law. Keeping peace means Ben eats a *great* deal of pain doing his work effectively." She smiles fondly at Ben, "I think he is mostly unaware of the pain he eats to find and forge peaceful outcomes. If Ben agrees, are you willing to try your hand, and your heart, at absorbing the pain of another?"

The woman looks at Ben who grins, shrugs, nods anxious ambiguity, and a querulous *heh, heh, heh*. She grins and confesses, "I don't know what I'm doing either, Sheriff, if that's any comfort to you." Ben nods, she bites her lip, and casts a quick plea to Hester. "Will you stand by me? To support me?" Smiling, Hester quickly moves to stand by the woman facing Ben.

Ben chuckles uneasily "I'm feeling a *little* alone here right now."

"I'll stand by you, Ben" calls a sweet voice borne on the nimble step of a natural dancer gliding to Ben's side to slip a hand under his elbow, smile up at him, and say "I'll stay right by your side."

Tipping back his head, Ben chortles, "I don't know if I'm more comforted, or more challenged by that."

The dancer grins, "It'll be fun finding out won't it? Pay attention. I want you to tell me *exactly* what it feels like to have your pain eaten." Ben cocks a dubious brow at the dancer, then turns to face the woman willing to eat his pain. Hester steps behind the woman placing her left hand on her spine level with her heart, her right hand on the woman's right shoulder. Inhaling fully, she slips into a trance to guide and feel the woman follow her there. As one the two inhale and exhale to ten heartbeats.

Those watching see the woman raise up in power, trusting Source to guide her in its correct use. As she exhales, they see her heart open to reveal its true passion and welcome it home. As one, they feel pain ease and flow, and as one, experience resolution and restoration in the crucible of love, each holding fast to the essential truth of wholeness in body mind and spirit. The dancer feels and yields to Ben's surrender and the melting closure that weeps from him. With him she receives the reviving breath, the measured treasured exhale, and the uprightness of body with the next breath of air. He bows chin to chest surrendering will and yielding to Spirit to release his burdens while time stands still to watch the silent prayer play with vital vigilance.

To Ben, each pain tormenting him is at once alien and as familiar as a twin, as fully known as another self, as true his own breath and the body that breathes it. At times pain racks him 'til he thinks his body will rip to sundered shreds as repairable as Humpty's shattered shell. All the while a guardian voice chants: *Breathe, breathe, breathe, all is well, all is worthy, all is whole, breathe, only inhale and exhale.*

In the way a coming storm changes temperature by tens of degrees in seconds, Ben's pain cools to be a strong element in his blood and body as health returns and possesses every cell and atom of his body/mind/brain. He finds whole health and respires in the giddy glad gratitude of irrational joy. He opens dewed eyes and smiles thanks into the ones across the circle.

The woman blinks "I did it," she whispers amazed. "I ate his pain." The statement as like a question. "I am *stronger* than I was before," she crows her joy. I *am* a healer!" she sings sweet surrender, "I didn't know that about me before;" she smiles serenely. "Now I know who I Am."

"Part of it, dear heart, only part of it, there is more for you to learn, accept, master and know," Hester assures stepping around to embrace her with a mother sister smile. *I'm a pain eater!* The woman mouths into Hester's ear and the two of them share a coming home joy laugh.

| Shawn Gallaway – The Light of The Flame |
| --- |

### Fight Dance

"Well, bat man is a dud for entertainment value," grumbles a dancer toeing the static form on the floor. "You *sure* he isn't dead, Luke?" Luke bobs his head in affirmation brows arched in petulant pique. The dancer shrugs,

"Let's *do* something then. Let's make something happen while we wait for the dead to arise. Or not," she says with innocent indifference.

"What do you want to do?" Luke asks giving her the attention she craves.

"Fight dance!" She shouts with an infectious cheerleader jump and smile. Some see crepe paper pom-poms fluttering though none are there.

"*Fight* dance?" Ben and Luke harmonize the puzzlement of all.

"Is that anything like the Schottische?" someone asks playing silly. Some chuckle, and all lean back to watch the theatre of the weird that is certain to play out.

The dancer is pleased with the spontaneously evolving theatre of the weird. "Not like the Schottische at all;" she refutes, and gives an impish grin "but it *could* be part of a fight dance if Schottische steps and moves were put into it," she demonstrates, improvising fight steps as she twirls about the circle slapping toes and palms where a shoe might stamp a Schottische step. "Who wants to learn the fight dance? It's no *fun* dancing alone," she whines

"You're making this up as you go aren't you?" Ben asks circling opposite matching her step and form as she moves. Eying and matching him she clacks imaginary castanets casting them to nearly snare Ben in her web. He shreds the web as she explodes into a back flip to snap up beside him reaching behind to slap the backs of his knees throwing him off balance, and with an impish grin nimbly back flips away.

"Okay, I'm getting the hang of this. I see how it works," Ben chuckles his signature *heh, heh, heh,* "All I have to do is stay on the *other* side of the room from you two and I'll be fine."

"Will that work for you" She coos from behind him light-fingering his handcuffs from his belt clip, "do you think?" she grins jingling the cuffs in his face.

"How do you *do* that?" He growls.

"The first, and perhaps the *only*, rule of Fight Dance is always keep them guessing, unsuspecting, surprised and off guard. Do you want to participate in this dance, or is complaining enough for you?"

"Sure," Ben snaps, snatching his cuffs away, "I'm teachable," he shrugs, "and I got some time." She twirls around him slapping the bottom of his baton with the sole of a foot so it leaps from its holder at his waist to arch over his shoulder where he catches it in astonishment.

"You won't be needing that," the dancer smiles, pushing him to his chair. "Leave the gun, the handcuffs, the knife, *and* the shoes under your chair. E*veryone*, make the circle bigger so the ladies can sit too, *or*," she entices, "can join the dance."

"If you show me how to get Ben out of his weapons," the dancer's young sister coos as she glides into the ring, "you can teach me *anything* else you want, Sister dear."

Luke clears his throat stepping lightly between the sisters "Start with what makes it a *fight* dance since no *weapons* are allowed, except, it seems, your fast feet and hasty hands." He grins a spin out of reach.

The dancer smiles executing a twirl then lighting fast, extends a shapely leg to clip her sister's knees lifting and rotating her into a full body flip in the air. She lands with a solid "whoop" of ecstatic triumph.

"Okay, that taught *me* how to flip, now teach me how to make someone *else* flip." Her grin is deeply wicked on such an angelic face. "Oh wait," she smirks down at her astonished sister *not* sleeping on the floor by the slumbering bat "I just did that didn't I?" Her giggle is strangely sinister and oddly infectious.

Luke leads with his toes slinking around the sisters eyeing them with devoted intent and a disarming smile. "Tell me about the fight dance, and since it is a dance, where's the fight? If it's a fight, where's the dance? And perhaps most important of all, "who leads?" He circles and spins to, with, and around the girls whirling one into the other in the grace of their improvised response. Smiling the light he bears, he thinks: *what fun if we all lead and follow, all for the joy of sharing with no expectation except to discover infinite opportunities for unexpected expressions of Truth that all is One Infinite and Expanding Whole, Wholly, Holy, and Here, and Now! It is good I don't talk out loud much.*

The sisters twin themselves to mirror to move counterpoint with Luke and with each other and are aware as one when Ben steps back into the swirling circle, moving with and challenging all of them "if the fight dance is a competition, what is its purpose? What's the objective? What's the prize? If our only goal is to show muscle and style and form, that is *far* too easy, we'd be bored before the hour is up. "What we need is a challenge, a goal, an objective to stretch us and to keep us engaged, here's what I propose."

Ben circles them like a kindly interrogator, playing the drama to the audience as he engages each in his play of powerful grace subtly enticing them into the circle. He grins bright delight, "By ancient Inca tradition the winner of every competition is *honor bound* to teach and train those he has defeated until each can stand against him as his equal. Teaching and learning would make this fight dance of yours a pastime worth doing, watching, *and* deserving of the time taken in doing it."

Jacob rises with a grin to join the circle "I admire that Inca tradition, Ben, but I propose a change." He tips a nod to each in the circle, "I will teach you hard and well, and one day," his grin a wicked challenge" you will stand *with me* as my equal."

The dancer slinks a step toward him "Next year, Jacob, next year. *This* year, I'll be teaching you. If you are focused, and practice daily, you can complete your training in a year's time," she smiles up at him, "and then be *able* to stand against me as my equal."

"Oh-ho-ho, *show* me, little girl, don't tell me, else I'll put my money on you being a skillful politician and *not* a collaborative Spiritual warrior." The dancer snorts at Jacob's back that hides the mischief in his eyes. He meets raised eyebrows, turns his hands palm up and feints bewilderment at their reaction.

"You are such a pot stirrer, Jacob. What can you add to the fight dance idea that makes it an enjoyable pastime – other than hot air?" a watcher poses.

Jacob shrugs a grin, "I don't know yet, I don't know the rules, or even if there are any. My bet is on the Inca having rules, watchers, and trainers, all we got so far is words, and some appealing dance moves."

The dancer huffs again, "then I shall be forced to teach you the toe slap dance."

"Oh, I am *so* in for that" cries the sister dashing to her side.

In the toe slap instant the bat shifts into his human form. "Oh look, the man in the bat is back," a sister observes. "Fortunately, its skinny naked body is tucked in the natal position so we can't see it." She studies the bat with a frown. "That silver eagle laid where it was before the shift might cause a body to curl into that protective pose." She nudges the man with a toe as her sister had done the bat. "It's still breathing," she observes, "and that is *still* all that can be said for its entertainment value."

The wall clock strikes two chimes. "Time's a passing," Jacob grumbles, "who's going to tell us what this fight dance looks like?" He claps his hands like a coach hustling his players to attention and focus, "what are the rules, what does it take to win, are there teams or is it every player for *her*self, are there style points, are you making this up as you go?" He demands of the dancer.

She grins, not apologetically, and shrugs, "well…, *yeah*! Everyone's sitting here like a bump on a log and that's as entertaining as watching a bat nap. I thought bats hung upside down in caves to sleep."

Jacob winks an evil grin "I think the man didn't expect to be unconscious just now, and his long sleep is *no* reason for you to propose something just as dull to pass time until he wakes up."

"Jacob, Jacob, Jacob," Ben intervenes, "in addition to rules, every good game needs at least two teams, some good players, some fair referees, a bunch of enthusiastic fans, and *few* critics. You obviously are not a player, nor a referee, nor even a fan, you, my friend, are a critic. You belong on the sidelines," he prods Jacob to his chair pushing him firmly into it, "where you can be as cantankerous as you please." The circle erupts in hoots of laughter. "Sit. Stay." Ben orders turning back to the dance.

"Okay, we had some good action going before our resident critic gave his review, let's make this fight dance competition worthy of watching and doing. "You, dancer, what are your favorite elements of a dance competition?" Caught off guard the dancer gapes drop jawed. "If you've lost your tongue and can't speak, *show* us!

"Come here, little sister, your elder needs some vision. Show us what you got while she evolves beyond the mouth-breathing stage." Ben narrowly ducks a toe slap to the head but is bumped off sides by the swinging hip of the slinking sister. *He, he, he,* he chortles triangulating himself between the girls.

"Luke, you showed us some good moves before, is that all you got?" Ben gripes provocatively. "If so, go lie down by the man in bat drag. You can be as dull as a lump of coal over there." He narrowly dodges Luke's jump kick to his head who then spins away to catch Ben's ankle with a foot to flip him airborne again. "Woo-*hoo*! What a great *move*, Luke! What else ya got?" Ben goads.

On a silent cue the sisters' dance in to separate the men mischievously inciting their competitive routine and introducing their own gymnastic gyrations to the evolving dance. Musicians among them improvise a driving beat, lilting tune, and sublime harmony to inspire the dance and the dancers. Wise elders watch and give points for style, originality and performance perfection. Soon the circle is filled with leaping, weaving, thrusting, pulling, shoving, tumbling, spinning, jumping, and laughing youths who break out to watch, cheer and take a breather while choreographing new moves for the dance of cosmic silliness before returning to the sphere of jubilant gyration. None recalls laughing so deeply and well for as long as they remember. All cherish this time as a favorite memory for as long as they live.

| Shawn Gallaway – We Dance |
|---|

## The Awakening

The chirping cries of a bat issue from the unmoving man in the natal position drawing eyes to the still form. Softly the twittering sounds evolve into tormented moans from a human throat that grow louder as the weight of the silver presses and burns.

"Anyone hungry for barbeque?" someone quips and is quickly silenced by glares around the circle, the dancers scowl and step away, the musicians lay their instruments aside.

"What have you done to me?" the searing man whimpers.

Doc leans back in his chair extending the soles of his feet to the man, "why son, we have given you one more chance to answer Jacob's question and tell all of us how one man can own another human."

The man moans "we've been through that and you took the word a slave over that of a free white man."

"Huh! You don't *look* free to me," Ben observes caustically.

"I *mean* I am not a slave, you dolt."

"'Dolt', I haven't heard *that* discouraging word since I was knee-high to a grasshopper." Grinning amiably into the face of the prone man, Ben sing-songs "sticks and stones may break my bones, but words will never hurt me." Seeing a human face shift to the face of evil is a disturbing demonstration, the hissed words of the silvered man are more unsettling still "your laughter is a sign of your *ignorance*."

"Well *that* was plumb mean," Ben pulls back with a grumble, "and me just trying to add a bit of levity to this *unfortunate* situation."

"There is nothing funny about this situation," the man snaps.

Eyeing the naked man livid with poorly contained rage Ben nods amiably and observes "that is a matter of perspective, son. From the angle of *my ignorance* the situation in which you find yourself, captured as a bat, allowed to shift to human form, pinned to a dusty floor by silver coins, and on top of that your impotent bullying, well, son, that is just plain rib-tickling *ri-dic-ulous*."

The pinned man growls "if I could get up, I'd...."

Ben's brows arch expressively, "*bite me?*" he growls. The man looks away with a sullen scowl as Ben's eyes narrow to a hard line. Reaching into a shirt pocket he pulls something out letting it drop into his palm, "I've carried a token for most of my career thinking someday I'd find someone I'd want to give it to. Today's my day, and you're my man." He tosses the thing so it lands lightly on the man's shoulder.

The man shrieks and writhes away and the token falls to the floor beside him, "a silver bullet," he yells, "you insensitive *brute!*"

"*This* from a man who enslaves and feeds on the life blood of *another*? It is plum hard to feel fairly judged by a man like you." Ben stalks resolutely to the prone man who flinches away. "I'll have my Lone Ranger silver bullet back since you *obviously* have no appreciation for the finer things in life." Ben's grin is devilish as he turns to his chair.

The silver studded man eyes the faces in the circle and finds them relaxed, alert, aware, and fully present without expectation or judgment. There is one outcome they anticipate and await. This is chilling to the man whose key talents are manipulation and control. *They have no stake in this, not one of them. Yet there is an outcome they will have, and will accept no other.* It rankles him, these nobodies without status, entitlement or authority binding him and deciding his fate with meticulous, merciless compassion. In face of the steadfast serenity he centers his considerable focus on life, liberty and the pursuit of freedom. Happiness, he has never known and discounts it as of little value.

Across the room an awakening sense of self-determination shreds habitual bonds of submission in the consciousness of the cocoa woman leaving her in a disconcerting clarity that she was *always* free to choose her own fate and thus to bear the consequences. Freedom and fate war in her as fierce as mythical dragons each bound till death to oppose the other. The winged serpents swoop, swirl, and spit fire, each intent on annihilation of the other and of all she knows and believes until the space of her is too narrow to contain their conflict, and feels herself hurled into a void beyond space and time. Doc senses her absence though she sits beside him still. He reaches to support her and she yelps suddenly elevated on an impossible trajectory from her chair, her left foot rides something unseen, her arms propeller in pursuit of elusive equilibrium. All feel the jolt of balance as her right foot is supported and she rises like a shot through the roof newly supplanted by infinity and its eternally spirited silence.

"*Dragons…,*" comes an awed whisper.

"*Who are you?*" The rider in another dimension asks to know.

"*Fre,*" replies the serpent beneath her left foot,

"*Edom*" says the other.

"*What's happening?*" The awed woman cries.

"*Perspective,*" breathe the dragons in one word thought. "*You were too close to your small human self to clearly see your options and make a wise choice so we spirited you away.*"

"*Options?*"

"*Yes. Fear is a human habit that practically predicts outcomes because fear always precludes options. What was the choice before you when we came for you?*"

"*Freedom,*" she pauses pondering, "*or fate.*"

"*Which would you have chosen?*"

She groans "*Fate, I suppose, fear habit. Doubt.*"

"*Name your doubt,*" demands one.

"*That I can be free to do what I choose, and to know that I can survive and even thrive on that.*"

"*Self-doubt.*" Breathes one, "*Is it possible the man you are with is possessed by the same fear?*" The infinite thrives in timeless silence and the dragons soar, spiral and spin in endless exuberant space beyond time, until the woman owns and allows the truth she denied, and the dragons return her to the chair where she began her quest. Doc lays a comforting hand on her wrist, silently reading her pulse and finding its rhythm and pace curiously more composed than before she left on her wild ride.

"Let the man free," The woman directs and expects it is already done.

"*What?*" The circle demands as one, all mouths agape.

The woman withdraws behind lowered lids, mourning the blamelessness of slavery and life at the mercy of a mean man. She understands the margins of being owned, she knows how to resist, how to win, and how to survive. "Slavery is not for the slow, the slight, or the submissive," she thinks. "Only the brave survive slavery." She eyes the man and speaks to the circle, "Look at him. The shackles that bind him are not the silver coins. He sold himself cheap before the Archangel dropped him where he lays."

The man struggles feebly to rise to her level. "Remove the coins," she snaps an order. "And give him his clothes. None deserve to suffer the shame of his nakedness. Especially him."

"Point taken," Luke agrees gathering the worn gaudy garments, dropping beside the man and lightly taking and pocketing the Walking Liberty coin and laying the jacket on the man's chest. The man gulps lungs full of air, his eyes wide with relief, doubt, and something oddly akin to fear. Next Luke removes the buffalo nickels that instantly return to their normal size and weight and flips them to Sheriff Ben. He takes the Silver Eagle quarter, then drapes the trousers over the man's groin and legs and sets the shoes nearby. That done he graciously returns the Silver Eagle to Counselor's palm.

### Revelation and Reckoning

When he is dressed the man looks at the woman and asks "Did – did you ride two dragons in – in space – like it looked like you did?" The woman nods and the man bobs his head with her, eyes wide. "I was afraid you'd say yes. I hoped you wouldn't. I never saw anything like that, not even on a bender after clearing the glasses after one of the master's shindigs."

"You *drank* the wine his guests left?" the woman asks incredulous. "Never mind. I don't want to know."

The man shrugs indifferently, "it was that or throw it away and that seemed a prissy waste."

The woman eyes him with a perceptive smile. "The master's car, tell me about that." He turns away and she crosses her arms cupping elbows in her hands, posing the patience of Eternity.

"You changed...," he offers an alternate telling.

"The car first. *After* that comes your time to ask questions."

"They didn't find us." He snaps. "I *said* they wouldn't find the safe hole and we'd be okay there."

She frowns at the memory, "did the master or the mistress know about the safe hole?"

Shaking his head no, he adds "I found it the day the lady had me clear out the canning room and throw out old fruit and vegetables to make room for the jars of fruit and vegetables harvested that year."

She smiles remembrance, "I'm thankful you threw the old food in the direction of the slave quarters. Even old vegetables and fruit in winter are better than none."

"And I thank you that the jars and rings were clean when ye brought them back for the next canning, it saved me a caning. The mistress could be a hard woman at times."

"Civil war..., was there *ever* a war that was civil? And looters on the front porch make even generous folks tightfisted and mean. The mistress was a good kindly woman before the war."

"She was that," the man agrees.

"Could *none* of the family be saved? The girls, the young boy?" The woman implores.

The man shakes his head quickly, "They knew how many were in the family, even the number of servants and slaves; it was dangerous business trying to save *anyone* let alone a whole family."

Her eyes narrow, "*How* did they know how many were in the family?"

"Looters. They kept their liberty by stealing and turning in the ones they stole from. When some of master's horses came up missing from the far pasture, I knew what was coming next. Men stole horses to sell to blue coats, and sold information about plantation owners and their families to carpetbaggers. Hungry people *cannot* be trusted. A son who stayed behind to run the farm was branded a Union man. Neither the yanks nor the Rebs had money to feed hostages, nor medicine to treat the wounded."

The woman watches him thoughtfully a long while and asks "*why* was no one but me and you in the safe hole big enough for the whole family?"

"Too much risk, I told you that," the man snaps clam tight closed.

"Too much risk for who?"

"If they'd come and found nobody in the house, they'd have searched first, taken what they wanted, then torched the place, watched while it burned, and shot anyone who ran from the fire. *Everyone* would have died then, is that what you wanted? This way at least you and I lived."

"You and me." Her eyes are clear solemn sad, "The master, his wife and children, the servants and slaves were taken away and everything of value including the contents of master's safe and the lady's jewel case. The safe hole *was big enough to keep them safe too.*"

"I'm telling you the carpetbaggers *knew* how many were in the family, how many slaves, how many horses and cows, if I'd tried to hide the family *we'd* have been at risk even in the safe hole."

"*How* did they know? Carpetbaggers never came that far south before. The master and his family were good people, they cared for the slaves and the servants, horses and stock animals. That's rare in the slave owning south. Someone turned them in for money, or freedom." her eyes narrow "Someone who knew when they'd come and had time to hide before they arrived. "Someone who *didn't* tell the raiders about the Rolls Royce and the *one* slave you hid with you. Tell me why you did that."

"I did it for you," he protests peevishly.

"You never did a thing for anybody unless you got paid for it. *Why* did you hide me and no one else?"

"You're like a daughter to me," he says softly serious, "a daughter I never had." He pleads into her eyes and she knows he speaks his truth and she does not understand nor believe a word of it.

"So, you think it is okay to feed off another human – a *daughter* – so long as you fancy they owe you?"

"No!" He protests, "It's not that at all! I owe *you*."

"*Why*?" She crosses her arms, and waits.

"You were born because of me." He admits in a whisper. A hush falls over the room. Even the wall clock waits without tick or tock for the remainder of the tale. "Before you were born, the master held a posh party and invited plantation owners and families and an old bachelor that couldn't keep a mate if she was deaf, dumb and blind. I owed a gambling debt I couldn't pay. The master wouldn't help, said he'd not countenance an employee gambling let alone lend or give them money to pay a gaming debt.

"The man I owned was at the party, horny old devil. He fancied your mother." The woman's eyes and mouth round in silent dread. Heedless of all but himself, the oblivious orator continues "the horny old wolf said he'd forgive the gambling debt on the spot *if* I arranged for him to have time alone with your mother during the gala. I said no, of course; and he threatened me, saying he'd see me in debtor's prison until I rotted unless I did what he wanted. When I hesitated he vowed to get me fired unless I made the arrangements *that night*. What's a man to do but what a man has to do? I told your ma a guest wanted to use the master's study and she needed to go there and make sure the master's papers were locked away and the room well cleaned. She'd cleaned the room that day, as always, and told me the study was spotless and that the master's papers were locked away as was his constant habit. The butler manages house staff so I ordered her to go and wait until I came to get her, which I did not do until the randy wolf returned and gave back my token." He mutters "You were born nine months later."

The woman, eyes round with shock, whispers: "I am the child of *rape*! My mother was raped *because of you*, who had charge of the wellbeing of the servants and slaves? Raped by a randy man she hated so you'd be excused of a debt you owed? How *could* you save yourself from the consequences of your ravenous lust for ill-gotten gains by betraying *all* the house slaves to satisfy your venial vile greed?"

"Only her!" the man defends dimly, "None of the other slaves were ever touched."

"*None*?" The woman cries, "Do you imagine no other slave was effected by your betrayal of duty to the master? Can you even *imagine* the other slaves didn't know what happened, didn't know when mother began to show that they too were at risk of betrayal by the very person the master entrusted with their well-being? You are a *despicable* human being!" She spins away screeching, "Can I *kill* him?"

Counselor places a calming hand on her arm, "*he* may deserve a quick death, but you do not; and our Sheriff Ben would be duty bound to arrest you for murder, and I, bound to hear your case and sentence you to prison for *premeditated* murder." Counselor allows time for reflection on the facts and evidence, then adds: "It's a hard sentence for you who have been through so much to be content with the sharp slippery pleasure of killing a man who wronged you and your mother."

Her eyes weep into his, "Mother could never *love* me," she wails, "She could not *be* mother to me. I was an orphan though my mother lived and breathed. The slaves shunned and punished her believing she went willing to the covetous man. She suffered that indignity alone and silent in her shaming."

Sheriff Ben clears his throat calling all eyes away from the stricken woman and to the drifter. "Tell us how it happened that you left your master's service."

Welcoming the relief, the orator reclaims his place at center stage. "Well sir that is a powerful curious tale in itself, and one I'm happy to share with you. As I said before, the carpetbaggers came and looted the house taking the master and his family away. I was able to save myself and this slave girl."

"And the Rolls Royce," Ben adds.

"Yes, the car too."

"Why didn't the carpetbaggers take the master's auto?" The woman probes regaining composure.

His smile is laudatory, "That's because I drove the car to the gully back of the house and covered it with brush so they'd not find it. Those greedy bastards would take that fine auto if they found it."

"Then you knew they were coming and had time to hide the car and prepare yourself?" Ben observes.

"Yes sir, that is a true story, and it was right clever of me if I do say so myself."

"*How* did you know carpetbaggers were coming?" the woman demands.

He pauses before answering, "You may not know it but gambling always involves hard spirits that loosen tongues and one of the gamers said he heard carpetbaggers were coming South looting, killing, and taking anything they could sell for liquor, so I prepared myself for what was to come."

"You prepared yourself by hiding your master's auto?" Ben asks conversationally and the orator nods agreeably, "and by taking the car title and one slave document from the master's safe?"

"Well sir, the way you phrase that is not kindly at all. It is downright unfriendly if you ask me."

"Which I didn't. My question had to do with *intent*, relating to that car outside, and this woman you brought with you who bears *your mark*." Ben softly hisses the last two words.

"Now see, that's just plain discourteous and judgmental the way you say it."

Ben cocks a brow coldly, "I'm in law enforcement; I'm not paid to be polite when questioning a suspect."

"A suspect? Suspect of *what*?" the orator demands.

"Theft of an automobile, theft of a slave. Selling out your master and his family isn't against the law in this state, but such treachery is reprehensible to good folks everywhere." The orator lowers his eyes but can't hide his unease at the direction the discourse is taking. Watching close by nature and training, Ben observes the orator casting about for an escape route, looking toward the door by which he entered the room. He feels more than sees Jacob's casual vigilance and winces at the thought of Michael's upright sword. He casts the front door option aside seeking a back exit and, for the first time sees the burly man standing like a wooden statue with a proprietorial air near the counter by the door leading to the back.

"You haven't met Smithy have you?" Ben asks tipping his chair back on two legs. "Smithy is a legend hereabouts because if he hasn't got the part you need, he'll forge it for you and it will fit better than the original. That Rolls need any parts before you take off again?" Silence resounds. "Since you will not answer my questions, I believe the lady has a question still unanswered. Do her the courtesy of giving her your answers while you consider your options."

"She's no lady," the visitor snaps.

"You don't treat her like one, but that's a whole other measure altogether, and by my lights you are a far piece from measuring up." Ben uprights his chair with a crack that echoes like a shot causing the man to jump anxiously. "Let me refresh your memory, the lady asked why you didn't save the master and his family. She asked what happened to them when the carpetbaggers came and took them away."

"I don't know," the orator sullen snaps.

"You don't know? Or you think it's safer to ignore the question?"

Hester steps to Ben's side laying a calm hand on his shoulder, "perhaps I can be of help Ben." She says pleasantly, then turns to the man. "Tell me about the master's family, were there children?"

Her conversational tone is disarming and the man readily replies, "yes, mam, he had four kids, three girls and a boy, he was right proud of those young ones."

She smiles "how old are they?"

"The boy was nine or ten, I guess, the girls were seven, five, and three, fine looking kids they were."

"You speak of them in past tense, why is that?"

The man starts, "because they were taken away with the master and his lady, I've not seen them since."

She nods "so in your mind they won't have aged in the six months since you left with this woman?"

"Well, yes, mam, they will have aged six months since then."

"What do you suppose happened to the family after they were taken away?"

"The carpetbaggers are beasts of a nasty nature, they'll have sold them as slaves is my guess."

"Slaves?" The cocoa woman gasps, "You sold them into *slavery?*"

"I done no such thing! I ain't responsible for what lawless carpetbaggers do."

Hester rubs her chin thoughtfully and observes: "I notice when you speak to me you use proper English as I imagine a butler at a plantation house might do; but when you speak to this woman you brought with you against her will, you use common language, why is that do you suppose?"

"I – I didn't notice."

Bobbing her head she observes "yes, I have detected that pattern in people who only respect up and always *dis*respect down." The woman catches Hester's eye and gives her a shrewd smile. Only Hester's eyes smile. She turns to the man in aged brocade. "Why do you think the family will have been sold?"

"They are used to eating well when they're hungry. An army moves on its stomach. The Yanks pay well for fresh food, the greys have nothing but confederate paper," he spits the words. "Soft potatoes with roots are worth more than a whole *box* of confederate money."

"I see you make it a point to be well informed." The man nods eagerly. "You said you thought the family was sold into slavery, who would purchase a family of soft plantation owners as slaves?"

"Uh –well – there are men who like fresh meat, and the master's girls were pretty young things."

"Oh, my poor sweet babies," the woman moans into hands shielding her mouth and leaving her eyes unmasked to clearly see the horror of the man's words and deeds.

Doc eyes the man as he clarifies with fierce candor "not just the girls, dear heart, the boy too."

"No-o-o-o!" She wails a supplication and denial. "No, no, *no!*"

Doc nods his misery "and the mother, and the father as well."

"*No!*" The woman screams. Jumping from her chair she stamps both feet and yells "*can* – I - kill - him?"

"He's not worth it, woman," snaps Counselor taking her arm and pulling her back to the chair indifferent to the tears now staining his jacket.

"Ben," Jacob inserts from across the circle, "maybe you could let him make a break for it and then you can shoot him trying to escape."

Ben grins "tempting, but it's not happening on my watch. Keep the Archangel on alert though."

"Oh like he *ever* sleeps?" Jacob grumbles grinning.

Hester rolls her eyes and turns back to the visitor. "Tell us about the car and the one slave you saved, why did you chose to do that?"

"I needed the car, and," he winces "the girl mattered to me, I care about her and her safety."

Hester can't make her brows *not* arch, "*Safety?* To have her blood sucked by a man who stole her, claims to own her, yet calls her *daughter?* Curious kindness you offer your kin. How much money did you get for selling the family to the carpetbaggers?"

"What?" The man snaps.

Hester shrugs indifferently, "I'm curious by what motivates a man like you, who claims no integrity nor morality, yet pretends to be a good and thoughtful man. Were you ever an actor?"

"Yes," the man smiles broadly "how did you know?"

Hester's brows bob in surprise, "Mother always said I was psychic," she says dryly, "perhaps that's it."

"Could you tell my future?"

Hester replies in solemn exasperation "I don't think that's a good idea today." A giggle arises in the circle followed by a chortle, then a guffaw and soon the circle is laughing and slapping their knees in glee.

"What's so damned funny" the orator demands red faced.

"You, that's what." The elder sister growls as she rises from her chair to stand before the orator. "Any fool can tell your fortune today and safely predict that you won't like it. Hester's no fool, *fool*."

"Well I ain't talking to you am I?"

The younger sister blasts from her chair to leap defensively before her elder. "*Don't* speak to my sister like she's a slave!" Her eyes menace, "or I'll *bite you* and I'll spit your blood in your face. Maybe you can use your bat tongue to lick it off and *drink it*." She hisses. "It may be your *last* supper." The orator turns a bilious green before her scalding threat, and searches the circle for a friendly face or a pair of soft eyes. Finding none and possessed of a consuming passion to be anywhere but here he calls plaintive to a nameless god who, surprisingly, comes to his aid in the form of a dragon sweeping him from his chair and into an infinity beyond the roof of a local Feed and Grain store.

"Well, whoda thunk it? *Another* dragon rider!" Settling back in his chair the man says, "Let's give points like this is a rodeo and him a bareback rider."

"He's got no experience riding bareback. I'll give him two minutes tops before he's dropped in the dirt." Ben growls, "Smithy, when *are* you going to sweep this floor again?"

"When a dang bunch of farmers quit tracking in plow dirt and grain dust, when I ain't busy all day fixing broken parts or forging new ones because your trucks are too old to have replacement parts, when…."

"Okay, okay, Smithy…," Ben grins behind a hand, "don't get your dander up, I'm just asking."

"Smart *ass*-king if you ask me," Smithy growls a surly smirk.

"I didn't, but thanks for sharing." There is a chortle, a giggle, then a snort, and soon the circle is laughing and hooting until Smithy can do naught but join, his barrel chest blaring like a blast forge. When the circle settles to return to watching the dragon flight, and calling points or penalties but no one keeping score, someone asks: "when you plan to have my transmission repaired so I can drive my truck again?"

"*Repaired*? Your truck is so damn old there are no parts to fix it anymore so I'm having to forge you a whole new transmission. Ya otta just get a new truck," he grumbles sotto voice.

"Hell, I'll do good to pay for the transmission rebuild let alone a new truck."

"That's what keeps me up nights worrying."

"You got a *forge*?" The woman asks short-circuiting the staple squabble.

Smithy looks around the circle for the voice and finds it in the face and eager eyes of the cocoa woman. "Course I got a forge, that's why I'm called 'Smithy.' I had a real name once, but I plumb forgot it. Why do you ask?" he looks into the eyes of the woman and gives free rein to his puzzled curiosity.

"Do you think…, I mean, could I…?"

"Spit it out, woman," he says with feigned vexation.

"Do you think I could make glass in your forge?" she asks in a rush of words.

"*Glass*? Why on Gods earth would you want to make something as common as glass?"

The woman flushes lowering her eyes timidly, then inhales and raises bold eyes to meet his. "Because I want to make beautiful things out of glass, and I need a kiln to do it." Her lip juts determinedly.

Smithy's curiosity flares like a heated forge and he asks as calmly as possible, "*why?*"

The woman blinks puzzlement and has no reply. Smithy shrugs contorting his face into perplexity, then rephrases his question *"what* do you want to make in glass?"

"Beautiful things – I already told you that!"

Smithy's head bobs and his eyes go round. "What *kind* of beautiful things do you want to make?"

"Oh," again she is without words to speak her dreams. Her face wilts, her eyes well for the weight of an idea that will not be cramped into words. "Have you any shop paper?" She asks instead.

"*Shop paper*?" Smithy repeats baffled.

"Yeah," she frowns, "brown paper you wrap things in when you sell them."

"Of course I do, there's a roll of it behind the counter." She beams a smile, jumps from her chair to dash behind the counter. "Did you *ask* if you could use some of my shop paper and I missed it?" He scratches the back of his neck to hide his mischievous grin.

He hears the woman's hands plop on the counter. "Can I *please* use some of your paper, Smithy?"

"Sure, how much you need? And what do you need it for?"

"I don't know how much. I will use it to draw things I can't say in words."

Smithy's eyes round and his brows raise. "Oh," he says to a circle of grinning curious faces. "Reckon you'll be done by the time the stranger returns from his dragon ride?" he wonders.

"Don't know. Why, does it matter? You got some charcoal?"

"*Charcoal*? I got a forge, woman, of course I got charcoal."

"Would you show me where it is?" Smithy laughs the way a father might at a trying daughter asking too many questions without answers. Rising he passes the counter waiving a brawny hand to the woman and hears her scampering after him. *"Daughter, whoda thunk it? And me without a wife."*

"I reckon you'll wants sticks of charcoal if you'll be drawing things that can't be explained." She arches a brow and tilts a grin. "And I reckon you'll want hardwood charcoal so it don't break unless you want it to. You know how to tell hardwood charcoal from soft wood, like cottonwood?"

"I sure do," she replies studying the charcoal sticks "hardwood burns slower than soft wood and is more black than grey like soft wood is," she says fingering a grey stick that crumbles at her touch. She then touches a black stick and picks it up with a brilliant smile. "This will do for now."

Smithy reaches into the ash pile to pick out more black sticks tucking them into a paper bag and handing her the bag. "Just in case you have a *lot* of things you can't tell but can draw."

Her smile is brilliant, "Thank you, Smithy, you're the best!" Raising to her toes she plants a kiss on his cheek and turns away quick so as not to see him blush. "Ready?" she asks pulling him along in her excitement to draw imagined beautiful things. "How about chalk, you got chalk?"

*I might just follow you anywhere you lead*, Smithy grins, then laughs and says "I got chalk too." Back inside the girl woman scampers behind the counter and begins slashing flowing curving lines on the sheet of shop paper totally losing herself to the heart and art of creation.

Curious at her focus, the Regaliaed One rises and walks to the counter to see what she draws with such power and purpose. Despite herself she sighs a smile disturbing the woman who stops mid stroke to look at her. "Oh, I'm sorry. I didn't mean to disturb you, but this is stunning. I couldn't contain myself. Finish dear, please finish. "May I watch if I promise to remain absolutely silent?"

Across the room Counselor chortles, "My darling wife, I have come to believe that it is utterly impossible for you to remain silent for any length of time. You even sleep out loud."

"Oh hush! Telling bedroom tales in public, shame on you." Though her tone is severe she makes no effort to hide her smile of shared pleasure with her husband. "Wait until you see the birthday gift you will give to me." Turning back to the woman she asks "you *can* make this in crystal can you not?"

The woman grins. "I can *if* Smithy will let me use his forge to make glass and blow the pitcher, will you?"

"That I will," Smithy agrees readily. "You *do* know how to use a forge don't you?"

"I sure do, Smithy, and before you ask, I know what I'll need to make glass, all of which is easily found, sand, soda, and ash, the ash can come from your forge." She grins impish "Can I have some of your *ash*, Smithy?" The room erupts in glee as Smithy's face reddens but not from laughter alone.

"Let me introduce myself," the watching woman smiles, "I am the Regaliaed One."

The woman blinks doubtful and says, "Your *name* is *Regaliaed One?*"

"Yes, dear. You would have to know my dear departed mother to understand such a curious name. It's not worth telling. Call me RO, like everyone else does." Touching a corner of the page, RO asks "may I?"

"Not yet," the woman blocks her hand, "it isn't finished." She smiles caressing chalk onto the paper pulling highlights on the round bowl and pouting the lip of the pitcher.

When she is done fixing and finishing she nods and RO takes the page and turns to walk to Counselor saying "Look, darling, at the birthday gift you will give to me."

Counselor studies the charcoal and chalk drawing for a long while and the woman holds her breath through the silence. "That is exquisite in its gracefully simple lines, it is no wonder you like it, but my dearest RO, could you lift and pour from a pitcher made of crystal *and* filled with your lemonade?"

RO strokes his cheek fondly "well, darling, if it's too heavy for me, then you will pour for me won't you?"

Counselor smiles up at her "I would walk to hell and back for you my dearest," he says. "Yes! I will pour for you, and I will pour making certain each guests has a clear view of your exquisite pitcher and they will be as envious of your birthday gift as they already are of your luscious lemonade." Hearts soften in the circle seeing the unabashed affection shared between the couple, and each silently pledges to love their mate with more genuine warmth and good humor.

"I must see the drawing" Hester says rising from her chair to step behind Counselor and peer over his shoulder. She is soon joined by others who also do not speak but smile in silent wonder.

"Pass it around so all of us can see" demands a sitter.

"No *way* is that happening!" RO replies. "It's drawn in charcoal and chalk. If someone blurs even one line or shadow I will have their head on a platter." She grins cheekily, "just like Salomé. I'll bring the drawing around so everyone can see."

As RO steps away, Counselor rises from his chair and walks to the counter. He leans across to whisper: "What you have created with charcoal and chalk on paper is not only functional, it is art. Although the piece is utilitarian, your work *will* command the price of art. When you have completed this piece, you will make my RO's birthday gift. I will set your expectations by paying you the price of art for both pieces. Thereafter, I will teach and coach you so that *all* of your glasswork is sold for the value of art."

The woman stares at him openmouthed. Fatherly now, he pats her arm, "The next thing you make for RO will be even more priceless," he breathes, "It's a thing she's wanted a long time and could not find. It will be a one of a kind." His eyes follow RO with an adoring light, then turn back to the silent woman to add, "RO had no way before today to have her vision made manifest. *You* can do that, and as God is my witness you will be paid its worth. Even if I have to work another decade to keep my word to you." He grins and pats her hand, "It is already done." As Counselor returns to his chair, Smithy hears the woman pull another sheet of paper from his role and smiles a heartfelt smile. *Whoda thunk I'd probably have a profitable glass forge instead of a make-ends- meet metal forge? The wonders of the Lord are boundless.*

### Return of the Dragon Rider

In the midst of the milling circle of friends, the orator plops unceremoniously to the floor from which he was swept puffing mighty bellows of air into and out of his lungs.

"That was quite a ride you took there, fellow." Ben comments, "For a while I thought you'd fall plumb off that dragon and be lost in space forever. Catch your breath and tell us about your ride." Eagerly the milling group returns to their chairs and settles in again, expectant eyes fixed on the returned rider.

"Well, sirs and ladies; that was indeed a unique experience and one I fondly hope never to again have."

"Was it bad?" the cocoa woman asks, concern gentle in her voice.

The orator studies the one he cruelly used and sees nothing but sincerity. He shakes his head smiling. "Only at first when I was hanging on for dear life and knew that dire dragon was doing all in its daunting power to unseat me and ditch me forever on some god forsaken planet. Which he did do, in fact.

"The first sunrise on that petite plain planet, the dragon chastised me right proper for abusing animals *so callously. His* words. I defended myself for I was the master's horse trainer, many of his horses won championships, and brought extra income from stud fees. The master had an eye for spirit power in horses; that he did. I was an important part of his success. Well that dragon filled its lungs, I feared, to shoot flames at me and burn me to a carbon crisp. Instead, he just thundered at me. Have you any idea what a roaring dragon *sounds like* in deep space? My ears hurt just thinking about that bellowing voice. My heart pains me remembering the lecture he delivered into my face at blow your hair back force and power. That daunting dragon *demanded* to know whether I had trained the master's horses with *equal* insensitivity to the body, *mind* and hide of the animal or if I had somehow, simply forgotten how to be sensitive to other living creatures than horses. Singed my hair ends it did, gave me a dark leathery tan in seconds. The dragon demanded I say honest and true if the only thing that mattered to me was the way *my training* showed up in the obedient body and mind of the animal; and, well, it was.

If something else mattered to me, the dragon demanded that I name what it was, and why it counted for me. Well that got my back bowed up and I informed the brute beast I was one of the *best* horse trainers the South ever produced. Thought I was bragging that dragon did, demanded I prove it. That set me to thinking about some of the horses I'd trained and recollecting the ways I talked to a new horse while I fed, petted, admired, exercised, groomed and curried it. I'd tell the horse all the amazing and lovely things I saw in it, and when they were preening and proud and eager, I'd set them to a run or another task to test and prove the speed, grace and pace. I did the same with the dragon as I talked, and soon enough all its scales were unruffled. I threw an arm over the dragons back while I told of doing the same to a horse to let the animal experience and practice the new and strange in a safe way. I scratched it soft where muscles connect, palming over the smooth shining hide and the long muscle of the legs; and just when I thought the dragon and me were bonding, real snotty like, that demon dragon demands to know how I can make such claims having torn a *dozen* of his finest scales from his back and shoulders. When he let me on his back again I did see not *one* damaged or dislocated scale on the bitter beast. He'd made his point though. And I proved mine or I'd not have been allowed on his back. *Fine* beast that one is, scales the color of morning sunshine and moss in a deep clear pond, with eyes of red and gold. What they say about dragons spitting fire from their mouths, I never saw that, though his eyes spit fire that burned through my heart and down into the roots of my soul. Made me weep. When the dragon saw my tears it gentled a bit and demanded I tell *how* I could tame horses to reins, saddle and rider, yet could not ride a dragon without ruining its *fine precious* scales.

"Well you don't have a saddle, or reins that I can see," I snapped back defensive and just as snotty.

"Oh like you'd have *noticed* anything but yourself?" the dragon snarled. That took me plum aback. I was speechless for the first time in my life. "*How?*" the beast demanded again, so I told him everything I did with a horse before I ever lay a blanket on its back as gentle and tender as a mother covering a sleeping babe, all the while doing the same with the dragon, whose heart is touched, I can tell. Now I know that dragons have hearts just like every other living breathing thing on God's green Earth, and on other every living planet and star beyond it too. It all made me smile, but that wee planet was as cold as hell is hot and my cheeks was plumb froze to ice. So I talked to the dragon warm and gentle and sweet just like I did the master's horses I trained to ride and race. That dragon took pity on me and puffed up his chest and cheeks, and I thought I was about to be scorched as hard and brittle as a lump of coal. Instead, that gold and emerald being puffed damp warm-hot air down on me and my wee planet until rain fell and grass sprouted and bushes and trees full with fruit hanging ripe and heavy on its branches, and rivers sang and splashed and played in an atmosphere much like other planets close to the sun, all warm and balmy it was.

But not a *hint* of game anywhere on that whole new Earth. Well, folks, I do like the taste and chew of meat so I complained to that dragon that evening. When he came back the next day, and every day thereafter, the dear dragon brought fresh meat of small birds and game, gutted clean as a whistle, and that marvelous monster carried them in its great mouth where they baked and broiled to succulent perfection in its juices. Thought I might like to stay there, but the dragon had other plans. I slept on that small paradise for seven nights, and every sunrise the dragon came to set me on an errand for the day and to prove it, I was to bring a token. Each sunset the dragon came for dinner and a chat.

"You weren't gone more than 20 minutes," Ben protests suspiciously.

"True as that may be, sir," the teller grins, "still I spent seven mornings and evenings on that island."

The room silently puzzles the teller's tale against Ben's fine point of time. "You seem to know a bit about the first Book of the Bible," Ben allows. "Tell your tale. There's a storyteller in you, and maybe you don't know that yet." All eyes return to the tale teller.

"Where was I? Oh yes, my first day with, or actually without, the dragon. We had a nice brunch, fruit, berries, tubers with grains and herbs, and we talked friendly like. Then without so much as an if you please, that brute beast grabbed me up in its claws and flew me up and away, dropping me in a small round boat without sail, mast, oars, or rudder, in the midst of an ocean with no horizon and only a hazy half-light to see by. Of course there was nothing to see, that being the first day of creation. At sundown the dragon came with food, and asked me to tell about my first day and what I'd learned, so I told him about the boat, which bored him *angry*, he seemed to think I was a complaining ingrate."

"*Imagine!*" The woman says politely.

He gives her a narrow look and returns to his tale. "I told of my day, not mentioning the feather; and there was little to tell without the boat and the endless sea in the tale." The teller grins impish, "So I'm making up stuff that might have happened but didn't, to fill up the hours from sunup to sunset, and all the while *not* mentioning the feather. The only interesting thing that did happen. At that moment the feather poked me in the head in protest for being ignored, or worse, forgotten." He laughs remembering the squirming impatience of the dragon over the forgotten feather.

"Unfortunately, I *still* don't know when to leave well enough alone," he can't suppress a giggle. "I baited the dragon until it wanted to bite my head off but there was the feather flashing fascinating contraries in delightful designs and he didn't want to damage the feather. He wanted it as his token of the day, and he wanted my experience of it. He didn't want to bloody it and gross it out.

"I live and breathe solely for the reason that I am to *strongly* warn everyone I meet against *ever* baiting a dragon." He shudders a shivering snigger remembering that he got away with *not* giving a token to the dragon and lived to tell the tale of seven sunrises and sunsets with the dragon. "As you know, on the first day, the Creator separated heaven from the earth and divided light from dark. Source made duality that day. That's it! And he saw it was good *because* without opposites things don't show up in physical form. All creation was ideated that first day, including that wee boat without oars, sails, or rudder where I found myself adrift on a sea without horizon in an infinite silence that echoed and reverberated with no sound at all. Silence whispers into the omnipresent ear of infinity and the dragon nowhere in sight. Though calm, I had a hazy foreboding of a forgotten mission needing completion by sundown and the niggling notion of a token I am to give the dragon at sunset. Since I had nowhere to go and no way to get there, I set myself to grasping the Divine Idea behind dividing light from dark and the essential duality of energy inhabiting physical form. The very *idea* of life in form invokes duality into creation inspired by the idea. That must be the lesson the master dragon wants me to take from his *already stupid* game of days.

"As I ponder alone and adrift it occurs to me that duality is essential to the physical world but isn't to the Infinite. The infinite has polarity, but not duality. But what's the dragon token if duality is the message of the day? I ask myself and fall into deep thought so focused I don't see the feather dancing, spinning and weaving about and above me and my boat, one half black, one half white each with a dot of the other, one at the top, one at the tip. As the apparently white feather danced and twirled it caught the light of day and the dark of night spinning and swirling the opposites into endlessly shaping possibilities of form, design and delight. *The dragon token*, I think. At my thought the feather shrank away, a ghostly ghastly ghoul howl of black horror and fright white. I couldn't help myself, I laughed out loud, and that flustered the flighty feather whose India ink black feathered part bled into the white of its pattern."

"Well then," I said to the fuzzy feather, "I see you have *costumes* to fit your mood. You change the pattern with your mood. I'm curious, what *do* you wear when you decide that you are a simply precious one of a kind creation, you *love* that, and you think it is perfectly true and suits you *just right*? If I could have been in any one of a dozen different universes to see and experience thousands of new and wondrous things, I'd trade them all for watching that feather fluff her stuff in crisp quick mosaics of black and white. '*Oh* my!' Is all I can say and she is suddenly shy. "You are the most brilliant thing I have ever seen." I'm thinking I'd found the perfect dragon token and I say: "The dragon will love you and prize you as a fluid flawless emblem of the first day of creation when God separated light from darkness. You are light *and darkness* in molten motion, a worthy token for the dragon on the first day of re-creation."

"It's all about you isn't it?" The feather sniffs turning away and showing mostly her dark side.

"You too," I retort. You *are* a feather after all. Nothing more than that either *if* no one ever sees you to appreciate you *and* your magnificent mutable manifestation."

The feather flutters into other possibilities, then poses pleasantly "where do you suppose your dragon pal might wear me? And do you think he will let me find my *own* place to ride his hide?"

"I think the dragon will let you find your own proud place *so long as* you make him look good at the same time. *This* dragon would wear you proud and display you as art. Dragons live forever you know. It is *good* to have a way to be your most amazing self, and a forever place to show yourself proud." Well, that about settled it for the feather drifted down and corkscrewed itself into a curl of my hair. Yeah, I know my hair has no curl, but then it did, and I'm telling you what happened, nothing more.

At sundown that day the dragon came and we had tea and talked of the day. All the while the dragon is studying the feather in my hair more than listening to me, so I commenced making up words and talking like I had something to say until the dragon caught my eye, raised a brow, and says "You are talking stuff and nonsense; and it offends me deeply that you think I won't notice." He sniffs his snit and thunders "What did you learn today, and where's my token? In that order, if you please."

"On the first day of creation, God called for light and saw that it was good, then God separated the light from the darkness covering the surface of the deep and called the light day and the darkness night. It occurs to me that

Spirit, first cause is without form and is forever integrally whole and therefore *must* have little functional awareness of *being* in a separate habitation the way a human has a sense of being in a physical body. Spirit just is. That is enough.

Except it's *not*. There is no *experience* in beingness, it just is. People *need* things to do, goals to achieve, things they can do to make the world a better place. They need understanding and will to deny habitual responses so better experiences show up in life. That's why Spirit created a shadow self that is *capable* of facing the polarity arising from inhabiting a mind with a conscious awareness of self that is separate from everything 'out there.' Everything is *intrinsically* at-One with Spirit, but man has ego mind that's wholly convinced that it is and forever will be, separate from everything else, including The One That Is.

"My dear dragon, the feather is the token of the day. And, *she* wants to find her own place to adorn your great scaly physique. Are you okay with that?" I demand letting on I wouldn't give it to him if not. It was a dumbfounded dragon that heard those words. The small skull beast could *not* comprehend a thing, anything, wanting to make it beautiful. Dragons may be magical and wise, but they are not smart. Well, finally, after a flighty flirtation by the flying feather, the dragon succumbed and let the feather find its place and enthusiastically welcomed it aboard when she suggested she perch on the ridge above its third eye and swing down before his great eye to show him all the options and both sides of decisions. *I will make you known as the Wise One among dragon kind for you alone shall see what I show to inspire wisdom and understanding in* every *decision, choice and change that comes. And,*" she hisses "*the one before you will see* only *a white fluttering feather, you cynical skeptical serpent.*"

The dragon apologizes profusely until the feather appears appeased and takes its place, then popped a few sharp poses, cocked me a brow and asks *"How do I look?"*

"Well, folks, sore tempted I was but I didn't grin or laugh. I wrestled both grin and giggle into a sincere face with a mouth saying in earnest awe: "you look *magnificent*!" The posing dragon freezes, cocks me a brow over a blasé eye and snaps "I *always* look magnificent. How do I look *with* the fabulous feather?"

"Even finer than before, and I *thought* that would be impossible," I said with a sincere straight face.

"*Don't* make that mistake again," the dragon drones dreadful, and I obey then and forevermore. The short story is that the dragon got his feather for a token and decided to be simply delighted at the idea of the feather choosing its place of adorning, beautifying and flattering, yes, he liked *all* of that, such a powerful and provocative serpent. Thus day one ended in peace and happiness.

"The dragon returns the second sunrise and after breakfast, sets the day's task for me, which is to understand and apply the Truth of what God did on the second day of creation, why God did that, and tell how that applies to me and my life, and, oh yes, bring back a token of my day's enlightenment. Then that sinister scaly serpent caught me up in its claws to fly far and fling me into the free floating coracle on the formless sea midway between never and forever. On the second day of creation, God separated water from water and set an expanse, between the water above and that below, and he called the low expanse water, and the firmament he called heaven. I could tell the water under my boat was liquid because my boat floated on it and it made my hand wet. I knew the water above was atmosphere, air, because I could breathe it. That got me to thinking that the water below represents the expressed capabilities of the subconscious mind which cannot think, but can ideate. So, the subconscious mind *needs* the conscious mind to decide on the idea and then to will and declare the word of it, thereby directing the idea to the subconscious where it can evolve and be made manifest. Something like the dragon marinating meat in its maw until it is cooked perfectly for eating.

So there I was the afternoon of day two with the idea and with no clue of a dragon token. I let that puzzle stew in my mind just like the first day while I had a wee nap in the boat and dreamed that a single drop of water coalesced from the sky above and fell into my boat at my feet. I sat there looking down at that drop of water and I saw an ocean in the drop. It surprised and delighted me and I spent a small eternity lost and contentedly adrift in that ocean in a drop.

"Until that danged dingbat bird came cross and cussing about some feather she lost the day before. Real calm like I ask the bird to describe her lost feather thinking it's a white feather because every feather on her body is white. Sure enough that dull bird said it was a white feather just like her other ones. I know she lies, but play along to see where she'd lead. I told her true and sincere that I had not seen a white feather before she arrived brilliantly full feathered with the ones she sought after. I said that if she was missing a feather I certainly couldn't tell because she looked perfect and perfectly handsome to me. Well that set her to preening, but I could tell something wasn't right with the bird and it wasn't physical, she was *lying* sure and clear. *Why* though? I decided to play her out and ask her to describe the missing feather in detail; and, as a kindness to me, to tell me why she would even want a missing feather back since she was perfectly, stunningly beautiful just as she stood. One more feather, I said, is *redundant*, it would spoil her peerless perfection. She pouted anyway, silly bird. I ask her again to describe the missing feather so I could tell the dragon about it and to tell why she wanted that feather so much. Which she did do, in *dreary* detail, not saying a thing about *anything* but a white feather.

"I was *really* wary now. Enough that I forgot all about the dragon's daily token and pulled my newly narrowed eyes from the gift potential of an ocean in the drop to the cawing bird flying stationary above me. "First, you must describe the feather to me in detail, and then explain to me *why* you are being so *simply rude to me* who never did you one single harm in all the moments you have known me! Well I may as well have hit the bird upside the head with a two by four for she commenced gasping, flapping and squeaky cawing screeching until she plumb run out of wind and fell like a boulder into my wee boat squashing the ocean in a drop, the way eons of heat and weight and time will do to a diamond. That transformation of substance was hot enough to blast the bird off and into the sky with such force the hot rock dropped from her thigh and into the ocean sinking into the infinite blue.

My dragon token of the day was gone, beyond reach and recovery. Dragons don't forget. And they have no functional grasp of linear time. When the dragon came at sunset, he met the mean bird and heard her criticism. The wise wyvern cocked brow, set a cold gold eye on her, and asked why one missing plume was so important to her she'd beard a dragon in its den for a solution.

The wise wyvern knew she'd lie. And if not lie, she'd at least not tell the truth, nor even drop a hint she knew the changeable nature of her feather.

"The..., the feather is..., um, white, all white." The white bird titters nervous and shakes a wingtip at the feather suspended over dragon's third eye. "Like the one in the middle of your head," she tries not to snap her beak but snap it does.

Dragon eyes up at feather, gives it a private grin and thought whispers *good job!*, then turns his wicked eye and a grim grin on the fat foul saying with a sad shake of his head "I'm afraid I can't help you, I have seen no pure white feather such as the one you describe.

"There's one on your *head*, you doltish dragon!" the hot hen retorts, losing her mind and jeopardizing her head in the bargain.

Dragon's eyes narrow and he purrs his in a way that sounds scarily like hissing "*why* do you want *my* feather which you sorely *abused* by dumping your dark angry thoughts and feelings into this *one tiny little feather;* and now you say you want it *back*? So you can abuse it more than *before*?"

The bird blinks owlishly three times in a futile attempt to process what the dragon said and the effect of it. It doesn't compute. "Oh!" she flaps wings in exasperation, "you don't get it do you, you myopic monster. What you see as abuse was me *honoring* her among all my feathers by preparing her to live well and prosper in the physical world where she will go, but I will not. Have you *any idea* how long it takes pure-as-the-driven-snow *me* to gather enough negative energy to make even one small dot of black on a feather? Oh, that won't have occurred to you will it, a wee small head on a gigantic body *can't* hold much brain can it?" The bird is teetering on the edge of insanity lost in the *story* behind her tightly coiled anger and the giddy power of *finally* having a place and an occasion to say it.

Sounding miffed the dragon snaps back "there's no need to be cruel or to say offensive things about someone you never met before." Leaning an elbow on a knee the dragon rests his chin in a paw and invites, "So tell me, why you went to such effort to collect *dark energy*? What will you do with it?"

"Easy for you to ask, you have enough darkness in your small claw to create massive black holes housing *dozens of* eternities." She peeps at the dragon whose jaw still rests in a paw, his maw set in an amused but patient smile, waiting for a reason, watching her feather flash mostly black into its third eye, and the bird takes another tack: confession. "The truth, you see," she says, "That one feather of all my brood has a dream of living on a place called earth that she says God will create on the fifth day but I'm just a mother so I don't know these things. My fine feather wants to be a bird God will create that day to fly above the earth and to sing joy songs every morning and evening.

"Well that's a noble cause," the dragon notes, "perhaps I can help."

"Help? You? How?"

"You can have some of my darkness. As you said, I've more than enough for one *infinite* dragon lifetime to feed your, oh wait, it's *my* feather. My forward looking feather that already has enough darkness to live long and prosper on the earth that God will make. What's an *earth*, does anyone know?"

"Read Genesis. You'll get the whole story there." The bad bird barks.

"Acting superior *always* makes me cross;" the dragon hisses, "and I'm *already* annoyed enough with you for abusing your feather, to broil you whole and eat you for dinner." The white bird goes a ghostly shade of pale and shivers in her pins as the dragon lounges into a more comfortable position and orders:

"Tell me about this Genesis story, especially the fifth day of it, and I will forget that you were mean to me."

The bird swallows hard. Three times, to finally get what she *really* wants to say back down her craw. She takes a deep breath, hits the high points of the first four days of creation, then tells the riveted wyvern about the Great One creating hoofed, clawed, and winged things on the fifth day, the day *her* feather would fall to earth to be a bird. Sighing a satisfied smile she ends her tale in rare peace and silence.

"The dragon's eyes narrow in thought. *The dim bulb bird thinks it's all about her like she's the center of the universe and all in it so the narrow eyes must signal anger with her.* The bird shivers simple silliness. The dragon rumbles: "Why don't *you* be bird that goes to earth on the fifth day of creation?"

The dumbfounded bird needs a moment to process that she's not on the dragon menu before she can process the idea the dragon presented. "Me?" she peeps, "Me go to earth as a bird?"

"Why not you? If not you, then who?"

"Oh. Well then, what sort of bird would I be?"

"A patio pigeon?" offers the dragon dryly.

"What's a patio?"

"I propose you become a parrot" I interrupt before the dragon can answer the patio question.

"What's a parrot?" the bird asks squinting in an effort to imagine one.

"I smile, I can't help it. I reply: "Parrots are magnificent birds with feathers in any color you can imagine and long bright plumes on its wings, tail, and head." Seeing her uncertainty I add: "It's better than being insipid snoozing snow white like you are now."

"I'm a beautiful white!" she protests petulant.

"Until the dragon puffs hotly "*who put all her own darkness* into this one small feather!" He inhales to cool down and adds sweetly to the bird, "If you'd kept it all yourself you'd already be a *fine* pigeon!"

"Don't ask," I order the pigeon, "you don't want to know." I assure before she puts a foot in the dragon's mouth. Her bird brain processes the sight of a mostly grey bird with bits and starts of black and white. She discards the image and the impetuous idea of perplexing a petulant dragon. That ended that.

The dragon took the white bird as his token for the second day naming her his assistant in mother *his* feather, and practicing its duality wisdom in preparing for the fifth day of creation and her debut on earth. The day ended well, but the petulant parrot wannabe would do naught but cluck over the trials of tending a feather she couldn't *reach* without being perilously proximate to a dragon's maw.

"On the third morning the dragon came with broiled game and we had our breakfast feast with fruit and grains I'd gathered the evening before and when we'd had our fill, the dragon asked me to tell about the third day of creation, so I told about the Divine One dividing water from dry land and causing earth to produce seed bearing plants and trees each seed according to its kind. The dragon nods agreeably, then clutches me in its claws and wings me back to that coracle adrift on a sea now separate from land and drops me there. That fine boat charts its course and soon lands me on a beach where honeymooners will one day go to begin their together lives in idyllic bliss and beauty. Before I set foot on the beach I knew that green is God's favorite color because every bush, tree, herb and fern were alive with greens of every shade and hue. Seeds are the third day gift of creation and the dragon's third day token.

"The abundance and variety of seed bearing things stopped me stunned. *How do I know and learn the seed for each seeding thing? Some are in pods, easy enough. Some in tassels of grasses, some cloaked in plump fine fruit, some nested deep in the earth among the roots of that green seeding thing? How do I collect and carry them? As thought staged this way, a woman gowned in green rises effortlessly and steps from a moss lined pool to move on a scented breeze to where I stand. She smiles and confides, "You ask the plant to reveal itself and all its power and vitality to you in a way that you will clearly know and remember the truth that each plant willingly teaches when you hear and speak its unique language of love. Do not be concerned over how you, in your puny mortal mind, will remember all the Wisdom I teach you. For the way I teach is by entering into willing oneness with you and you with me so that all my wisdom is already* your *wisdom. Your training is only, and vitally, to guide you in finding and loving the relationships of your life, to help you remember again with the truth of why you* chose *those interactions this time in which you live and the problems you came to find and heal in your walk of life on earth. Look around you, choose a plant that appeals to you, first with your eyes to see its shape and drape and the quality of its colors and the way it catches sunlight and rainwater, what it smells like when you're close and when you are far. When you are surely in love with the plant and honor its gifts and values, only then ask about her seed. When you love and value her seed much as she does, she will gift you with her seed. As is true with first love, in an abiding way, it is always first and for forever even though you will love another one plant and her seed, and then another. Each love is always first and forever for a plant and its seeds. You will easily and quickly collect the seeds you need for the dragons cache. Plants have short memories, lots of abundance consciousness, and an excess of love. Each mother will give you the perfect carrying pouch for her finest seed. All you do is ask and receive with gratitude.*

"I gave praise to every seed and root, and to the mother plant that gave it because the third day gift was one any man in his right mind would receive with humble and effusive gratitude from his sister wife on their marriage day. And so, the dragon token for the third day of creation was prepared, packaged and given by earth mother herself. When the dragon received and then explored his third day token he was squirmy pleased as a puppy being praised and given treats. When he left as the sun sank sanguine into the sea, I imagined that acquisitive dragon would spend his time visiting and seeding distant planets with his fabulous mother gift. The tale teller smiles reliving the sunset and imagining the dragon creating and attentively seeding lover's beaches with scented sensuous scenery and delighting in gratitude for the judiciously generous Earth Mother.

Into the celebrating silence the young dancer softly says with an infectious giggle "I saw the dragon seeding the beaches, and raising and planting mountains to gather and share life water with the Eden gardens he imagines and makes real." She adds with a shy girl grin "I spent time on one dragon beach, and a cabana boy brought me a lounge chair and fruit drinks whenever my glass was empty. I want to spend time on *another* dragon seeded island with maybe the same cabana boy."

"Daughter!" Counselor cautions, "you do understand your mother and I will go with you do you not?"

"Me too!" Says elder sister rushing to gush with her giggling sister, "but I want my own cabana boy."

"Daughter! Counselor restates to the elder dancer daughter. "*Why* did we have children, RO? Remind me again for I have forgotten and cannot name even one persuasive reason to have…"

"*Don't* say it father." The girls command in unison each clapping a hand over his mouth. "You *mustn't* say the words you were thinking, even in exasperation with us for imagining something wholly new and pampering, I haven't been pampered properly since I was a *baby*, daddy." Now she grins wicked, "In addition, you'd have to buy the tickets anyway."

Counselor chortles daughter delight and notes "The power of the purse, I still hold that…, for now."

"We *love* your generosity, Dad, we delight in the ways you please yourself by pleasing us, *after* mother, of course!" They roll their eyes, smiling all the while. "We wouldn't trade you for any other dad." The girls lean down to plant a kiss on each cheek. "Look, he blushes, that is *so* cute." Giggles one, then the other, enticing everyone in the circle to join the fun, even Counselor. Returning to their seats a dancer prompts the tale teller, "Day four…, hit it."

Grinning, the orator returns to his tale, "On the fourth day of creation God formed the greater gold orb and the lesser silver one and placed them in the sky along with all the firmament of stars, and then God divided light from darkness. He did that so he had a place to put the sun and its bright light, and a space to put the moon whose silver light reflects the sun's spiritual light into the night here, where humans abide, where the ghosts and goblins of our fear come in, and out, to play. See, the great gold orb of the sun is a symbol of spiritual light. Mother moon represents personal human intelligence, the intellect of man that can only reflect the light of the sun, or the son, either word and meaning works. The silver moon most intimately discloses Truth to mortals in our darkest hour, for only there, can the bright light and truth of Spirit be safely revealed to man.

"The star represents the first awakening of man when he apprehends and expresses the wisdom and power of the indwelling Christ Spirit. Just as the morning star heralds the light of the rising sun, so does the star of the mind first reveal the way to the wisdom and glory indwelling the son of man son of God. I got silver a star for mastering that fourth day lesson, it was dropped into my boat when the evening star first appeared, and that would be the dragon token for the fourth day of creation. That dear daft trivial dragon was by then *so* ornamented with bling things, feathers and trailing plants, that he went into a wardrobe tizzy just to deciding where to sport the star token. That great goofy wyvern was beginning to look *disturbingly* like a boy scout wearing all his merit badges.

"The dragon returned at sunrise on the fifth day wearing all his tokens (except that batty bird, which I *sincerely* hoped he'd basted and we ate, but I dared not say so) and when our repast was done he set me to my task for the day, and, as unceremoniously as ever, dropped me with a plop into my wee coracle that promptly spun about and headed for a distant speck of land so tiny I wasn't sure it was land at all, but maybe a mirage you see over water, or ghost dancing over land so flat you can see the curvature of the earth.

"Well on the fifth day of creation the Creator made the water teem with living creatures and created birds of every feather to sky wing and sing the sky and the trees and to my absolute delight my coracle delivered me with a soft thump and slide high up on a beach while I was caught up in a wave raised by a giant dolphin that caught me when I fell overboard and dove me deep in its fins breathing water as easy as it breathed air above the waves.

"Me? I was in utter that grew apace with each fathom the dolphin until we reached the deep floor of the ocean where the dolphin dropped me to walk about with the same ease as walking on land and breathing air, and *not* water. The ocean is a rich fertile place teeming with food of the sea that lives in a circle of life knowing that the one who eats is at one with what is eaten and what is eaten is assimilated and eliminated as the ideal food for another thing living in the sea. Assuming I needed a picture, Sea Mother spun her wheel of life showing a moving picture of one of the wondrous ways Sea Mother lives and thrives on manifesting abundance. It probably helps that Sea Mother can just as easily raise hard harsh energies that roil through and above her waters while she clears away a clutter of overly exuberant life forces accosting Earth Mother, and wresting from her what she willingly, and must, give freely and of her own accord.

"Mother knows man who cannot receive cannot give and is destined to take, and in some measure, to take by force and with anger. Guiding man through polarized dualities of the physical plane reveals the symbiotic balance of the Divine Law of polarity. It is a passion purpose of Sea Mother. More than anything she wants to teach the high heart art and key of *receiving* generously from a heart teeming confidence and forever full with delight. She wishes more passionately than anything, for man to find within himself in abiding consciousness of abundance knowing beyond doubt that all giving and receiving is meant to be equally sweet and joyful.

"It was Sea Mother who introduced me to the dragon's token for the fifth day of creation when she dropped me into a crab hole where I not only got my toes snapped but also found a hermit crab in my hand, looking up at me with round blue eyes (I didn't know they had blue eyes), like it knew me, like it knew I was the one meant to receive and to deliver its message. Before I could get proud for being a chosen one, the suddenly not-so-retiring crab informed me I was its *delivery boy, not* its messenger. Let me just tell you now, you can't out-crab a crab. After a mini eternity with the contrary crab I finally got it! My job, the hermit persuaded me, the one and *only* thing I was to do, was to take the confounding cross crab to the doubting dubious dragon and give it as my dragon token for the fifth day of creation.

"Faced with no alternatives, I opened a vest pocket invitingly and held it for the retiring one until it tucked itself securely in a pocket corner at the very instant I was whisked up and out of the water, into the coracle and slapped into a seat just as the boat rotated ninety degrees and zipped away toward a wee speck against a pulsating sunset with light rays shot like a great golden fan across the horizon.

"Much to my surprise the dragon was not pleased with my daily token and bellowed full blow at me: *Were am I to suppose put another fine ornament on my already exquisitely jewel encrusted, feathered and vined body?* The dragon leaned down eyes are level with mine and hissed: *Did you ever think about me? About how time consuming it is to* deal *with all these gewgaws and gems you bring every* blessed *day of creation?*

"Well, ladies and gents, you will be proud to know I kept a straight face, biting the inside of my cheeks bloody so they couldn't move to betray me. I kept my eyes down like I was well chastised so he wouldn't see my mirth. I was doing fine until my chest began to heave with the force of repressed laughter. The dragon asked: "Are you *crying?*" duly anxious and unsettled. That did it, I giggled, chortled, cawed and I croaked my glee so he could not see. He did see. And hear. He was not amused. Demanded that I explain myself, which is a *very* demanding role even for an experienced actor such as myself."

He catches and returns grins around the circle, then, with a palm up shrug, he adds: "I told the dubious dragon exactly what I thought of its consciousness. I intimidated the daunting dragon.

"It is unlikely that anyone ever had the temerity to grab the dragon by the whiskers, look him in the eye, and demand his gaze and attention. What *if*," I snarl soft, "you did *everything* you did with a keen sense of how it *might* affect people and trees and crops and streams around you when you did it?

"One day they'll call a space of a consciousness like yours a slash and burn or ground zero, and survivors will report the number of deaths that occurred there.

"You, my dragon pal, are *not* here to create a ground zero. You need a shift in perspective. What *if* you stop being controlling and let the token of the day choose where *it* would like to lodge in your commodious hide?

"Let me tell you what's in it for you, *witless wyvern*. That will help you decide that you *do want* to let the hermit crab choose its own place to hide. Hermit crabs *like* not being seen. You have no room to display a hermit crab properly." The dragon is dubious so I add the *piece d'resistance*, "They eat fleas."

"Crabs live on sand, what fleas…?"

"Sand fleas." I snap, "Hermit crabs love them. Dragon fleas are probably not *that* much evolved over sand fleas, although you *totally* deserve bigger, hungrier, and meaner fleas than other creatures. Now shut up and watch." I hold the hermit crab on my palm moving it close to the dragon's chest, slowing as it moves to my fingertips. When they're level with the dragon's heart the sand crab jumps off to wiggle and tickle below a dragon scale over its heart where it finds a momentary fill of its favorite fulsome fat fleas. The dragon purrs like a kitten evidently approving his choice to let the shy crab pick and choose the then current site of its Movable Feast.

"I love this crab," the dragon declares, "It's the best gift you have yet chosen and given to me."

"What if you offered the same compassion to yourself? What might change if you could say with equal sincerity that you love yourself? How would those changes show up in your world? The dim dragon didn't get it so I shouted at him like a *very* disappointed dragon rider and I might *never* again ride a dim bulb beast that couldn't stop navel gazing long enough to connect some dots that *go beyond* his belly and crusty hide.

"I demanded to know *why* a *real* dragon never applied the power of Imagination, or the gifts of the Divine Feminine to see, share, invite and inspire *her* evolving vision into the Divine Masculine. How *else* do you expect to excite your masculine aspects and choose and will to evolve and give birth to *one* loved and inspired new outcome?

"The light still doesn't come on in the dragons loft so I say preacher like, "It is a simple choice. Would you *prefer* being an uncommitted, know-nothing toothless dragon, or a dragon who has and does choose and serve its rider at the need?"

The dragon blinks a long silent while then says "I never thought of it that way. So how does this work, who teaches who what?"

I frown fierce and fiery "We teach each other and we do it spontaneously and respectfully, or it doesn't happen. You can go back to whatever pit you hole up in, just *take me home first*."

The dragon leers a grin "where's home?" He frowns, "*Why* do you want to leave before sunset the last day of creation? It's all the time we have to master ways to ride the wind as one being in two bodies.

"Home is here the heart is, I guess. If I ask you to be my wing-man do you know what I mean?"

"That I am your eyes, ears, and senses for what you cannot see, that I guide guard and protector when we go where you cannot safely go without me. Do you know what it means to be a dragon rider?"

"That I am your eyes, ears and senses for what you cannot see, that I go where you cannot go, and that I do for us all the things I can do but you cannot do. And, I do *not* live with you.

"Deal," the dragon slaps his hand on a rock narrowly missing the sand crab, "oh there you are my little hungry one. I didn't mean to scare you, I didn't know you'd jumped off me, here let me give you a lift, show me where you want to stop and burrow awhile." When the crab is settled in, the dragon yawns and stretches, "I and the little one will be off for the night, sleep well, we'll see you at dawns early light.

"At dawn the dragon returned and after we ate and chatted, the dragon sidles up to a boulder, settles itself, and tells me to climb up on the rock, which I do. I'm standing high enough to step over and onto its massive shoulders where the wings connect. I see my boots are new, soft leather soles and uppers to my knees. I hoped the dragon would let me keep those fine boots I'm still wearing my butler's shoes. Disappointing. Where do I step aboard?" I ask the dragon.

"Watch," the dragon replies commencing to raise and lower the elbows of its wings until I see the foot sized spots hollow on either side of its spine. The dragon looks at me with a full scale grin – disturbing – and invites me aboard. I step on and get the feet feel of his muscles as he raises and lowers wings, and rotates his head. Without him telling me to I drop my hips and ride his moves on my thighs like a jockey crouching in the saddle to ride balanced over the stride of the beast.

"The dragon steps away from the rock so I can feel and ride the muscles that move him over land. When that great beast began to raise, lower, tip and tilt its wings like it was flying I whooped a glee giggle. The dragon ran, flapped its wings and leapt into the air, waggled its cheeks to raise his black whiskers and slap them into my hands. Soon we were at cruising speed. I thought that. Until the dragon told me a true dragon rider would use his feet to guide the dragon to what he wanted and where he wanted to go.

"Oh," I say and gently heel my right foot into the right wing control panel, leaning right, lifting the right rein and, as the winged wonder raises into the sky. Curving my right shoulder back and up, I suck rarified air into my lungs, let out a whoop of wonder and joy, and in that instant the dragon joins me. I could feel the rumble of his laughter through the soles of my shoes.

"On the morning of the sixth day I got see my options for the day, and I heart chose the precise place where the big butt bird shaped a diamond and dropped it into the sea. My feet told the dragon where I'd go, and when we arrived, the beast shrugged me off its back and I fell headlong into the sea where a laughing dolphin caught me on its back, turned a wise eye on me, and plunged us into the depths below clicking, clattering and chattering me into a calm state of wondrous wonder at the bounty and teeming beauty of Mother Earth in her role of Water Keeper.

"I thank Water Keeper for letting me breathe liquid air and for the wise guiding company of her dolphin through my fathom fall through extravagant abundance of color, shape, form, and motion. The dolphin took me into a cavern shaped like an open clamshell. In the distant depths of the grotto a pearl glowed. Except it wasn't a pearl. It an open mouthed clam that held a pearl glowing from its core with iridescent light.

"Before that moment my hand never *wanted* a thing but my palms *ached* to cup that pearl inside them. I raised my eyes from the pearl to the eyes of the clam, old, wise eyes that spoke to me in feelings and thoughts reading me through and through. *Why this pearl? Why you?* Mother Clam posed and for a time I knew no answer. She knew it. She swept me up into her eyes so I could see me clear from *her* mind. Disturbing. And just the disturbance I needed for forever and a day, for I always thought of myself as not measuring up, not being enough, *always* lacking, always a day late and a dollar short.

"The man I thought I was had no *right* to touch this Pearl of Great Price and know the true value of it. Humbling. The son of man must follow the path of the Son of man and meet the death of all he holds dear to create a space where he loses his EGO and regains true Life. The man I'd become returned the gaze of Elder Mother Clam and asked *what makes the pearl so brilliantly clear and iridescent?*

"*A diamond,*" she sighs. "*It fell into our sea the second day of creation, and I took it up and swallowed it. It didn't suit me. Irritated me cruelly. I did what clams do against irritants, I sheathed it in nacre layer by layer day by day, every day of my long life.*

"Uh – it's the *sixth* day of creation – you ate the diamond no more than four days ago." Her wise eyes are wise to me and do not appreciate what she sees. Even the dolphin turns away like he never knew me and had nothing to do with my being in The Grotto of the Clam Queen.

"That *is* assuming the seven days of creation are 24-hour days." I add. Her eyes are withering. I whine like a punished pup. "Please, continue your tale, I see no less than a *quantum* of layers of luminous nacre on your pearl of great price.

"The clam leers a withering grin and probes "what will you *pay* to take my pearl?"

"I – I – I – have nothing," I say turning my pockets inside out.

"What makes you believe that *things* can purchase a pearl of great price?" The Mother Clam drifts into Dreamtime where time does not matter, and I go there too. There I learn the true worth and purpose of time lies in *not* putting linear limits on it. When I'd served my time and otherwise proved myself worthy of receiving, I told Mother clam that if she chose me, I would receive and deliver the pearl of great price to the dragon.

"Turns out Mother Clam knows the dragon and spewed the pearl into my hands in her dying breath. Humbling. I had my sixth day token for the dragon, all I had to do was get back to that far island where the dragon would meet me at sundown. The cheerfully devoted dolphin chattered a traveling chant, lifted me on its spine, and wave rode me back to my wee lush island to await the dragon and present my sixth day token."

The Tale Teller bows his head in profound silence awhile, "The dragon didn't come at sundown. I sat by my small fire in the solitary dark, dispirited, bewildered and bereft, now a Dragon Rider with purpose and no dragon transport to ride to its fulfillment. I rage and wail and moan, and in my angry tears I meet my father again yelling telling that I'd never amount to a damn, and that as lily livered as I am, I am no child of his; and I am small and powerless and alone again with my inadequacies. *What is the function of a dragon rider without a dragon to ride?* I wail bereft into the eternal still silent empty void of who I think I am, and as I sit abandoned alone watching puddling stars. They lean close and sing to me.

Shawn Gallaway – Shining Star

As stars sing and I re-member. I *forget* who I think I am. I plumb forget, not a memory thread left. Maybe who I think I am simply doesn't matter anymore. Maybe all my data points of self no longer connect into a scenario where I keep on being who I always was. Whatever the source, I had to start living like I want to be and express my true *I AM*. With stars listening close and playing a healing air, I'm thinking how I'd *like to be*, who I'd *admire* being, and *why* I'd admire being such a man.

"With no prelude at all, I *am* that man. I *do* admire him. On the Holy Instant of *getting* that functionally, I decide I will. If I am being given a chance to revision and reinvent who I think I am, I *am taking* it.

"At sunrise on the seventh day a spot crosses the face of the rising sun. With no data points to apply and nothing else to do, I wait to see what came of this odd sun spot. I see wings of the serpent emerge from the sun-shadow-spot, riding rising ray waves of light on its trajectory to me on my once again idyllic island. At the call of the dragon I respond, but not from my head. I leap on a nearby sunbeam, dance along it awhile, then quick step left to an adjacent ray and stride confidently from ray to ray until I meet the dragon in the heart of the sun on a new day of creation. We were One for the first time all over again. We speak of feats and deeds and dramas of the sundry paths and detours we see, choose, and walk in each and every One Holy Instant of time. The dragon asks *"Who do you think you are?"*

"I am breathless as a newborn and remain so until my body is bereft of air. The body itself must inhale to live and so I do. Over and again. That gave me a kick start of oxygen to ride on, and I *choose* wisely and responsibly *now*. I follow the Code of the Dragon Rider – which I somehow know by heart – to do with faultless faith in the One Source of All Life, everything that comes before me to do *this day,* even the acts and deeds that are *preposterously* beyond my ability. In authority of truth I know the answer and I reply with calm confidence. 'I AM a dragon rider. *Your* dragon rider. I came to change the world. I cannot do that without you because without you I cannot return to the world to be *able* to change it. Will you carry me back to the Feed and Grain?

"Sure thing." The dragon agrees, "Seventh day breakfast first. I brought a special treat for you, you will be pleased. It's something you *cannot* live without." The dragon pulls from his mouth a splendid small crystal goblet without a stem that catches and arrays rays from the rising sun. Turning away, he pours liquid into the cup, turns back with a *'Ta-da! Your favorite treat,'* and gives me the crystal chalice.

"I smile at the deep red richness of the wine and in gratitude, raise the cup to my lips already pursed for the first sip, and I gag, I retch, I puke, I spew, I hack and cough until my nose spouts like Spindletop before it was capped, until there is nothing liquid left in me. With seeping red eyes I take a gallant look at the piquant liquid and retch again until I cannot breathe and fall boneless to the sand. There I unleash and release all the tears of my life that I never cried before. I crawl to the surf wanting the odor washed away and there I collapse and heave more until I am gulping as much sea water as I'm spewing puke. Before I drown the watchful wyvern hooks a claw into the waist of my pants and drags me from the surf to sand still wet with my tears.

"When I can breathe again, I bawl and blubber over the EGO lies I believed and lived over my span of years. The agony of my sins of omission and commission and my obstinate fall from grace, my error thoughts and their outcomes, all are ghosts of the undead rising to dance with me while the dragon watches.

"When I recover and heal from boogying with my boogeyman bad guys, I lumber up, shake off the sand, and sit to talk with the dragon about the song of the stars and what I learned from it. After I confessed my sins, the serpent gave me the penance of practicing atONEment with my *sins*. He informed me that *sin* is an ancient archery term meaning to miss the mark, in this case, Oneness with the Source of Truth.

"AtONEment?" I sputter and the serpent launches into actually, a *rather good* lecture on the evil men do under the sway of accepting as true that they actually could fall from grace and could never recover. *Grace,* He explains, *is an eternal gift eternally given and forever actuated by the asking. There is no qualification, not one, of deserving, winning, or earning it. We exist and have our being in grace, yet we are more truly accurately, innocents unaware, caught in the fast hands of an angry god.*

"Did I say this all happened at sunrise on the seventh day?" Several in the circle nod. "The sun tarries awhile to watch what follows. I had to tell the dragon how every one of those mean petty nasty small thoughts came to serve me. "*Serve me?*" I shriek.

"Indeed they do. How?" The beast settles serenely into an easy slouch, lays its head on a paw to wait and to watch until I solve his puzzle.

Well folks, dragons may live forever, people don't. That is a vital thing to remember when working with a wyvern, particularly one who is probably a *Sensi* master warrior dragon or ascended master with no *concept* of space or time. I set myself to the dragon's task and a trivial eternity later I parse out all the *good* things about everything I once thought was bad about me, my life and the whole world as I knew it. The dragon then set me to the task of making all the things I named 'bad' come out of me and take a form so I could see and talk with them, and they *did* that!

Real stern like I ask each of my bad actors to tell me exactly how have served me. The short story is that *every one* of them said they came to protect me from the things *I feared* might, could, would, should, or ever *had* hurt *me*. They came to *protect me* from what I believed was true about me that I denied and repressed. I ponder the mission for a brief eternity, then thank my inside actors for their wisdom and service. For that loyalty, I gave each of them their freedom as a parting gift.

"They protest that they do not want to leave because there is nowhere else for them to go, they were formed from *my mind*, my beliefs and my fears. They are mine. They live in, always have done. I pretend to consider this and soon I feel their anxiety, for it is *their* fate of 'freedom' or 'protective service' I'm deciding. I rub my chin and I say '*if* I let you stay you must tell me *how* you will serve me in future'. They huddle awhile, and ask if I'm willing to experiment, to try thinking of as like dials and gauges on the dash of an auto. They are *not* there to alarm the driver, but to give *alert* to what should be done to keep all things working silent and smooth."

"Well *done*," the dragon professor approves. Sitting erect now he asks "Where's my sixth day token?"

"I give the dragon the glowing orb, and this time the enamored beast does not complain about excessive adornment but sets about placing the pearl on various parts on his body, head and paws, and liking *all* of them. With wisdom in my journey kit and no time for a navel gazing dragon, I hop on it like I always knew how to mount a dragon, and I ride that mythical worm like I always *was* a dragon rider. *This* darling dragon is, and becomes part of, *my own self.*"

In the profound silence that follows the dragon rider tale, the cocoa woman murmurs timidly, "What was in the crystal cup the dragon gave you to drink?"

Tale teller emits a bilious burp "blood.

"Human blood." They a share look of horror and without thought, the healing woman eats his pain, tasting the weight and hate of the daily dramas of his history, his story. She knows why he came to feed on the blood energy of others. Silent she asks to know why he came to see himself so needy of what lies outside of him that he blinded himself to the wealth that lies within. He is blinkered. His first semi-sane thought is: *I am a dragon rider! And you are dead on to my habit of quick offence and harsh defense. Retaliation in small doses.* He scowls tasting the gall of his bitter bile, *administered with a hard heart, fast fingers, and deniability.* He knows she heard. Nothing changed. Except *the pain is gone, almost as if she ate it.* You *did* eat it. She nods a wee wise smile. "Teach me," he whispers, "I *really* want to do that."

The woman starts back protesting "You didn't ask me to stop, or to know what happens to me when I eat your pain. It's all about you. You have no spare thought for any other being, man nor beast."

He eyes her, cocks a brow and replies, "If you taught me to eat pain, I would gladly eat your hard habit of thinking of yourself last and projecting your ever-last belief onto others. Then this conversation never happens because we have no pain left. We'd be holding only sweet and joyful memories that would weave into our mythic tales. That is my *only* hope when I'm back home fessing up to my Truth Ghosts," he grins, "while you stay here doing good, right and beautiful things. Yours is a better story."

Her smile is thoughtful and slow as she says "Maybe I *did* teach you to eat pain because I have none left. I am free as a bird and high as a kite. It's *all* good." She eyes him long and asks "what changed?"

Tale teller wells with emotion, sighs, and replies, "It was the star's song, *Shining Star,* I could not feel alone, nor even imagine being separate from anyone or anything. It felt so good and right, so true, and real, that I *chose* to believe that, and on my will, I changed. Listen..., and you will hear...."

| Shawn Gallaway – The Wind is Always |
|---|

Into the silence that follows, Time says, "I'm supposed to give you something from the dragon," he places a fist sized pouch in her hand, from which she draws a crystal goblet with no stem. The newly confirmed woman releases the anger reserved for the Great Deceiver that housed in the small hard heart of the man who would be Time. "Thank you," he says softly. "You should know that the dragon requires, and I will, go back to recover the family and their possessions, and return the Rolls Royce."

Across the circle the dancing daughters huddle and whisper, both sets of eyes round on the tale teller, "let's go see what's there," they nod agreement, rise, and walk to bend before the man, who squirms under their inspection. "I told you there was something there." "I told *you*," the other counters.

"*What's* there?" he asks covering his nose reflexively until a dancer slaps his hand away.

"It's a star. Wee, pale and indistinct until you remembered again with the saving grace of that sixth night when the star shone, twinkled and glowed like the first star, the leading star, the way shower star. Anyone knowing your star brand will clearly know when you fake truth or fiddle with facts or figures. I suspect the star looks like a mole then, a cancerous one." She gives him a pointed petite pout.

"Or," the elder options, "you can obviate that whole cancer scare by deciding to just let go of the script for your mean man self, stop investing your bright mind and light energy in creating *more* separation. Choose instead to just be and become a better man who is *worthy* of a living a good life. That means amending for the rapacious greed that led you to us in this place and time." She grins, "Oh, do remember to apologize to the dragon so he doesn't singe your tail feathers when next he sees you."

The eyes of the slapper sister narrow on his. "Think again about telling us the star song and the dire dragon drilling you with questions, and your responses to the wise wyvern. Just *think* about the feelings you were having and everything you were remembering and telling us. See, there it is again. Oh, how sweet, what a *divine* tattoo, and how telling too, for a clever tale teller."

"Oh," Jacob's head pops up, "I forgot to give you Michael's message that he left his master's mark on you. Said the mark was on the place where your bat body first made contact with the upright silver sword, and by this mark every man with eyes to see would know you and the truth of you." Jacob scratches his chin, "It seems that the way people see and know that truth proof could produce better outcomes, depending on you and your choices right now. So tell me, tale teller, will Michael's mark be an insignia of you and who you are, or an ugly abiding warning to be cautious in your company?"

The tale teller masks his nose and mouth below high arched brows, slides his hand slowly down his face and chin, remembers the man to whom the stars sang sad and soulful and sure and sure, he turns smiling eyes on Jacob and replies, "Well, sir, I do hope to meet that dragon again, as friend and master rider, not as piteous penitent; and I've a road ahead to travel that's littered with wrongs to make right, and rights to be won and celebrated. None of it can be done by the man I was. I'll be wanting to stay on Michael's Mark" he grins, "to best do, and to best undo, and all of that."

Into the hallowed silence that follows a voice calls: "I'll buy the master's slave," Smithy tips his head to where the woman stands, "and the tale teller trickster can take that money to the master too." He turns to Counselor "I reckon you can make the purchase legal?" Counselor nods, "and then, can you prepare her man-u-mission document, did I say that right?"

"You did, I can, and I will do all that is needful to make her free as the good Lord meant her to be."

"Well, former *slaver*," Ben teases, "I can help with the dragon's requirement that you see your master and his family restored to their home and life. I've been talking with the local law in Mississippi and they tell me the plantation house and barns weren't burned, some horses came back, some slaves returned and keep care of the house, farm and animals. When you go back with the gold and jewels you took and stowed in the boot of the Rolls. *Of course* I looked, it's my *job* to look!"

Ben grins, "it occurs to me that you can play the returning hero role and *maybe* get your old job back. "It is my *personal* wish, and I'll take it as a personal favor that you do all you can to persuade the master to legally free the slaves to leave – or to stay and be paid for their work."

"I'll remember your kindness Sheriff." The tale teller tips back his head to laugh at the curious turns life takes while you think you're managing it. "I'll call the master's horses along my way, you see I taught them to untie themselves from tie lines, to free themselves from stalls, and to come to my call. Never knew why I did that, but now I feel downright farsighted. I take it as my personal mission to win my family's freedom and see them safely back home again."

"On that note," Ben informs, "I'll give you an escort out of town and set you on your way to Mississippi; I've lined up mates along the way to keep watch over you and give you good speed."

"Thank you, sir, that's mighty fine help you give. In return, I will tell your mates along the way all the good news I find, and when I'm home I'll pass good news to the locals and ask them relay it to you."

"Deal." After they shake on the bargain, Ben asks, "What is the name that dragon gave you?"

"Time Turner, and I aim to live up to it."

"Good deal!" Jacob rubs his palms rapidly, "As you left on your seven day dragon cruise Smithy's clock chimed two bells." He nods to the clock, "Smithy's clock still says it's two o'clock. While you were out gallivanting around, we learned at least a dozen new dance steps, discovered an artist, saw her work, commissioned some of her art glass, and Smithy agreed, though not out loud, that the artist could turn his metal forge into a glass forge. Despite all that *time consuming* entertainment, Smithy's clock *still* says two o'clock, the sun still casts two o'clock shadows, and I for one, am six o'clock hungry. Would you *kindly* demonstrate for us what a Time Turner might do in an unlikely situation such as this?"

Time studies the unassuming face of Smithy's Big Ben wall clock, shakes his head and says "*that's* not the clock in need of righting." He turns away to long-leg across a nearly nearby galaxy to stop before a clock so towering tall it appears to curve back on its spine to admire an infinite blue sky puffed with cotton candy clouds and peppered with plump birds twittering and tweeting. The hands of the clock show two hours, same as Smithy's Big Ben. *Interesting*, Time thinks. Stepping to the cabinet he pulls a key from a pocket, fits the key in the lock, turns it, hears the click, and watches as the drawer slides open with a whispery whoosh and out steps a crane. The kind with wings and feathers. *Disturbing*! "What floor please?" the crane asks. "All the way to the top," Time replies and I does not know why.

Arriving at the heart of the mechanism he sees that it is broken in shatters and shards, and he does not know why. He asks, and the heart of Time responds: "I am Time," she wails, "I am infinite, everywhere present, even in the void where *nothing* is. Yet I am *required by man's* small concept of me to *only* move forward!" Time whines, "I'm the grandmother who lives too long in her estate while heirs and relatives impatiently await, or perfidiously plot, her sudden death. I am the temporal equivalent of *white noise*!" Time whines through her chimes. "I am used, scheduled, clocked and *measured!* I *will not* be proven!

I am *Time*! I am *eternal, without* boundary, form or dimension; my essence *cannot* be held in thought nor confined in concept. Ideas, now, ideas are formed by a brain firing neurons that have no shape or mass and no functional use for time. Ideas turn my key, they transport me, inspire me, give me utility, character, and cause; I can work with that. But," she glares, "I will *not d*ie! Nor will I be *man size* small! I took a work stoppage. It's an idea that will catch on. Until then, *Time is functionally dead*."

"Houston, we have a problem and it's bigger than eternities of neglected grandmothers. It won't be fixed by a crew of space techs, and while some ascended masters might help, there's nary one in sight.

"That's when I remember my name and I ask myself, what *would* a Time Turner *do* in a case like this? Well, I imagine such a man might sweeten the bitter tea Time's prepared for her solitary detention, so I start talking about all the things I admire about clocks and timepieces, the fine wheels and gears made of copper and other shiny metals, and how all hers need is a bit of cleaning and a nice oil rub. All the while, I'm doing what I'm telling her, so when she sighs a smile I ask "*doesn't that* feel better?*

If you take a quick peek inside here you'll see how much better you look too, why in no time at all you'll be humming, whirring, and tolling like a brand new clock. Listen to you, already purring like a contented cat. When I'm done here I'll polish your fine case and its fittings until you shine like sunrise on water." When Time chimes her next interval, she sings, intones, resonates and rings like a divine diva.

---

Shawn Gallaway – It's My Time

---

Oh, look, now Smithy's clock tick tocks too at exactly two past two.

## A Naming Convention

"You got a name, but I didn't," the cocoa woman praises and pouts in one expression.

"You got a name," come encouraging words springing on Luke's light feet. "I did?"

"You did. But it's not a christening name. It's the name of who you *are*. Your secret name known only to you and the One who gave it. Even though you don't remember it, you do know it."

"I do?"

Luke wears an assured smile for his dance around the one who does not know. "The dragons you rode spoke your name, do you remember it?" The woman shakes her head as he light toes round her. "What are the names the dragons gave you?"

She scowls, squinting, "They told me *their* names..., not mine."

Stopping his dance with a toe slap before her, Luke eyes her down, "*Stop thinking of a name suitable for a christening. Tell me the name of who you are.* What name tells *anyone* with ears to hear what you came to life to do?" The woman blinks thrice, and Luke enlightens, "Tell us the names of your dragons."

"Fre, and Edom," she scowls.

"Say it as one word," Luke coaches.

"Fre..., Freedom!"

Luke's smile is brilliant, "What did you do on that dragon pair?"

"I rode them."

"So you are...?" She eyes him silent. "Think *role* here," he jabs a finger at her, "*not* baptismal name."

"Freedom... *Rider*?" she measures for fit and beams, "my name is Freedom Rider, I *love* that name!"

"It is a name that will go down in history." Foresees Counselor. "Let's make history then. Time, you have a new name, one you have already proven, one that speaks well of you. Now that we have both names, we have documents to prepare and for you to sign."

"You're going to write these documents with a *pencil*?" Time asks aghast.

"It's a step up from charcoal," Counselor grumbles beneath a scowl. "What would you have me use?"

"You got ink?"

Counselor shrugs "Yes, and Smithy's probably got some, why?"

"Well, sir, if I can talk the owner of the fine geese keeping the sidewalks clean out of a feather, I'll cut and drill a quill pen for you to use preparing those *very* important papers you'll write today."

"No." Snaps RO. "You will not have *one* quill from my birds. You will need at least three. Will you trade me a quill pen for three feathers?" Time nods. "Come, time's a wasting, let's go pick quills, I'll introduce you to my girls." Time's eyes go saucer size as he mouths '*girls?*' then sprints after RO to pull quill.

"I gotta *see* this," Freedom says scurrying to the door, "it could be more fun than a calf scramble and a horse race in one rodeo." Cheerful voices trail her outside where RO and Time collect quill. When three are chosen they politely ask permission of the bearer birds to have the feather, and RO deftly plucks them from the air as they feather to her, one tucking in one hand, another in the other, the third twining itself in a curl to waft and wave stylishly as she moves.

Time smiles stepping lively with her and asks "the large sturdy goose feather, that's the quill I will cut for Counselor, correct?" RO nods. "The peacock feather, that would be to make a quill pen for you, am I right?" RO and her feather nod again, grinning now. "The third feather who's that for?"

"Freedom Rider," RO replies, "*any* great artist needs finer tools than chalk and charcoal, although they have a place among fine art media. She'll need at least one good brush too, can you also make brushes by chance?" Time nods, and RO smiles "what would you use for brush handles?"

"I saw some bamboo growing in the back yard of big house and if you know the owner, and she agrees, I'll come at the lady's convenience and collect a stalk or two for pen handles."

RO chuckles, clapping Time on the shoulder, "Somehow I think you know the bamboo is in *my* back yard," she grins, "and the lady agrees. Shall we cut it now? It needs time to dry a bit before the bristles are set in. Shouldn't the bristles be sable, do you think?" Time nods. "Good," she grins. My fur has been *years* in need of redesign, and now my dear conservative husband has good reasons to spend the money." Time tips his head back in glad glee as a regaliaed woman guides him safe along his giddy grace.

With ink loaded quill pen in hand, Counselor proudly prepares to prepare identification papers for the ones with new names. *Freedom first*, he thinks, collecting the money to purchase a healthy slave from Smithy, transfers her ownership to Smithy, then prepares her manumission document for Smithy to sign. "What a fine pen to work with," Counselor praises, "and what fine work to do with it. Time, you're next, for identification documents right?"

Time nods, clears his throat, "That's right, sir; but I got to thinking about games of chance the master and me admire and that some of them have time limits when the time keeper calls "time!" and rings a bell. It also occurred to me that the master won't know me as Time Turner and," Time grins "he values and manages his time so well that he would not admire having to learn a new name for me. I will take the name my master gave me, James Butler." Counselor smiles and sets quill to parchment.

"Well, can we call you Time while you're here? We just got used to the name." Ben grouses.

Time grins, "That would please me well, Sheriff."

## The Scrying Bowl

"Well, *energy sucker*, Smithy *said* the forge would operate exactly the same way it does when he's forging metal, it just has to be fired at the right temperature to melt sand soda and ash into a molten liquid. And, Smithy said the tools uses for shaping a crystal bowl would not need to be different nor even used differently than for forming a bowl out of metal.

"Why you talking small-self talk to me? Like you're trying to make me feel small and powerless so you can bully and push me around like before. I think you pulled a fast one on that dense dragon pretending you no longer *can* feed off the life force energy of others, all the while swearing off only the blood form of it. Why are you coming at me like my whole internal committee of doubting ghosts trying to scare me out of being strong and whole and powerfully *truly* me? Why you bullying me, new born into a new life, with ghosts of an old life and your abiding faith in what I *don't* know and how small and powerless *I am*? Why you feeding off my life energy *this* way acting like you're not getting high on it same as drinking my blood? You pulled a fast one on that dragon but I am *not* fooled. You're an energy *vampire*. Curled up like a pill bug with your hard scaly side out, looking at your butt hole, and telling me it's mine you see."

The former Time titters, chortles, snickers, then admits, "You're right. I spent a lifetime hiding behind the role of butler and doing everything right so I couldn't be corrected, even if my motive was bad." He tips a lopsided grin, "and, it's also true, Freedom, that when the Mistress had a broken glass or bowl, she asked me to repair it and if it couldn't be fixed, to liquefy it and reform it into a new bowl, glass or vase."

He looks to RO, "I never put gemstones into the molten crystal of a thing I formed, and never stroked jewels like wet paint into the design of a bowl, I want to *see* that done, I want to *help* do that, I want to be part of making that real. If you'll allow it, I'd also prize having a good peek into your finished bowl to see what I scry. Can I please help make your bowl, can I? I won't stop until you say I can help...." RO's silent stare stops him mid breath. He knows that she masters greater power than he, she uses her power more compassionately; and she does not suffer fools.

"I take your point, *Ms.* Rider. It is ROs bowl, her gemstones, her money that pays for making it, it's hers to decide if and how I can help, and if I get paid." He turns to go and pauses, "Thanks for letting me figure that out for myself, and for the kindness of not telling me what I *should* do, like I'd have done." Freedom smiles and waives him away.

"It seems you have had some experience in forming crystal objects and in heating and firing a kiln to the proper temperature to achieve the desired result." RO's voice turns him back, "Perhaps you *can* be of help, and there is a condition you will agree to before I accept you as one of my helpers. The condition is this: Freedom is a free and independent woman, trained and gifted with skills you do not have; and she is a woman. If you assist in this art I will do through my assistants, you will be compliant wholly and solely to the call and to the command of Freedom.

"Know this: you *will* be required to amend and atone for the persistent and pervasive domination of women by men, the utter submission of self that is required by men; and, for the physical, mental, and emotional abuse imposed on women by men. Furthermore, you will knowingly and willingly submit to this requirement as a personal atonement for the abuse you ruthlessly inflicted on Freedom. You will serve only at her request, you will perform ably, willingly, well, and *always* obedient to her direction to the smallest detail. Do I make myself clear?"

"Yes, abundantly clear, and *that* changes the proposition doesn't it? Freedom could be hard on me and justly so. She might punish me and give me paid for what I have done to her, and rightly so."

He studies her and her look of patient observation, feeling her energy of waiting without expectation, to see what comes next. *Powerful*, he thinks, smiling at who he sees from behind Freedom's clear tolerant eyes. He searches for the words: *indifferent, to outcomes, but* not *to the process.*

Holding smiling eyes on her, Time inclines his head toward RO, "I freely submit to Freedom's direction for it will come from her heart and *then* from her head, where vengeance, and passion for perfection, dwells. I promise, Lady RO, I will do all Freedom asks the way she wants it done with everything I have to give." Time chuckles, "Freedom should have been the one giving orders all the while I knew her. I'd have been a better man for it. But then, perhaps I wouldn't have met the dragon and learned how, and why, to consciously co-create a better world. Plus, I'd have missed the song of the stars, and the despair of knowing the truth of what kept me separate and mean; and I have been less the man I am today."

---

Shawn Gallaway – The Sword and The Shield

"Well, that's settled then." RO says, "Smithy, will you turn your forge into a glass kiln heated to properly fire and form crystal while there's still enough daylight to get the job done?"

"Yes, I will, *Mistress* RO," he grins mischief, and gets an arched brow in exchange.

"I will want the help of our resident Crystal Master," RO continues, "and *she* will require support from her assistant, Time, and, Time, please do what is needful to soothe the Eternal Mistress of Time so every step in this creative process is completed in order, and my bowl is ready to receive pure water before the moon rises tonight. Come, Smithy, lead the way to your forge and make it *hot, hot, hot.*"

The man once called Time falls in by Freedom and whispers, "she didn't even *ask* if it could be done, or if the Mistress of Time *would* even cooperate."

Freedom rings true delight, "in part that is because you already met and charmed the Mistress of Time, but more so because RO could always manage time to a tock and a tick. I suspect there is a Magi under that fine regalia she wears, and," she backhands him on a shoulder, "I bet you the Lady RO was a time turner before you even met the Infinite Clock, found the broken Heart of Time, shined, timed and tuned the box and clock and everything in it until the Heart of Time was a thing of beauty joy in the multitude of ways her theatre of infinite multidimensional time is *magical.*"

---

Shawn Gallaway - Surrender

---

Time is mute at the elbow of the wise Master and willingly follows her path to whatever she will do to create a stunningly magnificent and mystical Scrying Bowl for a woman who doubtlessly passed more lifetimes as Magi than as a mortal. The next man to tell me it is right and proper for a woman to be meek and submit herself to her man, I am going to hog-tie him and drag into Smithy's to meet Mistress RO and the Lady Freedom. If a tea time with our mad hatters doesn't set his mind right, he's not worth spit. *Meantime, we got a magical bowl to make and I'm not missing one fleeting moment of the making.*

---

Shawn Gallaway – All Shall Be Well

---

Smithy's forge is a transcendently enchanted place when the Crystal Master and her helpers step into a jubilant space emergent with an energy potent in power, transformation, and radiant fullness. Smithy, as Forge Master of epic fire and power directs by thought and eye, the shape, height, width, color and heat of each tongue of flame licking the caldron red gold in its fiery fervor to *be* a place of regeneration and transformation. *Fire of the Sun, Father Sky, bless and receive this offering prepared for you to thank you for making our work of transforming common elements of Earth Mother into crystal pure, clear, translucent and true with the pure passion of your love for Earth Mother.*

*Earth Mother, mother of wind, water, fire and earth, we bless and thank you for giving of yourself to guide us in transforming a vision into a thing of weight, shape, form, function, and great beauty and grace. Thank you for the gift of vision and for your inspiration of Father Sky to lend his volcanic heat to make flow that which is fixed in elemental form. Bless us richly, deeply of your graceful eye and guide our hands as we shape this transparent liquid of you into a crystal bowl of power, beauty and grace.*

*We thank you already for guiding each of us and your Lady RO in flowing and forming the twelve stones of power into a crystal flower of twelve petals each of different hue. Lady Earth, use us to form a bowl of far-sight, beauty and power worthy of your own hand and eye. Thank you Mother. I feel your presence, I see you flow slow stir the glass, I see the dross ebb away like water into sand. I see the crystal clarity of you settling into the infinite indefinite space between water and sky. My heart is full with your grace, and my forge never looked, smelled or sounded better. Thanks for that too, from me to you.*

His invocation complete, Smithy steps to the right, extends a hand to Freedom inviting the Crystal Master to step into her role in creation. She gazes into the pot luminous with liquid light in a color with no pigment, yet holding all shades and hues. Inhaling long and being in joy with the moment and those to come, Freedom exhales sub-audibly slower still, and when empty of air, she extends a hand to Time to join them at the forge. She smiles at RO facing them to her left across the forge and feels the flow of strength and confidence coming through her. *It is already done,* she smiles, *and it is beautiful.*

Those working the forge act and flow as three minds in one with six hands devoted to one purpose, and one vividly evolving vision of the art of glass. As one they know when the shaping is complete and they step back to gape and smile giddy like parents of a new babe and it the only one.

"Lady RO," says Time, "if the bowl shape meets your approval, it is ready to receive and embody your twelve stones of power."

"Oh! I don't know if I can do this. I've never done anything *remotely* like this before, oh...!"

"Mother! *Stop dithering* and just do it, or you will never have a thing you *always* wanted, and is now within your grasp. You're playing small doesn't *become us*! We – and you – are *worthy* of better."

RO pulls herself erect, "Thank you, Dear. You're right, of course, how silly of me." Reconsidering, she amends, "how utterly *human* of me. I rather *like* being silly. First, my team, Smithy, you are my forge master who has found the perfect flame to shape and form my bowl." She pats his arm, "you will find and hold the temperature of the glass so it's pliable yet firm while we spell gems to feather fluid along the center ridge of each petal. Thank you my dear friend, for being the rock you are for me, for all of us.

"Freedom, you are my artisan, my art glass master in the making, you will be my other self, outside and apart from who I am and from the role I play in the life of our town. Will you join the energy of your art with Smithy's fiery power, and fuse it with the art of mine, as together we do this thing that's never been done before?" Freedom beams her willing will.

"Time, we, Freedom and I, need you to keep the wheel rotating at the precise speed that best supports the flow of our work over time. Be at one with us as we meld this act of creation into form." Time nods willingly into the bow of a knight submitting to an oath by sword in support of a higher cause.

"Counselor, dear, you have the pave diamonds?" He nods, pats a vest pocket, and smiles at her artful application of order and process to create the space for new possibilities and outcomes evolving into a firmament within a bowl of crystal tinted with the twelve colors of power and light.

Resplendent with twelve succulent petals of color etched to catch reflect and reveal the power of the other stones is strewn with spiral galaxies of pave diamonds. When the basin of far-sight is alive and poised atop the placid dais of Smithy's kiln and filled with rainwater, the full moon rises.

Moon beams reflect dancing patterns of pure silver light across the water revealing only sights and scenes evoking soft sighs and smiles. Perhaps most blessed of all, the bowl of truth foretells only mythic futures where even the bad is good and the only outcomes perceived and seen are holy and whole for the sole body of One. The Master smiles pleased, and lovingly caresses His Master's Mark into the heart of each one.

---

Shawn Gallaway – All Shall Be Well

## The Angel Garden Reunion

The meeting room of The Angel Garden is set up with two rows of tables ranked behind the podium at the point where the center aisle meets two columns of chairs with aisles on either side. It is an unusual set up for a Daughters of Isabella meeting and each Daughter entering the space notes the odd setup. They shrug for this is not the first D of I meeting to be unusual because by nature, women are daughters, mothers, and sisters. All Daughters know that Mother Energy is essentially different from Father Energy. Ergo, if both are here, both are needed, though no one knows why.

Yet every Daughter knows that RO called this irregular meeting. All know RO is President the D of I. They also know RO doesn't waste time, hers, nor theirs. Daughters, you see, are never obedient. But they are compliant. In the case of this special meeting, they are curious, and curiosity always gets the cat. Plus, it's an excellent time to gather and share gossip and speculate on unknown outcomes, like the purpose of the two rows of tables flanking the podium.

Anything new and novel is worth speculation. It's a guessing game for women who discuss the possible outcome of the various options available. Sometimes women even wager on them. Some men, they imagine, may suddenly change and be attentive, helpful, and devoted life mates instead of....

Everyone knows what's not said. They've seen bruises make up can't hide. They've seen underfed children, they've heard the bourbon bottles in the trash at houses were the wife is not seen.

None of that's happening this evening. The ladies put their handbags on a seat, reserving it for when the meeting is called to order, then return to the wit and wisdom of their sister Daughters. 'What do you think the special meeting is about?' and 'What do you think those tables are for?'"

"I'm curious about the *purpose* of this meeting President RO called." A Daughter says to another. All nod agreement. "RO doesn't do anything without a reason. And her reason is always a good and helpful one.

"That *means* that the Daughters have a key role in determining the final outcome of whatever purpose it is that this D of I meeting was called. Anyone ever play 'Clue'?" All Daughters nod with fond smiles.

"What clues do we have?" All Daughters shrug, palms up. "Oh look, RO is here at last, let's take our seats and learn what's going on."

RO steps to the podium and welcomes all to the meeting. "I called this special D of I meeting so I can tell each and every one of you things that you will not believe." She waits for the Daughters to deal with the paradox of duality and then, one by one, to slip back into their unity as Daughters of the One.

"I know all of you are wondering about the tables behind me, and why they are here, so I will tell.... No." RO amends abruptly, "I will *show* you what you will not believe without seeing it, not even when you do see it. 'Believing without seeing' is a core D of I practice. Tee, hee, hee, there is a Judas in all of us.

"Ladies and gents, what I am about to show you is impossible. It cannot have happened." She gives her Wise Woman smile and adds: "Yet there is physical *proof* that the impossible *did* happen.

"My question is: Are you willing to accept *proof* of miracles?" The Daughters nod as one.

RO raises a hand, snaps a finger, and smiling men enter the back door carrying baskets brimming with fruits, berries, vegetables, tubers, and herbs. They put them on the tables and fade into the audience.

"Can I – can we taste of what's there?"

RO giggles and says, "Not while I'm talking, dear. Every one of you would be chewing and smacking your lips, and *not* listening to *me*! That is *not* why I am President of the D of I."

She looks at the Daughters, at the Knights, then Bam and Melt White, without whose help The Angel Garden project would not succeed. *It wouldn't even get off the ground.*

*What a lovely tight devoted group of people you have brought together, Earth Mother. We must swear them to silence. You know how obedient daughters are, and their husbands, sons, uncles, and cousins.*

*All of us are necessarily involved. Lead us through this twisted twining way of secrecy so your objective is achieved, and remains secret in our hearts long after our work is done.*

RO smiles, invites everyone to take a seat, and when all are seated and attentive, she begins with a question. "How many of you are wondering why I called this special meeting of the D of I?

"Are any of you wondering why Knights are invited to a special meeting of the Daughters?" All nod.

"It is because we need you. Every one of you – to help with a special project."

"What's the special project?" Someone calls out. All nod curiosity.

"First, let's discuss the confidentiality requirement for this meeting. What we talk about tonight, the votes we take, and what we will agree to do, will be held in the strictest confidence within this group. You will tell no one who is not here tonight about this meeting and the purpose of it.

"And, you will tell no one what happens afterward. Are there any questions?"

"I have one, and I think I speak for everyone when I ask you why the secrecy, what are we protecting?"

RO eyes him levelly, inhales fully, and replies calmly: "We are protecting a miracle."

"A miracle?" It is a single question gasped as one by Daughters and Knights. It's awhile before everyone remembers that RO won't talk again until all of them are listening.

A command and control figure in the group shushes everyone, tells them to sit down, to breathe deep, and just listen, "or the meeting could take all night." Curiosity always gets the cat, and curious cats always get quiet to watch and listen, just like the perplexed people do. Peeps are curious cats too.

RO smiles as she looks around the room catching an eye and sharing a smile with everyone in the room. "A miracle", she whispers. She smiles when all are silent and listening close. "So what miracle are we protecting then?" She asks each person there. No one has an answer.

RO smiles: "We are protecting the miracle of The Angel Garden, and to do that, we need your help. Every one of you."

"Then The Angel Garden is the miracle we're signing up to protect, is that right?"

"Yes."

"For those of us who don't know, what is 'The Angel Garden'?"

RO smiles, "I thought you'd never ask!"

"Well", the man grins, "I like to help out where I can. After you tell us about The Angel Garden, then you will tell us what we can do to protect the garden, is that right?"

"I love a skeptic! It makes a dialogue so much more vibrant and engaging. Any other skeptics here?" RO grins and looks to the doubter and says: "You are in good company, as you can see."

Without looking, RO reaches back, feels for a basket, reaches in and grabs a red bell pepper, holds it up and tosses it to the doubter. She looks around the room and asks: "Any *other* doubters?" All laugh and raise a hand. Bam and Melt pass a fruit or vegetable to everyone.

It it's not quiet for a long while though no one is talking. The sounds of flavor savoring fresh fruits and vegetables fills the room, and oohs and aahs are the most discouraging words heard in the room.

"Any skeptics left?" RO demands with a smiles for everyone is shaking their heads 'no'.

"You may wonder why Counselor and I called this joint meeting of Daughters and Knights." Most nod, some recall and remember but wait as the impossible tale unravels itself into the whole unit of one. RO shrugs. "I told you we are here to protect a miracle. And that the miracle is The Angel Garden."

"Can we see it?"

"Not today, dear. But the *last item* on the agenda for our meeting is Bam and Melt telling true tall tales about The Angel Garden, and *maybe* best of all, they brought their instruments. Anybody up for some pickin' 'n grinnin' and some tall tale spinnin' *when we have finished the meeting* agenda?"

RO grins. "Otherwise I will have to call Counselor up here to keep us on our agenda. *None* of you want my husband to have to come up here and be snarky with the lot of you."

Counselor stands, turns, and reports: "Where reason does not rule, faith is simply an *incredible* blessing that gives over and again. That's where we are folks. That's our choice point.

---

Shawn Gallaway – Choice Point

---

"Among humans, faith is at war with reason. Fallen ones like us, still fall from grace *because we do not ask*. The Master said: *You have not because you ask not.* The girl asked.

"Heck, as I hear tell, she *demanded* God save the garden, or they and their *neighbors* would starve. Her faith produced the abundance you see. You are her *neighbors*. She asked for you too. Every one of you."

Counselor grins amiably and adds: "I am asking every one of you for your help. I know you'll find this redundant, but you *will* swear as Knights that you will never speak of what you know, or what you will come to know." He pulls a forefinger and thumb across his lips and raises his hand in oath. All the Knights zip their lips and raise their hands in oath binding. The Daughters do the same.

Counselor turns to face RO with a smile of encouragement. He knows what comes next and that what comes next is impossible. It is simply unreasonable to think it *could* happen.

He knows that if anyone can sell a bunch of skeptics on believing in the impossible it is his lady wife RO. Plus, she'll make it fun, and laughter always softens the hard places inside a man. "You're up, RO."

"Don't dither, Mother," a smiling daughter cautions RO. "Make us proud. Again. Like you always do."

RO laughs, looks at the Knights and Daughters, turns her palms up and asks: "What's a mother to *do*? We need loads of volunteers to help in all sorts of ways. We need truck drivers with tarps to pick up The Angel Garden produce and bring it to the D of I storeroom.

"How many of you have trucks with tarps and are comfortable driving on country roads?"

She counts hands, looks to Counselor and says, "Looks like there are enough to rotate drivers by week day so we don't set a pattern to makes people curious." Counselor nods.

"Drivers, stay on country roads where you can, and don't stir up dust. Real farmer's *always* drive slowly on country roads just to watch things appear, change, and disappear again. They *see* the curvature of the earth. They *feel* the sunset melt them like ice in a cup, and they learn and know that when a man melts he free flows again.

"How many of you have pressure cookers? Oh, lots, that is so perfect!

"How about canning jars with rings and flats?"

"Canning jars we have," a Daughter offers. "And we have canning rings. But most of us don't have flats. We used them last time we had anything to can."

"We need to buy flats then, Counselor. How do we pull that off without spilling the beans that we have something to can when nobody *else* does?"

"Hum, I take your point. Okay, who has any ideas to offer?

"Well," Bam White says, "Me and Melt both can be practically invisible, and we both haul 'junk' for folks all over five counties. I reckon we could trade some boxes of flats here and there without anyone getting curious enough to ask why. Most stores that carry canning supplies got nothing to do with 'em but dust 'em. They'll be glad to pay us in inventory they can't sell. We'll trade for fresh flats when we can."

"Oh," RO exclaims, "That is *so* perfect!

"We'll be canning produce from The Angel Garden in the D of I kitchen. Who *likes* keeping kitchens clean and washing pots pans, jars, etc.? Oh, lots, that is *so* perfect! Thank you God!"

"Who's going to pack The Angel Garden produce for the drivers to pick up?"

RO grins and asks: "How many of you wondered the same thing?" She doesn't count hands. They're all up. "Well, I will tell you what you will not believe, and it's true. Archangels pack the crates, baskets and boxes and put them on the loading dock. They'll help load your trucks too."

"Loading dock? Archangels!" A wide-eyed man nods quickly and says: "Okay, *that's* really all I need to know about that." He shakes his head mourning: "I *do* wish I had a truck with a tarp though."

"Counselor, is there anything else you want to say?"

"There is. There's a table in the back with Volunteer Sign in Sheets. The sheet has a place for your name and phone number, fill that in. Check boxes to select the work you'll do, the frequency, and times you're available to collect and preserve the produce from The Angel Garden.

"Canning days will be all hands on deck at least within the confines of the D of I kitchen.

"Daughters, most of you will come with your Knight husbands. Talk it over so the two of you are on the same page when volunteering your best help times. Preserving food is more fun when it's a group effort.

"Daughter and Knight Couples who enjoys making jellies and jams? Oh, that is excellent! Ladies, can we be real? We'll talk by phone and get everyone scheduled so everyone gets to have fun pickling eggs."

"There are eggs?" Counselor asks. "I love pickled eggs. We're signing up for pickling eggs dear one."

"Done." RO agrees. "We're dealing with a miracle, people. We must have faith that we will have what we need when we need it. We know it our hearts, and that's where change happens.

"Daughters, talk with your Knight Husband this evening and call me tomorrow with your schedule.

"Okay, ladies and gents, have you got anything else related to our joint meeting this evening?"

"Well then, we go to our entertainment for this evening, Bam and Melt White, come on up, you two.

Everyone hoots and hollers until Bam and Melt are up front waiting for silence. Bam and Melt grin and wave 'hello'. "Thanks for helping out with The Angel Garden Project. Melt and I got different stories to tell about The Angel Garden because the girl wouldn't talk to me. She'd talk only with Melt.

"And," Melt adds, "Dad is the only one of us who talked with the dragon and so my dad is the one will tell the dragon tale."

Shawn Gallaway – The Source

"*Dragon?*" One bold man speaks for all, and his face shows the skepticism everyone else feels.

Except RO. And Hester, who's sitting in the back row keeping her head down. RO grins at the doubter and says: "Let's hold questions until the end of our agenda, or we will not finish in time. And then I will be cross." She pouts. "And that will make Counselor cross; and there's just no future in that. Deal?"

"Deal." The attendees agree in one voice.

"Bam," RO says with a small frown, "I think you begin." RO looks at Counselor who nods agreement.

"Well, Ladies and Gents, I reckon I gotta begin with the first in a series of impossible events. My first impossible event was to ride on a dragon, and I did not go *willingly* on that wild ride." He waits till the audience stops whispering '*dragon?*' and turns to face him again, eyes round with wonder.

"And, riding that weird wired wyvern made me the man I am today." He grins with them and goes back to his tale. "The dragon you see is the Thunderer."

"I thought Zeus was the Thunderer."

"Zeus is the Thunderer in mythology. Metaphysics teaches that thunder means the Perfect Mind, the Complete Mind. In metaphysics, thunder is a feminine power. Thunder is loved for bringing life." He smiles. "Thunder is hated for bringing death." Bam frowns. "Thunder moves in all creatures. Thunder is the 'I AM' voice that speaks softly in silence as perception and knowing. Thunder is the *real* voice crying out in everyone, and they recognize that voice for its seed indwells all and everything.

"Thunder says: 'I AM awareness of the Father. I know the hidden thoughts, the eternal mystery. I know the primordial consciousness. Because 'the Father abides in me and me in him', as The Master put it.

"Dragon is the Thunderer. And there was some powerful need for dragon thunder in The Angel Garden.

"I situated myself on the dragon and rode that wonderful wyvern as we winged so fast we broke the sound barrier which got me and the dragon into The Angel Garden. It was *not* a soft landing. It wasn't even one you'd fairly call a *hard* landing. We crashed in a belly-flop. And that is my prelude for the Lilly pond in The Angel Garden. See you can see the V of the dragon's ribcage where it fell, and on the other side, a V where the tail pressed a channel there.

The dragon likes lilies of all shape, size and color, and so it pulled all Earth Mother's lily gifts and planted them in the pond."

"And the water came from...?"

"Angel tears." Bam waits.

"Wait a minute, you said *"Earth Mother's* Lilly gifts'? There is only one God!"

Bam nods agreement, and argues: *"However* the Divine *One* made all and everything in his image and likeness, and there *is* duality in everything in life. So doesn't that *necessarily* mean there *must be* a female counterpart that is *not* separate from the One, but *is* separate from the masculine which is *also* not separate from the One?"

Bam offers a condolence, "And isn't that a *good* thing? I don't know what I would *do* without Lizzie, and Melt, and our girls. I personally *like* the dualities of life.

"I think I wouldn't find a reason to get up in the morning if I wasn't out looking for ways to help others knowing without proof that they'd help me when I needed help and they could help." Bam smiles and says: "I need your help. Every one of you."

He meets all eyes. "And I too need your vow of silence for what I am about to tell you, and what I have already said to you. As RO said earlier, we're here to create a space for a miracle. The Angel Garden produce is the miracle. We are here to preserve that miracle.

Counselor rises, turns to the door and calls: "Knights, join us please." Two dozen Knights enter with baskets and burlap bags and as they place the items, the Knight names what's in the bag or basket.

"Where did this come from?" Someone demands as the chosen Knights finish their work and take seats.

"I already answered that question," RO says simply. "Do you remember?"

"The Angel Garden? So there is such a thing! Where is it?"

"Well I *could* tell you," RO offers, "but you would first tell me *why* you want to know the location; and that is extraneous to the agenda for our meeting. You have a copy don't you?" The man nods.

"We are here to talk about *produce* from The Angel Garden, and what we will do to keep and to preserve it. You are part of the solution, or you are part of the problem. You choose. Make your choice now."

"I'll stay. And I'll remember the Knights Oath. And..., I want to peel an ear of that corn and eat it."

RO chuckles, "You are not alone. So, how are you at kitchen work, especially heavy lifting, the sort of things that need done during cooking, canning, and preserving?"

"I do all of that. How about the picking and packing?"

"Ah," Hester offers, "the Archangels do that and set the baskets outside the gate. That's covered."

"I am glad we're sworn to secrecy because nobody in his right mind would believe what you just said. It makes me feel like a kid again when I still believed in Christmas. When do we start?"

"You are not a patient man, are you? Well neither are we. We have an agenda. We're following it!

"Bam, pick up where you left off, please."

"Guys, angels don't have trucks. We need men with trucks and tarps to come to The Angel Garden to pick up the produce and bring it to the storeroom back of the D of I kitchen. When you load your truck, cover it with a tarp you tie down. Most of you are country boys, use country roads. Pretend you're rum runners if it adds zing to doing the same thing with something that's merely miraculous and *not* illegal.

"No caravans, please, caravans of trucks covered with tarps attract attention. Back up to the dock of the D of I kitchen to offload baskets and crates you brought in, and put them in the pantry off kitchen. Put peppers with peppers, corn with corn, gourds with gourds, and so on. Rows and aisles will be needed in the storeroom, and we don't know the quantity. Assume abundance.

"Next comes canning day," Bam says, "and it's back to you, RO."

"Daughters.... Don't you *love* being Daughters, *and* daughters?" She sees the nods all around. "Women are Earth Keepers. That is our role. It's why we created the D of I space that serves as a school cafeteria. School's on break, and we need it for preparing and canning produce from The Angel Garden. We need pressure cookers. Who has one?" She raises her hand and sees that most mother Daughters do too.

"How many would *like* cooking and canning together in a kitchen as big as this?" All Daughters raise hands, and most of the Knights too. By way of apology, the other Knights said they were *masters* at cleaning kitchens, washing dishes, pots and pans, and they really *liked* cooking and canning.

"How many of you are volunteering to help until we've preserved all the fruits of The Angel Garden?" All Knights raise their hands. All Daughter Mothers do too. RO smiles. "Excellent! Bam, you are up."

"I brought my banjo to accompany me in telling my impossible tale. Are you all up for some picking and grinning while I'm telling about riding a weird wild wyvern I did not want to ride?

"You see, the wyvern told me that my job was to coordinate getting The Angel Garden produce from the garden to the D of I pantry. That's it. A delivery boy."

Bam grins, "That is my living. This time I do it for a good cause and it help a lot of folks stay alive and maybe even to thrive. We need help though."

"I keep wondering as I listen, so I'm going to ask. "Are we trying to hide this?"

"No!" Bam scowls. "What we are *truly* doing is planning to maintain a low profile so *our town* doesn't appear in the news attracting unwanted attention and speculation about what we're doing, why, and *how*. How many newspapermen do you think would write that The Angel Garden is a miracle?

> Shawn Gallaway – Breathe A Little Magic

"Plus, the dragon said to do it this way, and the Archangels in The Angel Garden agreed. They pick and pack produce from The Angel Garden and put it on the dock for same day pick up. There's a loading dock there now," Bam says informationally. "The produce is grouped by type. All a drivers got to do is drive out, load the truck, tie down the tarp, and play slow rum runner on the way to the D of I pantry.

"If you see someone you don't know at The Angel Garden, it's an Archangel. Don't gawk. They'll help load trucks with berries first so they can be cleaned, cooked, and canned while they're fresh.

"They'll probably pick tomatoes and soft veggies the next day, and keep doing that until everything from The Angel Garden has been picked, packed, processed and canned by its best-by date.

"You might find it interesting to know the girl is the only person can freely go in The Angel Garden. Her mother still has to ask permission of the Archangels.

"And, if she asks, she receives, just like the Master said."

"Will we work on Sundays too?"

"Would a farm guy *expect* to work on Sundays after church too? Yes, of course he would!" Bam grins. "And your lady wife Daughter already knows that canning doesn't stop because it's Sunday.

"I said more than enough and it's Melt's turn at telling tall tales true and well, and peeps a mine, you won't believe this tale either. And you'll know it's true anyway. Come on up here, Melt."

When Bam tries to step away, Melt pushes him to the stage to sit, and says: "Cover my back, Dad. As you know, it's hard to tell tall tales true and well when you don't believe 'em yourself." Bam puts his hand on Melt's spine where it curves making room for the heart. Melt melts, and begins telling his tale.

## Shawn Gallaway – I Am The Love

"You're probably wondering what Dad doesn't know that I know, because Dad knows *everything* there is to know about everything there is. Am I right?" He sees nods and smiles.

"I know the girl's tale, because she only told it to me. And hear this, she told me if I ever told her tale I *must* tell it tall and true and *exceedingly* well.

"She actually *did* use that word. So there I was at Hester's because she'd called and said she needed my help. Help that only I could give. Help that only *I* could receive. That got me curious, so I went.

"Hester met me at the door and invited me into the kitchen where she poured water for us and squeezed a slice of lemon and of lime into the water. Tasty! We needed a tall cool drink before we could *accept* the tale Hester was about to tell. Believe – we did not. Then or now.

"In our trials we often forget that Faith is the gap-filler between hope and fear. The girl has *amazing* faith! The truth is that her faith has nothing whatsoever to do with the logic and reason. Faith and fact are *not* at war in the girl." Melt smiles melting hearts, opening minds, and making room for miracles.

"So there we were sitting on the cedar chest in front of a window overlooking the garden that I couldn't see, unless I did *not* look at it directly. What I *could see then* overloaded my mind, for in my mind I *knew* it was *impossible*." Melt rubs his palms up and down over his face and tarries a moment in silence.

"'Your faith is weak. Your doubt is strong', she said to me.

"She looked me in the eyes with gloomy grief, and said: 'You can't go into The Angel Garden. Your doubt would kill everything in it. *Then* people would *starve*'. She whispers 'I hoped you could help'." She turns to the window seeing things I *would* not see. I saw that. "I'm disappointed, that's all," she whispered.

"'The cat-fighting angels are horrid!' She said, palms against the glass overlooking the garden. I didn't ask. I waited, knowing she'd tell. That she *had* to tell.

"There were too many impossible things happening in The Angel Garden, and some of them are as zealous for evil as the snake in Eden's Glen. Fighting evil is outside her skill sets. She couldn't fight Archangels. Someone *else* had to do that.

"Turns out it was Hester who had to be Earth Mother to The Angel Garden. Dad didn't even know that at the time. Nor did Jacob. Not even Hester knew. Yet.

"The dragon knew though. Dragon is the Thunderer. Thunder changes things. Thunder means 'Perfect Mind', or 'Complete Mind'.

"For those of you who are wondering, yes, Zeus is the Thunderer. So is the dragon. Dragon is the sound of thunder.

"Thunder is a feminine power. If you ever see a dragon and don't know if it's a male or a female, default to female. Treat it like you would a *Lady*, a woman of high rank. That means treat it respectfully for if you don't, the dragon won't let you ride, and if you do manage to get on board, it will be a *wild* and terrifying ride."

Melt waits for silence to fall, then says: "Thunder is loved for bringing life. Thunder is hated for bringing death. Thunder existed before creation, it moves in all creatures everywhere.

"Thunder is the real 'I AM' voice speaking softly. Thunder dwells in the silence as perception, knowing. Thunder cries out in everyone and all recognize the voice for the seed of Thunder indwells everyone and everything. I AM is the voice of the father who knows hidden things. Thunder is the eternal mystery.

"The dragon is the guardian within that opens new realms to you. Thunder protects creation and helps manage emotions. Thunder helps us to act *only* from balance and self-control.

"The dragon took Hester into The Angel Garden – after it thundered through her for what she will tell you was an infinity of time during which the sun did *not* change position."

Melt reminds: "Dragon *is* the Thunderer who changes man's mind into Perfect Mind, Complete Mind. Hester will tell you the next part of the tale for she's the only one who can. Hester, you're up" Melt says stepping away.

It's no longer easy for Hester to be timid or rigidly reserved since her Dragon talk and her Dragon ride; and, she has a key role to play in preserving the fruits of The Angel Garden. She steps to the podium with a poised grace that wasn't hers before. "Thank you for being here, and for being willing to," She unexpectedly giggles, infecting everyone, "preserve The Angel Garden produce. I must start with my Dragon tale because the dragon reformed my mind about who I think I am. Before the dragon blowing my hair back and dropping me to my knees, I couldn't go into The Angel Garden. I did not *believe* what I could not see. I couldn't see mostly because my faith was too small. Not my faith in God. That I had.

"The faith I was lacking was my faith in *me* as a unique creation of the Divine across *all of time*. All my faith in *me* would fit into a thimble with space left. The dragon thundered that wee self out of me and made space in me for something new.

"In that Truth consciousness I went into The Angel Garden on the back of my wired weird wyvern savior. I was stunned by what I saw. The Angel Garden was ruined!" Tears brim in Hester's eyes but do not fall. "The Archangels sent to support and nourish The Angel Garden were fighting – as the girl put it – 'like a whole *basket* of cats from Kilkinney'.

It pissed me off." Hester giggles, "I ordered those two Archangels to come to me *now*, pointing to the dry dirt at my feet." They were angry. And, they had a common enemy now.

"Well, I am a mother! I'm not taking sass from a couple of fallen angels who aren't doing the jobs the Divine One sent them to do. And I'm not cleaning up after them either!" Everyone laughs aloud.

"I flew into The Angel Garden on the back of the Thunderer and I *knew* what I came to do. I *thundered* into The Angel Garden to save it. The Archangels listened to me, but not without a lot of grouchy grumbling. So I motherly asked the Archangels why they were naked as jay birds are on the day of their birth. Seriously folks, they were *clothed* in nothing but bruises, scabs, and powder dry dirt. And they had no shame." Hester shrugs, "Mothers don't put up with no shame sass from wayward children…, even if they are Archangels.

Hester smiles, "I did what any Earth Mother would do. I kicked butt and took names. I shamed the Archangels into being buddies and partners again.

"I did a disappointed mother version of 'ordering' them to clean up their act and just *do* the job the Divine One sent them to do to support and nourish The Angel Garden and then to restore it to what it was *before* their stunning fall from grace.

"And then I knew a thing I didn't know at all. I demanded: "Wasn't part of your mission here to cry Angel tears to water the garden?

"And then, motherly concerned, I asked them: "Where have you lost your wings?"

"Where are your beautiful bright white angel clothes?"

"Where are your white light halos?" They had no answer of course they were dim bulbs. They'd fully forgotten the reason *why* they were sent to The Angel Garden.

Hester grins, "You see, they both *thought* being assigned to The Angel Garden was a demotion from when Michael was the D.O.'s strong right arm, and Gabriel was Michael's strong right arm. More than that, Michael and Gabriel were best buds – before.

"However, the Archangel in The Angel Garden with Michael was named 'Gab-re-EL', and they *weren't* getting along well at all. All that dark energy and fighting filled the dome like Black Sunday. Or as the girl phrased it 'like a *whole basket* of cantankerous cats from Kilkinney'.

"Okay, I like this limerick so I'm saying it: 'There once were two cats from Kilkinney. They each thought there was one cat too many. So they fought and they fit, and they scratched and they bit, until instead of *two* cats there weren't any'.

"Well those Archangels had to straighten up and fly right and I did what any good mother would do in that situation.

"I shamed them. Brutally, caustically, sarcastically, the way *your* mother would have done had you gotten so out of line as to willfully destroy what God had made! *Really*? Not happening on *my watch*!

"Shame worked." Hester fans her hands. "Plus, I said no more 'casual Fridays' *any* day of the week. I expect you two to look totally angelic while you are here. And that *means* you do *not* have scratches, bruises, scars, cuts, or bruises on your bodies!" Everyone is laughing at Hester's delivery of her tale. She continues.

"You are not in The Angel Garden to bleed. You are here to weep tears of *joy* for have been assigned to The Angel Garden. It's a plum assignment, you *foolish, fickle* fallen angels!

"How *far* you have fallen from grace to even *imagine* that the Divine One would give *you* a demotion! *Que tonto! Que increable estupido!* He gave you a *plum* assignment. He even cherry picked it for you! And if you eat all the cherries I'm coming for you!" Everyone laughs and claps. Hester grins. "The Archangels laughed too, they laughed so hard they cried tears of joy..., like they were supposed to do from the beginning.

"Now The Angel Garden is whole and healthy again, and the Angels are proud and happy. I think they are the ones who are creating new plants in

The Angel Garden..., even *tropical* plants like papaya and pineapple. Who'd have thunk it?

| Shawn Gallaway – The Artist |
|---|

Hester waits until the applause and laughter stop, then, moist-eyed smiling, she says: "I want to personally thank each and every one of you for so generously dedicating your time and effort in the next few weeks to helping preserve the produce from The Angel Garden.

"Bam and Melt will be our distributors for the surplus canned produce." She pauses for the shock to settle and grins assurance. "There *will be* surplus, even if we generously share with our families, friends and neighbors. See those two Archangels are not just picking and grinning in The Angel Garden. They're creating new fruits and vegetables, and opening inner spaces for them to grow and thrive. And, we all know the Whites always follow heart guidance, and people in need that we don't know but they do, will also share the wealth of produce from The Angel Garden." She grins, "Let's call it a tithe. The Divine One does. And Earth Mother is always generous, true, and *unavoidably* at one with the One.

She claps her hands in girlish glee: "*Thank every one of you for being Thunderers!*"

# About the Author

When I was age three to four, I became wickedly angry about something, and Mom was no help. I went to the source, and I demanded to know why I agreed to come here and why I agreed to do this! The master said, "You have not because you ask not," and I took that to heart. I asked.

The divine one replied, "I can tell you everything you want to know about why you came to life, what you agreed to do, and even why you agreed to do that, but then you will have to forget."

"Why will I have to forget?" I demanded.

The DO was silent for an infinite eternity then replied, "So that you will live and experience the pain, the anger, the injustice, the slings and arrows of cruel fate that befalls humans in one way or another, at one time or another, while they still remain in their body, mind, and brain. Their earth suit.

"The spirit that inspires (the breath of life) and animates (quickens) the earth suit into life is, was, and always will be, infinite and eternal. A wise man once said, 'God is a circle whose center is everywhere and whose circumference is nowhere.'

"In truth, man cannot be outside of the presence of the divine. Yet, in the conscious mind of man, the source of all and everything is 'out there.' It does not indwell the body, mind, and brain of man.

"I gave mankind intelligence, reasoning power, and choice. Those gifts are placed into the conscious mind of man, where the co-creator lives. Man most deeply trusts linear thinking. Paradox.

"To give perspective, the electromagnetic energy of the heart center is five thousand times greater than the electromagnetic energy of the mind. The paradox is not opposing opposites. It's more of a two-step.

"The co-creator mind is designed to collect the facts, figures, and data points of the physical plane, even empirical evidence. It is designed to consider possible outcomes—the likely ones, the lovely ones, even the really nasty ugly ones—and take all that evidence to the heart center and be at peace with it there until the conscious mind knows what it wants, why it wants it, and all the ways and reasons that the co-creator chooses to make the world a better place than it was before.

"That's why you must forget now because only you can load up the co-creator mind of yours with all the good, the bad, and the ugly experiences of life. Only you can teach and invite your co-creator mind to join you in the heart center, and you can do that only when it is your time to do what you came to life to do.

"Then will you write Fibonacci Tales books."

2016.

"Welcome home again, crone of mine. Now is the time that you remember everything you forgot when I answered your questions of why you came to life and what you came to do.

"Now it is time to accept, and to know that you are eLBe. That eLBe is the author of the Fibonacci Tales books. That the Fibonacci Tales books will change the world, one reader at a time."

www.ingramcontent.com/pod-product-compliance
Lightning Source LLC
LaVergne TN
LVHW011933070526
838202LV00054B/4628